UNDER THE NORTHERN LIGHTS

Under the Northern Lights

TRACIE
PETERSON

BETHANY HOUSE PUBLISHERS

Minneapolis, Minnesota

To Merrill,
with love for your friendship.
You are a dynamic daughter of the King,
and I'm a bettet person for knowing you.

Books by Tracie Peterson

The Long-Awaited Child • A Slender Thread
What She Left for Me
I Can't Do It All!**

ALASKAN QUEST
Summer of the Midnight Sun
Under the Northern Lights

BELLS OF LOWELL*
Daughter of the Loom • A Fragile Design
These Tangled Threads

LIGHTS OF LOWELL*
A Tapestry of Hope • A Love Woven True
The Pattern of Her Heart

DESERT ROSES
Shadows of the Canyon • Across the Years
Beneath a Harvest Sky

HEIRS OF MONTANA
Land of My Heart • The Coming Storm
To Dream Anew • The Hope Within

WESTWARD CHRONICLES
A Shelter of Hope • Hidden in a Whisper
A Veiled Reflection

RIBBONS OF STEEL†
Distant Dreams • A Promise for Tomorrow

RIBBONS WEST†
Westward the Dream • Ties That Bind

SHANNON SAGA‡
City of Angels • Angels Flight
Angel of Mercy

YUKON QUEST
Treasures of the North • Ashes and Ice
Rivers of Gold

*with Judith Miller   †with Judith Pella   ‡with James Scott Bell
**with Allison Bottke and Dianne O'Brian

Chapter One

Last Chance Creek, Alaska

H ome."

Leah Barringer Kincaid sighed the word as the settlement they called Last Chance Creek came into view. It felt as if she'd been gone a lifetime instead of just months. But even as the relief of familiarity settled over her, another thought shadowed her joy.

"But it's not really my home anymore," she whispered as the dogsled drew ever closer to the village. She had just recently married, and though she and Jayce had talked about different possibilities of where they might make their home, nothing had been settled. Not completely.

This village—this house—was one she had shared for many years with her brother, Jacob. She could hardly expect that he would leave now, especially at this time of year. It wouldn't be prudent or beneficial for any of them to set out on their own in the face of the Arctic winter. A million thoughts rushed through her mind. So much would change now. She and Jacob had often talked about what they would do when one or the other of them married. Leah had always figured the house would belong to Jacob and she would move off to her husband's home, but where would that be? Jayce had spent time living all over Alaska. He spoke with fondness for Last Chance, but did he love it enough to remain?

"Lay-Ya! Lay-Ya!" Ayoona's voice beckoned to Leah. The squat old native woman waved and pushed her fur-lined parka back just a bit to reveal her brown face as she called to her son. "John! You look hungry. We got you supper."

Leah felt awash in emotions. Seeing Ayoona was like seeing her own grandmother. How she had missed her home. *And to think, there was a time when I wanted to be anywhere but here.* She remembered the restlessness as easily as she remembered her own name. The isolation of the Seward Peninsula was sometimes daunting. Winters were hard and long. Summers were fraught with dangers and endless sun.

John pulled the sled to a stop in front of his mother. "I need to see to the dogs, and then I'll eat."

Leah climbed out of the basket and hugged the old woman. "I've missed you so much. It's good to be home." The woman smelled of seal oil and smoke, and the combination made Leah smile as she pulled away.

"You got married," Ayoona stated. "Your man is a good man?"

"Yes," Leah said. "He is a good man. I love him very much."

"And he loves you. I know." Ayoona grinned, revealing several missing teeth against her weathered lips.

John interrupted their revelry. "I'm going to leave your things at the house," he told Leah. "I can help you get them inside after I feed and water the dogs."

"Don't worry about it. I can get the boxes inside," Leah answered, glancing toward the house. "I'll be fine."

"Your man can help," Ayoona said matter-of-factly.

"My man? Jayce is with Jacob. They're tracking down Jayce's brother Chase," Leah explained to Ayoona. "That's why John had to bring me home. Chase took Helaina Beecham at gunpoint. Remember her? She was the woman who helped Jacob last summer."

"I remember her," Ayoona said, nodding. "She didn't like it here. She strange—lived in your *inne* even when it was full of water." Ayoona referred to the summer ritual when most of the Inupiats moved into tents as the permafrost melted and caused flooding in the subterranean houses. Ayoona shook her head. "She didn't like our ways—our people." The words were matter-of-fact, and there was no condemnation in the woman's tone.

Leah smiled at the thought of Helaina Beecham up to her ankles in water. "I don't think she understood the people here, Ayoona. I honestly don't think it was a matter of like or dislike. She was probably terrified and uncomfortable with such a drastic way of life."

Ayoona nodded. "Not like you."

"No, not like me." Leah had always loved the people here, even if the place had grown wearisome.

John moved the dogs out. "I'll see you at the house, Leah."

"I'll be right there." She gave Ayoona another quick hug. "When I get things put away, I'll come tell you all about my time in Seattle."

"You bring your man too. We eat together."

Leah shook her head. "My husband isn't here, Ayoona. Like I said, he's trying to find his brother. The man is a killer and kidnapper."

"Your man is here." Ayoona pushed her parka back even farther. Her expression revealed absolute assurance that her words were true.

"Jayce . . . is here?" Hesitating, she shook her head. "He's here? You're sure?"

"He just got here. He came this morning," Ayoona stated with a smile. "Needed more dogs. Better dogs. Said he was only staying for a few hours, then going."

Leah felt her heart skip a beat. Jayce was here. They would have a few moments alone, and he could tell her what they had discovered so far. "I have to go," she told Ayoona. "I need to find him."

Ayoona grinned. "You won't have to look for long."

Leah fairly ran the distance from Ayoona's inne to her own home. The little structure of wood and sod had never looked more inviting. John had just finished offloading the crates from the sled. "I'll see you for supper," he told her.

"Thank you for coming after me, John. Ayoona said that Jayce is here. He came for more dogs. Jacob probably wanted his own dogs, though why he sent Jayce instead of coming himself is beyond me. Anyway, we'll be over in a bit."

"Jayce!" she called as she opened the door and went down the few stairs. The houses in this part of the world were partly buried in the ground for insulation and protection against the wind. She and Jacob hadn't buried theirs quite as deeply as the natives usually did their homes. Leah didn't like the feeling of being in the ground. She had also gotten Jacob to build their house with a shorter entry tunnel than those of the natives. Tunnels gave her a feeling of being closed in—trapped. She shuddered as she opened the second door to their house.

"Jayce! I'm home!"

She looked into the store on her left. There was no one there. The kitchen would be the likely place. The wood stove kept the place nice and warm and required the least amount of work. "Jayce?" She pushed back the heavy fur that acted as a door.

And there he was. Her heart skipped a beat as he turned from the stove. "Jayce," she sighed.

"Welcome home . . . Leah."

It was only then that she realized it wasn't Jayce at all.

It was Chase.

"You are Leah—aren't you?" he asked. His resemblance to Jayce was uncanny, but there was something about him that set him apart. Something raw and cruel. Something very, very evil. The skin on the back of her neck prickled, and Leah swallowed hard and leaned back against the doorframe. "What are you doing here?"

"Now, that's no way to welcome your husband." He grinned wickedly at her and took up the coffeepot.

"You aren't my husband." She turned to leave. Surely she could outrun this man. She'd get John, and he could take Chase in hand.

"I wouldn't go, if I were you. Otherwise your husband and brother, not to mention your dear friend Mrs. Beecham, might all be killed. I'd really hate to do it, but I will."

Leah froze in her steps. She turned very slowly. "What are you talking about?" How could he possibly have Jayce and Jacob?

He poured himself a cup of coffee and gave a nonchalant

shrug. "I suppose we could discuss that over something to eat."

"Ayoona is expecting us. She thought you were Jayce."

"Just as I hoped she would. I find that being an identical twin has its advantages. The heavy winter clothing doesn't hurt either. It's easy enough to hide a man's face when needed. But since it wasn't needed . . ." He let his words trail off.

Leah felt a shudder go through her. A million questions came to mind. "How did you even know about me—about this place?"

"Mrs. Beecham has been most helpful—without really meaning to be, of course. Not only that, but I've watched Jayce most of his life—or had him watched. Getting information on a man who is doing nothing to hide himself really isn't that difficult. I have well-paid friends who always seem happy to share their knowledge for a price. As for this place, I've been here before."

"How did you know about me—about Jayce and me being married?"

He looked at her and laughed. "You really are quite naïve—aren't you? You've certainly done nothing to hide your marriage. Besides, Mrs. Beecham told me about it—told me about Seattle and her clearing my brother through the use of fingerprints. She loves to talk, and I figure, why not let her? It's not costing me a cent, and it's valuable information."

Leah could have throttled Helaina. She had done nothing but cause trouble from the beginning. Now Chase was here, threatening everyone Leah loved, and there seemed to be nothing she could do but play along.

Leah felt a shudder go through her. "What have you done with my husband and brother?"

Chase took a seat at the table. "They're safe enough . . . for now."

Leah felt her anger overcome her fear of the man. "Where are they?"

Chase took a long drink, then settled back against the seat. "Look, you must be a fairly smart woman. I doubt Jayce would marry a ninny. He always did have to have the best of everything. But be that as it may, being smart, you must know that I'm not about to divulge any secrets that might help you to betray me. All I will say for now is that they are safe. Safe for the time. What you do or don't do will determine if they continue being safe."

Leah decided it couldn't hurt to temporarily play his game. "What do you want?"

"I want dogs and provisions. Mrs. Beecham eats a lot, and we left town in a hurry—as you probably know—not exactly prepared for this sudden change of weather. I figured to get blankets and warmer clothes. You know, sometimes a person's survival depends on little things." He swept her body with his gaze.

Crossing her arms against her chest, Leah wished fervently she could wipe off the smug expression Chase wore. He clearly had the upper hand. If she told the village that he was Chase instead of Jayce, he would most likely be taken into custody . . . but not without a fight. But more important, she might never find Jayce and Jacob. Or even Helaina. Leah felt bad that she held very little concern for the woman, but with her brother's and husband's lives at stake, Helaina ran a distant third—especially considering all she had blabbed to Chase.

"So how do we resolve this?" Leah finally asked.

"You do what I say and no one will get hurt. We will pack a sled and head out in the morning. I figure a night of rest and . . . warmth will be to our advantage." He dropped his voice low. "I'm very much the same man as my brother. So it would hardly be wrong for us to ... well ... enjoy each other's company."

"You're nothing like my husband. Jayce is a good man with a strong conscience to see right win over wrong. He loves God, and you clearly love only yourself," Leah said, shaking her head. "I might help you get dogs and supplies, but I won't betray my husband by allowing you any part of me."

"And if I insist?"

Leah's knees threatened to buckle. She was shaking so hard she was certain Chase could see her tremble. With a false sense of bravado, she squared her shoulders. "Then I suppose we all die."

He studied her for a moment. "Keeping your marriage bed untainted means that much to you? What has Jayce done to deserve such loyalty?"

Leah refused to back down. "He's a trustworthy man, and he's had my heart since I was nineteen. I love him very much, and I won't betray him, even to save my own life."

"But what about doing it to save his life?"

It was then that Leah realized this was all a game to him. He was enjoying the play of emotions on her face—the frustration and fear in her voice. He seemed to feed off of it.

Leah could stand no more. "I have supplies to bring in and put away. The villagers believe you are my husband. For now I'll let them believe that. But if you do anything to cause me grief, I'll tell them all, and you'll be imprisoned."

"Not without a fight," Chase said, laughing.

"I think we both realize that," Leah replied. "But you do not know these people like I do, and there you are at a grave disadvantage. You'd do well to remember that. Now I'm going to bring in the supplies—otherwise everyone here will know that something is wrong."

She hoped her words sounded believable. She certainly didn't feel convincing. Walking back out of the house, Leah contemplated what she could do. The options seemed so few. She didn't want to risk the lives of the people here, but she didn't want to give Chase any advantage.

"So where does this stuff go?" he asked.

She hadn't realized he'd followed her out, but it made sense. He wanted to keep track of her—to keep an eye on her so that she couldn't cause him any harm. "It goes into the room on the left."

He easily hoisted one of the heavier crates. It drove home the point to Leah that this was no city-born dandy. Chase was strong and well muscled, or he'd never have been able to handle that box. There had to be at least one hundred pounds of supplies in that crate, and yet he acted as though it weighed no more than a pair of *mukluks*.

She followed after him, carrying a smaller pack of goods. She tried to pray but found the words were jumbled and made no sense. Surely God would understand the situation and know her heart. Leah feared for her brother and Jayce. She longed to see them again—to know they were safe.

While Chase went back for the last of the goods, Leah began to put things away. How had Chase managed to capture Jacob and Jayce? No doubt he had used Helaina as bait. Leah suddenly felt very angry with the younger woman. She'd been nothing but trouble from the moment they'd met. *If not for her, things would be different. If not for Helaina, we would never have had to endure the trip to Seattle and the fear of Jayce hanging for offenses committed by his twin.* Leah seethed. The rise of her anger fueled her body as she tore into the crate. None of this had been their fault. Everything could be

17

squarely placed on Helaina Beecham's shoulders.

"This the last of it?" Chase asked as he put a small wooden box on the counter.

"Yes." Leah hoped her clipped tone would indicate her unwillingness to discuss anything further.

"We need to establish how things are going to be. Especially since we don't want to give anyone here the wrong impression," Chase stated. He leaned against the counter and watched Leah. It gave her an uncomfortable feeling, almost as if he could see through her layers of clothing—even past her flesh and bones to her very soul. It was like he could read her every thought.

"You need to act as though nothing is wrong when we go to eat with your friends."

"I'll fix us something here. I don't want you around my friends."

"That will never do. If you reject their hospitality, they will assume something is wrong. We can't have that, now, can we?"

Leah stopped putting cans of milk on the shelf and looked at Chase. "I'm not going to give you away." *At least not yet.*

"Good. I'm glad to hear you say that. I'd really hate to have to hurt you—or them. But I can hardly sacrifice my life because of sentiment. I haven't survived this long by letting my heart run the show."

"I seriously doubt you have a heart, Mr. Kincaid," Leah said, returning to work.

"Ah, but there you are wrong, my dear sister-in-law." He came up behind her and took hold of her shoulders. She froze in place. "I have a heart, and I can be quite considerate—when extended the same respect." He forced her to turn toward him, then reached out to lift her chin so that she would look him in the face. He stroked her cheek and seemed to study her reaction.

Leah steeled herself against his touch. She wouldn't tremble and give him the pleasure of seeing her fear. "I won't play your games, Mr. Kincaid. I will give you as much respect—as you put it—as I can, but I won't dishonor my husband or my God."

Chase laughed and let her go. "So now God is your sole possession? I thought He was available for everyone."

Leah nodded very slowly. "He is. But since I'm the only one in this room who hasn't rejected Him, I figured it suited the situation well to claim Him as my own. You are more than welcome to surprise me and prove me wrong."

He walked away, chuckling. "I would never attempt to prove you wrong on this point, Mrs. Kincaid. I hardly have need for God, much less one that you claim possession of so fervently."

Leah watched him walk away, and for the first time since learning about Chase Kincaid and the things he'd done, she felt sorry for him. It was little wonder he did the things he did. He had no use for living a righteous life. He had made his bed in hell, and it seemed to suit him just fine.

Chapter Two

J acob held up the pot of coffee. "Want some more?"

Jayce looked inside his mug at the settlement of grounds and shook his head. "Nah. I think I've had enough."

They'd taken shelter from the strengthening wind and had decided to make camp among some dwarf birch and shrub willows. Snow had fallen off and on for the last two hours, but it was the bone-chilling wind that had the dogs sleeping with their noses buried between their hind legs. Jayce was glad for the warmth of their tent. The camp stove helped considerably, as would the furs and wool blankets they'd brought from Nome.

"The dogs aren't going to last long," Jacob said matter-of-factly. "I've been checking them over. They weren't in the best shape to start with, but they were all we could get on short notice. I figure, however, we're not that far from Last Chance. It might be wise to head that way and put together a couple of good teams."

"But what about the trail? We'll lose it altogether if we leave."

Jacob put the pot back on the stove. "This wind and snow is burying the last of it, anyway. I seriously doubt we'd be able to pick up on it in the morning. If we get fresh dogs and better provisions, we might be able to hit the trail again and find someone who's actually seen Chase."

Jayce considered this idea for a moment. "What about Helaina?"

"Look, I don't like it any better than you, but I'm telling you, these dogs aren't going to last long. If we spend any more time attempting to run Chase down, I think it will kill half of these beasts."

"How far do you figure us to be from Last Chance?"

"Probably two, maybe three, days."

"And the dogs will hold out that long?"

Jacob shrugged. "Most will. I think there's one that might not. We can always put him in the basket."

Jayce nodded. "I guess it makes sense. We'd also get to see that Leah made it home safely. I hated sending her back on her own."

"I'm sure John got word to come for her. There were a good number of people heading north to Teller, and I'm sure they would have rested at Last Chance. Some have family there, and you know they wouldn't have missed a chance to share some time together."

"Sure. It'll put my mind at ease, nevertheless, to see that she made it home without any trouble."

Jacob smiled. "Me too. I can't imagine life without her. Of course, now that she's your wife, I guess I'll have to."

"I never had the kind of relationship with my siblings that you two share. I was born into a brood of vipers. They were all about what they could get for themselves. My father used to say that if his casket had gold plating, my brothers and sister would pry it off before putting him in the ground. I suppose I'm the odd man out in the family. Although I'm hardly a saint, as your sister will attest. I had my selfish ambitions as well." Jayce looked out into the darkness. "It's just that I seemed to realize, as I grew up, that selfish ambitions were hardly the way to live amicably with family or friends. Of course, I came to Alaska because I had no desire to live with my family—amicably or otherwise."

"Were you and Chase never close? I thought twins were always ... well ... like one soul or something." Jacob almost seemed embarrassed to have asked such a question.

"Chase was ambitious from the start. Mother used to tease that the only reason I'd been born first was because I was bigger and had blocked Chase's way." Jayce smiled at the memory. "I told you, didn't I, that we were born on different days in different years?" Jacob nodded and Jayce continued as if he needed to explain. "I was born at the close of the calendar year at three minutes till midnight in 1882. Chase was born four minutes after midnight on New Year's Day. He had to be cut out. He was all wrapped up in the umbilical cord, and he and our mother nearly died. Somehow, Chase has had to do things the hard way ever since."

"Some folks are like that," Jacob admitted. "I know I've had my hardheaded moments. Still, it's difficult to imagine two such different brothers."

"Like I said, my other brother and my sister are no different. Eloise always acted like she had somehow been robbed in being born a woman instead of a man. She was the firstborn, treated like a pampered pet. I remember she actually talked of going to college to simply irritate and offend our mother. I knew nothing would ever come of it, however. Eloise was lazy and concerned only with finding a wealthy husband who could spoil her as father had done."

"What about your other brother?"

"Clyde? Well, he's really just a more subdued version of Eloise. He demands his own way, but he's more subtle in controlling situations." Jayce shifted, as if the ground had suddenly become unbearably hard. "I don't suppose it really helps matters now to speak ill of any of them. It's enough to say we weren't close. I envy you the relationship you've had with Leah."

Jacob smiled. "Leah is loyal to a fault. She will never bear you a grudge or desert you. You've got a good woman in her. I will miss her, but I couldn't be happier for her to have found true love in you."

Jayce only missed Leah more at Jacob's warm description. "I wish I hadn't wasted so many years." His words were laced with regret.

"You can't go around bemoaning the past," Jacob said sternly. "It won't serve any good purpose. God had a plan in all of it."

"I suppose He has a plan in all of this, too, but it's sure hard to see it for myself."

"I really admire you for your willingness to go after your own brother, Jayce. I know I've said it before, but I figure you deserve to hear it again."

"Well, at least a dozen times a day I find myself wanting to turn around and head as far away as I can get from Chase."

"You know, I can go on without you," Jacob suggested. "After we get back to Last Chance, you could stay there with Leah and care for the dogs and store—maybe get in some good trapping. I can go on and find Helaina and Chase."

Jayce considered the proposition for only a moment. It was tempting, but he knew he couldn't leave Jacob to bear a burden that was clearly his responsibility. "No. I have to do this. I'm grateful for your help, but if you want to stay in Last Chance, I wouldn't hold it against you."

"No. I'm in this for the duration. This likely isn't a surprise, but Helaina . . . well, I've come to care for her a great deal. I don't know what her feelings are, but I feel I must try to save her from Chase."

"I figured as much, even without Leah mentioning it," Jayce said, smiling. "But Helaina's not like us. I seriously doubt she'll ever stay in Alaska. Are you prepared to go to the States for her?"

Jacob shook his head. "I don't know how to live down there anymore. I can't see myself doing that."

"So what will you do?"

"I don't know," Jacob answered honestly. "I suppose I'll let her go once we find her. I just pray she's safe and that Chase hasn't . . ." His words faded off, but Jayce understood the fears Jacob had. Chase had proven he had no regard for life; what would stop him from assaulting a woman's virtue? Still, that had never been Chase's style in the past. No one had yet accused him of such things.

"I don't think Chase would . . . hurt her." He drew a deep breath, pondering his further response. "Everything Chase has done up until now has been against men. Helaina got in the way and made herself an easy target. I'd honestly be surprised if she's even with him now. I figure Chase has probably set her free somewhere along the way. As soon as he felt safe and out of the reach of the law in Nome, I'm thinking he probably dropped Helaina off at the nearest village. He wouldn't want to be bothered with her—she'd serve no useful purpose. He'd probably just consider her inconsequential."

"Not if she ran her mouth," Jacob said, frowning. "You know Helaina. She holds no fear of men like Chase. I think she actually gets her energy from encountering them. If she goes on telling him about her connection to the Pinkertons and how she's there to catch him, Chase might get the idea that he can hold her for some kind of ransom. He might even believe the Pinkertons would trade him his freedom for Helaina."

"I suppose it's possible. I can't be sure from one minute to the next what Chase will get a mind to do." Jayce wondered what he could say that would offer his friend some measure of comfort.

"We may have made a mistake in leaving those Pinkerton agents in Nome." Jacob leaned out the tent opening and tossed the remains of his coffee. Cold air rushed in, causing Jacob to hurriedly close the flap. "There's strength in numbers." He secured the tent and crawled back to his pallet.

"True, but they would have become a liability to us. They're not cut out for an Alaskan winter. They weren't even wearing decent boots. They would have slowed us down—or worse, died on us."

"That's probably true, but I can't help feeling we would be better prepared to deal with your brother if we had more men."

"There's no way of telling what we need in order to deal with Chase," Jayce admitted. "But I know we've made better time on our own. Those agents will be just as happy filling in for those deceased officers, and the police chief seemed real happy to get the help."

"I suppose you're right."

Jayce laughed. "Of course I'm right. After all, this is the same argument you gave me back in Nome."

"Thought it sounded familiar," Jacob said with a smile. "Besides, I guess the objective is to stop Chase. I can't keep second-guessing everything else or I'll never be focused enough to get the job done."

"Chase has a way of stealing a man's attention. It's like ... well ... sometimes I swear he can read my mind—even from a thousand miles away."

"Hope not. That would give him too much advantage in this situation."

Pulling up a thick wool blanket and heavy fur, Jayce settled in to go to sleep. "You know, I remember a time when Chase wasn't so bad. He was about eight years old and he'd come down with the measles. He was pretty sick. I guess we all thought he might die. Chase was pretty scared, but he kept telling our mother that he didn't want her to take care of him because he was scared she'd get sick and die too. Mother was undaunted by the threat, telling Chase that he was her child, and she would see him through this crisis as she had seen him through others. Chase told her that if he lived, he would be a better boy."

"So what happened?" Jacob asked, nestling into his own pallet.

"He was good for a time. Really seemed to have a changed heart. Up until his bout with the measles, he'd often lied and cheated at school, was even given to petty thievery and assaults to get what he wanted. My father was at his wits' end trying to figure out what to do with him. I think Chase was close to being sent to a military academy.

"For a few months after his recovery, Chase walked the straight and narrow. Then one day he just seemed to put it all aside. He grew angry and hateful, and none of us ever knew why. It just got worse after that. Father threatened him, Mother cajoled him, Mrs. Newfield, our cook, promised him her best goodies. Nothing worked. Chase just seemed to go bad."

"Something must have happened to make him that way. Especially if he had been good for a time. He had to have seen that being good accomplished more than being bad," Jacob countered.

"But see, that's the thing," Jayce said, shaking his head sadly. "I don't think it did merit him more. I think people still treated him like the same old Chase. They expected the worst from him, and I think after a time, he just decided to meet their expectations."

"I guess I can understand how that would happen. Expectations are hard to live up to—or live down, in this case. It's always hard to imagine what causes a person to choose the wrong path. I know even for myself, some choices just seemed a little short of good—not really bad. You know what I mean?"

Jayce nodded. "I've been on some of those paths myself. I knew a decision wasn't completely in keeping with what was right, but it wasn't really all that bad. Just tilted the wrong direction a little."

"Yeah, and you can convince yourself that they aren't tilted at all if you try hard enough. I know when I ran away to go find my father, I convinced myself that it was a good thing I was doing. See, we'd gotten word that a man killed in an avalanche might be our pa, but we couldn't be sure. People carried letters back and forth for folks all the time, and this man had a letter from our father. I needed proof—one way or the other—of whether our father was alive. Never mind that I had to defy all of my authority figures to do it, and hurt my sister. She confronted me about it too. Leah was never one to just let you out of a situation—not if she thought it was for your own good. I gave her a necklace and told her I didn't want her to give up on the dream. I needed for her to keep dreaming, because all of my dreams were gone." Jacob sighed.

"I'll never forget the way she looked at me the day I left. I knew she'd forgive me in the long run, but there was such a sense of betrayal in her expression that I very nearly didn't go. Still, I left because I felt I had a good and righteous mission. Maybe a lot of bad choices are made that way."

"Maybe, but that can't be Chase's excuse. He's broken the law so many times that he cannot doubt his choices are wrong. Maybe when he was eight years old or even a young man of thirteen, those choices were not clearly understood. But a man of nearly thirty-three must surely know the difference. My only hope is that in going after him—in capturing him and turning him over to the authorities—I might see other people safe from his antics."

"It won't be easy when the time comes," Jacob said.

Jayce stifled a yawn and nodded. He closed his eyes. "I've had a hard time coming to terms with potentially killing my brother, but if it saves the lives of innocent people, then there really is no choice."

"You're not the one killing him," Jacob said softly. "He's made his own choice to live this life. He's bearing the consequence of those choices—or will bear it. You had nothing to do with that."

"But I have everything to do with hunting him down." Jayce rolled to his side and tried not to see the image that had haunted him since leaving Nome. It was the shadowy picture of his twin hanging from a gallows. Even more unnerving was the fact that the scene only served to remind him that Chase would have allowed Jayce to suffer the same fate and probably have had little regret for it. The thought angered Jayce, but it also gave him cause to check his heart.

This cannot be about revenge, Jayce told himself. *Chase has caused me unknown damage and heartache. He's given me a reputation I did not deserve. But this cannot be about revenge. I could never live with myself if I found that to be the motivation of my heart. It has to be about justice and saving other people from my brother's threat. Nothing more or less.*

Chapter Three

Leah finished packing food provisions in a crate just as Chase came into the store. She hadn't been able to get all of the supplies put away because Chase had forced her to come and help him handle the dogs.

"Are you nearly done?" he asked, sounding strangely nervous.

Leah looked up as she secured the pack. "Yes. Did you see to feed for the dogs?"

"Yes," he murmured, not sounding at all like the confident man she'd been dealing with.

"Good. Take this and load it on the sled. I need to grab a couple of traps and the rest of my things. Then we can leave."

"Traps? Why are you taking traps?" He sounded suspicious, but Leah could hardly be bothered. If she allowed herself to think for even one moment about the gravity of the situation, she might well back out and expose Chase.

"We'll need to stretch our supplies as far as we can. Especially where the dogs are concerned. If the pulling gets hard or the distance extensive, the dogs will need more food. Then there are Jayce, Jacob, and Helaina to consider. Have you provided for them? If not, we'll need to see to that as well. I have no way of knowing where you are taking me or when you plan to let us go. We can hardly survive for long on what we can carry out in one sled basket." She thrust the heavy bag at him. "This will last us a couple of weeks at best, even a shorter time once we join the others."

"Should be sufficient for two," Chase said, easily hoisting the bag to his shoulder. "I have a place up north. Near Kotzebue. We shouldn't have too much trouble reaching it before supplies run out."

"But what of the others? If this is sufficient for two, what about Helaina, Jayce, and Jacob?"

He shrugged. "I don't figure to take an entourage with me. One hostage will suffice."

Leah felt her knees tremble. Somehow she knew she'd be the one hostage he'd choose. She drew a deep breath to steady her nerves. "Nevertheless, I'll take the traps. Fresh meat will keep us alive and the furs will be useful for trading or even using in our clothes." She went to where she stored the traps and pulled out two. One larger and one smaller. Checking them for defects or problems, Leah was finally satisfied that she had all she needed.

"Lay-Ya!" Ayoona called from the front door.

"That's what I hate about the north," Chase declared, turning to go. "Nobody ever knocks."

"There's no need when you care about each other as if they were family," Leah replied. "Just go load that, and let me deal with business here." He cocked a brow but said nothing.

"Lay-Ya, are you here?" Ayoona pushed back the fur. "Oopick is with me."

"Good. I need to go over our arrangement and make sure you have everything you need." Leah watched as Chase allowed the women to come into the room before edging carefully around them.

"You ladies are looking lovely today," he said with a devilish grin. "If I weren't already head-over-heels in love with my wife, I would surely come a-courting." Oopick smiled, but Ayoona ignored him. She was far too intent on speaking to Leah.

"Lay-Ya, it's not a good time to travel. There are bad storms coming. You should stay."

"I know," Leah said, nodding. She had seen the signs herself. "Chase . . . Jayce is of a mind that it won't cause us any real trouble." She hoped neither woman would think it strange that she'd stumbled over Jayce's name. "I've taken good provisions and a sturdy tent. We should be all right."

"You won't get far today. The wind is going to blow in plenty soon," Ayoona said matter-of-factly. "Tent won't do you good. You tell your man to find something better."

"I will," Leah replied. She knew Ayoona was worried. "Oopick, thank you so much for being willing to watch the store. These last couple of crates are what's left to put on the shelves." Leah pointed behind the women. "Just write down what everyone buys and pays. We'll go over the books when I get back." *If I get back.* The thought startled Leah, but she held fast to her calm façade.

"John and I will take care of everything," Oopick replied. "He will take good care of the dogs, and I will run the store."

"And you'll both stay here, right?" Leah questioned. She knew that Oopick and John would be hesitant to enjoy the Barringer hospitality. They were never ones to take pay or reward for simply offering a neighborly service.

"We will stay, but we will bring our own supplies. You will need yours for the winter. John plans to hunt tomorrow, so maybe there will be plenty more meat when you come back."

"When you be back, Lay-Ya?" Ayoona asked.

Leah shrugged. "I don't know."

"Where you go?"

She shook her head. "I don't know. Likely Kotzebue. Jayce wants to surprise me. He has a place up north," she told them, hoping that if her husband and brother escaped and showed up in the village, someone might be able to help direct them to where Leah and Chase had gone.

Ayoona shook her head. "Bad storms there too."

Leah knew the old woman was probably right but said, "I'll be back before you know it. Take care of each other." She hugged Ayoona and then Oopick. She didn't want to admit it, but deep in her heart, the situation felt bleak and increasingly hopeless.

Ayoona and Oopick had barely gone before Emma Kjellmann showed up. As a missionary to the frozen north, Emma seldom made it to the States. She was eager for a discussion with Leah.

"Is the coffee on?" she asked as she popped her head in.

"I think there's a bit left," Leah admitted. She knew Chase would be in a hurry to leave, but she hadn't had a chance to even visit with Emma since coming home. She led the way to the kitchen, holding back the fur for Emma as she passed through.

"I heard you were heading out again and figured I'd better come over before you left. I wanted to hear all about Seattle and about your wedding. I saw your husband outside, and he sure seemed happy. Guess our prayers were answered and God worked all things together for good."

Leah buried her surging emotions, hating to mislead her dear friend. She wanted to believe Emma's words with all of her heart, but at this point that thought would not even begin to register in her brain. Nothing seemed to be for good at this point. "God does know what He's doing," she replied, more for her own sake than Emma's. Leah took up a cup and poured Emma a cup of coffee. "Hope it's warm enough. We let the fire die out since we're leaving."

"I'm sure it will be," Emma said, taking the mug. "Say, I heard you brought back supplies. I hope you thought to bring sugar. I never did get enough in my shipments. They were always running short, and I hate to think of going through the winter with no more than I have."

"I did bring some, but it probably won't be enough to suit the likes of Bryce and Nolan."

"Ja, my boys, they like their treats," Emma admitted. "I spoil them too much, but their papa is just as bad."

"I'm sure he is, but he's a good man."

"Your man is good too. I remember our talk last spring," Emma began. "I remember how you worried he might never understand your heart—never love you. But God knew what would happen." She was grinning from ear to ear. "Did you have a lovely wedding? Oh, I wish you would have gotten married here so I could give you a party."

"It was a nice but very simple ceremony," Leah remembered fondly. "I wore a beautiful white muslin dress. I brought it back and will show it to you sometime. It seemed silly to buy such a thing, but Jacob insisted. He felt I deserved a special dress for my wedding day."

"Ja, I agree. A woman only gets married once. She should look as pretty as she can. My mama and sisters made me a beautiful gown. It was white with tiny bluebells embroidered around the hem."

"That sounds lovely," Leah commented.

"I'm sure you made a beautiful bride. I'm surprised your husband can bear to be away from you at all."

Leah suddenly felt very compelled to tell Emma the truth. She opened her mouth, determined to explain the situation, then closed it again. Chase had no scruples, no fear . . . and would take Emma if necessary. He would even kill her if she got in his way. Leah couldn't risk that.

"So was it a pretty day?"

"Hmmm?" Leah looked at Emma. "Oh, the wedding. Yes and no. It had rained in the morning, but it cleared off and that made everything seem lovely and clean. The autumn weather there was quite nice. Not too cold or too warm."

"Oh, I almost forgot to tell you," Emma interjected. "My little sister, Sigrid, is coming to live with us next spring. She's agreed to come and teach school."

"That is good news. Where is she now?"

"She lives in Minnesota with my parents. She teaches there at a big school. She's very good."

"What caused her to agree to come here?" Leah couldn't imagine a young woman just up and coming to Alaska to teach school.

"I begged her," Emma admitted. "I miss my family so much. Bjorn said we could go back next spring, but he wanted someone to be here to take care of the house and such. Sigrid agreed to come for that purpose, and then the more we wrote back and forth, the more she realized it might behoove her to come and teach. She checked into the requirements and will come through the government. Isn't that wonderful?"

Emma's delight was contagious. "Yes, I am sure you will enjoy her visit," Leah said, laughing. "So you plan a trip home next year?"

"Ja. My parents are anxious to see the children. They've never met Nolan or Rachel. I just want to sit on my mother's porch and snap beans and talk about the old days. I want to eat her cooking and have a mound of fluffy scrambled eggs for my breakfast. Oh, and my mama's fresh curds and whey."

"It all sounds wonderful. We certainly enjoyed our share of delicacies in Seattle. I'd almost forgotten what beefsteak tastes like. And, I have to admit, I ate more than my share of eggs and fresh fruit. Oh, the oranges and bananas were incredible," Leah remembered. "The man whose house we stayed at had a taste for both, and the house was never without them. I could only wonder at the cost, but he insisted we all partake." Leah offered Emma a grin. "I didn't have to be asked twice, but I'm sure they were expensive."

"Ja, I can imagine. I sometimes miss those things enough to leave here forever."

"I hope you won't," Leah admitted.

"Probably not. Bjorn says there's much of God's work to be done. He sees good changes in the people. Less drinking and fewer superstitions. The village is more peaceful. Remember the murder that took place the year we came?"

"I remember not only that, but the ones that came before your arrival. Up here the law means very little to some. And to others . . . well, Inupiat justice is sometimes very swift and without concern for white man's ways."

"We've tried to teach respect for the laws, but when you've lived here for generations and haven't had to worry about the government, it must be hard to have to take on someone else's ways."

"It's hard to know what's right," Leah said thoughtfully. "Eventually more people will come to this area. Alaska will probably be made a state soon. They're already working hard to see that happen. Once they convince people to move north, Alaska will fill up like the States. I fear for the natives then."

"I do too. My grandparents were missionaries to some of the Indian peoples in Montana, before it was a state. They told us stories of how the whites lied and cheated those peoples."

"Adrik . . . you remember he's married to the woman who helped raise Jacob and me?" Emma nodded. "Adrik is part Tlingit, and he's talked of the abuses he's seen his people endure. Of course, there are good white people." She smiled. "I try to be one of those myself."

"Ja. It's sometimes hard to gain their trust," Emma said, finishing her coffee. "I sometimes feel we have accomplished very little."

"You've both done great work here. The north needs you." Leah would never want to keep them from going wherever God directed them, but at the same time, she didn't want to lose her friend to the south.

"There is other news," Emma said, smiling. "We're going to have another baby. I'll probably deliver in May, just before break-up. Then we'll travel to Minnesota in June."

"That is wonderful news. Maybe it will be a little sister for Rachel."

"I'd like that. Rachel doesn't seem so much a baby anymore. She's walking and talking. Always running after her brothers."

"I wish I could see her. I wish I were going to be here longer," Leah said with regret evident in her voice. "I would love to have a nice long talk, for there's so much to tell you about. My visits with Karen in Ketchikan, the ship blowing up on my trip home . . . God really showed me a great deal. I hope we'll get a chance to discuss it when I get back."

"Where are you going?"

Leah knew she would have to be careful. She wanted to give as much detail as possible without endangering Emma. "I'm not entirely sure, but Jayce says we'll head north—he has a place up there somewhere. He mentioned the area around Kotzebue."

"You aren't going to move there, are you? I couldn't bear it if you left us for good. And it's such a long way to travel."

"I don't plan to be gone long, and I certainly don't plan to move there," Leah said. "Truth is, I've had enough travel to last me a lifetime. Now I'd just like to settle down and stay put."

"So why go?"

Leah thought for a moment. Maybe if she shared some of the true details, it would help to save her life—and the lives of her brother and husband. "Jayce has a twin brother—an identical twin brother." She said the words with a strong emphasis on *identical*. "Chase is a criminal, and he's kidnapped a woman and she must be rescued." She again emphasized her words, this time focusing on *kidnapped* and *rescued*.

"Chase is very dangerous. He has killed several men. Two police officers were gunned down in Nome before he took this woman. Jayce and Jacob went after her." Leah lowered her voice and spoke even more slowly. "They will need to hurry or Chase may get beyond their reach."

"Leah, we need to go," Chase said as he bounded into the kitchen, looked momentarily at Emma, then back to Leah. "I didn't know you had company."

"Oh, I snuck in while you were admiring Qavlunaq's baby." Emma gave him a big smile. "Maybe you'll have your own baby to admire this time next year."

Chase laughed. "I certainly would enjoy that."

Leah felt her face grow hot. "I wish I could visit more, but like Jayce says, we need to head out. Bad weather is moving in, and Ayoona says we'll need to find some reasonable shelter before we get too far."

"You can always put the trip off another day or two."

"No," Chase said firmly. "It's important we leave now." He came up behind Leah and took hold of her shoulders. She couldn't help but stiffen. Chase and Emma didn't seem to notice as Chase continued talking. "There's something that needs my attention not far from here. If I don't leave today, it could be too late."

Emma laughed and got to her feet. "I usually find there's nothing that cannot wait another day. But, of course, Alaskan winter changes everybody's schedule."

"He's right. This is really important," Leah said, remembering Chase's hostages. She broke away from Chase's hold and went to hug Emma tight. "Pray for me. Pray for us."

"Ja, I will pray. God be with you." She headed out without another word, but there was a strange look on her face that gave Leah hope that perhaps Emma had noticed things were not exactly right.

Leah turned to Chase. "I'll grab my pack." She hurried to her bed and picked up the bag. Throwing it on her back, Leah couldn't help but frown. She had hoped to arm herself with a gun, but Chase had cleared those out prior to her arrival. She cast a quick glance over the room, wishing there might be something else that could aid her on the way.

"I'll take your bag," Chase said.

Leah nearly jumped out of her skin. She hadn't realized he'd followed her. "I can manage it just fine." She jerked away from him and set out for the door. He took hold of her arm, however, and pulled her back. Leah resisted him as he tried to draw her closer.

"I certainly hope you didn't say anything to your friend that would . . . well . . . slow our progress."

"I wouldn't risk Emma's life that way," Leah said, growing very still. She met his gaze and narrowed her eyes. "I'm not a fool, Chase Kincaid. You'd do well to remember that."

He looked at her oddly for a moment. "I have never figured you for one, even if you did marry my brother." He let go of her arm. "Is it true the old woman believes the weather will turn bad on us?"

"Yes. She's seldom wrong. You can see the signs for yourself. The wind has shifted and increased, the temperatures are colder, and the skies are growing darker on the horizon. Anyone can see it bodes ill."

He shrugged and turned toward the door. "Then we'd better hurry. We've got a lot of distance to cover and apparently a shorter time to do it in than I had planned. Come on."

Leah followed him, but all the while her mind searched for ways she could leave her husband and brother a message, if they returned. She hoped fervently that if they did show up, they would be able to follow the signs. Signs. Leah thought of the word for several seconds. Hurrying back to her chest, she threw open the lid and reached for a red checked tablecloth. It had been placed here for mending, but now Leah thought its purpose would be better served in tattered pieces.

"Leah, come on!" Chase called. His voice betrayed his frustration with her.

Leah took the tablecloth and stuffed it inside her parka. The layers would add warmth when the weather turned bad, and hopefully she could find ways to leave pieces of the material along the trail for whoever might come to her rescue. *If* anyone even realized she needed to be rescued.

Chapter Four

B y the time Leah got to the sled, Chase was studying the western skies. She could sense that things were not shaping up well, and apparently he was pondering the same thing. Looking at him as if his answer didn't matter, Leah asked, "Are you sure we have to leave today?"

"Unless you want your loved ones to die," he replied in a gruff manner. He didn't sound the least bit happy.

The dogs yipped and danced anxiously in their harnesses. They loved to run and couldn't understand the holdup. Behind them, some forty other dogs yelped and howled at the injustice of being left behind. Trying to forget the situation for a moment, Leah leaned down and scratched the lead dog behind the ears. Marty, who had been a fun-loving pup, had turned into a first-class leader.

"So what's it to be?"

Leah was surprised he'd asked her opinion. "You know the answer to that." Leah didn't even bother to look at Chase. "I'm willing to brave the dangers."

"Are you sure ten dogs will be enough?"

Leah looked at the team. They were some of Jacob's best, known for their strength and predictability. "These are some of the strongest. They are very experienced, and I wouldn't expect trouble from them. Some of the others are less reliable."

"I suppose I'll have to take your word on it. My own experience has taught me much, and they seem capable." He acted as though he was about to walk away, then turned back to her. "By the way, I want you to drive the dogs. I want you busy," Chase said, climbing into the basket. "Besides, they know you better. No sense starting out with animal troubles."

Leah straightened and eyed him with a frown. "But I have no idea where we're going."

"North. I told you that much. Head north as if you were traveling to Mary's Igloo—you do know where that's at, don't you?" Leah nodded and he continued. "I'll let you know when it's time to veer off the trail."

Leah pulled on her sealskin mittens. There was nothing to do but cooperate. She pulled her pack from her back and secured it in the basket beside Chase. It would be far easier to manage the dogs without the cumbersome weight on her shoulders.

She freed the anchoring hook and jumped to the runners in one motion. "Ho, Marty! Hike!"

The dogs began to bark in earnest as they strained against the weight and pulled the sled into motion. Leah felt the wind against her skin and realized she'd forgotten to wrap a scarf around her face. She considered trying to manage it and the team but knew that would never work. The dogs were just starting out, and their enthusiasm was much too high. She would need all of her skills and focus to control them.

Besides, it's not that cold, she reasoned. *We'll stop for a break soon enough, and I can deal with it then.* But Leah knew that normally she wouldn't have forgotten such a precaution. Alaska was a harsh companion at times, and often unforgiving. Jacob had always reminded her that a person had to pay attention to every step, every inch of land, every breath. There were just too many potential problems.

If I hadn't been so upset with this situation, she told herself, *I never would have forgotten to secure my scarf.* She pulled the parka farther down, cutting some of the chill. Her mind flooded with questions and thoughts. She wondered how she might facilitate an escape once she found the others. Timing, no doubt, would be one of the more critical issues.

Having made the trip to Mary's Igloo many times with Jacob, Leah was somewhat familiar with the territory. The coastal flat-lands broke into small hills from time to time, and in the distance the mountains created a daunting barrier to the interior. Of course, there were ways through those places as well. There were always ways around obstacles—if a person paid attention.

Leah had lived in this area for over ten years, and in that time her training had been intense. She thought of the ways Ayoona had assisted her in learning the vegetation, especially beneficial herbs. She and Oopick had also worked to teach Leah about watching the weather, the seasonal signs, and even animal tracks and behavior. Living successfully in Alaska was all about observation.

Leah was glad for the opportunity to drive the sled. The work gave her something to think on other than her circumstance. But even with this job, she couldn't help but let her thoughts drift. Jacob and Jayce were out there somewhere. Chase knew where they were and knew what he planned to do with them. Leah, too, wanted to make plans—to think ahead to that moment when they might all be free again.

"Lord, I don't know what I'm supposed to do in this," she whispered, knowing that Chase would never hear her with the wind and his own insulated parka distorting the sound. "Please help us, Lord. Keep Jacob and Jayce safe and help them get free from whatever place Chase has put them. Help Helaina too." She said the latter almost as an afterthought. Her feelings toward Helaina were still too emotional and raw. She blamed Helaina for all this, and it was difficult to feel sympathy for the girl. *I've defended her so many times—to so many people. Just yesterday I defended her to Ayoona, and now I feel so angry.* It wasn't easy to consider Helaina, however, without thinking of her brother.

Jacob cares for her very much, Leah reasoned. *What if he rescues her and decides to marry her? I'll have to accept this woman as family.* The thought made Leah uncomfortable. Helaina was a woman who loved the noises and the smells of the city, who talked often of her home in New York and of the life she missed. Jacob would never want to be a part of those things. Jacob loved the land and the wide-open spaces.

Leah sighed. Maybe nothing would come of Helaina and Jacob's relationship. After all, she couldn't see either one of them coming to terms with where they might live. And if they couldn't come to terms on something that simple—how could they ever hope to make a marriage work?

They stopped the dogs and had a small lunch nearly three

hours later. The winds were growing fierce and the skies had turned a leaden color. Winter had come early to the Seward Peninsula, and the snow and cold were more intense than usual. It felt and looked more like January than nearly November. "We should find a place to take shelter. It would be good," Leah said, "to find a nook away from the direct flow of the wind."

"Do you have a suggestion?" Chase asked, finishing the last of the boiled seal meat Leah had given him.

"I haven't been up this way in some time," Leah admitted. "But I'm thinking we need to hurry. It's already starting to snow, and the wind will soon whip it into a blizzard."

Chase got to his feet. "Then let's move out. Get us as far as possible, and if a good place to camp presents itself, then take it. Maybe we'll make better time tomorrow."

Leah nodded and readied the dogs. They needed little encouragement. They were still eager to move ahead, and Leah found their enthusiasm matched her own. Perhaps they knew they were going to find their master soon.

By early afternoon the snow still fell and the temperatures had lowered even more. But the wind held back, almost as if God blocked it with His hand. At least that was how Leah liked to think of it. Thoughts like that helped her feel less lonely.

Leah was about to give up hope of a shelter when she spotted a place between a couple of small hills. She urged the dogs in that direction and felt only moderate relief when the cut seemed to offer perfect protection.

"Help me get the tent up or we'll both be in for it," Leah called as the wind seemed to pick up a little. "I can't do this by myself."

Chase didn't hesitate, much to her relief. He took up the

canvas and held it in place while Leah drove the stakes into the frozen ground. It wasn't easy to do, but in about ten minutes they were able to raise the pole to secure the tent. The wind whipped at their refuge in a merciless fashion, despite the hill's meager protection.

Leah finished securing the dogs while Chase took their needed supplies into the tent. Listing the tasks in her mind, Leah realized there would be much to do before she could rest. She needed to melt snow for the dogs to drink, as well as some for herself and Chase. Next she'd have to fix food for them all. Perhaps she'd just throw the dogs some frozen fish and worry about something warm later.

She crawled into the tent as the snow grew more blinding. There was no hope of keeping the snow completely out of the tent, but Leah tried her best. "I'm glad you agreed to stop," she said, securing the tent flap.

"It's no problem for me," Chase said, lighting a seal oil lamp for warmth. "I'm not the one waiting for my return."

Leah frowned. "How can you be so callous about human life? About the death of others?"

"Everybody dies, Leah."

She looked at him as she pushed back her parka. "Yes, that's true enough." She pulled her mittens off and let them dangle on the cording that attached them to her coat. "You just seem intent on helping some of them die sooner than they might ordinarily have."

He shrugged and gave her a cold-blooded smile. "We all have our jobs to do."

Her anger spilled over like the river during spring breakup. "I've never met anyone as evil as you."

He looked almost hurt. "Evil? You have the audacity to call me evil? Your friend Mrs. Beecham runs all over the world trying to catch me for the purpose of putting me to death. Why is it acceptable for her to kill me, but not the other way around? Then, too, what about the world at war? Soon America will no doubt be a part of that European fiasco. What about that evil? Will you so readily condemn those who fight, as you condemn me?"

"They fight for a cause—for their countries, for their homes."

"And I, too, fight for a cause," Chase protested. "My cause— me. I've never had an easy or simple way. Yet I find a way that works for me—an unconventional way, I suppose you could say."

"What way? Thievery? Murder?"

Chase's expression seemed confused for a moment. He considered his words, then shook his head. "I don't expect you to understand. You've set yourself against me and will not be persuaded to feel sympathy for my cause."

Leah could hardly believe his words. "Is that what you want from us? Sympathy?"

Chase again shrugged. "Sympathy is a start. At least sympathetic people do not have the tendency to seek your life."

"I'm sympathetic when one of the dogs gives birth to pups that aren't healthy enough to live. But I still put them out of their misery." Leah's words were delivered in such a cold, even manner that they frightened her. When had she become so lacking in compassion for the life of another human being? How could she call herself a Christian and still feel such hatred?

Hoping Chase would drop the subject, she reached for one of the food sacks. "Dried salmon and crackers should make us a decent supper," she muttered.

"So are you trying to tell me that you would kill me if you had the chance?"

Leah looked up to find Chase watching her. She considered his words for a moment, then shook her head. "I wouldn't kill you. You're the only one with the knowledge of where my husband and brother are. Not to mention Mrs. Beecham. If I killed you, I'd have to go find them myself."

Chase laughed. "That's very true. I'm glad you realize that I have the upper hand in this situation. The people you love so much will die if you fail to completely cooperate with me."

Leah felt a chill run down her spine. Chase had a way of taking the fire from her anger. "I never said I wouldn't cooperate with you."

Chase studied her for a moment and nodded. "Just so long as you remember the facts. I feel as if I must constantly remind you."

"I need no reminding. I need my family back safe and sound."

They existed in silence after that. Chase seemed to doze off and on, while Leah recited Bible verses and poetry, and prayed. An hour or so later the snow abated and the winds calmed. Leah found herself surprised by this turn of events. She had fully expected the storm to rage on for hours, even days. The thought had grieved her, leaving her worried for Jacob and Jayce.

"I need to feed the dogs," she announced. "I'm also going to set some traps. Hopefully we'll have fresh meat in the morning."

Chase leaned up on his elbow and narrowed his eyes. "Remember, if you try to get away from me, I'll kill them all. Then I'll go back to the village and kill your friends there."

"I gave you my word, Chase. I told you that I would cooperate until I knew that Jacob and Jayce were safe." *But only until they're safe.* "I'm not going to do anything to jeopardize them."

With that, Leah pulled on her mittens and secured her parka hood. The chilled night air hit her face and lungs and took her breath momentarily, but it quickly refreshed and invigorated her in a way she had not anticipated. She felt strength replace the defeated spirit she'd known only moments before.

Leah held up a lantern to see in the darkness. She fed the dogs, then walked well away from the camp to set and bait the two traps she'd brought. There was always the danger of encountering a wild animal, but at this point, the risk was worth taking. Chase wasn't about to see her armed for protection.

"I don't know why he's done this," she said, trudging through the snow with her traps and lantern. Finding a promising spot, Leah stopped and set to work. She prayed as she hid the mechanisms in the snow. "Lord, I don't know what we need, but you do. Please help me to help Jacob and Jayce—even Helaina. Please show me what to do—and when to do it."

Walking back to her tent, Leah was startled by a sound that rose up behind her. She turned quickly, half expecting Chase to have followed her. Instead, the noise sounded again, only this time her gaze went heavenward. There in the night skies danced the northern lights in impressive displays of reds and greens and whites. The sky was ablaze in color.

For a moment, Leah felt her breath catch. The northern lights were one of the most beautiful sights she'd ever known. She'd never gotten tired of this wonder. She remembered seeing them for the first time as a teenager; one of the sourdoughs in Dawson City had told her that if you whistled the lights would move faster, but though she'd tried it, Leah didn't think it worked. Still, she had to admit that the display was breathtaking. It made her feel as though God himself were swirling the skies with some heavenly paintbrush.

"Oh, Father," she whispered. "It's almost as if you are speaking directly to me—as if you want me to know for sure that you are here for me." Leah felt her heart grow warm in her chest. "It is a sign for me; I'm certain of it. A sign that I shouldn't give up hope. You are here." Her voice lowered to a barely audible whisper. "You are here for me."

A peace she'd not known since finding Chase in her house at Last Chance washed over her in waves that matched the pulsating rhythm of the aurora. She had no idea how she would deal with Chase once he finally reunited her with her husband and brother, but Leah felt more confident that, when the time came, she'd know instinctively what to do.

The evening passed quickly, despite Leah's discomfort with such close quarters. When she announced her desire to sleep, Chase tied her hands and feet together, then secured the rope loosely, but effectively, behind her back. Leah didn't protest his actions. She knew he needed the reassurance that he would remain in power. She wanted him to have no reason to doubt her full cooperation.

"You're a beautiful woman, Leah," he said as he pulled a fur around her. He touched her cheek. "We could really benefit each other nicely on this trip."

Leah tried not to react as her stomach churned at the very thought of Chase's intentions. "I have nothing to offer you, Chase. I belong to your brother."

He frowned but moved away from her. "That can always change," he muttered. He said nothing more, nor did he try to touch her again.

Leah drifted off to sleep feeling her peace of mind slip away. If he came to her in the night, she would be defenseless. *God, please keep me in your care. Guard me through the night.*

When she awoke in the morning, Leah felt stiff and achy from having been stuck in pretty much one position all night. Still, she was determined not to complain. Chase slept soundly in front of the tent opening. No doubt he thought this would be just one more barrier to keep Leah from escaping.

"Chase, wake up. I need to check the traps and get the dogs readied for the day," she said as she struggled to sit up. It was impossible. "Would you please untie me?"

"It's still dark outside," Chase muttered.

Leah laughed. "It's going to be dark for several more hours, but I still need to tend to things. Unless, of course, you don't plan on our leaving before it's light."

Chase yawned and unfastened her bonds. "If it were up to me, we'd forget about the others all together."

His words frightened Leah. She suddenly thought, for the first time, that perhaps he would do just that. "I don't want to forget the others. You know that full well." She pulled the rope away from her feet and hands. She decided to say nothing more. "I'll get a fire going. If we've managed to catch something in the trap, I'll do a quick skinning and cleaning and put the food to cook for our breakfast."

Leah didn't wait for a response. Instead, she hurried to secure another oil lamp to light her way outside, then left Chase to his own devices. The dogs stirred and began to whine for their breakfast. She gathered dried brush and took pieces of driftwood that she'd packed on the sled to start a fire. Once that was going, she put a pot of snow on to melt, then set off to check her traps. By the time she returned, the snow would be melted and she could add more to the pot.

There was no other sound except for the sorrowful howls of the dogs. They were grieved that she would go off along the trail without them. Especially Marty. She could hear his distinct cry even as the others joined in.

The first trap revealed a fat fox. Leah smiled. She would save the skin for trading, should they come to a village, but feed the meat to the dogs. It would stretch their meager breakfast and make a hearty addition to the frozen fish. The other trap revealed a hare. Not as fat as the fox, but a good enough size to feed Chase and herself a couple of meals. She would boil the animal, and they could drink the broth and have some of the meat for breakfast. Later in the day they could have the remaining meat for lunch. The skin would be nice to save as well. If she didn't sell it, Leah knew it could be useful to them for lining their clothes or making additional protection for their feet or hands.

She had been working for nearly an hour when Chase finally came outside. It was still very dark, not even hinting at dawn.

"What time is it?" he asked, yawning. "I fell back asleep. Good thing you're a woman of your word." He stretched and sniffed the air. "What's that?"

"Snowshoe hare. I caught one in the trap, as well as a fox. The dogs made quick order of the fox meat, but our rabbit will make two nice meals for us."

"Smells delightful. I guess your traps came in handy."

Leah looked up from the camp stove. "Yes. They always have in the past. If you're ready for something to eat, I can pour you some of the broth. I figured we'd drink the broth and eat a bit of the meat, then save the rest for lunch. Does that meet with your approval?"

"I'll tell you after I see how full I get on broth," Chase replied, sitting down on the ground beside her.

They ate in silence, but all the while Leah kept wondering where they would travel and how far they would have to go. "So are you holding my husband and brother at Mary's Igloo?" The tiny town, if it could even be called a town, had once been a fairly well-populated place. It had originally been called Kauwerak, but when gold came to the area in the early 1900s, a name change had come about due to an Eskimo woman named Mary who offered refuge and warm meals for the miners who were in need.

"They aren't there," Chase said flatly.

Leah felt the food stick in her throat. She quickly grabbed some water to wash down the lump. "Why are we going there, then?"

"I didn't say we were. I just said that was the direction you needed to go."

Leah drew a deep breath and let it out slowly. "I see. So how much farther will we go? Surely it does you no harm to tell me now. We're far from Last Chance. There's no one for me to give the secret to."

"I suppose not," Chase replied, "but I know you to be a very ingenious woman. After all, your survival skills rival mine or any other man I know. If I were to tell you where we were headed, there would be little to keep you from doing me in and slipping away to find them on your own."

"But I gave you my word."

"A lot of people have given me their word before, Miss ... excuse me ... Mrs. Kincaid. I don't trust you or anyone else."

"Maybe that's your problem," Leah replied rather flippantly.

"Well, now it's yours as well," he answered, getting to his feet. "Be ready to leave in ten minutes."

Leah watched him walk away. She had no idea where he was headed, but no doubt he'd keep an eye on her the entire time. With a sigh, she quickly went about breaking camp. Within the requisite ten minutes she was ready to roll out. As Chase made his way back into camp, the skies overhead revealed signs of dawn.

"Let's be on our way," he announced, motioning her to the basket. "But this time, I'll drive the dogs."

Leah had no choice but to accept the arrangement. But as she settled into the basket, she felt a despairing chill settle over her once again. Gone was the peace from the night before, and in her heart she cried out again for God to help her.

I'm not a very faithful child, Lord, but I'm trying. Please help us. Help me . . . help Jayce and Jacob. Lord, I don't know what else to do. I just need for you to show me.

Chapter Five

W hat are you saying, Emma?" Jacob looked in disbelief at the woman. "Jayce hasn't been here until now. Not since last summer."

"But he was here. I saw him. He was here with Leah. They left together."

Jacob looked to Jayce. "It must have been your brother."

Fear for Leah mingled with anger—no, rage—at Chase. Jayce clenched his fists. "I'm sure you're right. Which way did they go?"

Emma shook her head. "I don't understand any of this." The bewildered woman took a seat at her table. "I thought Leah wasn't acting herself, but since she'd just arrived and was so tired ..."

Jacob sat down across from her. "Emma, think back. Tell me everything."

Jayce joined them. He feared any kind of delay, but it was evident they needed more information.

"Well, Leah came home with John. They only arrived a few days ago. The man we thought to be Jayce arrived a few hours ahead of her. We thought from the things he said that he was you. He seemed to know us—at least he acted as though he knew us."

"My brother is a consummate actor. He has fooled an entire nation into believing we are one and the same."

"He was very nice," Emma said, shaking her head. "I would have expected . . . well, he didn't seem bad."

"Chase has a way of putting people at ease and making them believe whatever he wants them to believe," Jayce said. "Don't feel bad."

"Well, he certainly had me fooled. He seemed quite kind and very loving toward Leah. Are you sure she would know the two of you apart?"

Jacob laughed. "Leah would know. She was probably under some sort of threat. At least that's my guess."

Emma nodded. "She did tell me that your brother was in trouble. She mentioned his kidnapping Mrs. Beecham."

"What about Mrs. Beecham—Helaina? Was she here as well?" Jayce questioned.

"No, there was no one but your brother."

Jayce and Jacob exchanged a look of concern. "That's probably how he gained her cooperation." Fear for Helaina edged Jacob's tone. "Leah knew your brother had taken Helaina. If Chase played on this—well, she would probably have done whatever he asked her to do."

"Which was what?" Jayce looked to Emma again. "What were their plans?"

"Leah said they were going north—Kotzebue was mentioned, but she didn't know anything for certain. She said he had a place up north. I asked if she was going to move away from us, and she assured me she wasn't. Oh, I wish I'd paid better attention."

"Chase spent last summer with the *Homestead* exploration group. They were in Kotzebue for some time trying to get native help. You don't suppose he really has a cabin up there, do you?" Jayce turned to Jacob for answers.

"I can't imagine Chase being open enough to confide any such news. If he told her Kotzebue, it's probably just a diversion."

Emma began to twist her hands. "I can't believe this. It's so awful. Leah with a murderer."

Jayce's fear and anger mounted. Chase had gone too far this time. What little sympathy Jayce might have mustered for his brother fled in the realization that Leah was now in jeopardy.

"I wonder what he did with Helaina," Jacob muttered.

Jayce realized Jacob was now pacing instead of sitting with them at the table. "I'm sure she's fine. Chase would have had no way of knowing Leah would return to the village. If he came here merely to get supplies and new dogs, he probably put Helaina somewhere for safekeeping. Somewhere with friends or someone he could pay to watch over her. Maybe he promised them extra food or needed supplies."

Jacob stopped. His face appeared to be chiseled in granite. The expression was one of barely contained rage. "He could have just killed her."

"I don't think he'd do that," Jayce said, shaking his head. "Think about it, Jacob. He knows someone is after him. He had to figure that a search team would be assembled. Besides, Helaina would have told him that we would personally come for him. She knew we were only days behind her arrival into Nome."

Jacob seemed to consider this and calm. "That's true enough. Still, I don't trust your brother."

"I don't trust him, either, but I trust his sensibility when it comes to self-preservation. He won't do anything to jeopardize his safety and survival. Keeping Helaina alive while he gathered supplies and dogs would be in keeping with his manner of doing things," Jayce assured. He could only pray that he was right. It did seem reasonable that Chase would conduct business in such a manner, but it also seemed just as much like Chase to eliminate any extra problems. Jayce would not tell his friend that, however.

"So he came here, and they took ten dogs and supplies," Jacob reiterated. "Emma, did Leah mention how many supplies they were taking? Did she perhaps say that Chase had told her to pack a certain amount of stuff?"

Emma frowned and closed her eyes. "I don't think she ever mentioned it. We only talked briefly. I told her my sister was coming in the summer and that I was expecting another baby. I told her we had plans to go to the States in the summer. I just ran on with talk about me. I feel so ashamed." She opened her eyes, revealing the tears that had welled.

"Emma, this isn't your fault," Jacob said. He came to her and put his hand on her shoulder. "No one blames you for this. Now tell me, did anyone else talk to Leah before she left?"

"Ayoona and Oopick did," Emma recalled. "You might talk to them about how that went. Ayoona's a very astute old woman. She might have noticed something amiss."

"That's true," Jacob said, looking to Jayce. "She might have known something was wrong but not been able to figure out what it was."

"We'll talk to her," Jayce said. "So let me get this right. They left two days ago with ten dogs and a sled packed with goods and headed north—but you know nothing more."

Emma nodded. "I'm really sorry." From one of the other rooms a baby began to cry. "That's Rachel. She's not been feeling well. If you'll excuse me, I need to tend to her."

"You go ahead, Emma. Jayce and I have bothered you long enough. Thanks for helping us."

"I wish I knew more," Emma said, getting to her feet.

"It's all right. It's more than we knew before this," Jacob replied.

Jayce nodded. "It's very useful."

Walking away from the missionaries' house, Jayce couldn't help but feel a tremendous sense of frustration. It had been such a surprise to arrive at Last Chance and find Leah wasn't there. The first people they spoke with had no idea where Leah had gone, but then they'd happened upon Emma as she was hauling in chopped driftwood for her stove. Jayce wished that Emma's comments had given comfort instead of dread.

"We'll find her," Jacob said. "We'll find them both. We're smarter than Chase, and we know this land better than he does."

"But you don't know him. He has an uncanny knack for learning and surviving. I mean, look how long the Pinkerton agents were after him. He knows how to take care of himself, but he doesn't have any regard for others. Now he has Leah and Helaina. I want to be encouraging about this, but I don't know how."

Jacob nodded. "I know. I feel the same way. But if we despair, we might be inclined to admit to defeat and give up."

"I'll never give up." Jayce was resolved to the pursuit of his brother. "If I have to follow Chase all over the world, I won't give up. He's made this more personal than merely pretending to be me. He's taken the woman I love. He's taken the very heart of me, and I won't stand for it."

———————

Karen Ivankov awoke with a start. She sat up in bed and tried to listen to the silence around her. It wasn't even light yet, but something felt very wrong. And then she remembered: She'd had a horrible nightmare about Leah falling through the ice. She was a young girl again—about the age when Karen had taken over guardianship.

Leah was flailing against the water and Karen had tried desperately to reach her, but it was impossible. Then in her dream she saw Jacob walk out across the ice to help his sister. Karen called to him, admonishing him to crawl on the ice to better distribute his body weight. But Jacob wasn't listening and fell through the ice as well.

"Are you all right?" Adrik asked with a yawn.

Karen turned. In the darkness she could only make out her husband's outline. "I had a bad dream about Jacob and Leah. I can't seem to shake the feeling something's wrong."

She could feel Adrik turn over. He reached out to her. "Come here. I'm sure it was nothing."

"I don't know." She snuggled down in his arms. "It seemed so real. Leah fell though the ice, and then Jacob fell through. I couldn't help them, and they were going to ... well ... die. I just knew they were going to die."

"Sweetheart, they've already been through life-threatening circumstances. You're probably just dreaming this because of what happened this last summer. Leah and Jacob are no doubt doing just fine. Besides, Jayce is there to help Leah now. He'll help Jacob as well. Don't worry about them. God has it all under control."

Karen cherished the warmth of her husband's arms and felt a small amount of relief as he pulled her closer. Perhaps he was right. It was, after all, just a silly dream.

"So what do you think about my taking that railroad job?" Adrik asked, changing the subject.

"What exactly would you do for them?"

"I'd help the teams that are planning out the route. I'd hunt and trap for them and help them find their way through the forests and such. The governor doesn't want to see the line fall apart again, for there's been a great deal of money put into this venture. The project has halted twice now, and if it stagnates again, he's afraid it will never be completed. He trusts a handful of his old friends to help get the track . . . on track." He grinned at his play on words.

"But you'd be gone for a long time," Karen said, thinking in earnest about the job offer.

"Well, that's what I wanted to discuss with you. I've been thinking about it, and well, I think you and the children should come with me. Move to Seward at least, or better yet, north to the mouth of Ship Creek. There's a huge population there—nearly two thousand people. It's mostly tents, but I'd build you a house."

"I thought you said it would only be temporary."

He frowned. "It would be temporary."

"Temporary as in years? No one is going to build that railroad overnight. Then, too, there's talk about setting aside lands for a national park. No doubt they'll want you to stick around and help with that. Before I know it, they'll decide to run the line all the way to the Arctic, and I'll be wearing a fur parka year-round."

Adrik laughed. "The Arctic would be a very ambitious project to say the least. There's an awful lot of rough terrain between Seward and Fairbanks; just getting it that far would be a miracle. I'm not completely convinced that a railroad line would ever be prudent in Alaska. The marshy ground in the summer would never support the tracks. They'd have to figure something out to ensure its endurance. Just look at all the trouble the earlier builders had. They used green wood and lighter rails. There are a great many places where the line will have to be rebuilt before they can ever move forward to new land."

"But they'll find a way. I know they will." Karen's tone held a sound of resolve. "They built the train over the White Pass," she reminded her husband. "That train line has lasted since 1898, and from all I've heard is still in decent order."

"But most of it is on solid rock. This project is entirely different. I'm not sure what the politicians and railroad barons have in mind, but it's going to take more money than any of them can possibly imagine. Supplies too. I had a letter from Peter Colton just the other day. He's been commissioned to haul supplies from San Francisco to Seward for the railroad. There's going to be good money in it for him, but he agrees that the men involved are really underestimating the cost. Thirty million dollars was originally invested, and those men haven't seen a dime of profit yet. I figure once they get further along, they'll see just how expensive this project is going to be. And to what purpose is it all being built? It's not like this line will truly amount to much."

"Maybe they figure more people will come and settle the territory if they offer more civilized means of transportation," Karen offered.

"Maybe, but if you want my opinion, they're asking a lot. Most folks in the States aren't going to be able to adapt to the isolation. Most are used to the bustle and comfort of city life. You remember those comforts."

"Chicago was a long time ago."

"Not long enough. Now Ashlie talks of nothing but going to the States—to cities where she can enjoy all that the world has to offer."

"Our daughter craves adventure," Karen replied. "It's in her nature to be that way. She has a father who constantly seeks such things."

"Ah, as if her mother never enjoyed those things at all. Wasn't it just the other day you were telling me how bored you were?"

"That was just for the day. I thought a trip to Ketchikan would provide a nice diversion. I wasn't planning trips to Chicago."

Adrik laughed. "Just think about it, Karen. I won't take the job with the railroad if you're against moving to Seward. I can't be that far away for that long. I want my family near me."

Karen leaned up and kissed Adrik's bearded face. "I want to always be near you, my love." She felt much better now. She could almost laugh at her earlier fears. Almost. "Adrik?"

"What?"

"Would you pray with me for Jacob and Leah?"

He chuckled. "You know I will. In fact, you know the moment you spoke of your fears, I prayed for them."

"I know," she sighed. "I just want to hear the words out loud."

———

Jacob's anxiety was causing him to make mistakes. Mistakes, he figured, that might cost him his life if he didn't start paying attention. But as he loaded the sled for their trip to find Leah and

Chase, Jacob found it nearly impossible to focus on the task at hand. His sister was in grave peril. Helaina too. It was bad enough when only Helaina was at risk, but now Leah faced an uncertain future.

I don't know why any of this is happening, Lord, but I pray you'll give me the strength to overcome Chase and his plans. Jacob prayed on but felt little comfort. Sometimes he wondered if he lacked the faith to make things happen. Sometimes he just wanted to sit down with the Bible and not get back up again until all the answers were clear. But even as he'd think these things, Jacob knew there were no easy answers and sometimes, even when a man put forth all kinds of effort, God's ways were still a mystery.

"Jacob, some of us have been talking," John said as he brought Jacob a requested dog harness. "We want to help find Leah."

Jacob took the leather strapping and met his friend's sober expression. "John, that's more than I can ask of anyone."

John shrugged. "So you didn't ask. We decided on our own. We're going to go with you."

"But there's a lot still left to do to make sure the village will get through winter."

"We dried a lot of salmon, more than we ever have in the past. We have seal and whale meat. We're doing good for the winter. We can't let Leah die."

Jacob felt the words cut to his heart. "No. We can't let Leah die."

"So we want to go and help get this man. He needs to go back to the authorities and leave us all to go on with our lives. He's caused a lot of problems."

Jacob nodded but was silent.

"What about that other woman?" John asked.

"Helaina?" Jacob shrugged. "She's in danger too. Chase Kincaid is a ruthless man. He doesn't care who he hurts so long as he gets his own way."

"If he kills them," John said sternly, "I will hunt him like *nanook* and kill him too."

"I don't want you to make pledges like that," Jacob replied, shaking his head. "Chase is as crafty as the bear, but he doesn't need to be gunned down by us. We need to let the law take care of it."

"Sometimes the law can't help you up here. Sometimes the law can't help you at all."

"It may seem that way," Jacob answered, "but God still expects us to obey the laws of the land. Unless, of course, the legal authorities want us to go against God's law. Then we have reason to make a stand." He sighed. "No, we have to trust that God will see us through this, John."

"I don't want to see Leah hurt. She's a good woman," John said, turning to go. "We'll be ready to head out when you are."

"John, I'll only agree to your coming if you promise to head back if we don't pick up the trail within the week. Will you promise me that?"

John waved. "I give my word. I think we'll find them, though. We've got the best tracker in the village going."

Jacob laughed. "And who would that be?"

John gave a sly smile as he glanced back over his shoulder. "Me, of course."

Chapter Six

The cold cut through Helaina and numbed her hands and feet. The old man who watched her vigilantly night and day seemed not to notice her misery, although Helaina had mentioned it more than once.

"Please could I have a blanket or a fur?" she asked once again. "Just something, please. I'm freezing."

She knew the temperature had dropped steadily since Chase Kincaid had taken her from Nome. She had tried hard to keep track of the days, but the darkness was confusing, and the old man seemed to keep no clock or watch.

To her surprise, the man brought her an old wool blanket and dropped it on the ground beside her. With her hands and feet bound, she had great difficulty in wrapping the warmth around her body.

For days now she had plotted and planned how she might

escape, but the problem of her clothing always ruined her plans. She was hardly dressed for Arctic winter, yet that was what she would face. She really had no idea of where they were, but Chase had told her he was taking her north, and from what she could figure by watching the sun, it seemed to be true.

The other thing that concerned her was her own health. She felt weakened by the meager meals and poor conditions he'd forced upon her. Her head ached and she'd developed a cough. It wasn't going to be easy to escape under any circumstance, but if she truly were ill, it would make matters much worse. One thing she could count on: Chase would have little, if any, sympathy for her situation.

Helaina tried not to think about what would happen when Chase returned. He'd been nothing but a problem since her brother, Stanley, put her on Chase's trail. Stanley had warned her that Kincaid was a master at keeping himself out of the hands of the law, but Helaina hadn't taken him seriously enough.

She thought back to the high price she'd paid to get the ship's captain in Seattle to take his freighter into the dangerous waters of the far north. She had given him the ridiculous amount of money he'd demanded, although she thought, in some ways, the man saw her request as a challenge. Could he get his ship up and out of Norton Bay before the winter froze him in?

She might have been able to talk him into undertaking the mission for a lower price by challenging his abilities, but Helaina had not had time to appeal to the man's ego. And so she had paid his price and had gotten to Nome ahead of Jacob and Jayce and the Pinkerton agents her brother had sent along.

I wanted to redeem myself, yet now here I sit. And I can't even be sure Jacob and Jayce even know anything about my kidnapping. They may have no idea that Chase took me, and even if they do, they may have no desire to come after him and save me. The thought sunk in as a crashing wave of defeat. What if no one cared that she'd been taken? After all, Stanley was thousands of miles away and still recovering from the wounds Chase had given him earlier in the year. What if Jacob, Jayce, and Leah arrived in Nome and realized Helaina's fate, but upon talking it over, decided to head home instead?

"This is impossible," Helaina muttered.

"You talkin' to me?" the old man questioned.

"No. Not really." She thought to appeal to the man's sympathies. "What if Chase doesn't come back? I'm out here—wherever here is—all alone. Will you help me to safety?"

"No," he replied quite simply.

Helaina frowned. "No? Just like that—you won't help me?"

"Can't help you."

"But why?"

"Chase said to keep you here. I keep you here. You stay here, and then Chase come back for you."

"But," Helaina argued, "what if he doesn't come back? What will you do then?"

"I kill you," the man said with a shrug. "Chase said to kill you if he don't come back."

Helaina couldn't hide her shock. "What? What are you saying? You would just murder me in cold blood? What kind of man are you?"

The old man shook his head. "I go trapping. You talk too much."

"Please don't go. I need to talk to you about this. Look, I'm a very wealthy woman. I could pay you generously if you let me go."

The man just continued pulling on his parka. He appeared to

have no interest in Helaina or her money.

"Wait, please. I need to talk to you. I need you to help me. Please ..." Helaina's words faded. The old man had never given her his name, so she couldn't even appeal to him by using the smallest expression of familiarity.

"Can't help you."

He headed out the door, leaving Helaina so overwhelmed that she burst into tears. Why was this happening? What had she done to deserve such consequences?

She thought about Jacob's faith in God and wished for at least the twentieth time that she had such a faith of her own. At least then maybe she wouldn't feel so alone. She thought of her house-keeper in New York. Mrs. Hayworth had a deep faith in Jesus. She often spoke of the love of God—a love that followed her out of church on Sundays and accompanied her throughout the week, as Mrs. Hayworth loved to say. But for Helaina, it had never seemed real—never important. Now, however, alone in the wilds of Alaska ... alone with a man who planned to kill her should her murdering captor not return, Helaina thought God seemed very important.

She gazed around at her surroundings, then attempted to adjust the blanket around her shivering form. Jacob would laugh if he could see her now. He would chide her for showing up in Nome without sealskin pants and a fur parka. He would note the silly leather boots she wore—quite suitable for Seattle's weather, but most inadequate for Alaska.

Drying her tears, Helaina pulled and tugged against the knotted ropes that held her fast. She had rubbed her wrists raw, leaving blood on the rope as a constant reminder that she was helpless to overcome this obstacle—this adversary. When had she ever known such a situation? When had money not been able to buy her out of difficulties?

The door to the cabin opened and an old woman Helaina had never seen entered the room. She held in her arms a stack of fur clothing. "This for you," she said, placing the garments on the dirt floor in front of Helaina. "You dress more warm now."

Helaina held up her hands. "I can't get dressed trussed up like this."

The woman stared at her for a moment, then went to the door. She called out in her native language, and it was only a moment before the old man reappeared. She jabbered for several minutes, the old man arguing her comments. Then finally he waved his hands as if to shut her up and went to Helaina. "I untie you, but you get dressed very fast."

"I will," Helaina assured him. Getting loose of her bonds and being given warm clothes seemed like a momentary victory for her situation.

Helaina did as instructed, hurrying to don the heavy pants and parka. There were no mukluks to help warm her feet, but at this point Helaina decided to be grateful for what she had. As the old man replaced her bonds, Helaina thanked him for the clothing.

"I appreciate your kindness. I wish you would tell me your name. I think that as much time as we've spent together, we should at least know one another's names. I'm Helaina Beecham."

The old man looked at her and grunted. "I don't talk to you. You go back and be quiet now. I get our food."

Helaina tried not to be upset. She shrunk back against the wall to the blanket and pallet that had become her prison. Cherishing the warmth, she actually dozed off. She tried to reason a plan for escape as she fell asleep, but the pain in her head seemed to intensify, and her chest hurt when she breathed deeply. The symptoms were starting to worry her. *What if I grow ill and die? Will anyone ever find me? Does anyone even care?*

———

Leah felt more frustrated as they traveled. Chase not only wouldn't share any details of his plan with her, but for the most part he refused to let her out of his sight. Leah had wanted to leave bits of cloth in case someone, preferably Jayce and Jacob, tracked after them. Her constant prayer was that by now they might have escaped and that they would learn the truth and rescue her. And they would need her to mark the way.

But with Chase continuing to watch her, Leah had a hard time marking their route. She did what she could when Chase allowed her private moments, but mostly she left great messes when she trapped animals. She tried to make sure the site appeared some-how very human in origin so as not to be mistaken for a mere animal kill. Still, she knew the odds were against her.

Leah had more than enough time to let her mind wander, which of course was very dangerous. She began to consider the situation in greater detail and worried that perhaps Chase had already killed Helaina and that he'd never taken Jayce or Jacob captive. What if it had all been a lie? A lie given because of his surprise at finding Leah in camp before he could slip away. This filled her with dread. Chase had no proof of holding Jacob or Jayce, and yet he was smart enough to know that Leah would fully cooperate with him if she thought that complicating the situation would endanger their lives.

That night as they made camp, Leah prayed to better under-stand her adversary. She figured that a conversation with the enemy might best serve her purpose.

"Why do you hate Jayce so much?"

The question clearly took Chase by surprise. He didn't even take time to try and hide the truth from her. "Because he's made my life unbearable."

"How?" she fired back.

He studied her for a moment, but Leah lowered her gaze and busied herself with food preparation as she expanded her question. "How could one man make you so miserable that you would do the things you've done?"

"You have a brother. Hasn't he ever made you mad? Taken something that belonged to you?"

Leah frowned but refused to look up. "No. Jacob wouldn't hurt me that way."

"Well, Jayce would—and he did. He hurt me by means of his very existence."

"How so?" She dared a quick glance. Sometimes seeing the man look like such a mirrored reflection of her husband was uncanny and unnerving. It was best not to look at him for overlong.

Chase grew quiet for several minutes, then finally spoke. "My brother was the perfect son who grew up to be the perfect man. He could do no wrong. At least he could do no wrong in the eyes of my father, while I could do no right."

"Would you share an example?" She braved the question only because she was hopeful it would somehow help her case.

"My entire life was an example. Jayce learned quickly and easily. Jayce was fearful of punishment and obedient to the laws, whereas to me laws seemed to only be in place for the purpose of breaking. I thought it all rather silly. Jayce had his way of looking at life, and our parents praised him for it and his accomplishments."

"But they didn't praise you?"

Chase looked at her hard. "No. I cannot remember a single word of praise. I remember once when I startled one of the scullery maids as I came down the servants' stairs in the kitchen. She dropped an armload of dishes and I helped her clean up the mess. My father came in as we were finishing up and demanded to know what had happened. I explained and even took full blame for what had happened. I wanted him to see that I could be responsible. Instead, he chided me—no, he yelled at me—for having come down the servants' stairs. He told me I knew better and that this had been caused by my disobedience. I was never so angry with the old man as I was in that moment. It changed everything . . . forever."

He grew quiet and closed his eyes. Leah felt sorry for him and opened her mouth to speak, but closed it as he continued. "My father could have chosen to praise me for helping the maid, for being a man and owning up to my mistake, for being honest. But instead he condemned me. I have an entire lifetime of similar circumstances that play themselves out in my memories. But things were always different for Jayce. Jayce made good marks in school. Jayce saved his money and made wise purchases. Jayce showed ambition and a flair for business. I had none of these abilities, and it only caused my father to hate me more."

"I cannot imagine a father hating his child."

"Then you didn't know my father." Chase's words were full of venom and bitterness. "It wouldn't have mattered who held me in esteem. My father would have used it against me or to show me some object lesson."

"I'm sorry," Leah murmured. And in truth she was. She felt sad for the little boy who must have tried his best to please.

"I don't need your pity," Chase countered.

"That's good," Leah said, handing him a plate of food, "because I offer you none."

He raised a brow. "You are a queer woman, Leah."

"I suppose that could be said of me," she responded. "But I'm also honest. I don't lie."

"Everybody lies, Leah. It isn't possible to live life without lies."

"That is where you are wrong, Chase. Honesty is the only way to live life. If I wrap myself in lies, I'll have nothing but misery. My mother taught me at an early age to cherish the truth—and I do."

"Then tell me the truth now."

She looked at him and shook her head. "I don't understand. Tell you the truth about what?"

"Why did you marry my brother?"

She actually chuckled at this. "Because I love him. I've loved him since I was nineteen."

"That's your truth?"

Leah thought about the question a moment. "No. It's not just *my* truth. It's *the* truth. Jayce is a generous and loving man. He has worked hard to earn a good reputation, for which he's had to fight equally hard to clear—thanks to you. I suppose that's what bothers me the most," Leah said thoughtfully. "For hating a man as much as you claim to hate Jayce, I can't help but wonder why you would so clearly associate yourself with him. Associate yourself so much, in fact, that you take on his personality, his likes and dislikes, even come to Alaska. I think rather than hate Jayce, you truly esteem him—love him. I think you desire more than anything to be like him."

"Hardly that," Chase said, looking away. "I competed with Jayce all of my life. First for our parents' affection and later our teachers' attention. I have known nothing but misery from him, and frankly, it would not bother my conscience in the least if he were to meet with a terrible accident. An accident that ends his life."

Leah tried hard to keep the fear from her voice. "But that's where I believe you're wrong, Mr. Kincaid. I think that you'll go forward in life only so long as Jayce goes forward. I think when you come face-to-face with the prospect of killing your twin, you won't do it, because there is just too much of yourself in Jayce. It would be like killing yourself."

"But we're all killing ourselves in one way or another, Leah. So what if my standards are different from yours?"

Leah shook her head. "You are wrong, Mr. Kincaid. I'm not killing myself. I'm trying hard to survive—no thanks to you."

Chapter Seven

Leah found it impossible to know exactly where they were. She had tried her best to keep a mental picture of their trail—mapping the route in her mind as they continued north and east. To the best of her knowledge, Leah figured they had skirted Kotzebue Sound by some distance and now were moving into interior lands, away from the sea. The weather had calmed somewhat, but from the look of the skies overhead, Leah figured it would begin to snow most anytime.

The other thing that had her worried was the fact that winter had come rather early and hard. She was concerned that the bears would be desperately hunting for food to fatten themselves for winter. She saw signs of bear from time to time but said nothing. If Chase was as smart as he claimed to be, then he'd no doubt see the tracks and scat.

But more than the bears, Leah feared the natives. The tribes that lived farther inland were often warring with the coastal people. There were very few members on either side who would tolerate the others. Some had pacts and agreements that allowed for one or two specified people to come and trade goods, but this had been born out of desperation for foods and furs, not because of any great love between the nations. Now as she and Chase moved farther from the coast, Leah couldn't help but wonder if there would be repercussions for this intrusion.

"You do realize, don't you," Leah began as they readied to move out after a modest lunch, "that the tribe in this area isn't very accommodating toward strangers."

"I have friends in these parts," Chase said, completely unconcerned. "I wouldn't worry about it."

"But I do." Leah pointed to the sled and then to her own clothes. "They will clearly associate us—or at least me—with the coastal natives. There are many hostilities going on between some of these people. They may not realize you are friendly to their party until it's too late."

"By my calculations, we have less than two, maybe three hours to go. I'm telling you it isn't a concern."

Leah shook her head. "We have two or three hours until we reach the others?"

"That's right."

"And what are your plans for us then?"

He shrugged. "I'm not entirely sure. I have a place up north, but this was where I left Mrs. Beecham."

Leah frowned. "What of the others?"

Chase laughed and gathered his things. He checked the rifle he always kept close, then motioned her into the sled basket. "There are no others."

Leah froze in place. "What are you saying?" The tightness in her chest made her realize that she was holding her breath. With a loud exhale and gasp for air, she questioned him again, aware her greatest fear was unfolding. "What are you saying to me? Where is my husband—my brother?"

"I have no idea." He again motioned her to the basket. "I haven't seen either of them."

"But I don't understand. You came to the village knowing they wouldn't be there—otherwise you wouldn't have posed as Jayce."

"I came there because it was close enough to get the supplies and dogs I needed, and Mrs. Beecham had already informed me that my brother and yours were after me. I figured the last place they would look for me would be in Last Chance."

Leah was completely confused. She momentarily considered pushing Chase to the ground and attempting to take off with the sled, but she found she could not move.

"We're wasting time, Leah. Now get on that sled. I'm taking us to where Helaina has been kept. If she's still alive, I'll decide then what to do with the two of you."

Leah moved slowly to the sled. "*If* she's still alive? What do you mean by that? Why wouldn't she still be alive?"

"Because she's a woman, much like yourself, who asks way too many questions. Frank has probably grown quite tired of her by now. It wouldn't surprise me at all if he's already killed her."

Leah swallowed down the bile that threatened to rise in her throat. "Who is Frank?"

"He's a murderer and a thief. Much like myself. You could say that we're kindred spirits. I met him on my trip north last summer. They call him Cutthroat Frank because he likes to do just that—especially while people sleep."

Leah didn't know what to think. For all she knew, Chase could be lying to her again. She took her place in the basket without asking anything more, knowing she needed to formulate a plan. The situation had changed. Helaina was the only person at risk now.

No, that's not true, she thought with a heavy sigh. *I'm at risk, and I have no one but myself to blame for believing a man who's made it his goal to be the best of liars.*

"Is it much farther?" Leah called back to Chase. "The snow is growing worse, and before long we won't have any light at all."

"It's just over the next ridge, if I have my bearings," Chase shouted over the wind.

Leah could see that the dogs were tired. They hadn't had a decent meal all day because Chase had been unwilling to allow Leah to feed them more than a few scraps of frozen meat. For all he seemed to know about driving a team, Chase acted rather unfeeling—even ignorant of their care. When one of the dogs had slowed his pace due to sore feet, Chase had merely shot the dog rather than let him be taken off the line for rest and Leah's ministerings. The act had grieved her greatly, but it once again served to drive home the realization that Chase had no regard for life, human or otherwise.

As they topped the ridge, Leah could see a small cabin. There was a light in the window—a traditional method of helping weary travelers to find their way to safety. But this cabin didn't represent refuge. This might well be the place where Leah and Helaina would meet their fate.

Oh, God, Leah prayed, *help us now. Help us to be wise about our choices—to see what we should do and when.*

Chase brought the team up alongside the cabin and threw out the hook to anchor the dogs firmly. Leah didn't think at this point it was as needed as other times. The dogs were spent. They were more than happy to collapse on the ground for rest.

"Get inside," Chase commanded. He grabbed hold of Leah as she jumped out of the basket.

"I need to take care of the dogs."

"No. Get in the cabin."

"But . . ." She saw something in his expression that halted her words. "All right." She turned toward the cabin door, surprised when it opened and light spilled into the dusky twilight.

"Frank, it's me," Chase called. "Come take care of these dogs for me. I'm half frozen."

The old native man looked at Leah, then grunted. She could see he wasn't happy with the task but nevertheless appeared to accept that it had to be done. Up here, dog teams were the difference between life and death at times. Surely this man understood the need to see the animals well cared for.

Chase pushed Leah through the door of the cabin. She might have fallen, but as if pulled up straight by unseen hands, Leah steadied herself and lifted her eyes to gaze straight into the face of Helaina Beecham.

"Leah!" The woman's expression seemed to be one of hope, until she caught sight of Chase. "You."

Chase laughed. "Miss me, darling?"

Leah stepped to the side. She could see that Helaina was bound by ropes. She could also see that the cabin was small and held few places where escape might be possible.

"You are despicable. Do you realize how long you've been

gone?" Helaina questioned before falling into a fit of coughing.

"Well, it sounds as though I've been gone long enough that you've talked yourself hoarse and grown ill in the process."

"Why is she here?" Helaina questioned, regaining her wind.

"She's my additional insurance against my brother's attack. See, after listening to you, I'm just not all that convinced that Jayce will care at all what happens to you."

Leah saw Helaina's expression fall. "But my brother will care," Leah quickly threw out. "He's the one you need to fear in this situation. You've not only taken his sister, but you've taken the woman he cares for."

Helaina looked at Leah oddly, but Chase seemed not to notice. He laughed, but it sounded rather nervous to Leah. "It seems I'm always paying for someone's affair of the heart. Well, let him come. I have a rifle and plenty of ammunition, thanks to your store in Last Chance. I'll deal with him when he gets here—if he gets here."

He motioned to the corner where Helaina sat. "Leah, I want you to sit there and wait for my return. I'll tie you up if I need to."

Leah shook her head. "You don't need to. You know I've pledged my cooperation."

Chase narrowed his eyes. "That was when you thought I had your husband and brother. Now that you know I don't, there's really no reason to expect your good nature. Still, it's enough for you to know that I will kill you and Mrs. Beecham if need be. Now sit there while I bring in some of our supplies."

Leah immediately sat and said nothing more. She didn't want to give Chase any reason to believe her anything but obliging.

When he'd gone, Helaina turned to her. "I don't understand

any of this. How did Chase capture you?"

"It's simple enough. He came to Last Chance thinking it would be the only place people wouldn't expect him. He took you at your word that Jacob and Jayce would be after him. You've really got to learn the benefit of keeping some things to yourself. Anyway, he figured no one would be at our home in the village. So he went there to secure dogs and supplies. Apparently he'd been there before because he knew his way around—at least in part. He very nearly pulled it off without a hitch, except I showed up and caught him in the act."

"But why were you there? Where is Jayce . . . and . . . Jacob? Where are the agents my brother sent to Alaska?"

"Jayce and Jacob thought it too dangerous for me and asked that I remain in Nome until someone from the village could come take me home. Jacob sent word via some relatives of our villagers who happened to be heading north. It took longer than I'd hoped, but John finally came for me. As for the Pinkertons, they're in Nome. The two officers Chase shot in Nome died of their wounds. The police chief wasn't in great shape, either, and needed help. My brother felt the agents would be liabilities as he and Jayce moved out across the territory. The agents were ill-equipped and knew nothing of survival in the frozen north. It seemed the best decision."

Helaina nodded. "No doubt. So there's only Jayce and Jacob to come for us?"

Leah leaned back against the cabin wall. For so long she had figured her brother and husband to be prisoners, and while she had hoped they might escape, she hadn't really believed this scenario to be possible.

"They'll come," she said softly. "I just don't know how soon or in what manner. They may have headed back to the village to restock and reorganize."

"But they'll not give up?"

Leah heard the desperation in Helaina's tone. "No. They won't give up."

"Because of you," Helaina said, sounding rather defeated. She, too, fell back against the wall. "They hate me, don't they?"

Leah considered the question. "They aren't happy with you, Helaina—that's for certain. Your actions caused problems for everyone. It caused the death of two good men, and now it's risking the lives of other good men. What in the world possessed you to leave ahead of us and pull that stunt in Nome?"

"I had a job to do."

"Your brother had relieved you of that job, as I recall."

Helaina was undeterred. "You are just as determined a woman as I am. I know that if you were given a task, you would seek to accomplish it no matter the cost."

"I wouldn't risk the lives of other people. Not just to satisfy my ego."

Helaina opened her mouth to speak but instead fell into a fit of coughing.

Leah could hear the hacking, unproductive sound. "Does your chest hurt—down deep?"

"Horribly. Every breath cuts me like a knife, right here." Helaina pointed to her lower ribs on the left side.

"It's probably pneumonia. I have some herbs, but I don't know if Chase will allow me to treat you."

For several moments Helaina said nothing, and then she surprised Leah with her question. "Why did you say that Jacob cared for me?"

Leah was quiet a moment before saying, "Because I believe he does, even though it wasn't my right to say so. I said it because I wanted to ensure that Chase knows you are as important to my brother and husband as I am. Otherwise, I'm afraid he might very well kill you simply to be rid of the responsibility."

Helaina nodded. "I'm afraid he might just do that. He has no conscience."

"Be that as it may, we have to figure a way to outsmart him."

"Yes!" Helaina seemed to gain momentum. "We have to capture him and get him back to Nome, where my brother's men can take him into custody."

Leah eyed her for a moment. She was completely serious. The thought of capturing Chase was far from Leah's mind. "I meant only that we need to find a means of escape. Turning the tables on Chase and taking him hostage is not in my plan."

"But it must be. He's a criminal. He's the reason your husband nearly died for crimes that were not his doing."

"No, Helaina. You are the reason my husband nearly died for crimes that were not his doing."

Helaina looked stunned by Leah's words. "You can't mean to hold that against me. I was doing a job. I realized there were discrepancies and I worked to resolve them. I am also the reason your husband's name was cleared."

"I suppose so," Leah replied, "but I still fail to see why I need to play bounty hunter. I have no desire to risk my life to capture Chase Kincaid. I want to figure a way out of here and do it as quickly as possible. Either you're with me or you're against me. What's it to be?"

"Please listen to me, Leah," Helaina said, lowering her voice. The pained expression on her face indicated the cost of talking so much. "I know this is a difficult situation, but I need you to help me. Chase must be taken into custody or he will continue to kill. He's proven that over and over."

"My point exactly. We need to get away from him and let others who are more qualified take that matter into hand."

"But I am qualified."

"You're also desperately sick. If you don't get treatment . . . and soon," Leah said quite seriously, "you'll most likely be dead within a week."

Helaina shook her head. "That cannot be. I'm not that sick."

"You are. You're burning with fever—it's clear by the glazed look in your eyes."

"I'm freezing in here. I can't possibly have a fever."

"You're chilled because of the fever. I know it makes no sense, but you can trust me on this one. I know medicine, and I know you're sick." Leah reached out her hand and touched Helaina's forehead. "You're burning up."

Helaina refused to give up. "Leah, I know I can make it with your help."

"But the only help I'm offering you is for escape. I'll gladly help you to sneak out of here and head home. But I will not lift a finger to help you apprehend Chase. Do you understand me?"

"No. I don't understand any of this. My brother nearly died at the hands of Chase Kincaid. Your husband nearly faced the gallows because of this man. Now your own brother will put his life in jeopardy to save you and me, and you selfishly worry only about saving your own life."

Leah had taken all she could stomach. Her anger toward Helaina had only grown as the woman continued to argue her point. Folding her arms against her chest, Leah closed her eyes and prayed for strength to hold her tongue and not lose her temper completely.

"You can't just ignore this and hope it will go away," Helaina said in a gruff whisper. The men were returning and at the sound of the door crashing open, Leah startled. "They aren't going to just leave you alone to plan our escape."

Leah threw a glare in Helaina's direction, hoping that Chase and Frank would be too inundated by the winds to hear what the ninny had just said.

"If you don't hold your tongue," Leah said, leaning against Helaina's ear, "I'll only plan *my* escape."

Chapter Eight

G od bless our girl," Jayce said, holding up a strip of red checked material. "I don't know how she's managed to do this with Chase no doubt watching her every move, but I'm glad she did."

"She's resourceful," Jacob agreed. "It's evident she's been trapping along the way. The kills have been clearly made by humans. There are trap marks by the tree."

"So she's at least allowed that much freedom," Jayce said, analyzing the situation. "Still, I wonder why she hasn't tried to get away from Chase."

"No doubt he's keeping her tied up most of the time," Jacob offered. "I can't see him allowing her any real freedom. He has to know she's dangerous—at least in the sense of being able to care for herself."

"I'm betting he's threatening her as well." Jayce shook his

head and walked back to the sled. "He's probably told her that if she so much as raises a finger against him, he'll kill her."

"But Leah wouldn't be afraid of that." Jacob came to where his own dog team waited. "I'm guessing that if there's a threat, it's against us or Helaina. Leah wouldn't be cautious in regard to herself, but she would endure hell itself to see you or me safe."

"Yeah, you're probably right." Jayce was in no mood to contemplate his brother's way of doing things, but he knew it was important that they keep a clear picture in mind when dealing with Chase. The more they considered what was driving him and why, the better off they'd be in the long run.

"Where do you suppose he's going?" Jacob asked.

"I keep asking myself that. We know Chase spent time up north this past summer; he must be returning to a place he's familiar with."

"I can't figure out how he knows so much. It's almost as if he can read your mind. He's able to mimic your interests and abilities enough that he took your place on the *Homestead* last summer."

Jayce nodded. "All I can figure is that he's been watching me. Maybe shadowing me throughout Alaska. Maybe he's even lived up here for a time."

"Well, we know he hasn't spent all of his time up here. After all, you've been sighted all over the world . . . or rather Chase has been sighted."

"I know." Jayce sat on the edge of the basket and pulled out some jerked meat to eat. "I guess none of it makes sense—maybe it never will."

"Right now the only thing I care to make sense out of," Jacob said, moving toward his dogs, "is where he's heading and what he plans to do once he gets there."

———

Leah took the bowl from Frank and nodded. "Thank you."

"Why are you thanking him. That . . . that . . . meat," Helaina said in a tone that wavered between disbelief and disgust, "is spoiled."

Leah waited until Frank left the room before answering. "It's seal meat and yes, it's gone a little rancid, but it will give you strength. It's part of the supplies I brought, and it won't be that bad. You need to eat it."

"I won't." Helaina turned up her nose and fell back against the wall.

"You have to or you'll never have the strength to leave when the time comes."

"I already told you—without Chase, I won't go."

Leah frowned and popped a piece of the seal in her mouth. "Suit yourself."

Helaina said nothing for several minutes, then finally she reached out to take a piece of the seal. "I can't go without him, Leah. You need to understand this and help me."

"I won't risk our lives to capture him. That is a job I'm happy to leave in the hands of Jacob and Jayce. They are stronger and better equipped to deal with someone like Chase. I would think that by now you would have learned that lesson. Your brother and several other Pinkerton agents were unable to keep up with Chase, much less capture him. You should know it won't be easy to turn the tables on him and take him captive. He has ammunition and weapons, and he's not afraid to do what he must in order to serve his own purpose."

"It doesn't matter." Helaina coughed quietly. "I can't leave without him."

"Then you'll most likely die on the trail."

Chase chose that moment to come into the cabin. Leah was relieved to see that he'd brought her pack. "Is this what you wanted?"

Leah nodded. "Feel free to go through it. I have no weapons. There are just herbs and remedies that I thought we might need on the trip. I believe Mrs. Beecham has pneumonia, and I would like to give her some medicines to help her. Would that be all right?"

Chase opened the bag and began to rummage through it. "I don't know why you should bother." He looked up at Helaina, his expression void of emotion. "If she dies naturally, it's one less murder in my name."

"You can't just keep killing, Chase. You have to stop this madness and—"

"And what? And they'll overlook the other murders and let me go? If I let you save Mrs. Beecham, will they show me mercy and only put me in prison to rot away the rest of my life instead of hang me?"

"I can't say what they'll do or not do," Leah admitted. "I just thought maybe you were tired of such things. Wouldn't you like to stop killing?"

He threw her the bag and laughed. "Killing people is no more or less important to me than any other survival skill. Do you tire of trapping and killing animals for meat or does the possibility of an empty belly or death on the trail keep you going? I won't be taken alive—you both must know that by now. I'm backed into a corner by those who hunt me. And you, Leah, above all others, should know what trapped animals are capable of doing."

He was right. She did know. A trapped animal was capable of chewing off its own leg to get itself out of the trap. Chase Kincaid was the kind of man who would do whatever it took to keep himself free.

"Fix her whatever you have to, but then we're going to be on our way. I can't just sit around here and wait for Jayce and your brother to catch up to me. I figure once we put a few more days and storms behind us, they will be hard-pressed to find any kind of tracks."

Leah knew the storm from the night before had probably obscured any sign of their trail. She could only hope that the bits of cloth she'd tied to the dwarf birch near their camp the night before had survived the winds and snows.

"I'll need some hot water," Leah said before Chase exited the house.

He turned to look at her, sizing up the situation. "I'll have Frank bring you some."

With that he was gone and Leah took up the pack to search its contents. "Well, are you any more convinced of the futility of staying?"

Helaina shook her head. "I cannot go without him. You do what you have to do, and I will do what I have to do."

"If you're still alive to do it," Leah said rather dryly.

———

"I've been thinking about what you said regarding the railroad job," Karen said as she poured Adrik a cup of coffee. "I think if you believe it to be the best thing, we should do it. I think the boys might actually enjoy going north. Ashlie will be difficult about it, but she would give us trouble even if we did nothing more than stay here."

"I'll talk to her," Adrik said, smiling. "She'll come around."

"When do you want to make the move?"

"We should probably go before it gets too cold. We don't have to worry about the harbor freezing, but the waters will get rough. I don't want to place anyone's life in jeopardy."

"Well, after praying about this, it seems to be the right thing to do," Karen said.

"I think we have to accept the very real possibility that Alaska will be a completely different place in a few short years. We might as well do what we can to have a say in its development. After all, we know the land better than those from the States."

"True. I think there are those, however, who won't care what the truth is about this land. Besides that, what about the war in Europe? It shows no signs of letting up and being resolved. Did you see the article in the paper from Seattle? The one about that English nurse the Germans murdered?"

"How could I not?"

"What kind of people does it take to kill a woman who worked to help so many? Edith Cavell was the head of the nursing staff there in Brussels."

"Yes, but she aided the enemy, as far as Germany was concerned."

"She helped her countrymen and others to escape prison camps and certain death. I know she was an enemy to the Germans, but she's a hero in this country. I just can't believe that anyone would put a woman to death for simply helping people to live."

"The situation seems to be escalating out of control. Boys are dying and the world seems to be in the fight of its life. Makes me glad to be so far removed."

"But with aeroplanes and trains coming to Alaska, it won't be that way for long."

Adrik tossed back the coffee and got to his feet. "No, I suppose it won't. Still, I'd rather have some kind of say in what's happening than to turn away and pretend it won't come if we ignore it."

"I agree," Karen said with a sigh. "I just wish it weren't the case. I've truly come to love the north, just as my parents loved it. Their missions work up here to the Tlingit people was something I didn't completely understand. In my youth I thought them rather mad for leaving the comforts of the real world." She grinned at this reference. Ashlie often chided her parents that she deserved to at least try life in the "real world" before being forced to spend the rest of her life in the frozen north.

"The real world," Adrik repeated and nodded. "I can't say I've ever seen such a place, other than what we have right here." He frowned and looked at Karen. "Perhaps we should consider sending Ashlie to live with some of your family in the States."

Karen could see he was serious. It was the first time they'd really discussed the possibility. "She won't be happy with the move to Seward—that much is true. Still, I hate to see our family separated."

"She's almost grown. Maybe we could get her into a regular school down there and let her see just how the *real* world operates."

Karen considered it for a moment. "If you think it's for the best."

"What do you think?"

Karen got to her feet and came to where her husband stood. "I think Ashlie will leave us no matter what. Perhaps if we send her on our terms and with our blessing, she'll feel less rebellious and more appreciative of what she already has."

Adrik nodded. "Why don't you send a telegram and make some arrangements? We'll send some extra money with her. That should see to her physical needs."

"My family would never take money from us—you know that." She was still surprised by Adrik's sudden turnaround. Never before had he advocated sending their daughter south. Perhaps it was all God's timing, she thought.

"Well, try to send it anyway. If nothing else, tell them to keep it for Ashlie's return trip home."

Karen sighed. "If she ever does come home."

Leah helped Helaina into the sled basket. Chase had demanded they leave immediately, and while Leah knew Helaina was in no shape to travel, there was nothing she could say or do to persuade Chase to stay.

"My brother will be closing in. I can feel him coming."

Leah shook her head. "He won't stop just because you keep pressing on. You've crossed a line this time. You have to know that."

Chase shrugged. "I was always crossing lines as far as Jayce was concerned." He motioned to Helaina. "Is she going to make it?"

"I doubt it," Leah stated matter-of-factly. "You're taking her out into the elements, and the trip will only get rougher. She's very sick. I think you should leave her here."

"I can't. Besides, Frank would kill her for sure. He says she talks too much. He'd cut her tongue out at the very least."

Leah refused to show any shock at what Chase said, but inwardly she shuddered. "Very well. I'll do my best to help her. But it won't be easy."

"Nothing in my life has ever been easy," Chase said bitterly. "I don't know why this should be any different."

"Did you get my traps repacked?" Leah asked, looking at the sled basket.

"They're near the back. Can you both ride in that basket?"

Leah looked at the sled and nodded. "It'll be hard on the dogs. The going will be slower."

"I've added the dogs I stole out of Nome. They aren't the quality that your brother has raised, but they'll get by and give us a better time of it—at least for a while."

"All right, but they're also going to require more food. Does Frank have some for you to take along?"

Chase laughed. "Frank has very little to spare for any reason. We'll get by. You'll trap us something nice and perhaps I can shoot us a caribou or bear. Bear seem to be plentiful around these parts, and they make good eating."

Leah nodded. "It'll take a bear to keep this brood in decent shape to make the trip. I don't know where you plan to take us, but be advised, these dogs won't last long without a decent supply of food."

"It's duly noted. Now get in that basket with Mrs. Beecham. Perhaps your added warmth will help her to heal."

"And if she dies?" Leah questioned.

"Then let me know so we can dispose of the body." His callous attitude reflected the deep void in his soul. "I'm sure the dogs would love it."

They moved out quickly, Chase sparing no consideration of the team. Leah felt sorry for the brood. They were well rested, but their rations had been quite meager. Chase hadn't even allowed Leah to care for them; instead, he'd relegated her to play nursemaid to the fading Helaina.

"Where does he intend to take us?" Helaina asked groggily. The medicine Leah had given her had caused her to breathe a bit easier, but it also induced sleep. Frankly, Leah was glad for the silence.

"I don't know. I tried to get him to leave you behind. I thought maybe Frank could get you to safety, but Chase insisted you be a part of this journey."

"Good." Helaina nodded. "I can ... watch ... him that way."

Leah shook her head and eased back against the basket. "You can hardly watch the passing scenery, much less keep track of Chase Kincaid."

"I haven't found anything," Jayce said in complete frustration. "How about you?"

Jacob studied the landscape a few more minutes, then answered. "There's nothing here. Maybe John will have had a better time of it. He really is the best tracker. He should be back soon."

Jayce pulled off his eye protection and stared out across the white landscape. He was grateful for the little wooden slit goggles Jacob had given him, but at the same time he felt they restricted his vision too much for close-up work like tracking. "There's got to be some signs ... somewhere. Two, three people can't just disappear without a trace."

"The storms have wreaked havoc with the trail, Jayce. You know that as well as anybody. We might as well just sit it out and wait for John. Hopefully he'll have some good news for us."

They waited for nearly an hour before John and most of the others returned. "We killed a bull caribou two miles up. I left a couple men to prepare the meat. We need to feed the dogs." John smiled and added, "Need to feed me too."

Jacob nodded. "Any sign of the trail?"

"I think so. I found some tracks buried deep. Looks like they went that way." John pointed toward the northeast. "I know some people up there. Bad folks. Not good."

"Just the kind of company my brother prefers," Jayce said, repositioning the goggles. "How about I head out that way on snowshoes, and when you get the dogs taken care of you can catch up to me. The day is clear and bright. You shouldn't have any trouble tracking me."

"It would be better if we stayed together. We don't need to lose you as well."

Jayce picked up his gun. "We can't let them get much farther, Jacob. You know that as well as I do."

Jacob put out his hand and touched Jayce's shoulder. "I know. But I also know there is strength in our numbers. We have food and we have good trackers. We need to be sensible about this. You and I know this territory to a point, but John and his men know it even better. This is their homeland. Not for five or ten years, but for a lifetime. We have to trust them."

Jayce understood the logic in what Jacob said, but he didn't like it. Leah was out there somewhere, and Chase was her captor. He cringed when he thought of what might have already happened. He didn't trust his brother to be honorable ... even though he said otherwise to keep Jacob from worrying about Helaina. Chase was a man who would take whatever pleased him, but he was also a man bent on revenge. How better to avenge the wrongs he considered done him? He would know that in hurting Leah, he would hurt Jayce more than any other way. He would also know that Jayce would never stop coming for him if he did hurt Leah. And perhaps that was what Chase wanted more than anything: He wanted Jayce to come for him. Maybe he even wanted Jayce to end this whole miserable thing. There was no way of telling.

Turning away in defeat and frustration, Jayce waited for Jacob to finish securing the dogs. *Lord, this isn't easy. In fact it's the hardest thing I've ever done,* Jayce prayed. "I ask that you protect Leah from my brother. He's evil and he cares nothing about anyone but himself."

"Did you say something?" Jacob asked, coming alongside Jayce.

"I was just praying," Jayce said. He drew a deep breath and let it out slowly. "Are we ready to move out?"

"Yes."

Jayce started to walk away, but Jacob stopped him. "John says we're very close. He doesn't think they're very far now."

Jayce nodded without turning around. "Good." He said nothing more. In his mind he wondered how the matter would resolve itself when they found Chase. Jayce hated the thought that he would have to kill his brother in order to free Leah, but deep inside his heart, Jayce was convinced that it would probably be the only way. "Let's get going."

Chapter Nine

The weather cleared, but the shortened days gave them less and less sunlight by which to traverse the land. Leah constantly looked for landmarks that might help her find her way back home. She tried to memorize the trail, as well as figure out ways in which she might actually escape Chase. She needed dogs and a weapon. Those things would ensure her success. Without either, she wasn't convinced she could make it.

Helaina seemed no better. The herbs were causing her to sleep, but she was still feverish. Leah could only pray that God would help them. There was very little chance that Leah could get the sickly Helaina away from Chase, even if a moment of escape presented itself. Of course, Helaina had already stated on several occasions that she would not go.

Chase stopped them for the night and, after allowing Leah to help him set up camp, tied her up with Helaina. "You don't need to trap tonight. We need to leave no sign of our being here. I won't even have a fire." He stared out into the growing darkness as if sensing his brother's presence.

"I'm going to backtrack and make sure we've left no signs along the way," he told her. He gathered a small pack and slung it on his back. "Keep quiet."

"What if we're attacked?" Leah questioned. "You've seen the bear tracks, not to mention wolf and lynx. There are plenty of animals out here—no doubt hungry animals."

"The dogs will raise a ruckus if anything comes near. If that happens, I'll hear it and come back. I won't let anything happen to you." He leaned down and touched her cheek. Leah jerked back, causing him to laugh. "I could make you just as happy as Jayce has."

"Hardly," Leah replied.

He eyed her for a moment, then glanced at the sleeping Helaina. "In time, I'll prove it to you. We could be quite happy up here together. You know the land and the people. I have skills as well. Once Jayce and your brother are out of the way ..." He let his words trail off.

Leah looked away lest he see the tears that were forming. She had noticed Chase watching her more closely. His eyes held a kind of hungry look that she had never seen. Chase frightened her more and more, and she knew her escape must come soon or he might well act upon that hunger.

Helaina stirred and opened her eyes a short time later. With Chase gone, Leah leaned down to speak. "We have to get out of here soon," she told Helaina.

"I told you, I can't go." Helaina fell into a spell of coughing and gasping. The pain was evident with each breath she drew.

"You can't stay," Leah replied. "You're very sick. I need to get you to safety."

"I'm feeling much better. Look, while we're on the trail it should be easy to overpower him. There are two of us."

"Two of us who are tied up. What do you suggest? Should I gnaw through the ropes?" Leah's sarcasm was not lost on Helaina.

Helaina struggled to sit up. "I am better. I feel stronger. Just help me in this. We can overpower him. Then you can get us back to Nome."

"No. I want no part in taking Chase prisoner. I've told you that before. I won't risk our lives that way. We need to get away from him."

"I've been thinking," Helaina said. "We can knock him over the head while he sleeps. Then we can tie him up."

"Again, how do you propose to do this when we are tied up nightly?"

Helaina nodded. "I've been thinking about that too. You are allowed to prepare dinner each evening. You could hide your *ulu* and retrieve it after he goes to sleep."

The thought had already occurred to Leah, but Chase always kept close track of the tools she used. Especially in skinning the animals and preparing the meat. "Chase said that I can't trap tonight. He's not even going to allow us a fire for supper. He's too worried about Jayce and Jacob spotting us."

"Well, he'll want food sooner or later. When he does, you can hide the knife. Or wait . . ." Helaina said, glancing around. "What about your herbs? Might you have something in there that could put him to sleep? That would be perfect. You could put it in his food."

"How do you propose I do that without putting it in our food as well?" Leah questioned. "Chase is hardly going to eat food that we refuse to touch. What then?"

"There has to be a way, Leah. I'm sure of it."

"Like I said, he's not even allowing for a fire tonight, much less for me to prepare food. We'll probably eat nothing more than dried salmon and crackers until he feels we're safely out of Jayce and Jacob's reach."

"Just keep it in mind, Leah. Sooner or later he's going to want something hot again. I'm sure of it. Just be ready for the moment."

Leah thought about Helaina's suggestion long into the night. By the time they were on the trail several hours before dawn, she was beginning to think there might be some merit to Helaina's plan. She could put herbs in the food, after setting some food aside for herself, then drug not only Chase, but Helaina as well. It wouldn't be easy to pull off, but so far it was the best plan Leah could come up with.

When they stopped again the next evening, Chase seemed far less concerned about being spotted. He allowed Leah to go set her traps but followed her at a distance. His gaze never left her and Leah hated the feeling. When she walked back to where he was standing, Chase seemed quite lost in his thoughts. At least she'd thought him to be. When she walked past him, however, Chase reached out and pulled her without warning into his arms.

"Let me go," she said, struggling against him.

"You're really very beautiful. I can see why my brother would fall in love with you. I can see why he would hunt me down to take you back."

Leah fought his hold, but Chase was much stronger. "Leah,"

he murmured against her ear. He slipped his hand inside her parka. "I want you."

The lust and desire in his voice froze Leah in place. "Let me go, Chase. You have no right to touch me like this."

He pulled back to look in her eyes. In the growing darkness, Leah could barely see his face, but she could feel the intensity of his stare. "I've always taken what I wanted," he said, his voice edged with anger. "I want you, Leah. And I mean to have you." He forced her to the ground and threw himself on top of her to hold her still. "We can do this the easy way or with great difficulty and pain. It's up to you."

"It's never been up to me," Leah said, still struggling against him. "You took that choice from me back in Last Chance."

———

Jacob stared out across the landscape as the first hint of light touched the horizon. Their progress had been slow but steady. The day before they had managed to find the cabin where Chase had held Helaina and Leah. They had waited in the dark, keeping watch, and when the old man tried to sneak into their camp, John had wrestled him to the ground. The old man had admitted everything. He had told of knowing Chase from encounters with him earlier in the year. He had admitted to being well paid in supplies to hold Helaina while Chase went for additional goods and animals.

Jacob wasn't at all sure what they should do with the man and his wife. He knew they couldn't leave them unrestrained or they might well come after the party. On the other hand, they couldn't just tie them up and leave them to die. Finally John had come up with a solution. He arranged for two of his men to transport the couple to the nearest village. John had an arrangement with a village just to the west of where they were situated. He felt certain that once his men presented the couple and explained the situation, the village elders there would take the matter under consideration and keep them prisoner until the proper legal authorities could arrive to arrest the old man.

"I know they're out there somewhere," Jacob muttered. He gazed to the skies. "You know where they are, Lord, and I'm just asking that you keep my sister and Helaina safe, and that you would guide me to their hiding place. We need your help now more than ever."

"He's getting better at covering his tracks," John said as he joined Jacob on the ridge. "But he's not as good as he thinks."

This caused Jacob to smile. "How far ahead of us are they?"

"Three, maybe four, days. They're still following a straight path," John said, pointing. "Heading north. Just like they've been doing since they left that old man's place."

Jacob nodded. "We're not gaining on them quickly enough. Dare we push on, even in the dark, and trust that they will continue this path?"

John looked north across the horizon. "I cannot say, Jacob. If we trust that and they go west or east, we will lose a lot of time."

It was the very thing that Jacob had already considered. "But if we don't start taking some chances soon, we'll never catch up with them. They have the lead and the advantage of knowing where they're headed. We can't just follow at this slow pace and hope to overcome them."

"Then I would go north. We can keep pushing ... travel during the night. When light comes, I can check for signs."

"I think that's our best chance," Jacob said.

"Our best chance for what?" Jayce asked, joining them.

"We're going to press on through the night. We'll change out drivers and rest in the basket as the other one drives. When light comes, John will check for signs and see if we're still on the right trail."

"But that's a big risk," Jayce countered. "What if we lose the trail in the night?"

"We were just discussing that," Jacob admitted. "But if we do nothing, we'll never gain any ground. We've noted that they are moving steadily north. Hopefully they will continue that way, but even if they don't, we can always backtrack and find where they changed course. I'm just afraid if we don't take a chance, we won't catch up with them until Chase reaches wherever he's headed and has a chance to dig in and defend himself against us. We'll have a much better situation if we can catch him out here on the open trail."

Jayce nodded. "I suppose you're right. I trust your judgment in this."

"We need to go," John stated firmly. "We will go fast and travel round the clock. I'll get the dogs ready." He headed back to the teams and Jayce followed after him.

Jacob watched them walk away. He wished fervently that he had a better feeling about their situation, but he couldn't muster up much hope. He felt a deep sense of dread and frustration. The old man back at the cabin had told him that Helaina was very sick and he figured she'd die. The thought of it troubled Jacob's heart like nothing else. If she died, he knew a part of his heart would die as well.

Leah tried not to think about what Chase had done to her. She had hoped ... prayed that he would not take such liberties. She had wanted to believe that there was some good in Chase—something buried down deep inside that would keep him from hurting her. But she'd been wrong.

Now as she sat in the basket with Helaina, she wiped at the tears that would not stop flowing. How could God let Chase rape her? She'd tried her best to be kind and share God's love with Chase. She had presumed that in return, God would keep her from harm. Wasn't that the way it was supposed to be? If she trusted God, put Him first, and did everything in accordance with the Bible, God would protect her. But He hadn't.

Trembling, Leah tried to regroup her thoughts. It was bad enough to feel hatred toward Chase, but worse still to feel such isolation from God. She tried to rationalize that what Chase had done needn't change her—shouldn't steal away her peace and faith in God's goodness—but the more she thought about what had happened, the more she could still feel his hands on her body. And the more she relived what Chase had done, the more she longed to kill the man.

She drew a ragged breath and forced down the lump in her throat. *How can I ever face Jayce again? How can I ever hope for him to comprehend what this means? He'll never understand or want me after this. Chase has been nothing but a thorn in his side since they were young. Now this has happened.* She shook her head. Jayce could never want her back after this. She would be better off dead.

Chapter Ten

Karen struggled with her fears for Leah and Jacob. She couldn't shake the premonition that they were in some kind of danger. She tried to pray about it, but often she felt her prayers reached no higher than the ceiling. Adrik offered comfort and support, but Karen knew it was a burden she would carry until she found out for certain they were safe. Now standing at the Ketchikan dock, preparing to bid her firstborn good-bye, Karen didn't know if anything would ever feel safe or normal again.

"Mama, you mustn't worry," Ashlie declared. "Cousin Myrtle said she would take good care of me."

Karen tried to smile. Her elderly cousin had written an enthusiastic letter upon learning that Ashlie had a desire to travel south. Myrtle had pledged to be the best of chaperones, assuring Karen that Ashlie would be properly dressed and arranged in the third pew of the First Seattle Lutheran Church every Sunday. Furthermore, she would pay for the girl to attend a very fine finishing school there in the Seattle area.

Knowing that Myrtle was left a wealthy, but childless, widow, Karen had no doubt that the old woman was lonely and in need of someone to spoil. Ashlie, on the other hand, was a young woman in need of an adventure. The two seemed mismatched, but Karen felt a peace about sending her daughter to the older woman. At least as much peace as a mother could have when parting with her only daughter.

"I know you'll be fine," Karen said. She reached out to touch an errant wisp of her daughter's strawberry blond hair. Ashlie had pinned it up in a very adult manner and topped her coiffure with a dainty hat she'd actually made. Karen was impressed with the girl's skills but knew it wouldn't matter now if she complimented her on such. Ashlie's mind and heart were set on the journey to come.

Karen forced a smile. "I can't say this is easy. One day you may be a mother, and you will know just how difficult such a separation can be."

Ashlie hugged her mother tightly. Karen thought perhaps she did this more for herself than for Karen. "I know it's not easy for you, Mama. I'm just grateful you are allowing it." She pulled back and looked into her mother's eyes. "I don't want to appear as though I don't care about your feelings . . . but I'm just so excited. I feel as though everything good is about to happen to me all at once."

Karen nodded and smiled. How could she not be enthusiastic? The child's excitement was almost contagious. Even her brothers were jostling around the pier in animated wonder.

"Well, as soon as your father returns with the Reverend Mulberry, I suppose you'll board the ship." Karen looked across the crowd of people to where the southbound *Horatio* was docked. "You mind your manners and listen to whatever the reverend tells you. I don't want any bad reports on how you caused him undue worry."

"I will be as good as the boys on Christmas morning," Ashlie teased. "But I still don't see why the reverend has to travel with me. I'm almost sixteen."

"Ashlie, this is not a civilized land. For all of our pretenses at being one, we hardly come close. Of course, from what I remember of so-called civilized lands, they could be far more dangerous than anything you've grown up knowing." She hugged Ashlie close again. "Oh, you will be careful, won't you?"

Ashlie laughed. "Of course I will. Now stop worrying. Remember what you said about worry being a sin? You said it was like saying that God couldn't do what He had promised. It was like calling God a liar."

Karen drew a deep breath and nodded. "I guess I thought you weren't listening to such things."

Ashlie grasped her mother's arm. "I was listening to that and a whole lot more. Please . . . don't be afraid. I'll come and see you soon. You'll see."

Karen knew she had to be brave. She squared her shoulders and drew in another deep breath. "I know you'll have a wonderful time. Don't forget to write to me and tell me everything."

"Papa's coming!" nine-year-old Christopher declared. "See! There he is with the reverend."

Karen turned to look in the direction her son pointed. Sure enough, there was her bear of a husband towering over the rather petite Reverend Mulberry. They looked almost comical in each other's company. As they approached, Karen put on her bravest smile. "Reverend, it's good to see you. I can't thank you enough for acting as a traveling companion to our daughter."

"It is I who am blessed," the older man said, pushing up wire-rimmed glasses that perpetually rested on the end of his nose. "How could I refuse such sweet company? Or such a generous donation to bettering my own quarters. I don't believe I've ever had a stateroom to myself. I think it all so fortuitous that I should be traveling home to Illinois just when you needed a companion for your daughter."

Karen looked to her husband and back to the reverend. "God knew exactly what we needed, and it was our pleasure to improve your journey. You are, after all, guarding one of our most precious gifts."

He nodded. "Indeed, Miss Ashlie is a remarkable girl. I've no doubt she will excel in her finishing school."

"You have the address and money I gave you to hire transportation to Myrtle's house?" Adrik asked Ashlie.

"It's all right here," Ashlie declared, patting her small purse. "I shall keep it with me at all times."

The final boarding was called for all passengers bound for Seattle. Ashlie looked momentarily panic-stricken, and then the expression was replaced by one of sheer joy. "It's time!" She threw herself into her father's arms.

Karen watched the scene play out, feeling almost as though she were watching from a dream. Ashlie tousled Christopher's hair and then embraced him for just a moment. The boy was clearly embarrassed by the whole thing and squirmed out of her hold. Oliver, suddenly quite somber, allowed the hug and even offered Ashlie the briefest peck on the cheek.

"I'll miss you both," Ashlie told her brothers before turning back to her mother. "I'll miss all of you, but I've wanted to do this for so long."

Karen smiled and embraced her daughter one final time. "I know you're happy, and that pleases me. But I feel as though I'm sending a part of my heart away. Guard it well." She felt tears fall and didn't try to hide them. She needed Ashlie to understand the importance of this moment.

"I promise I will, Mama," Ashlie whispered against her mother's ear. She pulled back and saw the tears. Instantly her eyes dampened. "We're a fine pair," she said, barely keeping her voice from quivering.

Karen nodded. "A fine pair indeed."

The reverend had moved to the gangplank, where he waited patiently for Ashlie to join him. Adrik prayed for their safe journey, then handed Ashlie's small bag to her. "I'll miss you, my girl. Don't forget to write to us in Seward, care of the railroad. We leave the day after tomorrow."

"I won't forget."

And then she was gone, moving up the gangplank, Reverend Mulberry at her side. They appeared to be chatting comfortably, neither one too concerned about the people they were leaving behind.

Adrik came and put his arm around Karen's shoulders. She felt comfort at his touch, but her tears would not stop flowing.

"Are you all right, Mama?" Christopher asked. He patted her hand as if to help. Oliver came to stand in front of her beside his brother. He simply looked up at her, as if ascertaining her well-being.

"I'll be all right, boys." She hoped her voice sounded

reassuring. She wiped at the tears with her handkerchief, then spied Ashlie and the reverend at the rail. They were waving good-bye along with many other people. Karen waved her handkerchief rather than shouting her good-bye because words would not come. *How can I let her go, just like that? Send her thousands of miles away ... Oh, Ashlie ... please be safe. Please be happy.*

"Your boots are smoking," Chase said, sounding rather startled. "Do you not see it?"

Leah looked at the mukluks and realized her fate. Sitting beside the fire, she'd not even noticed that her mukluks were being singed by the flames. She pulled her feet back and powdered them with snow. Bitterness corrupted her thinking. She was making mistakes at a time when she couldn't afford to make them. She could feel Chase watch her; still, she did her best to ignore him— to pretend he simply didn't exist.

"How is Mrs. Beecham today?" Chase asked.

Leah said nothing. Helaina was still quite ill, and Chase already knew it. He was simply trying to engage her in conversation. Leah felt certain he regretted what he'd done to her. But he could never regret it as much as she did.

Leah stared at the fire, her shoulders hunched, her face kept down. As Chase squatted down beside her, she cringed inwardly but held her ground.

"Look," he began. "I don't know what to say. I can't change what happened. I ... well ..." His voice faded as he seemed to consider what to say. "I didn't intend for it to happen. Not really. I know I've acted inappropriately since we first met, but ..."

well . . . you must understand, what happened wasn't a reflection on you at all."

Leah's head snapped up. This was nothing like the man who'd tormented her since forcing her from Last Chance. She looked at him in disbelief. "You sound as though you're offering conversation over tea and cakes. As though the offense was something as simple as a stolen kiss. You didn't intend for it to happen . . . it isn't a reflection on me. Is that supposed to make me feel better? Is that supposed to make it right?"

Chase shook his head. He no longer looked as much like her husband as he had when she'd first met him. Worry, fear, even exhaustion marred his features, and the beard he'd grown on the trail also altered his face. He seemed to hold less power over her now. . . . It was almost as if he'd done the worst to her that he could, so what was left to fear? Death would have been a kindness, as far as Leah was concerned.

"I know it can't make things right," Chase said, getting to his feet. He paced out a space on the opposite side of the fire. "I don't know why I did what I did. I wanted to hurt you . . . but not really even you. I wanted to hurt him." He looked at her hard. "I wanted to hurt Jayce."

"I don't care," Leah said evenly. She had never intended to get into a conversation with this hideous creature. She looked down at the fire again.

"You should. The hate between us will probably kill us both."

She shook her head, still not looking at him. "The hate has already killed you. You aren't a human being anymore. You're an animal. You kill and maim at will. You are like a rabid dog gone mad and you need to be eliminated."

"So the good Christian now wishes me dead?"

This caused an anger in Leah that she had not expected. Leaping to her feet, she jumped the fire to claw at his arrogant face. "You have no right," she said, flailing as he fought to control her. "You lost your right to compassion and kindness when you took from me what you had no right to take."

"But that's what I'm trying to say." He pushed her back, almost pained at the contact of even touching her. "I took from Jayce. Not from you."

Leah saw the emotion in his eyes but didn't care. She balled her hands into fists. "I am Jayce and he is me. When you harm one of us, the other bleeds. You are a fool. You have no idea what you have done. The war between you and your brother has only grown more intense ... more destructive. Jayce will never let you live now. Not that I care. I only hope your actions don't get Jayce hurt in the process."

She could hardly believe her own venomous words. There was nothing of the love of Jesus in her heart at that moment. Her anger and wounded spirit refused to be calmed by the comfort she knew could be hers.

Chase seemed genuinely stunned by her reaction. Perhaps he had thought to merely apologize and seek her forgiveness. Maybe he believed her a simpleton because of her religious beliefs. Whatever his reasoning, there could be no doubting her thoughts now.

Chase straightened. "I can't undo what's happened. What's done is done."

His matter-of-fact words served only to further irritate Leah. "Oh, it's not done, Mr. Kincaid. Not by a long shot. Jayce will come for you. He will come because of Helaina and because of me. And when he finds out what you have done to us ... he will even the score."

She turned and walked away, going to the tent where Helaina slept. Leah was certain the woman was dying. There simply wasn't proper medicine to treat her sickness. Leah crouched down and crawled inside the tent. It was surprisingly warm. Leah had lit a pot of seal oil for light and heat, and the results were quite satisfactory. Reaching out, Leah touched Helaina's forehead and felt that the fever still raged. If she couldn't find a way to ease the temperature, Helaina would no doubt die.

Leah shook her head. If only Helaina would have done what she was supposed to do. If only the woman would have been obedient to her brother.

"This is all your fault," Leah said, shaking her head. "I hate you as much as I hate him. I don't care whether you live or die. You've brought this on yourself."

Leah regretted the words the minute they were out of her mouth. But perhaps more than that, she regretted the ugly hate that festered, out of control, in her heart. There seemed no way to overcome it. She was a prisoner to those feelings, as much as she was a captive of Chase Kincaid.

Chapter Eleven

Leah's mind was made up. Botanist Teddy Davenport, dear friend from the gold rush days, had sent Leah a nice shipment of herbs that weren't available in her part of Alaska. He knew of her medical work in Last Chance and had kindly sent the herbs, along with instructions for their use, to help in her cause.

She had some of these herbs with her now. One of them was belladonna—deadly nightshade, as some called it. A little bit could be used to relieve respiratory spasms. In fact, she had used some to ease Helaina's cough. A little higher dosage could be used as a sedative for surgery. More still could cause death.

Leah would simply slip some belladonna into the food that night and put Chase to sleep. Once he was asleep, she would take Helaina and they would head out. She'd tried to focus on the trail as Chase pushed them ever farther north and into the interior. She'd never journeyed this direction and hadn't even heard Jacob tell tales of such trips. It would be difficult to escape and make an easy path home, but to do anything else might well end her life . . . or Chase's.

The rage she felt toward Chase terrified Leah. She tried to calm her spirit, but she found there was no reasoning with herself at times. Just as soon as she'd convince herself that everything would be all right—that Jayce would still love her and that she would heal from the damage done by Chase—her anger would resurface, and Leah found herself wishing fervently that she could exact her revenge.

The days were shorter than ever. Leah had lost track of the time but knew that if they continued north they would soon have no daylight at all. That would make travel very dangerous. She felt certain Chase couldn't be all that capable in such circumstances.

Chase brought them to a stop earlier than Leah had expected. He'd grown careless of late—no longer going back to see that the trails were obliterated, nor concerned about having a fire at night. He had even allowed Leah to begin trapping again, although the catches had not been good.

Tonight, Leah thought, *tonight I will end this one way or another.* She tried to think of exactly how to handle the situation. She would set the traps and hope that perhaps something could be caught before she needed to leave the area. She would prepare Helaina's medicated broth and while measuring out those herbs, would add the belladonna to the main dish. The trick would be to put aside some food for herself—food that hadn't been tainted. She couldn't risk putting herself to sleep along with Chase and Helaina.

"Will you set the traps tonight?" Chase asked in a gentle tone. Since the assault, he had strangely gone out of his way to ease the tension between them, but Leah wanted no part of it.

"Don't I set them every night? At least every night that you aren't too fearful to let me out of your sight?" She wished immediately that she could take the words back. Perhaps she should force herself to be nice to him—just long enough to put her plan into motion. *No,* she thought just as quickly. *He'll know that something's going on if I treat him well. I have to continue with things just as they are or it will ruin my plans.* She looked at him from the corner of her eye and set her jaw. "So are you letting me set them tonight?"

"I see no reason to do otherwise." He seemed rather thoughtful for a moment. "You always manage to make us good meals. You're a good cook."

She hated his patronage. She knew his words were only intended to sooth his own guilty conscience, and Leah refused to give him such comfort.

"Your flattery means nothing." She glared at him. "You are still worse than an animal. I'll not absolve you of your sins."

"But what of forgiveness?" Chase asked, surprising her. "Doesn't your God require you give forgiveness when people seek it?"

"Lately my God has required a great many things of me," Leah answered. "If He wants me to forgive you, however, He's asking too much."

She stomped off toward the sled basket, where Helaina slept. The traps were tied to the side toward the back. Leah reached out and touched Helaina's forehead. To her surprise it seemed the fever had lessened considerably. Leah checked the younger woman's breathing. It appeared much less labored, more even. Perhaps Mrs. Beecham was on the mend.

"How is she?" Chase asked, coming up behind Leah.

Leah jumped and moved away as though he might touch her. "She's very sick. I've already told you that."

Leah turned to go, but Chase questioned her again. "Should I put her in the tent?"

Leah hated that he was asking her opinion. He was doing this only to force her into conversation, thinking she might crack under his kindness and give him what he seemed to crave more than anything: her pardon.

"I think she'll be warmer and more comfortable in the sled." Leah kept her answers short and without emotion. She walked away without waiting for him to respond and was glad when he said nothing.

With the traps set, Leah went back to their cache of food and began to unwrap the supplies. She thought of what she was about to do and realized that she had no concern for Chase's well-being. She knew the herbs she would use could kill if too much was consumed. She knew, too, that some people reacted violently to the medication. She'd seen a man die in their village when he'd had such a reaction. But her heart was hardened. If Chase died, she'd consider it justice and nothing more.

The wind picked up, causing the flames to dance in their campfire. Leah watched the show and thought of a time long ago when she had sat at her mother's knee before their hearth. She could almost feel her mother brushing out her hair . . . almost hear her speak.

"*Leah,*" her mother had said, "*sometimes life is very hard. It doesn't mean God no longer cares. It's just the way things are at times.*"

"*But it seems unfair,*" Leah had replied. "*If God loves us so very much that He would send His Son Jesus to die for us, then why not keep the bad things away from us?*"

Her mother had leaned down and kissed her on the top of her head. *"I wish I had an easy answer for you, my love. God has His reasons. They sometimes seem cruel, I know. But I promise you, Leah, even when things seem confusing and wrong, God loves you. He's still by your side, holding your hand—guiding you through the painful times."*

Leah didn't realize she was crying until droplets fell onto her hands as she prepared the hare she had saved from the previous night. She wiped at her cheeks with the back of her sleeve and tried not to think about the memory of her mother. The thoughts would not leave her, however.

Life might have been very different had her mother lived. Leah might never have come to Alaska. She might never have known the sorrows and betrayals that had haunted her days. Jayce Kincaid might never have entered her life, and without him there would certainly have been no Chase.

But would I trade away the good along with the bad? The question permeated her hard façade. There were many wonderful things that had also come her way. The love she knew with Jayce had been the fulfillment of everything she had hoped for. Would she throw that away as well?

"But that's all ended now," she said, not meaning to speak the words aloud. She looked up, wondering if Chase had overheard her. Yet he was nowhere in sight. Sometimes he took himself away from the camp, but never for long. Often he was trying his best to hunt food, but for some reason the game was quite scarce in this area.

Leah turned her attention back to the broth. Ayoona had given her some dried *mazué*—Eskimo potatoes. Leah had hoarded them away for times when the food was scarce. The mazué were good by themselves and could even be eaten raw with seal oil. This time, however, Leah thought the added treat might entice Chase to eat more than a small portion. Cutting the roots with her ulu, Leah made a list in her head of things she needed to do in order to make her escape plan work.

I will need to hide the knife so that I can cut my bonds if Chase ties me up tonight. Her hope was that the belladonna would work quickly and Chase would fall asleep long before he thought of securing Leah for the night.

I will also need to collect the traps and anything that might be in them. She glanced at the basket. Helaina continued to sleep, but Leah figured to wake her and get some of the drugged broth down her. She couldn't risk having Helaina awaken and raise a fuss about their leaving Chase behind.

Leah portioned out some of the broth and left the rest of the soup to cook. She put another dose of belladonna in the mixture and stirred it for several seconds. This should keep Helaina asleep and cooperative.

Going to the basket, Leah arranged things so that she could sit beside the sick woman. "Helaina, wake up. I have some broth for you."

To her surprise, Helaina managed to open her eyes. "Are we there yet?"

"Where?" Leah was surprised by the woman's question.

Helaina shook her head. "I don't know. I can't remember. I just . . . wondered . . . why we'd stopped."

"We've stopped for the night, and no, we aren't there—wherever there might be. We're still in the middle of the wilds." Leah lifted a spoonful of broth. "Now take this. It will make you feel better."

"I do feel better," Helaina replied. "I don't feel so cold."

"I think your fever broke. I can't be sure that it will remain gone, but for now it seems to have passed. That's why you must take your medicine."

"Thank you for taking care of me." She swallowed the broth and closed her eyes. "That's very good. What is it?"

"It's just a concoction of things," Leah replied honestly. "I used what I had available. You have to keep up your strength."

"I know you . . . are . . . unhappy with me," Helaina said before taking more of the soup. "I'm sorry for the . . . trouble I've caused. I hope you'll forgive me."

Leah grimaced. Yet another person asking for forgiveness, as though that might suddenly make everything fine. She spooned more soup into Helaina's mouth, hoping to silence her, but it didn't work.

"I know your faith is strong. I know you will forgive me, but . . . well . . . sometimes I think I don't deserve forgiveness."

Leah focused on the bowl. "There are times when everyone feels that way. I think people especially feel that way when they know just how wrong they were to begin with."

Helaina shook her head. "I know I went about things in the wrong . . . way." She yawned and Leah knew the herbs were working.

"Forget about it. You need to stop talking and eat."

Helaina gave up the discussion and Leah breathed a sigh of relief. She hadn't had to lie and tell Helaina that she didn't feel like forgiving her and then wrestle with some argument about why Leah was obligated to forgive.

By the time the bowl of soup was gone, Helaina was once again unconscious. Her heavy breathing suggested a very deep sleep. Leah felt a huge sense of relief as she returned to the fire and checked the soup. Everything was ready. All she needed now was for Chase to return. Leah pulled out the portion of meat and broth she'd hidden for herself. She slipped a few pieces of root into her own mixture and stirred it before sampling.

"It smells marvelous," Chase said, once again slipping into camp without a sound.

"It's ready."

Leah continued eating her own portion, hoping he'd sit down and serve himself. To her surprise, he did just that. She tried not to look anxious as he began to eat. He ate nearly half a bowl before commenting further.

"It tastes as good as it smelled. I could eat the entire pot."

"Do as you will. I have all I want." Leah hoped her words sounded indifferent. She didn't want him to suspect a thing. Not until she was long gone.

Chase dished himself more food and sat back. Leah finished her bowl and grew nervous about what to do next. She had slipped the ulu under the fur on which she sat and hoped Chase wouldn't ask for it as he usually did after their meal was concluded.

"You know, when I was a young man we ate very well. After my father made his fortune, we had the best of everything. I remember sumptuous meals. Huge roasted baron of beef, five and six side dishes with gravy and sauces that made your mouth water just to see them on the table. Oh, and the bread ... Our cook could make the flakiest rolls—nothing like the sourdough we get up here." He yawned but continued eating.

Leah thought to show him that she felt just as tired. She faked a yawn of her own and forced herself to lean in a relaxed manner near the fire. Chase seemed completely at ease as he continued with his memories.

"My favorite things were the desserts. Oh, we had such wonderful creations." He smiled. "I'm sure I'm boring you—that's
why you're so tired. I'll get the tent set up as soon as I finish
here."

"Don't bother on my account," Leah said with a yawn. "I plan
to sleep in the basket with Helaina. She'll need my warmth. I've
no desire to share the tent with you any more than I have to."

Chase frowned. His eyelids seemed heavy. "I'll have to tie you
up."

"Why should tonight be any different?" Leah asked sarcastically. She changed the subject then, hoping to keep his mind occupied elsewhere. "How long must we continue this journey? Where
are you taking us and when will we finally be there?"

Chase shook his head and downed the last of his meal. "Not
long now. I have a cabin not far from here. It's on the river. It's
plenty warm with lots of wood. It'll keep us well through the
winter."

"You expect to keep us there all winter?" Leah questioned.
"Then what?"

Chase seemed to struggle to think. Leah thought he looked
almost puzzled at her question. "I don't know what we'll do then.
We have to deal with Jayce first. I know he will come. It might
take him a while, but eventually I'll have to deal with him."

"Jayce will hunt you down. You can be assured of that."

Chase put the bowl down and rubbed his eyes. He couldn't
quite keep them open. "What . . . what have you done? What have
you put in the food?"

Leah laughed, but the sound was choked and unnatural. "I've
put in deadly nightshade, some mazué, and the last of our snowshoe hare."

"Nightshade!" He tried to get up but fell back down. "You've poisoned it. You've ... decided ... to kill me."

"Kill you? Why, Mr. Kincaid, as much as I would love to see you pay the ultimate price for your crimes, I have done no such thing. I certainly don't need your death on my conscience."

He fell sideways and struggled to keep awake. "I should shoot you now." He pulled the gun from his coat, but it fell from his hands even as he attempted to raise it.

Leah sat up and watched him fight against the herbs. "It's no use, you know. Belladonna is quite potent. You will be asleep for several hours. More than enough for me to take Helaina and the dogs and leave."

He let his head fall hard against the ground. The jarring prompted him to open his eyes for just a moment. "You'll leave me to my death."

"Maybe," Leah said, getting to her feet. She came to where he rested and picked up the gun. The temptation to put a bullet through his head was strong. The smell of his breath against her face, his hands on her body, his pleasure despite her pain ... the memories begged for her to kill him.

For a moment Leah wrestled with her conscience. She wanted nothing more than to put an end once and for all to this miserable chapter of her life. But would it end? If she killed him now, no one would blame her. They would take into consideration the kidnapping and the rape, and the great possibility that Chase had planned to kill both her and Helaina.

But even as Leah fingered the cold metal of the revolver, she knew she couldn't shoot a defenseless man. She looked at Chase, his expression now relaxed in sleep. He deserved to die, but she'd leave that for someone else.

Without another thought, Leah slipped the gun into her pocket and went to work. She collected her things and loaded them in the sled. She thought to leave Chase without anything, but she couldn't do it. She knew the cruelty of the north. She portioned out a few supplies and left him a knife. There was no possibility of leaving him the rifle or the revolver. It would be dangerous for him to be left without a gun, but Leah couldn't risk it.

The traps were empty, just as she'd figured they'd be. There hadn't been enough time. She gathered them, securing the bait for another time, and tied the traps back on the sled. Her last order of business was to offer Chase some sort of protection from the elements. She stoked up the fire, then took one of the furs and a wool blanket and secured them around his body. It wasn't much, but she couldn't bring herself to do more. In several hours he would awaken and his fate would then rest solely in his own hands.

The dogs sensed that the journey was about to take a new turn as Leah adjusted their harnesses. They moaned and yipped as she rubbed their heads and spoke to them in soothing tones.

"We're almost ready, boys. Come on now, don't fight me." She pushed one of the big wheel dogs back into place as he tried to dance around her. He bumped up against the basket and yipped but finally obeyed Leah. It took only a few more tries before she finally had him strapped securely in place.

With this done, she hurried to light a lantern. It wouldn't help much, but it would give her a sense of the path and their surroundings. Hopefully it would be enough to ward off any dangerous breaks in the trail.

Leah felt her heart racing as she rocked the sled to release it from the ground. The crusty snow gave way easily. She then released the snow hook. "Hike!"

The dogs pulled against the weight easily. Leah circled them around the camp, her gaze resting only momentarily on the sleeping form on the ground.

It's what he deserves, she told her guilty heart.

Chapter Twelve

The tracks head back to the west," John said, coming to join Jacob and Jayce. "We were lucky the dog went lame or we'd have missed it for sure."

Jacob scratched the dog's head. "Well, Brownie can't pull anymore. He'll have to ride." The dog yipped as if to contradict this statement.

Jayce looked to John. "How far behind them are we now?"

"I think maybe just a day or so. Those trails were pretty fresh."

Jacob straightened. "What about villages? Did you find anything in the area?"

John nodded. "Just north and west of here. Not far."

"Do you think they might have seen them?" Brownie strained against Jacob's hold. "Do you think Chase would have gone there?"

John shrugged. "If the villagers were out, they might have seen them, but I don't think Chase went there. Tracks keep going west. I don't think it's a trick."

Jacob considered the words for a moment. "Well, why don't we go there? The dogs need to rest. We've been pushing them pretty hard. We can drop off Brownie, and maybe someone there will know something more. Hopefully they'll be friendly and offer us a meal as well."

"I don't see the harm in it," Jayce replied. "As long as it doesn't take too much time. If John thinks we're just hours apart, I think we need to push on as soon as possible."

"I agree," Jacob said. "I think we'll have an easier time of it without having to worry about Brownie. We can always pick him up on the way back or even trade him for supplies. He's a good dog and he'll heal just fine."

"Maybe they trade information too," John said with a grin.

"We should be cautious." Jacob turned to lift Brownie into his basket. "I've heard rumors that the tribes around here are fighting amongst themselves."

"I'm willing to take the risk," Jayce said, moving to his dog team. "Let's go."

Jacob tied Brownie in the basket. The poor dog was miserable and began howling up a storm as Jacob resumed his place behind the sled. The injustice of it all left Brownie miserable, but he finally settled down in the basket.

They approached the village cautiously. Heavy clouds were blocking what little sun could be had, but it was easy to see that the people were not feeling in the leastwise threatened by the appearance of Jacob and their party.

They exchanged greetings, and Jacob listened as John fired off a rapid line of questioning to the man who seemed to be in charge. The man shook his head vigorously, and John continued with additional questions.

Though the dialect seemed a little different than that of the natives of Last Chance, Jacob caught a good portion of the conversation. Apparently the man had not seen any strangers in the area, and especially not any white people. He would have remembered such a thing. Jacob and Jayce were, in fact, the first whites he'd seen since summer.

Then one of the other men spoke up. He had seen a sled moving west, and it appeared there were at least two people, but he had no idea whether they were white or not.

"How long ago was this?" Jacob asked in the man's tongue.

The older man smiled and replied, "Yesterday morning."

Jacob turned to Jayce. "That has to be them. We should give it all we have to finish the job."

"I agree. I say we let the dogs rest a short time, then immediately put ourselves back on the trail."

"I have to fix my sled runner," John threw in. "I don't need long." He headed off toward his sled.

Jacob went to work seeing to the dogs. Several villagers brought him hot water, and one even prepared a nice fire for him. Jacob began mixing a hot meal for the teams, but all the while his mind went back to the time he'd spent alone with Helaina while they were in Seattle. He thought of how irritating she could be— how headstrong. But at the same time he couldn't help but feel sympathy for her. She had endured so much, and all she really wanted was a way to fill the emptiness left by the tragedies of life.

If she could only come to terms with the fact that God loves her, that she needs Him. But of course that would take time . . . and maybe seeing it with her own eyes, instead of hearing stories about it. Jacob had known many people who were that way. They could hear people's stories all day long, but until something actually happened to them personally, it just didn't make any sense. He figured Helaina would be that way.

As the wind picked up and the temperature grew colder, Jacob wondered if Helaina and Leah were warm enough. Leah knew about this land and had no doubt dressed appropriately. Ayoona had mentioned that Leah had packed the sled, so Jacob felt confident she would have taken ample supplies. But Helaina knew very little of the far north.

With the dogs fed and resting, Jacob noticed John was finishing up with his sled runner. John had been more than a brother to him, offering to take time away from the village and his own family in order to find Leah. So much time had passed, however, that Jacob felt he needed to release John from any obligation.

"You need help?" Jacob questioned as he came to where John sat working.

"No. It's not too bad. I got it fixed now."

Jacob looked around for some of the other natives. "John, I think it's time for you to head back. We've been gone a lot longer than you'd planned."

John's round brown face took on an expression that suggested he was considering the comment. "No. I won't go," he finally said.

"But you have a lot of people depending on you."

"They got others to depend on too. We had great hunting this summer and the salmon were good. We dried a lot of fish. Leah only has you and her husband . . . and us. We stay and help you."

Jacob knew the act came as a sacrifice, no matter what John

said. He was deeply touched. "You're a good friend, John. I won't forget this."

John looked at him and nodded. "In Alaska you don't forget."

———————

Leah sensed the dogs' excitement. Something was urging them on. They had picked up the scent of another animal—perhaps a hare or fox. She held fast to the sled, working her best to slow and direct them. She felt their anxiousness. They were headed home—they were free. She wanted to put as much distance between herself and Chase as was possible, but she knew the dogs were her lifeline. She couldn't let them wear themselves out.

"Whoa, Marty!" She felt the pace slow. Then without warning the dogs picked up speed again. They began to bark and fuss as they raced across the snow.

Leah feared she might lose control of the animals and decided to show them who was boss. Her muscles were weary of the work as she fought to manage the sled and team. "Whoa, Marty! Whoa!" She stepped down on the brake hard.

Again Marty heard her command and lessened the pace. This was all Leah needed. They were good dogs, generally as eager to please as to have their own way. Putting her full weight on the brake, the team slowed and finally stopped at Leah's insistence.

Leah anchored the sled and stretched her aching shoulders. She tried to calculate the time. Heavy clouds were making the day gloomy and nearly as dark as evening. It seemed they had been traveling for at least four hours since their last stop. Leah could always tell because of the way the middle of her back began to hurt after that amount of time on a sled.

"Where are we?" Helaina asked groggily. She tried to sit up, but Leah wasn't ready yet to do battle with her.

"Stay where you are. We're taking off in a minute. We're just resting the dogs."

Helaina stretched up. "I think I feel better. It doesn't feel so hard to breathe."

"That's because of the medicine I've been giving you. I have some more you should take." Leah went to where she had what remained of the stinkweed concoction. "It would probably taste better hot, but you need to drink this down."

"Is it going to put me back to sleep? I don't want to sleep. I need to make plans for capturing Chase. Where is he, anyway?"

"It isn't important." Leah shoved the bottle into Helaina's hands. "Drink this now." She pushed Helaina's hands toward her mouth. "Hurry. A storm is moving in and we need to get going."

Helaina drank the mixture and yawned. "Leah, you aren't making any sense. What's going on?"

"Look up and you'll see for yourself. The clouds are thickening, the wind is picking up. Already the temperature is much colder than it was just a few hours ago. Now settle back down. We need to be on our way."

Helaina had no sooner eased back on her furs than Leah wrapped a scarf around her neck, adjusted her parka hood down, and called to the dogs. "Up, up, boys! Hike!" She pulled the hook and gripped the sled as they once again headed down the trail.

Leah thought that Helaina was trying to say something to her from the basket, but she pretended not to notice. She figured that once Helaina realized the full impact of what Leah had done, there would be little or no peace. For now, Leah just needed time and distance to feel safe.

But safety wasn't to be had. The dogs began frantically barking. They pulled toward the right, but Leah held them fast. "Haw! Haw! Marty, haw!" And then she spied something coming out from the side of the trail. It was nearly fifty yards ahead, but the outline was one Leah recognized immediately.

"Whoa!" She held fast to the sled and jumped on the brake at the same time. "Stop, Marty!" He had no interest in stopping. Leah did the only thing she could think to do. She threw one of the snow hooks and prayed it would catch and halt the team.

At first it didn't catch, but the drag helped enough that Leah could get the team under control. Finally the hook caught in a snow-covered tussock, jerking Marty backward as it did. They were stopped. And none too soon.

A grizzly stood not twenty yards from them. He seemed very interested in the dogs. Much too interested. Leah figured he was a young male who hadn't made it to a den prior to the snowfall and storms. Sometimes the animals were confused and remained out of their winter dens, seeking additional food.

Leah reached for the rifle and squared it against her shoulder. The meat would be good to have. She'd hate to take the extra time to dress out the beast, but it would definitely benefit them. After all, she had no idea how many days it would take to reach home. She had no idea which path would get them there in the most direct route.

Breathe, she reminded herself. Jacob was always chiding her for holding her breath whenever she was about to shoot. She forced a deep gulp of air into her lungs and sighted the swaggering animal. *Breathe. Just breathe.*

The dogs were frantic now, pulling at the sled, trying to get to the bear. The bear lowered his ears and then his head. Leah wasted no time. She squeezed the trigger before he could charge.

The bullet hit the grizzly in the shoulder. She worked the lever to eject the casing. The reassuring click of the next round loading gave her renewed confidence. She took aim again and fired.

This time the bullet grazed the bear's head. He'd had enough, but rather than drop, he turned and ran. The dogs howled in sorrow that they could not give chase. Leah, however, was fretful over what she should do. A wounded rogue bear was nothing to leave running free, but she was limited on ammunition and on knowledge of the area. If she left this trail to follow the bear, she might get hopelessly lost.

She took in a deep breath and relaxed the rifle. Her heart was pounding so hard she could feel it and hear it in her ears. There was no time to waste, she reminded herself. She put the rifle away and reached for the hook. They needed to press on.

Chapter Thirteen

With the village nearly three hours behind them, Jacob noted the thickening clouds. They would have to either press on or make camp. He felt a deep sense of frustration. The terrain was unfamiliar to them and the threat of complications were everywhere. He brought the dogs to a stop, hoping to rest them and confer with the others as to what they wanted to do. As if he didn't already know.

"Why are you stopping?" Jayce asked as his team came up behind Jacob.

"Look at those clouds—a storm's gathering. I figured we should discuss what to do. Do we press on?"

"Of course we press on," Jayce declared as John came to join them. The other men waited with the sleds.

"If Brownie hadn't gone lame we would have missed them turning west," Jacob offered. "What if they change direction again? We might waste a great many hours."

"I can check the trails," John offered. He looked up at the sky. It was just starting to snow. "Looks bad."

"Feels bad too." Jacob didn't like the sense of foreboding that permeated the pristine beauty around them.

Then the silence was broken by the sound of a single shot ringing out. All three men looked toward the north. It wasn't that far away. A second shot rang out. Jacob stiffened and looked to Jayce.

"Let's go!"

The other men ran for their sleds while Jacob offered a prayer and pulled his sled hook. He felt sick in the pit of his stomach. He couldn't help but wonder if Chase had killed Helaina and Leah.

Two women.

Two shots.

Jayce could hardly bear the images racing through his imagination. Chase had to be responsible for the gunfire. He could believe no other explanation. Never mind that it could be a hunter from the village foraging for food. His gut told him that Chase was somehow involved.

If he's hurt her, I'll kill him.

Jayce thought only of his wife. His heart seemed to beat in a rhythm that called her name.

Le-ah. Le-ah. Le-ah.

He tried not to think of how reasonable it might seem to Chase to end the lives of his hostages now that he was this far north. No doubt Chase figured he'd thrown off any pursuit. *If he thinks that, then he doesn't know me at all,* Jayce thought.

He clenched his jaw. Throughout this pursuit and search he had tried hard to keep an even temper. He'd tried to pray that somehow God might turn his brother to the truth before his life ended. Now that Jayce had put his faith in God, he hated to think of his own brother dying and going to hell. His entire life had been spent worrying about and dealing with the trouble Chase got into, but this was something he couldn't help him with. Chase would face his Maker on his own. Maybe sooner than he planned.

Jayce might even be the one to end Chase's life. Especially if he just killed Leah. A fire started somewhere in the pit of his stomach and spread. Why had this happened? Why couldn't Chase have been caught by someone else? Jayce felt so torn. He knew this had to be done. Chase had forced Jayce's involvement when he posed as his brother during his crimes. But still, it seemed so unfair—so unnatural that one brother should turn against another in this way.

They moved along the trail for two, maybe three, miles when a dog sled team came into sight. The view was somewhat obscured by the snow. The team approached them from the opposite direction and there seemed to be only one person on board—and that was the driver.

Jayce did nothing to slow his dogs. He wanted to close the distance as quickly as possible. If the driver was his brother—if Chase had done the worst—Jayce knew the responsibility should be his to bear.

But as he drew closer, Jayce realized the figure was too small for his brother. Disappointment washed over him as he figured the driver to be a local native. He was ready to give up hope when Jacob called out, "That's Marty in the lead. It's them!"

Jayce looked again and realized that the driver was a woman.

"Leah." He barely breathed the name. He stepped on the brake and called to the dogs. "Whoa! Whoa now!"

The dogs were none too eager to stop; after all, there were other dogs to meet up ahead. But Jayce got them stopped in short order. He was in no mood to brook nonsense. He secured the hook and stepped from the sled. He allowed the other driver to approach and pushed back the hood of his parka as he waited.

The driver stepped from the sled and pushed back the shielding hood that kept her face obscured. Jayce instantly recognized his wife, although she looked quite tired. She locked gazes with him and shook her head ever so slightly. Jayce covered the distance between them in long, easy strides. He pulled her into his arms and held her tight.

"Thank God you're safe. I feared the worst." His voice broke. Jayce buried his face against Leah's hair and silently thanked God for her return. Leah said nothing at all. She stood rather stiff in his arms, neither embracing him nor rejecting him.

Jayce finally pulled away and took Leah's face in his hands. "Are you all right?"

Leah looked at him for several seconds. She almost seemed to be searching him for some answer. "I left Chase drugged. He's back to the north—at least he was. That was last night."

"We heard gunshots," Jayce began. "I feared the worst."

"I shot a bear. It only wounded him."

"But you weren't harmed?"

"The bear ran off. He didn't have a chance to attack me or the dogs."

Jayce felt a strange sensation wash over him. She hadn't answered his question. She looked away from him as Jacob came up. Something wasn't right.

"Leah. You're a sight for my eyes," Jacob said, hugging her. Again Leah remained rather stiff, almost as if she were separating herself from her brother.

"Helaina's very sick. She's there in the basket. She's better than she has been, but I think she has pneumonia."

Jacob went immediately to the sled. Jayce moved closer, mainly to be at Leah's side, but he figured he might as well see Helaina for himself.

"She's had some stinkweed tea. She should be waking up soon," Leah said in a rather monotone voice. "I had to keep her sedated or she would never have cooperated."

Jacob looked at his sister. "What do you mean?"

"She intended to take Chase into custody. She wanted me to drug him and bring him back for her. I refused."

"I'm glad," Jayce said, putting his arm around Leah. "Chase is very dangerous. He might have hurt you."

Leah looked at him as if she might comment, then turned back to Jacob. "I'm out of herbs. I can't help her anymore. She's been so ill, I thought for sure she would die."

Jacob knelt down on the sled. He put his hand to Helaina's cheek, but she didn't stir. "There's a village a ways back. We can get her there. Maybe they have medicines to treat her."

John finally interrupted them. "The storm is bad, Jacob. We should make camp. After that, I can look for a closer village."

"There's a rogue bear out there somewhere," Leah reminded them. "I shot him twice. Hit him both times, but the second shot was just a grazing blow to the head."

John nodded. "We'll find him. Bear like that will be dangerous."

Leah shrugged. "I've got a tent. I'll set it up."

Jayce watched her, sensing that there was something very wrong with his wife. Perhaps it was just that the entire ordeal had worn her out. She had endured great physical demands, as well as emotional ones.

Leah was already pulling the tent from the sled as Jayce joined her. "Let me help you." She cringed slightly as he reached toward her. "Are you angry at me?"

Leah looked surprised. "No. I'm . . . I'm tired. We need to get the tent up quickly."

He nodded but said nothing. What could he say? What should he say? Leah seemed a completely different woman. He helped her put up the tent while Jacob and John were busy putting up their own shelters. When they finished, Helaina was starting to rally. Jacob lifted her from the sled and took her to Leah's tent.

"Why are you bringing her here?" Leah asked. She was already busy unrolling the bedding, while Jayce worked to set up the oil stove.

"I don't suppose it would be appropriate to have her lodge with me," he said rather sheepishly. "John's tent is already pretty crowded, so I figured some of the guys could share my quarters. I know you and Jayce would probably like your privacy, but this seems the best solution."

"She can stay with us," Jayce replied. "We'll soon be home and have all the privacy we need. It's all right. She'll need Leah's help."

"She wouldn't have needed anyone's help had she just listened to her brother," Leah snapped. She quickly turned away.

Jayce exchanged a rather confused look with Jacob. Leah's attitude puzzled them both. "I see she's waking up."

Helaina moaned and struggled to open her eyes. Jacob gently positioned her on one of the pallets Leah had just arranged.

"Helaina, it's me, Jacob. Wake up."

Helaina murmured something and tried to stretch. "I hurt so much." She opened her eyes and seemed startled to find Jacob. "Where are we?"

"I'm not entirely sure," Jacob said with a grin. "Alaska is about the only answer I have."

"That's a very big answer," she said, rubbing her neck. "Oh, I'm so sore. Everything hurts. It has for days—maybe weeks. How I long for my warm feather bed in New York. I think I'd sell my soul to be back home."

Jayce saw the sobering affect this had on Jacob. "Look," Jayce interjected, "we need to finish caring for the dogs. The storm is really building."

Helaina looked past Jacob to where Jayce was kneeling. She studied him for several moments, then looked back to Jacob. "That's Jayce—right?"

"Right." Jacob appeared to recover his good nature. He smiled again. "You don't think I'd let Chase share a tent with you if I had any say over it."

She relaxed a bit. "Where is Chase? I hope you've tied him up good."

Jacob looked to Leah and then to Helaina. She hadn't missed the exchange. Fighting to sit up, she squared her gaze on Leah. "You did tie him up—right?"

Leah narrowed her eyes. "I told you for days that I had no plan to help you capture Chase at the cost of our success. I left him on the trail. I left him there drugged and asleep. He has a knife and a pack of food, a fur, and a wool blanket."

"Leah, how could you!" Helaina's voice was weak but clearly angry. "I had a job to do and you interfered." She began to cough.

Leah balled her fists. "You nearly died. I should have let you, for all the gratitude you show." With that, Leah left the tent.

Jacob and Jayce were stunned by Leah's words. They had never known her to be so ugly with anyone.

"She blames me for all of this," Helaina said. The coughing dissipated and she fell back against the pallet. "I deserve it, but I don't like it." She closed her eyes. "I can't believe she let him go. Now I'll have to start all over."

"You have to get well first," Jacob said firmly. "You're still very sick."

"I'm going to help Leah," Jayce said, noting that Jacob had the situation under control. Jayce slipped from the tent and felt the blast of Arctic wind against his face. The darkness and storm made visibility nearly impossible. "Leah?"

"I'm here," she said. "Getting the supplies from my sled."

He walked against the wind, feeling the icy particles against his face. Jayce pulled his parka hood closer.

Leah met him halfway. "This is all we need."

"Let me take it." She gave the box over to him without protest. "Hold on to me while we make our way back. This weather is not going to show us any mercy, and I don't want to lose you again."

"I'm fine. Just get the supplies to the tent." She spoke out against the wind, but to Jayce it almost seemed to be an angry demand.

Rather than argue, he pressed forward. They were soon back in the tent, but Jayce was completely uncomfortable with the way Leah was acting. She wanted very little to do with any of them. Something had happened; he was certain of it. He put the box on the tent floor beside the stove and considered his options. If he took issue with her now, she would have to explain in front of Helaina and Jacob. Obviously that would be most uncomfortable.

"Do you have anything for Helaina's cough?" Jacob asked as Leah rummaged through the box.

She shook her head, not even looking up. "I told you. I gave her the last of the tea. I'll put some water on the stove. The steam will help her. Otherwise, she needs to just rest and not talk."

Jacob nodded, but Jayce noticed Leah's attention was focused on the stove. The wind howled mournfully outside. The small tent shook rather violently but held fast.

"What do you have to eat?" Leah asked no one in particular.

Jacob replied before Jayce could answer. "We have some fresh reindeer meat. We traded for it back at the village. I'll go retrieve some from John. We can definitely feed you well."

Leah plopped down on her pallet as Jacob opened the outside flap. Cold air rushed in, causing the seal oil lamp to flicker and nearly go out. Jayce watched as she did her best to protect the flame. His glance then went to Helaina, who watched him very closely.

"It really is me—Jayce," he told her. "I'm not sure how to convince you."

"It's uncanny how much alike you two look. With the beards, it's even more difficult to distinguish who's who."

"Jayce looks nothing like Chase," Leah said angrily. "His eyes are completely different. Their mouths and noses aren't alike at all."

Jayce laughed. "We're identical twins, Leah. Of course we look alike."

She devoured him with a look that nearly froze him to the ground. "Don't ever say that again. There is nothing about you that is like him. Chase Kincaid is evil. He's an abomination with no conscience—no concern for others. You might have come from the same mother, at the same time—but that doesn't matter."

Jayce held her gaze for just a moment, but it was long enough to see the terrible pain in her eyes. In that moment he was certain that his brother had deeply wounded Leah. How deeply and through what means, he couldn't be sure. Unfortunately, his imagination ran wild enough to believe Chase capable of most anything. And that frightened him more than he cared to admit.

Chapter Fourteen

J acob watched Helaina's labored breathing and felt dread wash over him. What if she died? What if the storm lasted for weeks instead of days and they couldn't get her help?

Jayce had suggested that Jacob remain in their tent so that he could keep an eye on Helaina, and for that Jacob had been very grateful. He struggled with his feelings for this woman. Helaina still didn't understand the need to turn her life over to God, and without that, Jacob couldn't be more than friends. Now with her fighting just to stay alive, he worried that she would die without having found God's peace for her soul.

But Leah's attitude troubled him deeply as well. She was strangely quiet and aloof. She had cooked for them but then went to her pallet, turned her back on the rest of them, and went to sleep. Now, nearly ten hours later, she was still sleeping. Her behavior was unlike anything he'd ever known.

"Coffee?" Jayce asked him.

Jacob looked up and realized he'd been staring at Leah's back. He saw in Jayce's eyes that he held some of the same worries. Jacob looked again to Leah.

"Do you think she's all right?"

"I don't honestly know. I was hoping you'd tell me. You've known her a lot longer."

Jacob shook his head and lowered his voice. It was a big tent, but not that big. The last thing Jacob wanted to do was offend Leah for talking about her as if she wasn't there just six feet away. "I've never seen her act this way. Not even when you left her back in Ketchikan. She's always spoken gently—kindly—of everyone. Even when she was angry, I've found her to hold her tongue."

Jayce nodded. "That's what I figured. I don't know ... I mean ..." He fell silent. "Forget it." He still held the coffeepot. "Want some?"

Jacob extended his tin cup. "Sure. Doesn't seem to be much else to do while we wait out this storm."

He sipped the brew slowly, enjoying the warmth. Just then Helaina stirred. Her fever had returned in the night—no doubt because they had nothing with which to stave it off. She opened her eyes.

"When we reach the train station," she said in a low, raspy voice, "will you see to my bags?"

Surprised by her request, Jacob said nothing for several moments. "Helaina, it's me—Jacob."

She narrowed her eyes as if to see him better. "I'm sorry. What did you say?"

Jacob leaned a little closer. "It's Jacob. I'm here to help care for you."

"Oh, I was having the strangest dream. I was riding in a buggy and ... we ... we ... well, I can't remember."

He smiled. "It doesn't matter. Would you like a drink? I have some tea for you. It's not the same as what you've been drinking, but it will help warm you."

"Tea would be nice."

Jacob turned to Jayce, who immediately went to work making the tea. When he returned his attention to Helaina she seemed to be a little more coherent, so Jacob asked, "How are you feeling? Is it still difficult to breathe?"

"No, not as much. I don't know why ... I'm still sick."

"Leah thinks it's pneumonia. That's very hard to overcome. I know—I had it once myself. I wound up in bed for three weeks."

"I don't have three weeks. I need to get better so I can finish my job."

Jacob shook his head and took the cup of tea that Jayce offered. He helped Helaina sit up and steadied the tea for her to drink. "There is no job for you to finish, Helaina." He tried to keep his tone gentle.

She drank some of the tea, then fell back against Jacob's arm. "I've let Stanley down."

"He doesn't feel that way. He's worried that you'll be hurt."

She closed her eyes. "I don't know what to do. I'm just so tired."

"You needn't worry about it, Mrs. Beecham," Jayce said. "I plan to go after him myself. You need to recover, and maybe by the time you are well we will have Chase in the hands of the Nome authorities."

Jacob wasn't sure if Helaina heard this or not. She seemed to have gone back to sleep. He loved the feel of her cradled in his arm. She seemed so vulnerable and helpless—not at all the bossy, arrogant woman he'd first met in Nome.

Just then John peeked in through the inner tent flap. "I'm gonna water and feed the dogs. You coming?"

Jacob placed Helaina back on her pallet. "Yeah, I'll be right there." He pulled a blanket over Helaina, then reached for his gloves. "You'll keep an eye on her, right?"

"You know I will. I'll watch them both."

"I'm worried about them," Jacob admitted, "but I keep trying to pray through it. God has a reason even in this, I keep reminding myself. I just wish I understood better why any of this had to happen."

"Sometimes we don't get answers," Jayce said, looking sadly at Leah. "I guess we just need to be patient. Sometimes the only thing to do is wait."

"I guess," Jacob said, but his heart couldn't accept this. There had to be something more he could do to help his sister and Helaina.

Leah listened to her brother and husband's conversation. She tried to take comfort in their words but found she couldn't. She felt such a mix of emotions: guilt for having left Chase on the trail and feeling he deserved nothing better; anger that God would have let things get so out of control—that He would take her to a place where she was helpless to keep bad things from happening.

She felt sorrow for the way Chase had ruined things for her and Jayce. Bitterness for the loss of a good future—for truly she did not know how she could go on with Jayce once he learned the truth.

She finally rolled over after Jacob left to help John with the dogs. Jayce was watching her as she opened her eyes.

"Hello," he said softly. "Did you sleep well?"

Leah thought the question absurd. How could she sleep well in the middle of the horrors that had become her life? Nevertheless, she tried to be civil. "I suppose."

"Would you like some coffee?"

She sat up and stretched. Her body ached from the long hours in one position. "Yes." Coffee actually sounded quite good.

"Are you hungry? I can warm you up something, or we have jerked meat and smoked salmon." He smiled and handed her a tin of steaming coffee.

"I'm not hungry." She drank the coffee slowly, happy to have something with which to occupy her mouth so that she wouldn't have to talk.

"You look better. The dark circles are gone from your eyes."

Leah didn't know what he wanted her to say. She could barely look at him without being reminded all over again of Chase and what he'd done. She longed to just go home, but she could hear the wind still wailing outside their shelter. Who knew when the storm might abate?

"Can you ... well ... talk about what happened?" Jayce asked hesitantly.

Leah felt sorry for him. He seemed almost afraid of her. "There's not much to say."

"Jacob and I went back to Last Chance for dogs and supplies. We learned that you were gone and that everyone thought I had already been there. I take it Chase told them I was your husband?"

Leah looked at the cup. "Yes. He wasn't expecting me to arrive in the village. I think he thought I would be with you."

"I'm sure he thought he could fool everyone."

"He did. No one suspected a thing," Leah replied. "Not that I would have wanted them to. If they would have known it was Chase instead of you, they might have gotten hurt."

"I suppose that much is true. Chase wouldn't have cared who he harmed. We followed your tracks and found the markers you left us."

"I couldn't do much. He watched me all the time."

"I don't understand why he took you."

Leah gave Jayce a look of disbelief. "For protection—to keep the others from learning who he was and coming after him. Because he's a selfish, evil man. How many more reasons does he need?"

"I suppose those things crossed my mind, but it seems that traveling with one woman, let alone two, would slow him down. We honestly worried that he would kill Helaina as soon as he got far enough away from Nome to feel safe."

"She nearly killed herself."

"I can see that. But I can understand that she wanted to complete her job. I don't like what she did, but I can reason through why she would take those chances."

"She did what she did because she's as selfish as Chase," Leah said matter-of-factly. "None of this would have happened if she'd just gone home with her brother."

"But that's not true, Leah. I would have gone after Chase even if she had gone back to Washington. You know that I labored over that decision, but I felt it was my obligation. I'd hoped that it would help keep other people from suffering at Chase's hand. I still feel that way."

Leah nearly dropped her cup. "What are you saying? You can't still plan to go after him."

"I have to. This must come to an end. Chase has hurt too many people. Why, he came in and stole you right out from under the noses of people who'd known you for ten years. He hurt you as well. That's easy enough to see."

If you only knew, Leah thought. She drank the last of her coffee. "You can't go. He hates you. He plans to kill you. Frankly, I think he means to put an end to your life and assume your place in society."

"But obviously that would be difficult."

"Why? He's performed all of his heinous acts under your name. If he convinces people that *you* were the evil twin, then there will be no reason to cause him further grief."

"Leah, listen to yourself. You aren't making sense. Helaina's brother has no doubt already shared the truth with the Pinkerton Agency. They know the fingerprints they have on file belong to Chase and not to me. As they compare evidence from all of Chase's crime scenes, they will have other proof as well. Chase can't win in this situation, and I won't live in his shadow all of my life."

"That's the way he feels about you. That's why I know he will kill you." Leah tried to contain her frustration at Jayce's ignorance. "You can't go through with this. You can't."

"I'm sorry you had to endure so much," Jayce said, suddenly changing the subject.

"I don't want to talk about it," Leah replied. "I want you to promise me that you won't go after Chase. I need you to just be done with this here and now."

Jayce's expression told her his answer before he spoke. "I can't. You know I can't. Especially now."

"Why especially now? Why should it matter so much?"

"Because he took you. Because he will go on believing himself capable of taking whatever he wants. You know it's true."

Leah did know, but she wasn't about to admit it. Not if it meant Jayce would risk his life to go after Chase. "Maybe so, but I also know his hatred will drive him to destroy you. He told me stories, Jayce. Stories of when you were young. He hated you even then. He blames you for everything wrong in his life. You can't fight against that. He only cares about seeing you dead."

"And you think me such a poor example of manhood that I couldn't be the one to put an end to this? Do you honestly give him more credit for ability and brains?"

Leah heard the hurt in his voice. "No. I don't give him credit for those things. I give him credit for his blinding hate. There is a rage and hate so fierce inside of your brother that he will never stop trying to satisfy it. But the only thing that will ever ease it will be your blood—or his."

———

The storm eased the next day. Leah awoke to a strange silence in the absence of the wind, then immediately noticed the missing warmth of Jayce sleeping next to her. He hadn't tried to be overly familiar with her, and for that Leah was grateful. She felt strange in his arms, almost confused. She knew it was her husband—knew that Jayce and Chase were two different men—but at the same time there were just too many similarities. It was as if Chase had cursed her somehow. Could she never again be alone with her husband without remembering what Chase had done—how he had touched her? She shuddered and closed her eyes tight against the memories.

I can't live like this. I have to find a way to get beyond this—to no longer remember anything about it.

Sitting up, she pushed back the blankets and looked to where Helaina slept. With a heavy sigh, Leah went to the woman. She didn't want to hold such fierce anger toward Helaina. The woman was sick and needed help. If Leah didn't offer her healing skills, Helaina might yet die. That was something Leah knew she couldn't live with on her conscience.

"Helaina?" Leah felt the woman's forehead. It was cool. "Helaina?"

Helaina stirred and opened her eyes. "What's wrong?"

Leah shook her head. "Nothing. I just woke up and wondered how you were doing. It sounds as though the storm's abated. Jayce and Jacob must be outside readying things for us to leave."

"But if we go, we'll lose track of Chase."

Leah squared her shoulders. "Haven't you learned your lesson about that? What in the world possesses you to continue with such nonsense? Chase Kincaid is a dangerous man who wouldn't think twice about killing you."

"But he had every chance . . . and he did nothing," Helaina said in a weak voice.

"He did plenty." The bitterness was evident in Leah's reply.

"So you're awake," Jacob declared as he entered the tent. He had a tin plate of steaming meat. "John's enjoying the calm after the storm. He cooked this up for you."

"Where's Jayce?" Leah questioned, moving away from Helaina.

Jacob's joyful expression contorted to a frown. "He said he left you a letter explaining."

"Explaining what? What are you talking about?" Leah looked back to her pallet. Jayce's things were gone, but a folded piece of paper was propped up against Leah's mukluks.

The answers came to her without Jacob speaking a word or without opening the letter. Jayce had gone after his brother. Leah shook her head and yanked on her boots. "Fine. If this is the way it's to be, I don't know why I even bothered to marry him. It's obvious that we are totally wrong for each other. He doesn't trust me to know the truth of this situation, and he won't listen to anything I have to say."

"Maybe it's more an issue of honor," Jacob suggested. "He has a job to do—he's pledged himself to do it."

"She said the same thing," Leah said, pointing her finger at Helaina. "But you don't want her going out there after Chase. What's the difference, Jacob?"

"The difference is, she's a woman and she's very sick. Jayce and Chase are brothers. You know how Jayce has suffered over his decision to go after Chase. It's not easy for him."

"It hasn't been easy for me either," Leah countered. "You probably just urged him on. That's it, isn't it? You wanted to keep Helaina safe, so you encouraged Jayce to get out there and capture Chase."

"You're talking crazy, Leah. No one has more influence over Jayce than you. You know very well that he's struggled with his decision to get involved in this. You told me so yourself, and now you're acting as though it's the first time you've heard it."

"I'm not the crazy one here. Crazy is going after a man who wishes to see you dead. A man who hates you so much he would stop at nothing to hurt you. Nothing."

"That makes it all the more logical for Jayce to want to go after him. He can't very well spend the rest of his life looking over his shoulder for Chase, now, can he? You're being completely self-ish about this, Leah."

Leah could hardly believe Jacob's words. "You don't under-stand any of this. You never will." She pulled on her parka and stormed from the tent, ignoring Jacob's comments and protests.

The sun shone in a washed-out manner against pale blue skies, but Leah hardly noticed. She looked across the small camp noting Jayce's dog team and sled were gone.

He's really gone. He's left me to hunt down his brother—not even know-ing what Chase has done. Chase has taken my virtue, my purity, and now he will take my husband as well.

Leah actually tried to pray. *Please, God, keep Jayce from death.* The words seemed to echo in a hollow manner within her worried mind. She wanted to believe that God still cared—that He was truly faithful and knew exactly the wrongs that had befallen them. Leah wanted to trust that He was able to deliver her and Jayce from this nightmare, but it hurt so much. She felt betrayed—deserted. Her soul ached from trying to battle the demon that threatened to completely destroy her heart and mind.

She sunk to the ground. "Oh, God, help us. Help me."

Chapter Fifteen

J ayce pushed north in the direction from which he'd seen Leah
come. The snowfall had covered the trail, but he was certain
that if he continued in this manner, he would find some sign of
his brother. The crisp air stung his nostrils and ice formed on his
mustache and beard. It was considerably colder than when they'd
first started the journey. He wondered how long they'd actually
been gone; he'd managed to lose track of the days in his worry
over Leah.

Slowing the dogs, he tried to find some sign of the trail. There
was nothing, even though this had looked to be a main thorough-
fare, according to John. The snow had clearly buried the evidence,
and the dogs were tired from battling the trail. Jayce knew it
would be easier for them if he cut the trail for a while. Jacob had
taught him this during one of the other storms.

Jayce halted the dogs and let them rest while he took up his snowshoes. It wouldn't be easy to break the trail, but it would help the animals, and that was of the utmost importance.

"Come on, boys," he said, taking hold of the gangline. Jayce worked to clear a path wide enough for the dogs, all the while looking for any sign of his brother having passed this way.

He tried not to think of how angry Leah would be when she awoke and found him gone. After her comments the night before, Jayce knew there would be no reasoning with her. A weight settled over him. Marriage was hard work, and he and Leah had scarcely had time alone together since their wedding. Chase had come between them in so many ways.

"All of my life you've caused me trouble," Jayce declared, as if Chase could hear him. "All of my life you've tried to exact some kind of revenge on me, and none of it has ever made sense."

Eventually the snow evened out and Jayce could see that it wasn't as deep. He took off his snowshoes and positioned himself behind the sled once again. The dogs were happy to have their head again. The lead dog, especially, seemed to have renewed energy for the day as he pulled eagerly against the weight.

The next morning Jayce felt his cause rather hopeless. There was no sign of Chase. Any tracks he might have left had been covered by the wind-driven snow. Jayce studied the landscape for any discrepancies and found none. He thought perhaps Chase had taken a different direction. If so, Jayce would be hard-pressed to figure out what direction he'd gone.

"Lord, I need your guidance. I need to know where to go and how to find my brother."

Jayce continued to search the trail. There was an abundance of dwarfed birch and willows. Rounded tussocks, dangerous to the sleds when hidden in the snow, were barely visible in areas where the wind had drifted the snow. It was a lonely, desperate country.

Clouds moved in, subduing the light. Soon it would be night and another day would pass without Jayce having anything to show for it. He let his mind drift to Leah. He knew Jacob had promised to get her back to Last Chance. Jayce could only hope she'd been cooperative and sensible. He couldn't endure it if she tried to come after him and got hurt.

Up ahead the trail seemed more notable. There looked to be signs of activity. There were numerous animal tracks. Snowshoe hare, fox, and even a wolf or two. Jayce felt for his sidearm. It might be nice to hunt something down for his supper. He didn't relish the idea of eating smoked salmon and crackers once again.

Then he noted other tracks. They were human.

Chase.

Jayce didn't dare even breathe the name lest it somehow jinx his search. Once again he halted the sled. Leaving the dogs anchored and resting, Jayce walked ahead, following the tracks. There seemed to be something wrong. The tracks were staggering first in one direction and then another. There was no real sense to their pattern. If they did belong to Chase, perhaps he'd grown ill or was hurt.

Glancing back, Jayce could see he was a considerable distance from the dogs. He didn't like that idea and retraced his steps back to the sled. Once again he took hold of the gangline and led the dogs himself.

The dogs were agitated. They were good at sensing trouble, and Jayce couldn't help but wonder if he was walking into an ambush. It would be like Chase to feign illness or some other trouble. Jayce pulled out his revolver just in case.

The tracks veered to the west. The path was more open here,

but the tracks were just as strange. It almost seemed as if the one who'd made them had been dancing instead of walking. What could it mean?

Another ten yards and a stand of stunted spruce revealed that someone had taken refuge beside them. A blanket remained behind as evidence. Jayce anchored the dogs and went to retrieve the piece. He held it up against the dimming light and felt his breath catch. Blood!

Jayce looked around him, searching past the spruce and the other vegetation. Someone was injured. If not Chase, then someone else. Either way, they would clearly need some kind of care.

Jayce hurried back to the dogs and pulled the hook. "But what if it's a trick?" he questioned. The lead dog cocked his head and gave a whine, as if to question Jayce in return. "What if Chase left this and it's just animal blood?" His mind raced with questions. "But why would he do that? What would he hope to gain?"

Jayce moved out with the dogs, still wondering at the situation. He felt his skin prickle. Every sound seemed magnified—every movement was suspect.

The path came to a creek. The ice looked solid enough, but just as Jayce was about to cross it, he noticed that there was a smaller trail that ran alongside the frozen water. For reasons that were beyond him, Jayce turned to follow the path. It wound back and forth as it followed the outline of the creek. Snow had drifted here and hid any tracks.

Jayce stopped the dogs and knelt several times to see if he could brush away the snow and spy any clues. There appeared to be nothing and he pressed forward cautiously. The dogs sensed his concern and began to whine. One of the swing dogs let out a mournful howl that caused Jayce to seriously consider turning back. Something just didn't feel right.

When they rounded the next bend, Jayce spied something on the trail up ahead. He stopped and strained to see. It appeared rather furry. He thought of Leah's wounded bear and drew a deep breath. Perhaps the thing had come here to die. Then again, maybe it wasn't dead yet. Jayce gripped the rifle tighter and began to walk slowly forward.

As he drew closer, however, he could see it wasn't an animal at all, but rather a man. Native, from the looks of his clothing. *But it could be Chase,* he thought. He felt a catch in his throat. He held his breath. Was this a trap?

Halting the dogs, Jayce secured the sled, then gingerly made his way to the man on the ground. "God help me," he murmured as he poked at the man with his toe. The man didn't move.

Carefully, Jayce reached down and rolled the man over. He jumped back at the reflected image of his own face. Only this face had been cut—sliced several times by some sort of animal. The pattern suggested bear. Perhaps Leah's rogue bear.

"Chase, can you hear me?" Jayce leaned down to ascertain if his brother was yet alive. There was a faint heartbeat and shallow breathing. The man was barely alive.

Helaina's recovery was slow but steady. Leah managed to secure healing herbs at the small village where Jacob had left Brownie. She faithfully tended Helaina, saying very little and offering nothing more than medical care.

"You can't just go on like this," Helaina said that morning as they prepared to head out once again. Jacob and John were busy with the dogs, so she thought it the right time to speak to Leah.

Although Leah looked up from her packing, she said nothing. Her expression seemed to challenge Helaina to continue. "I know you're angry at me, but if anyone has a right to be mad, it's me."

"And how do you figure that?" Leah was clearly intrigued.

"We had Chase Kincaid at hand, and you let him get away. Now he's off doing whatever he pleases."

"It's not enough that this obsession of yours has cost me everything I care about," Leah said frankly. She stared hard at Helaina, and it was easy to see the disgust in her expression. "I wouldn't even be here if it weren't for you. You have no right to condemn my actions."

"But you have the right to condemn mine? I hardly see where that is fair."

"Nothing about this trip has been fair. Fair doesn't even enter into the picture. You are a selfish, self-driven woman, Mrs. Beecham. Had you not had to have your revenge on the world for the loss of your husband and parents, you might have done the sensible thing and settled down to remarry and have a family."

"This isn't about my family," Helaina retorted angrily.

"No, but it is about mine," Leah countered. She squared her shoulders and put her hands on her hips. She appeared to wait for Helaina to comment on this. Instead, Helaina refocused on Leah's role.

"You have to understand—by leaving Chase, you put us days behind in his capture. He might even escape all together. All you had to do, once he was drugged, was tie him up and throw him in the basket with me. It should have been fairly simple."

Leah looked at her oddly but said nothing. Helaina continued. "He'd be here now, on his way to justice, and your husband would be at your side. Do you not see how you are the cause of your own misery?"

"You are by far and away the most ruthless and uncompassionate woman I've ever known." Helaina bristled at this but allowed Leah to continue. "Your own brother suffered because of you. You weren't there when he discovered what you'd done. He was heartbroken to realize you would probably end up dead. How he must be suffering even now—not that you would care."

"I care," Helaina said, surprised at Leah's words. She'd tried not to think of Stanley or how she'd disappointed him.

"You care only so long as it doesn't cost you anything—as long as you can get your own way in a matter." Leah pulled her long dark hair over her shoulder and began to braid it in a furious manner. "You are a spoiled woman who is used to having her own way. You have a separate set of rules designed for yourself. The rest of us have to do your bidding or you use your rules against us."

"I don't have any idea what you're talking about. I've only worked to see justice done."

"You've worked for revenge. You've worked to prove something to yourself and to your brother. I'm not even sure you know what it is you're trying to prove, but it drives you on—and God help the man or woman who gets in your way."

Helaina felt the words stab deep into her heart. Was this truly how Leah perceived her? How others perceived her? "You don't understand—"

"Nor do I want to," Leah interrupted. "I spent far too long trying to understand. Trying to forgive you and give the matter over to God. I tried to pray for you, to help you get well, and now I have to contend with your condemnation once again."

"I'm not condemning you. I merely wished that you hadn't left Chase behind." Helaina's words came out rather stilted. "I might have a different way of doing what I think to be right, but that doesn't mean I can't appreciate your position."

"It's not my position that worries me now," Leah replied, securing her braid. "My husband is out there facing that monster. Jayce is a kindhearted, loving man who has labored with the decision to track down his own flesh and blood. You only care about getting the job done, but my husband has to face that he's sending his own brother—his twin brother—to his death. Imagine someone asking—no, demanding—that you send Stanley to his death."

Helaina felt tears come to her eyes. Leah was right. She hadn't really cared about Jayce's feelings or how it might affect him to hunt down his brother like some kind of rabid dog.

"I'm sorry," she whispered.

Leah looked at her for a moment and shook her head. "Sorry doesn't change anything. It doesn't bring Jayce back here safely, and it doesn't return the things that have been lost or stolen in this."

Helaina had no idea what Leah meant, but she tried to ease the tension. "Look, sorry may seem to just be an empty word to you, but I truly mean it. I'm not one to offer it lightly. I know I've been demanding in this matter, but look at the harm Chase has done. Do you want to be responsible for his continuing to kill and wound? I couldn't live with myself if I didn't at least try to see to his capture."

"There are a lot of things I can't live with," Leah replied in an eerie calm that unnerved Helaina even more. Leah grabbed her parka and left the tent without another word.

Helaina, much to her own surprise, burst into tears and buried her face in her hands. "What have I done? What do I do now?"

Leah felt as though a noose had tightened around her neck. Every word, every thought that had been exchanged with Helaina had drained Leah's sanity and energy. She hated herself for the things she'd said, for purposefully trying to make Helaina feel the same depth of pain that she herself felt.

"I would be better off dead," she whispered as she stalked off away from camp. She looked to the skies overhead. "Why not just kill me? Why must I suffer more? You've proven your point. You've shown me how wretched I am. I already believed it. I'd already asked for your help and deliverance, and here I am—angry and ugly. It's no use for me to go on. I can't be helped this time." She began to cry, the tears that she'd held back on the trail refusing to abate.

Leah fell to her knees. She pounded her fists against her thighs and let out an anguished sob. It was all just so hopeless. How could she ever be alone with Jayce and not see his brother and remember what he had done to her? Those memories would never fade—they were permanently planted in her mind like hidden dynamite that would go off when she least expected it.

Her nature had fought against the anguish and sorrow in order to survive, but Leah no longer wanted to survive. What was the point? If she couldn't love Jayce and give herself to him without fear of the past, what was the sense in living?

Chapter Sixteen

Helaina heard someone come into the tent and presumed Leah had come back to continue her attack. Looking up, she was surprised to find Jacob instead. "What are you doing here?"

"I heard you crying. What's wrong?" He knelt down beside her. "Are you feeling worse?"

"I feel terrible, but not because of my health." She wiped her eyes with her hands. "Your sister thinks I'm a horrible person."

"Leah said that?"

"Well, not exactly that." Helaina looked away and tried not to remember what Leah had said about Jacob loving her. She saw no proof of that, and she figured now that Leah had been lying in order to worry Chase.

"Then what did she say?"

Helaina bit at her lower lip. She wasn't entirely sure she

wanted to have this conversation. A part of her reasoned that Jacob might offer comfort, but at the same time another part suggested that he might confirm Leah's statement.

"Please tell me. I want to help if I can," Jacob said, reaching for her hand.

Helaina pulled back quickly. "She said I was selfish. She said that I was the cause of all of this." She waved her hand. "She blames me for everything—for her being kidnapped, for Jayce being forced to go after his brother, for . . . for . . . everything." The tears came again. "I only did my job. I only did what I thought was right. No one seems to understand my motivation. . . . my reasoning in this."

Jacob sat cross-legged a few feet away but said nothing. It was almost as if he needed to hear more before he could comment.

"I know that no one wanted me to leave Seattle alone, but I had to show Stanley that I was still trustworthy and capable. He had given me a job to do, and I had done it fairly well to that point. After all, I'm the one who figured out that Jayce Kincaid was not the man we were after."

"That was a good thing, Helaina, but had you just talked to some of the rest of us—even questioned Jayce himself—you probably would have learned that without having to send us all the way to Seattle."

"But that's not how things are done in apprehending criminals. All criminals suggest they are innocent. Every man or woman who ever broke the law has some excuse as to why it wasn't their fault or why they shouldn't be charged." She pushed back her long blond hair, wishing fervently she'd at least attempted to attend to it before Jacob's arrival. It had been so long since she'd had a bath or any chance to clean up. She knew she must appear a frightful mess. Perhaps that was why Jacob looked at her with what seemed a suspicious expression.

"Even guilty," she continued, "Jayce Kincaid would have declared that he had nothing to do with those crimes, and his statements would have been no different than any other criminal I've helped to apprehend. So you see, it isn't quite as easy as you'd like to believe. I had a job to do, and I did it."

"All right, so we set aside your deception from last summer and focus on Seattle," Jacob said softly. "Your brother relieved you of your job. He forbade you to go to Nome. Yet you disregarded his decisions and went ahead on your own. You didn't even wait for us."

Helaina realized she couldn't deny his words. She thought for a moment. It suddenly seemed very important that she make him understand. "Have you never felt responsible for something? Something that you had to see through to completion?"

"Of course."

"Well, this was no different. I knew Stanley had relieved me because he felt the job too arduous for me. Perhaps he even felt that I wasn't as cunning and smart as Chase Kincaid."

"You know that isn't true. He took you off the job because he finally came to his senses and realized you could be killed in the process."

Helaina painfully got to her knees. "But he knew that from the beginning. He was always nervous about sending me, but Chase had already defeated several agents. He'd nearly killed Stanley, so he knew something had to be done. He figured Chase would never expect a woman."

"No doubt that was true," Jacob replied. "But it wasn't

sensible. Chase is much too dangerous ... as you've learned the hard way."

"So you think Leah is right? You think I'm just selfish and self-centered?" She felt tears stream down her cheeks and hated herself for such weakness.

Jacob looked to the floor. "I think you were wrong."

"Explain yourself."

He lifted his gaze to meet her eyes. "I think you acted out of a desire to accomplish something for yourself. You were motivated not by justice, but by a need to fulfill some imaginary mark you had set for yourself."

"It wasn't imaginary and it wasn't just for me," Helaina argued. "Chase is a dangerous man who needs to be stopped. I felt responsible—I needed to finish the job. I wish you could understand that."

"I wish you could understand my point of view on this as well."

She looked at him questioningly and sank back to her pallet. "What do you mean?" She suddenly felt drained of all energy. Her illness had definitely taken its toll.

Jacob didn't answer right away, and for several minutes Helaina thought he might refuse to speak. Finally, just when she'd given up hope, he began.

"I don't think Leah has a right to put this all off on you. However, I do believe Leah innocent of any wrongdoing. I don't think you have a right to blame her for not apprehending Chase. It wasn't her obligation or desire. She was afraid for her safety and for yours. She knew that without proper treatment you would die. You do realize that, don't you?"

"I know I was sick, but I've always had a strong constitution. I would have recovered."

Jacob shook his head. "Do you honestly think you're invincible? That you'll live forever? Because without accepting that Jesus died for your sins and that He wants you to repent of those sins and turn to God, you can't live forever."

She stiffened. The last thing she had expected was a sermon. "I asked you if you believed your sister was right in calling me selfish and self-centered. I didn't ask for a theological discussion."

Jacob looked sadder than Helaina had ever seen him. She instantly regretted her words but knew there was no way to take them back. She opened her mouth to speak, but Jacob beat her to it.

"I don't want to have a theological discussion either. You know, I feel sorry for you, Helaina. People care about you—genuinely care—but you push them away because you're terrified of being disappointed . . . hurt. God genuinely cares, too, but you've lumped Him in with the rest. You're afraid He'll disappoint you as well."

"This isn't about God. It's about your sister."

"No. It's about you."

———

Leah fell asleep despite the rough ride. In her dreams she saw Jayce and couldn't help but feel joy at his affection. He told her how much he loved her, but as Leah started to reply, his image faded. Soon there were other faces. Ayoona and Oopick, Jacob and Karen. Leah felt as though they were all trying to tell her something, but she couldn't make out the words. It was as if they all spoke a language she couldn't understand.

Then the dream shifted and Leah was a little girl running in the mountains. She felt free and exhilarated by the mountain air. She thought for a moment she might lift right up into the air and fly. It was a marvelous sensation.

"Leah?"

She knew that voice. Turning, Leah found her mother. She smiled and waved. "I'm here, Mama."

Her mother smiled. "Leah, do not forget who loves you."

"I won't forget, Mama. Look, I've picked you some flowers." Leah held out the bouquet, but the blossoms withered and blew away. She frowned. "They used to be beautiful. Now they're ruined." Leah began to cry. "I'm ruined too."

"No, Leah. You aren't ruined. You are beautiful, and you are loved. No one can change that." The voice was no longer her mother's; rather, it was a deep, comforting voice that seemed to come from the skies. Could it be God?

"But Chase did those horrible things to me," she sobbed, suddenly seeing herself as a grown woman in rags. "Look at me. He's destroyed me."

"Chase had no power to make you, and he has no power to destroy you, Leah. You have already chosen who holds power over you. Remember?"

Leah awoke with a start. For a minute she feared everyone in the party had experienced the same voice she had heard. She pushed aside the furs and came up from her place in the sled. Buried there in her warm cocoon, no one knew whether she was awake or asleep. She glanced over her shoulder to John. She had chosen his sled so that Helaina could ride in Jacob's. John didn't seem to even notice her there. No one paid her any mind.

No one had heard the voice. She realized she was panting and eased back into the furs. Could the words have come from God? The bitter pain that had hardened her heart felt lessened.

"Chase had no power to make you, and he has no power to destroy you, Leah. You have already chosen who holds power over you. Remember?" She heard the words echo in her head as though they were being freshly spoken.

"Chase has no power over me unless I give it to him," Leah murmured. Her heart picked up speed. "I know who holds power over me." A tiny spark of hope began to burn. Chase had only touched her physically because he had imposed that upon her. She had no choice. But she was allowing him to touch her spiritually and emotionally, and she had a choice in that.

"I won't give him that power," she whispered. "I won't give him that part of me." The words gave her renewed strength. The shackles seemed to fall away. The ember of hope burst into a flame. "I'm not ruined." Tears fell hot against her cheeks. "I'm not ruined."

————

Later that night, Leah felt she had to face Helaina again. She had hoped Helaina could stay by herself so Leah could share Jacob's tent, but Jacob insisted the women stay together. Knowing this, Leah knew she had to apologize for having lost her temper.

"I've brought you supper," she said as she came into the tent. Helaina looked up. "What is it?"

Leah put the tin plate on the floor in front of her. "Reindeer stew. It's the last of the meat. John and one of the other men plan to scout ahead and hunt. I'll be driving John's sled tomorrow."

"It smells good," Helaina admitted and sat up to eat.

"Look, I want to say something," Leah began. She sat down,

hoping Helaina would understand that this wasn't just a quick, insincere comment. "I need to apologize for losing my temper this morning. I was wrong to do that."

Helaina looked up in surprise. "Were you also wrong to say the things you said?"

Her tone seemed rather hard—almost smug, but Leah refused to let it put a damper on her newly found peace of mind. "No. I meant what I said this morning." Helaina's expression fell and Leah continued. "I spoke the truth."

"Maybe your truth." Helaina pushed back the plate and shook her head.

"Truth is truth. You're the one who believes the law is the law. Why should it be so hard to understand that it's no different for truth?"

"Laws are established and written down. There is only one interpretation—one meaning."

"Then why must there be judges—Supreme Courts to review the laws and the cases involving those laws?"

"Look, this isn't about that. You called me names—said I was selfish and self-centered."

Leah easily remembered her words from the morning. "And your actions have proven to be such. You focus on yourself—not God or anyone else. I apologize for getting angry about it and saying things I might otherwise have kept to myself. But that's all."

"So this is about God. Just because I don't believe the same things you believe, I'm wrong?"

"Helaina, I'm not here to condemn you. I don't even want to argue with you." Leah got to her knees. "But I hope someday you will understand that vengeance belongs to the Lord. You will never find satisfaction in your schemes for revenge—at least not the same kind of satisfaction you could find in belonging to someone who will never change—never disappoint."

"How many times do I have to tell you or your brother, I'm not in this for revenge?"

"Do you suppose if you say that often enough, it will be true?" Leah didn't wait for an answer. "Helaina, I wish you would truly consider the matter with an open heart. You want revenge for Stanley—for the pain caused him. You want revenge on Chase because he's the one assignment that you've failed to fulfill. You couldn't catch him. Just like you couldn't keep your family from being killed."

Helaina gasped. "How dare you? You have no right to bring them into this."

"Maybe not, but I think if you consider it, you'll see the truth for yourself." Leah got to her feet and moved to the door. "I'm sorry if I've offended you, but rather than worrying about yourself, I'd start thinking about poor Stanley. All he knows is that you've disappeared into the wilds of Alaska chasing after a madman. If the Pinkerton agents were able to get word to Washington from Nome, then Stanley will truly be grief-stricken. He won't know if you're dead or alive, but given Chase's record, he'll assume the worst. Instead of worrying about the one that got away, it might be good for you to remember those you still have."

Leah left Helaina to ponder her words and hoped that the younger woman would see and understand. Walking toward the fire, Leah met Jacob's questioning expression.

"Was she hungry?"

Leah shrugged. "I don't suppose she has her appetite back just yet."

"What about you?"

Leah sat down beside him. "I ate. It was quite good."

"Are you feeling better now? You seem ... well ..."

"Less caustic?" she asked, throwing him a smile. "I'm sorry for the way I've acted. This little adventure in my life has taken its toll. I'm ready to go home and be quiet. I'm still not myself, but I'm trying to regain some peace of mind."

"God can give it to you, if you let Him."

Leah nodded. "But we've been at odds lately. I feel frustrated that He would allow all of this misery into my life. If He loves me, how can He allow me to suffer so much?" She genuinely wanted answers.

Jacob gazed into the fire. "But God didn't spare His own Son misery and sorrow. Why would He spare us?" He turned toward his sister. "Look, I think that things happen—all things—for a reason. Those reasons are sometimes painful to deal with ... to understand. I think, however, that it's all a part of trusting God more. It's easy to trust Him when things go right. Then your faith has no need to grow. Understand?"

"I think so. I guess I just didn't want to grow that much." She forced a smile. "So many times in my life, I've had to grow up before I felt I was ready. Like when Mama died, and then Papa died, or when Jayce refused my love. Now with all that's happened, I feel that again I've been made to face things that I wasn't ready for."

"But God will take you through it. He will never leave you nor forsake you. The Bible says so. These problems are only momentary. They won't last forever."

Leah nodded. "I know you're right. I need to look forward to my future with Jayce instead of looking back at the sorrows of the past."

"Exactly." He shifted his position and suppressed a yawn. "Look, I've been thinking about that as well. I want you and Jayce to take the house. I'll build a small place close by. It'd be nice if you'd still cook for me from time to time." He gave her a rather pathetic look that suggested pleading.

Leah smiled. "You know I will, but we could surely work out something so that you don't have to go building a house in the dead of winter."

"Maybe I'll stay with someone until spring."

"You can stay with us," Leah countered. "We can set up a room for you in the store. There's plenty of room in there. So long as we learn to respect each other's privacy, I don't think there will be any problems."

"Well, maybe until spring," Jacob said, nodding. "You should know, though, I've actually thought about returning to Ketchikan."

"Why?" Leah was genuinely surprised by this statement.

"Adrik asked me to consider it. He says there's going to be a lot of new job opportunities. The government is going to pick up that plan to build a railroad to Fairbanks. They've already gotten started and have asked Adrik to come in and help them."

"Help them do what?"

"Hunt for the workers, mainly. I think he'll also help with the natives."

"But he's Tlingit and Russian," Leah replied. "The railroad will go into Athabascan country."

"I know, but Adrik said he has friends there and feels he can offer help as an interpreter. He suggested I come and take care of the homestead in Ketchikan or even come work with him."

Leah considered this for a moment. "It's hard to imagine you leaving Last Chance."

"Well, I haven't completely decided. Captain Latimore still wants our help with the Arctic exploration. I wouldn't mind giving that a chance either. I know Jayce is still very interested. We talked about it on the trail."

"I guess I hadn't thought about either of you leaving."

"You were invited as well."

Leah shook her head and reached her hands out to the flames. "I've had enough excitement to last a lifetime. I don't want any more."

For several minutes, Jacob said nothing. "What happened out there? With Chase?"

Leah swallowed hard. The old feelings tried to creep in, and she closed her eyes. "Please don't ask me." Her voice was barely audible. "I can't talk about it. Not now—maybe never."

Chapter Seventeen

Jayce managed to get Chase into the tent before the wind picked up and the temperature dropped. He carefully arranged his brother's injured frame, then went to work melting snow for water.

The weather threatened more snow, and Jayce worried about finding his way back to the village at which they'd stopped. He'd seen no other sign of civilization and given Chase's desperate state, this furthered his concern. For all he knew there could be a village just over the next hill, but then again, he might head off in the wrong direction and be hundreds of miles from any kind of help.

As Chase's body began to thaw, he started to move and then to moan. Jayce moved to his side with a bit of melted water and one of his old shirts. He ripped the shirt into strips that he could use to dress Chase's wounds. The only problem was that there were many cuts.

"Chase, can you hear me?"

His brother's head moved, but he didn't open his swollen eyes. Jayce took one of the strips and dipped it in the water. He touched the cloth to Chase's bloodied lips, hoping to trickle a little of the clean water into his mouth.

"Chase. It's me, Jayce. I'm trying to help you, but you need to wake up."

With a tenderness he didn't truly feel, Jayce lifted Chase's head ever so slightly. How could this man have gone so wrong in his life? How could he have forsaken the training and upbringing of good people to live a life of crime and murderous hate?

"Chase, I'm going to give you a little water." He squeezed the cloth onto his twin's lips. Some of the water ran into his bloodied beard, but a little made it inside.

Lowering Chase back to the pallet, Jayce began to tend the wounds. All the while he talked to his brother.

"I don't know why it had to come to this. It seems such a senseless waste of a life. You were always clever and good with mastering skills when they were of interest to you."

Jayce felt certain the nasty rips in Chase's face and upper body were made by a bear. Perhaps it had been Leah's rogue bear or one of the Arctic polar bears wandering inland. If it was Leah's bear, he would have been wounded and more dangerous. He would most likely attack without provocation. Chase would have only had a knife with which to defend himself. The fight would have definitely been unevenly matched, even if the bear was injured.

The water bloodied in the bowl rather quickly, and Jayce found himself in a dilemma. If he tossed it outside, it might attract the killer bear to join them. If not the bear, then perhaps wolves would be attracted to the scent. On the other hand, Jayce hadn't brought a lot of supplies and utensils with him. The bowl was much needed and Chase required more care.

Jayce finally decided he had no choice. He braved the wind and cold to walk some twenty yards from the tent. He carried the bowl and lantern in one hand while balancing his rifle with the other. He wasn't about to take a chance that the bear was still in the vicinity, just waiting.

The night was amazingly quiet. Only the wind offered any sound across the frozen tundra. The skies were heavy with clouds. No stars. No moon. Yet Jayce's thoughts were focused solely on his situation: He was in an unfamiliar area of the territory and his brother was fighting to live. Neither of them were in a good position. Jayce still needed to figure a way back to civilization, and Chase . . . well, as best Jayce could tell, Chase was dying.

"But you were coming here to take him to his death anyway," Jayce spoke to the silent landscape. "Isn't it better to see him die here than wait for him to be hanged?" There was no comfort in such thinking; what Jayce really wished could never be. He would trade most everything he had to see the years turned back and his brother's heart remade. "But that isn't going to happen. This is the life we have chosen. He chose his way, and I chose mine. It can't be undone now."

He made his way back to the tent and refilled the bowl before sitting back down at Chase's side. His brother lay very still. Jayce wasn't even sure he was breathing. He put his hand on Chase's chest and felt the very shallow rise and fall. At least he was still alive.

But to what purpose? Jayce felt almost torn in nursing his brother's wounds. He felt certain that without the medical attention of a doctor, Chase would most likely not make it through the night. It seemed heartless to pick and prod at his wounds. Even as Jayce contemplated this, Chase began to stir and then to cough.

Jayce heard him make a gurgling sound and rolled Chase slightly to his side. Blood poured from his mouth, causing Jayce to jump back a bit, while Chase struggled to regain consciousness. His eyes opened slowly. They were lifeless dark pits that seemed to see nothing.

Jayce put his hand on his brother's shoulder. "Chase, it's me. It's Jayce. You've been wounded." He helped Chase ease back on the pallet. "Can you hear me?"

"I . . . do." The words were barely audible.

The wind picked up, blowing fiercely against the tent. Jayce was glad for the small refuge but couldn't help wishing he could close his eyes and wake up in another place—another life. He suddenly hated where this one had taken him.

"You've been attacked by something. You're in bad shape."

"I . . . know."

"I'll make you some tea in a minute," Jayce said as he went back to tending Chase's face. "These cuts are very deep. I'll have to make a salve for them and see if we can keep the bleeding from starting up again. The head wounds are the worst. Whatever got you seems to have chewed on your head."

"Bear." Chase looked Jayce in the eyes. "Big bear."

Jayce nodded. "Leah said there was one moving around."

Chase tried to smile, but it looked most macabre. "Leah safe?"

Jayce was surprised by the question. "Yes. She and Helaina met us on the trail. Jacob and some of the men from the village took them home."

"Not you."

It wasn't really a question, but Jayce felt as though Chase were asking why he hadn't gone with them. "I had to find you. You knew we'd come for you."

Chase closed his eyes and drew a couple of wheezing breaths. Jayce set aside the bowl of water and went to the stove. He made a cup of strong tea and tested the temperature. He worried that it would be too hot for Chase to handle and went to the tent flap to retrieve some snow. He only opened the very bottom of the flap to keep the cold from stealing away the warmth. Stretching out, he grabbed a handful of snow and quickly plopped it into the cup. The tea sloshed over the sides, burning Jayce's hand momentarily. The pain caused him to remember Leah. There was so much he wanted to know—needed to know. How had Chase hurt her? What had he done and said that left her so devastated?

Jayce secured the flap and came back to Chase. His brother had opened his eyes again and watched him intently. "I have tea. I'll help you sit up a bit. It should help to relax you."

Chase gave the tiniest shake of his head. "No."

"Look, I'm just trying to make this better for you. Contrary to what you believe, I don't want to see you in pain."

"Lot of pain."

"I'm sure you're in a lot of pain," Jayce replied. "This tea should help."

"No."

Jayce felt a sense of frustration but put the tea aside. "Have it your way. You always have."

Chase tried again to smile. "Never had ... it ... my way."

Jayce sat back and shook his head. "I don't know how you figure that. You've done nothing but run our family for years. You know it's true. Now that you're finally incapacitated, you have no choice but to listen to me. And since the weather has turned foul on us, we have nothing better to do than talk."

"You were . . . the perfect . . . one."

"No, I wasn't perfect." Jayce toyed with the sinew that attached his mittens to the parka. "I didn't have time to be perfect. I was too busy trying to clean up after you. You were always causing me trouble, and I really resented it. I guess now that I have turned to God for my answers, I should ask your forgiveness for the hatred I felt toward you all these years."

"God . . . doesn't . . . care."

Jayce looked at the wounded man. "He does care. He cares more about you than you've ever cared for yourself. You were always taking chances with your life—with the lives of those around you. You've lived a reckless existence, and now you've no one to blame but yourself for this mess you're in."

"Can blame . . . you."

Jayce laughed and shrugged. "Sure. Go ahead and blame me if it makes you feel better. I doubt it will, however. Why you ever believed that made things better is beyond me. You've blamed me all of your life for one misery or another. And you know what's sad? In most cases I was your defender."

Chase's eyes seemed to widen a bit. "Didn't . . . ask you . . . to be."

"I know that."

"Hated . . . you . . . doing it." Chase grimaced and closed his eyes against the pain. Jayce leaned forward, and Chase immediately opened his eyes again. "Don't . . . touch . . . me."

"Don't be ridiculous. You'll die if I don't help you."

"I'll die . . . anyway. You'll . . . see . . . to it." He was panting the words, yet they came out stronger than the others.

Jayce said nothing for a moment. What could he say? He knew

Chase was implying that Jayce would see him hanged. And if the rest of the family ever found out the part Jayce had played in this strange little play, there would be no living with any of them. Not that he would anyway. It was one of the reasons Jayce had chosen to hide out in Alaska. His siblings had no desire to follow him here. Only Chase had braved the elements.

"When did you first come to Alaska?" Jayce found himself asking.

"When you came." The words came out all run together.

Jayce cocked his head to one side. "That was a long time ago. You mean when I first came here after Mother died?"

"Yes."

"But how did you follow me? I didn't even know where I was going."

"You . . . weren't trying . . . to hide."

"That's true enough. Still, why would you do it?"

Chase tried to lick his lips, but the effort, coupled with talking, seemed too much. Jayce, without waiting for Chase's approval, took one of the clean strips and dipped it in the tea he'd made. Coming back to Chase, he put it to his brother's lips and dampened them.

Chase made no protest, so Jayce took the opportunity to do it again. That seemed to be enough and Chase raised his left hand ever so slightly as if to wave off his brother's efforts.

Jayce presumed the conversation would end. Chase was in no shape to continue, and it would probably be best if they both got some sleep. "We'll need to get out of here at daybreak. Better rest for now." He started to clean up the area.

"Had to leave . . . you were leaving."

Jayce turned at Chase's comment. "I don't understand."

"If I stayed . . . they would know . . . who I was."

Jayce thought a moment, then realization dawned. "You mean if you stayed with everyone knowing I had gone, and continued to pull your pranks and commit crimes, there would be no doubt that you were the culprit. Is that it?"

"Yes."

Jayce shook his head. "So even then you were planning a life of crime?"

"It . . . suited me."

"But why? You were wealthy. You had a good inheritance from our father. All of us did. I never understood the way you each squandered what you had instead of investing it or buying something useful like a home."

"You . . . were . . . the perfect son." His eyes narrowed, and Jayce clearly saw the hatred there. "Turned . . . Mother against me."

"But I wasn't trying to be perfect, and it had never been my intention to turn Mother or anyone else against you. You did that all on your own." Jayce felt his ire grow. "I was merely trying to do the right thing. Our mother was alone and needed protection from all of you. You robbed her blind. She loved you and you took everything she had."

"I . . . never . . . did."

"I know you did. She gave you her inheritance. She gave money to each of you after you went through your own fortunes. She ended up so deeply in debt that she had to sell the house in order to make things right with her creditors. Don't tell me you didn't do that. Don't lie to me—not now."

"I . . . would have . . . helped her."

"It doesn't matter now what you would have done. It's in the past." Jayce took a deep breath to ease his anger. There was no sense in getting mad at a dying man.

"You'll ... soon have ... your way ... your revenge."

Jayce looked at his brother and shook his head. "I never wanted revenge. That's never been what this was about. I wanted to keep you from hurting people. You'd already killed, and then in Nome you killed again. I couldn't let that go on for the sake of those innocent people. But it's never been about revenge."

"It ... will be." Chase gasped for air and seemed to fight against some imaginary grip as he clutched his chest as best he could.

Jayce feared Chase might die any moment. "You need to make your peace with God. You cannot die without making things right."

"No." Chase moved his head from side to side, the movement ever so slight.

"Chase, God wants to forgive you your sins. The Bible says that He sent His Son, Jesus, to die for those sins so that you could have everlasting life. He can wipe away the blood and thievery. You can die a forgiven man with a clean slate."

"And ... you?"

"I don't understand. What about me?"

"You ... forgive ... me?"

Jayce thought about it for a moment. He had wrestled with such thoughts while on Chase's trail. Could he forgive his brother for stealing his life ... ruining his reputation ... kidnapping his wife? It would take a supreme effort on his part, but Jayce knew he had to try.

"I want to forgive you, Chase. I won't lie to you and say it's easy. You've given me nothing but a life of misery and heartache. You've grieved me at every turn. We could have been close.... I really resent that we couldn't have that. You might have been my most trusted confidant, but you chose instead to put a wall between us. You destroyed what might have been. What I hoped could one day be salvaged, you destroyed by your deception and lawless acts."

Jayce rubbed his bearded chin and held his hand against his mouth for a moment. When he pulled it away, he gave a heavy sigh. "I want to forgive you, because it's the right thing in God's eyes. God will forgive you if you ask, and I must as well."

Chase gave a strange laugh. "You won't . . . forgive."

Jayce narrowed his eyes. "Why would you say that? You know nothing of who I am, Chase. Through God's power, I can do all things. The Bible says so. And since I believe that to be true, I have to believe that with God's help, I can forgive you."

Chase shook his head. This time the movement was more pronounced. "I . . . had . . . Leah." Jayce saw him watch for a reaction. Even in the midst of his pain and suffering, even though he was dying, Chase was commanding the moment. "I . . . forced her."

Jayce couldn't move. He couldn't breathe. To hear his brother's declaration—his admission of guilt—was surprising and devastating. Jayce had suspected this bitter truth, but to hear his brother's confession made him want to strangle the remaining life from him. He thought of his wife and how she must have suffered. *No wonder she didn't want me to touch her. No wonder she was changed.*

Jayce took his time and spoke in a measured fashion. "I knew you had hurt her. I could see in her eyes that she had been deeply wounded. I suspected . . . that you . . ." His words trailed off. He wanted to cry for Leah but knew he had to be strong. He was determined that Chase not have the upper hand in this matter.

"You ... can't ... forgive." Chase paused and fought for air. "God ... can't forgive."

God, help me, Jayce prayed. He wanted to hate Chase. He wanted to let the hatred fester up inside and give him the strength to deal with the matter man-to-man. In that moment it seemed like retribution was the only thing that would get Jayce through the pain. Yet even as he thought this, he knew that it wasn't the right answer. God wanted Jayce to rely on Him. Though the trial was worse than any he had ever known, God would be the one to see him through—not anger or revenge.

Jayce looked at his brother and found his eyes closed. He thought for a moment that Chase had succumbed to the pain and lost consciousness, but then it became obvious that this wasn't the case.

Jayce leaned over and touched his hand to Chase's chest. There was no movement. Jayce quickly felt for a pulse. There was none. He sat back in stunned silence.

Chase was dead. He was dead and Jayce had not forgiven him ... nor had Chase turned to God. A dark cloud settled over Jayce. He wanted to believe that Chase's death signaled the end of misery for him and Leah, but he knew it wasn't true. Chase had come between them in the only way possible. Jayce could hardly bear the moment.

"I've failed. I've failed Chase. I've failed Leah. And I've failed God."

The anguish rose up inside him like the rushing winds outside. With a scream born of pain more intense than a human being should have to endure, Jayce clawed blindly at the tent flaps and staggered from the tent into the dark Arctic cold.

Chapter Eighteen

L eah resented the time Jacob spent with Helaina. Watching
them now as Jacob helped Helaina to warm herself by the
morning fire, Leah knew she would have to figure some way to
separate them. Jacob already cared much too deeply for this
woman, and Leah knew that Helaina would only hurt him.

She's a selfish woman who would never stay in Alaska for him, Leah
reasoned. *I cannot let Jacob fall in love with her. It will be no different than
the pain I suffered with Jayce when he didn't return my love.*

Leah tried to imagine how such a rejection would alter Jacob's
sweet nature. He possessed such a strong faith in God that no
doubt he would turn to the Lord, but Leah also felt confident that
he would sequester himself away from everyone, and she couldn't
bear the thought of losing him that way.

She gathered her things and started repacking John's sled.
He'd gone on ahead of them to hunt. Leah prayed he'd be

successful, as her traps had proven less and less fruitful as they'd drawn near the Kotzebue Sound.

"You're sure quiet this morning," Jacob said, coming to help her take down the tent.

"Well, you aren't." Leah regretted that her voice held such a snide tone.

"What's that supposed to mean?"

Leah stopped and looked across the short distance to where Helaina sat. Leah lowered her voice. "She's nothing but trouble, Jacob."

"Let me be the judge of that." He pulled up the tent stakes using the end of a small pick.

"But I'm afraid you won't be a very good judge this time."

"You know me to be a cautious man when it comes to dealing with people," Jacob countered. "You should trust me to be the same this time."

"But your heart may not listen to your head."

Jacob laughed. "What makes you think that all my decisions and choices are made with my head?"

"I suppose that I don't, but this is one of those times when I think it will be dangerous for you if you let your heart rule. She's not for you."

"I think I'm old enough to decide these matters for myself. I didn't come to you and tell you that Jayce wasn't right for you. And I think I would have been well within my rights to do so. After all, I knew the pain he'd caused you all those years and how much it had altered your life."

"This is totally different."

"Is it really?" He pulled out the remaining stake and looked up at her. "I don't think it is."

Leah walked a short distance from the camp and motioned to her brother. Jacob finally got up and followed her. He shoved his hands into his pockets and waited for Leah to speak.

"Helaina has done nothing but lie to you and me. She's caused us so much trouble. You cannot let yourself fall for her schemes. You were the one who warned me about her in the first place. Go back in time to those first minutes you met her in Nome. You know that she's going to cause you nothing but trouble. If she plays on your emotions, it will only be to benefit herself and capture Chase Kincaid."

"You think so lowly of me? A woman can't fall in love and be kind to me because of that love?" Jacob sounded genuinely hurt.

Leah shook her head. "You know that's not what I think. You are a wonderful man with a big heart and a loving nature. I don't want to see you used for any reason, but especially not for her games. Helaina Beecham is another story. She's manipulative and self-centered. She's here for just one reason, and I don't trust her."

"But you don't have to. This is really up to me."

"Look," Leah gazed back over her shoulder as Helaina began to cough. "She's sick. Let's leave her at the next village. Someone there can help her. They can treat the sickness, and when spring comes, they can get her out on the mail ship."

"Listen to yourself. You would deny the woman our Christian hospitality just because you fear I'll lose my heart to her? That isn't like you, Leah. You used to be far more compassionate."

"I used to be a great many things. All of that has changed now. This trip has cost me too much."

"I know," he said softly. He reached out to touch her, but Leah pulled back. "I wish you'd tell me what happened. Maybe talking about it would help you to get over it."

Leah pushed the old feelings aside. She had to fight this—had to overcome. Chase didn't have power over her unless she gave it to him. "This isn't about me. It's about you and . . . her."

Leah paced a few steps farther from the camp. She was desperate to help Jacob see the truth. "Look, all she's been able to talk about is going back up north. She wants to catch Chase to prove to her brother that she can do the job. She's obsessed with it. She will do whatever is necessary to get the help she needs. If that includes duping you with emotions and flowery words, then she'll do it. I've no doubt in my mind."

"Leah, this isn't your business." His words were stern and his expression held such a serious look that Leah felt instantly reproved. "I'm a grown man. I know how to look out for myself. If it's of any comfort to you, I have no plans to take a wife just yet. But even if I did, I would hope you would respect my wishes and be happy for me, no matter the circumstance."

With that he gathered the stakes and tent poles and rolled everything into a neat bundle. Leah stood watching him. She couldn't make herself join in. She was fearful of what she might yet say, and Jacob had made it clear he wanted no more advice.

They broke camp about twenty minutes later. One of the men from the village led the way in his sled, while Leah followed and Jacob brought up the rear. Leah couldn't help but wonder how she might yet put distance between Jacob and Helaina. She didn't trust anything about the younger woman and figured that even now, Helaina was plotting how to get Jacob's cooperation.

"I have to stop her," Leah whispered against her scarf. "There has to be a way."

There has to be a way to get Jacob to help me, Helaina reasoned as the sled moved easily over the trail. She knew he cared about her physical well-being. He'd checked on her many times since finding them, and he was always happy to share her company. Helaina had not yet broached the subject of hunting down Chase Kincaid, but she was watching for her opportunity.

He will help me. I know he will. He wants to see this matter resolved. I'm sure of it.

She pondered the situation, wondering how to set it all in motion. She had no confidence that Jayce would find his brother, let alone capture him and bring him back for the authorities. It wasn't that she didn't think he wanted to see justice served, but Helaina figured he had no real motivation to try too hard. After all, as Leah had already pointed out on many occasions, it was very hard for Jayce to decide to pursue his brother.

Perhaps I can hire Jacob as a guide, she thought. *I have more than enough money, and if he knows that I'm determined to go with or without him, maybe the promise of wealth will entice him.*

But even as she contemplated this, Helaina knew that Jacob Barringer was not a man to be purchased—not at any price. To be honest, she liked that about him. He wasn't easily swayed by feminine wiles or cold hard cash. She found that refreshing. In fact, when she'd first met him in Nome, it had been a challenge just to get him to talk to her, much less put any trust in her.

Snuggling down deeper into the furs, Helaina smiled at the

memory. Jacob had wanted nothing to do with her. He had hardly been willing to look her in the eye. She'd thought then that it was due to some criminal intent or complication in his life. Usually the men who avoided such contact were up to something devious, but with Jacob it turned out to be more of a protective issue.

She yawned and let the pleasant memories spill into her planning. Last summer Jacob had been so good to help teach her how to work with the dogs and how to keep house in the Alaskan wilderness. She could still remember the trials she'd faced enduring the smells of butchering and then tanning the hides. She was mortified to learn that Ayoona wanted her to save urine in order to pour on the hides. This would cause the hair to fall out and leave them with a clean skin. Helaina shuddered still to think of the stench.

It was definitely a strange existence in Last Chance, but Jacob had made it all bearable. The only truly bad times she'd known were those days when he was gone off hunting or delivering dogs. Those were lonely times for Helaina. She hadn't been able to connect with anyone else in the village, save Emma Kjellmann.

Knowing there was little she could do at this moment, Helaina allowed herself to doze. As Leah kept saying, rest would see her well faster than most anything else.

They stopped around one o'clock to rest the dogs and eat a little lunch. They were near water, but Helaina had no idea where they were. All she knew was that every hour took her farther and farther away from Chase Kincaid.

"So where are we?" she asked Jacob as he helped her from the basket.

"On the Kotzebue Sound," Jacob answered. "We'll follow it around a ways, at least as far as Kiwalik, and then maybe south to

Candle. There are some good trails, and if the rivers are frozen solid they'll make a good path for us."

He walked to the small fire that Leah had built. Helaina followed him as he added, "It won't take us long to get back to Last Chance if the weather holds. We know this territory at least. It's always slower going when you don't know where you are."

Helaina sat down on the ground. She had no strength and was frustrated by her weakness. *There was a time when I could walk five miles without even getting winded,* she thought. *Now I'm reduced to collapsing after just a few feet.* Still, she refused to show Jacob any weakness.

"I feel much better," she told him. This much was true. "I'm sure I'll soon be able to—"

"Look, it's John and the others," Leah called.

Helaina looked in the direction Leah pointed. Sure enough, John and two other men were making their way to camp. They were dragging something behind them.

"We were blessed," John announced. "On the ice we got a seal. He was sunning himself. He's small, but he'll taste good."

Leah clapped her hands together. "That is a blessing. How wonderful. The dogs will eat well and so will we."

Helaina watched as the men approached the fire. Jacob helped John with his pack. The Inupiat stretched. "We'll have to butcher him fast in case nanook comes to see."

"Nanook?" Helaina said, trying the word. "Bear?"

Leah turned with a look of exasperation. "Yes, bear. The polar bears will be tempted to take away our little catch. Here, near the water, there's a greater danger. There could even be other bears and animals who'll smell the kill." She turned back to the men. "I'll get the pots out and cook up some of the meat."

"I'll help you get it cut up," Jacob said, crossing the camp. The dogs began to catch the scent of the seal and started to bark and whine. "They want to help too."

John laughed, as did Leah. Helaina merely sat back and realized she truly didn't belong in this country. She felt as though she were an uninvited guest in a party of strangers.

I can fit in too. I am strong and resourceful. I can do what I have to do. She tried hard to convince herself that she could belong anywhere she chose to belong.

"I'll start gutting him, John," Jacob said. "You all get some coffee. I'll have Leah fry up the liver for you."

"Too bad it not summer," John said, picking up a tin cup. "We'd make soured liver. Good eating."

Helaina shuddered. The thought of eating the seal meat wasn't as troubling as it used to be, but she remembered Ayoona making the soured liver. They put it in a dish and left it in the sun for days. After it had soured—or spoiled, as Helaina believed was the case—the older people would relish the flavor. Trying not to show any displeasure, she turned to Leah, who was busy filling pots with snow.

"Do you . . . well, that is . . . is there any way I can help?"

Leah looked at her for a moment, then shook her head. "No. You're still sick. You'll just have a relapse if you start working too hard."

Helaina didn't argue with her. She had no strength for work and was glad for the directive to remain idle. After all, it would give her time to continue thinking on a plan. She had to figure a way to convince Jacob to help her return to the north. There had to be a way.

Jacob worked quickly with the others and soon had all of the dogs fed and watered. As he sat down to enjoy some boiled seal meat, he found Helaina taking an unusual interest in him. He felt a warning bell go off in his brain.

"You look really tired," she began. "Can I get you anything?"

"I'm fine, actually. And I'm not that tired. Maybe you're just seeing me through tired eyes." He smiled, hoping she would take the joke in a good-natured fashion.

She smiled, and he went back to eating as she spoke. "I think lying around doing nothing makes a person tired. I shall endeavor to exercise a bit more when we make our stops."

"Just don't overdo it. You have plenty of time to rest up and regain your strength."

"Yes, but I want to help more. I know I've been a terrible burden."

"You haven't been a burden at all," Jacob replied. He didn't want Helaina to feel bad; after all, she couldn't help that she'd caught pneumonia.

He ate in silence for a time after that. It seemed that Helaina was content to rest and enjoy the quiet of the day. Jacob knew they would be pushing out soon, so he motioned to the sled. "We'll be heading off in about fifteen minutes. You might want to get yourself comfortable."

Helaina nodded. "I have some urgent personal matters to see to first." She got to her feet rather slowly. "Don't leave without me."

Jacob laughed. "We couldn't do that." He watched her move away. "Don't go too far. We don't want you having to deal with nanook."

"Indeed not," Helaina called back, "for you would have to

come to my rescue, and you've already worked very hard today."

Leah approached him as Helaina left the camp. "See what I mean? She's flirting with you."

"So what? There's no harm being done to either of us." He finished the meat and handed Leah the tin plate.

"It's dangerous and you know it. She's going to presume a relationship with you that doesn't exist."

"You worry too much. I'm a grown man, Leah. I wish you would stop worrying over me like a mother bear with cubs."

Leah wiped the plate with snow. "Jacob, I think we should leave her in the next village. We can always make arrangements for her once we get home. Or you could even go to Nome and contact those Pinkertons, and they could make arrangements for her."

"Leah, we've discussed this before. You aren't being reasonable."

"Neither is she. Mark my words: She'll try to force you to help her with Chase. If we just drop her off at one of the coastal settlements, there are bound to be missionaries who can help get her back to the States."

"You know that Helaina wouldn't be comfortable with that."

"Be comfortable with what?" Jacob and Leah turned in surprise to find Helaina had already rejoined them. "What wouldn't I be comfortable with?"

Leah took a deep breath and exchanged a glance with her brother. "I was telling Jacob that for your sake, we should leave you in the next village. We can get you better care, more herbs, and warm accommodations. Then we can arrange to have you picked up when the mail ships are running again."

"No!"

Jacob shook his head and got to his feet. "No one is being left behind. We'll get Helaina back to Last Chance and then send her home in the spring. We can surely find someone who can put her up for the winter. Emma has that new addition for her sister, so maybe she would let Helaina stay there in return for helping with the children. Leah, didn't you tell me she's expecting another baby? Emma would probably love the help."

"I don't want to stay in Last Chance," Helaina said firmly. "I need to get to Seattle or San Francisco. From there I can get in touch with my brother—perhaps even take the train back to Washington, D.C., and rethink our strategy."

"See, I told you she wouldn't be content to remain in Alaska," Leah said, packing Jacob's plate with the others.

"I need to get more help," Helaina admitted. "I need to convince Stanley that I can handle the situation and secure more agents to assist in Chase's capture. Then I'll return to Alaska."

Jacob frowned at Helaina's statement. He tried to ignore the woman and returned to readying the sled for travel, but she followed him. Leah came along as well.

"Jacob, I can't just leave this matter to Jayce Kincaid. He won't be able to bring Chase in. Not if he was as tortured by the situation as you made it seem."

"My husband can handle the matter," Leah replied sternly. "You need to remember your place."

"Bringing Chase to justice is exactly my place."

"No it's not," Jacob said. "Look, you were relieved of your duties. You are still sick and very weak. Don't think I don't know it's taking every ounce of strength you possess just to stand here."

"I'm much better. By the time we get to Last Chance, I'll be perfectly able to travel to Seattle."

Jacob shook his head. "But there will be no transportation south. We're frozen in until spring breakup."

"But I have money."

"Helaina, your money won't matter. There are no ships into Nome this time of year."

She was undeterred. "Then where is the nearest year-round port? Take me there. You have dog sleds, and you told me once before that you've made the trip across the interior. So I'll pay you to take me now."

"Jacob isn't going to risk his life trekking out across the interior of Alaska for your selfish needs."

"Leah, I can handle this." He saw the look of anger that crossed his sister's face. She wasn't one who liked to be reprimanded, much less in front of someone like Helaina. He held up his hands. "Ladies, we're wasting time. Leah, you need to finish loading up John's sled and get yourself settled in the basket. He can drive now. Helaina, you need to get settled here."

"Fine," Leah declared, stalking off toward John's sled.

He thought the matter settled and turned to go, but Helaina had taken hold of him. "You can't just leave me stranded like this. I need your help to get south. I need more men to go north on the search with me."

Jacob felt a deep sorrow. "Helaina, what you need and what you want are two entirely different matters."

She looked at him oddly. "I don't know what you mean."

He gave a sigh. "I know you don't, and that's your biggest problem."

Chapter Nineteen

That night Jacob found himself actually contemplating Helaina's request to go across the interior. Adrik had suggested Jacob come to Seward and join him working for the railroad. If he took Helaina, she could catch a ship out of Seward and head south. The harbor never closed and would be the perfect place to get transportation to either Seattle or San Francisco, given the large volume of goods that were being shipped back and forth in association with the railroad.

He went as far as to take out pencil and paper and try to figure the cost of such an expedition. It would be harsh and difficult to deal with the weather and unpredictable land. There were mail trails that could be followed, but even these would present dangers.

"What are you doing?" Leah asked as she joined Jacob at the fire. Most of the others had retired to their tents and sleds.

"I was just thinking about getting Helaina to Seward."

"What? Are you crazy?"

He rubbed his bearded chin. "Not the last time I checked."

"Jacob, you can't do this. It's much too dangerous. It's not like this is any real emergency."

"But maybe it would be better for everyone concerned to get Helaina on her way. You want her away from me, after all." He watched her frown. How could she argue such a point—she was, after all, the one who had made such a big issue of it earlier.

"I want her away from you, not isolated with you for a month or more." Leah sat down and tried to reason with him. "Jacob, it would be costly and dangerous. You know it would. The dogs would be pressed to their very limits, as would you. The winter has come early and the weather has been unpredictable. You could find yourself in trouble within days."

"Again, thank you for the vote of confidence."

Leah slapped her palms against her sealskin pants. "You know this isn't about you and your ability. It's about it being November—nearly December in Alaska. You wouldn't suggest anyone else take such a risk, so why take one yourself?"

"I didn't say that I would. I'm just trying to think of what would be best for everyone concerned. Helaina won't give us any peace so long as she's determined to get to the States."

Leah's jaw clenched. "Helaina needs to learn some manners."

"Be that as it may, you should remember your Christian charity. You were the one who gave me such a difficult time of it when I wanted nothing to do with Helaina. Now you're angry because I'm being kind."

Leah blew out a heavy breath. "I'm not trying to be difficult, Jacob. I'm just worried."

"You needn't worry about me. I've been through much worse than Helaina Beecham." He grinned and added, "If she's the most difficult thing I have to contend with, then my life will be rather simple."

"I seriously doubt that."

"I was just thinking that I could take her by sled to Seward. It would be a long and arduous trip, but Adrik would like to have me join him there anyway. We talked about the potential of it when we were in Sitka."

"But you also have the Arctic exploration to consider. Have you given up on that idea? Captain Latimore will return in June and expect you to be a part of his team."

"I know. I haven't given up on such plans. I want to pray and seek what God wants me to do in regard to both options. I feel that God has a purpose in presenting both possibilities. I need to consider which might be best for all parties concerned. Including Helaina's desire to get to a ship."

"Helaina desires a great many things. Too many, if you ask me. She wants Chase captured. She wants to show the Pinkertons how capable she is. She wants you to make all of her obstacles go away."

Jacob actually laughed at this. "I wish I could. I wish I could set her free from the shackles that bind her, but only God can do that. She thinks she needs so many other things, when what she really needs is Jesus. She has no peace of mind—no hope for anything past the performance she can give."

Leah frowned. "I suppose I haven't been too concerned with her spiritually, though I did seek her forgiveness for my mean spirit."

"Then you should understand," Jacob replied. "I want to help her see the truth. It isn't a matter of allowing her to manipulate and have her own way. I want her to see that Chase and the original job she was given to do are no longer the reasons she's still here. She focuses on this because it's all she has. She doesn't know how to be fulfilled any other way."

Leah put another piece of driftwood on the fire and stretched out her hands to the flames. "I can see the truth in that. I've suggested as much myself. I told her I believed she was seeking revenge for the past."

"As have I." Jacob leaned forward. "I don't know what the Lord would have for me regarding Helaina. I do care about her . . . deeply. I never thought I would, given our initial introduction."

"But she's—"

"Just hear me out." Jacob looked at her hard. "I care about her. I can't help it. I won't pursue it because she doesn't love God. She sees God as some sort of adversary. I couldn't pretend that doesn't matter. You know me well enough to realize that."

Leah nodded but remained silent. Jacob gazed into the flames and tried to figure out how to say what was on his heart. "When we were in Nome, you helped me to understand that often I allow my ability to discern people and their motives to keep me from caring about them—about their souls. I know that isn't why God would give me such a gift. Helaina is hurting. She's still trying to figure out why she was left behind when all that she loved, short of Stanley, was taken from her. She needs to understand that God isn't the enemy here, and that terrible things will often happen to the children He loves, but it doesn't alter His love for those children."

Leah still said nothing, and Jacob looked up to find her crying. "Leah?"

She looked to the ground. "I'm sorry."

"Don't be." He scooted closer and hesitantly put his arm around her. She didn't push him away and Jacob breathed a sigh of relief. "Talk to me."

"I don't think I can."

"Of course you can. I love you. You're my little sister. We made promises to each other a long time ago. Remember? We promised to be honest with each other and to take care of each other. Of course, Jayce has the job of caring for you now, but I will always love you."

Leah sank against him and he tightened his hold on her. "I used to think God would keep me from bad things. I remember asking Mama why God didn't protect us from evil men and evil things. I asked her if God wasn't strong enough. She told me that God was always able but that sometimes things happened as a means to bring Him honor and glory. Like remember when we were at that revival meeting and the minister talked about the missionaries who had been killed by the natives when they went to Africa?"

"I remember. He said the missionaries hoped that their story would bring people to God."

"Yes, and even as they were being tortured to death, they praised God. That did inspire me, Jacob. I thought how wondrous it would be to have that kind of faith. To be put in the flames— to die for the cause of taking the Word of God to people who had never heard it. But at the same time, I couldn't understand it. I still don't. Those people were serving God. They were living for God, trusting Him for direction. They were being good to other people, and ..." Her voice broke. "They were trying to do the right thing."

"But still they died. Died in God's service," Jacob whispered. "And you were trying to do the right thing. You were living for God and trusting Him, and yet Chase came and took you away."

"Yes." She grew very quiet. For several minutes she said nothing, so Jacob merely waited. Finally, she looked up. "He forced himself on me, Jacob."

The words were delivered matter-of-factly. Jacob had no doubt they were true. "I'm so sorry, Leah. I wish I could have kept you from that."

Leah bit her lower lip and drew several ragged breaths. "He . . . well . . . I . . ." She shook her head and leaned back against her brother.

Jacob simply held her for several minutes, waiting until she felt able to speak again. He knew it would be important for her to talk.

"I didn't tell Jayce," she finally said. "I couldn't."

"You'll find the strength when the time is right. Jayce will understand."

"How can he? I don't." Leah sat up. "I don't understand why God would allow that to happen. I even tried to help Chase know more about God—about salvation. I tried to be helpful to Helaina even though I blamed her for our even being in that situation. I tried to have a good heart. Do you think my anger at Helaina caused God to punish me?"

Jayce shook his head. "I don't think God works that way, Leah. I think what happened was the result of Chase's evil ways. This is a corrupt world. There is evil that lurks and waits to cause harm in the lives of the innocent."

"But we pray for God's protection. The Bible is full of examples of people who were protected in times of trouble. Why not me, Jacob? Why not? What did I do that was so terrible that God wouldn't hear my prayers?"

Jacob felt a lump form in his throat as he looked at Leah. She pleaded with him for answers that he didn't have. "I believe God heard, Leah. I don't believe He rejected your prayers. Remember that even while there were times when people were protected in the Bible, there were other times when they were not. Paul went through many trials. He was stoned and thrown in jail. He was shipwrecked and beaten, yet Paul loved God and God loved Paul. And what about Job? Job was a righteous man and God allowed him to be stripped of everything but his life. And Job wished that had been taken, as well, because of his physical infirmities."

"He promised that though God had slain him, Job would still trust Him. I remember that verse," Leah said. "And I do want to trust God. I didn't at first; I felt angry. I felt that God couldn't possibly care about me anymore—that He didn't love me. I know that's not true, and I still love Him, but I don't understand any of this."

"And God has never promised us that we would understand. He has His plans, and ultimately they will deliver us into a peaceful and perfect place. But, Leah, that place isn't here on earth."

She nodded. "I know. I guess that's why I would just as soon have died."

Her words pierced Jacob's heart, but he didn't reprimand her for them. Her pain was already so great. "I don't know if I could bear that loss," he said simply.

"You know, Chase was actually sorry afterward. I couldn't believe it, but he was. He kept trying to find a way to get me to let go of my anger and absolve him of his guilt. It was almost like nothing else in his life had ever made him feel the need to make a thing right. But I couldn't deal with him."

"I can understand that."

"I honestly wanted to kill him, Jacob. That really scared me. I've never wanted to end anyone's life. Never. How can I be such an awful person? I left him out there to die."

"He is already a dead man, Leah. One way or another, he will pay the price for the things he's done."

"Jacob, what am I going to do? When I look at Jayce, I see Chase. How will I ever be able to ... be a wife to Jayce again? I just keep thinking of that and I can't reconcile it. Chase didn't just steal a part of me; he's taken what's most important to me. He's taken my happiness with Jayce."

"They might look alike, Leah, but they aren't the same man. You know that better than anyone. Jayce has a heart that is full of love for you. You should have seen him when he realized that Chase had kidnapped you. He was a driven man. He wouldn't rest or even consider turning back, no matter how hard things got. He loves you."

"But once he knows the truth," Leah countered, "that love may fade."

"Then it isn't love at all, because the Bible says that love endures all things."

"Maybe, but I think it's asking a lot of Jayce."

Jacob laughed, surprising them both. "Sorry, but I think Jayce would say that loving you is easy. I know he'll be angered by this, but his anger won't be directed at you."

"I realize that. I figure his anger with Chase will be greater than ever."

"Maybe to a point, but his real rage will be directed at himself."

"Himself?" Leah shook her head. "But why? This wasn't his fault."

"But he will feel like it is. He'll second-guess his decisions and choices. I know I would. He'll think that if he'd only gone back to Last Chance with you instead of going after Chase, you wouldn't have gotten hurt. He'll think that if he would have just told someone sooner about Chase being in Alaska, then Helaina might actually have caught him early on. He'll have a million questions that have no answers, and all of them will point to his failing you. You have to be ready for that."

"But he didn't fail me."

"You don't need to convince me, Leah. You'll need to convince Jayce."

––––––––––

The next morning Jacob found a moment to be alone with Helaina. "I want to talk to you."

"Good. Have you thought about getting me to Seward?" Her expression was hopeful and her tone excited.

"I have considered it," Jacob began, "but the answer is no. It would be a very dangerous and expensive trip to make."

"But I have plenty of money."

Jacob smiled. "That still leaves it dangerous, and I doubt you have any tricks in your bag that would prevent that."

"But you know this land and the people. I trust you. I believe you could get us through without any mishaps."

Jacob looked back at the camp. He had purposefully asked Helaina to walk with him to get away from the others. Now as they readied the dogs and sleds, Jacob knew he couldn't waste time.

"I appreciate your trust in me. I'm honored that you think so highly of my skills and abilities. But that belief won't keep things from happening to us. You know how difficult this trip has been, and John has known the people and most of the terrain. Yet still some of the men have suffered injuries, and you are fighting to recover from pneumonia. Leah had to shoot a bear. There are just too many unknown factors."

"So don't take me to Seward. Help me instead."

"Help you?" He knew what she would say, but he couldn't help but ask the question.

"Help me capture Chase. I'll pay you. You can hire other men to help us. We can get supplies and head back to where we left him. Surely there's a good enough tracker among you all that he could pick up the trail again."

"Helaina, you need to let this go. You can't continue like this." He looked at her and saw the set of her jaw. She was in no mood to hear him out—at least not on this subject. Jacob let his gaze travel to her lips. He wanted nothing more than to kiss her. Kiss her and make her think about something other than Chase Kincaid.

"Jacob, I'll pay you whatever you want. I have more than enough money."

"Helaina, this isn't about money. It's about the fact that I care about you. I care too much to be the one to help you risk your life. I care too much to help you continue this unhealthy obsession to find Chase Kincaid. I won't do it. Not for ten dollars or ten thousand." He left her to contemplate his words and walked back to the sled.

Helaina stood frozen in place as Jacob walked away. Normally she would have gone after him and tried to argue her point, but given what he had said about caring about her, Helaina found it impossible to move. What did he mean by those words?

She watched him speak to Leah and then go to check out the lines on his dog team. He was a handsome man. She'd conceded that some time ago. And she had to admit that no one had ever taken as much time to reach through her façade of self-sufficiency.

She heard the words in her head. *"It's about the fact that I care about you."*

She shook her head in confused disbelief. "But what did he mean?"

Chapter Twenty

Leah felt exhilarated at the thought that they would arrive home that evening. John and Jacob had discussed their location and felt confident that if they didn't stop too long for rests, they could have the group home not long after nightfall. The very idea appealed to Leah in a way she couldn't explain. It seemed like she had been on this journey forever instead of just weeks. She supposed it was due to having been gone all summer, only to return and be forced onto the trail by Chase. It really had been months since she'd been able to just sit down and work on her sewing and enjoy the sights and sounds of her own little house. Now it was nearing December, and she longed only for the peace and comfort of Last Chance. She wanted to celebrate Christmas with Emma and Ayoona, and she desperately wanted to feel the peace that she'd once known.

Feeling rather useless with the packing done, Leah walked

away from the camp just far enough to crest a small hill. She looked over the frozen valley and sighed. Alaska was a beautiful and diverse territory. She thought of growing up near Ketchikan. The thick forests and large amounts of rain left the area lush and green. The temperatures were mild year-round compared to other parts of the territory. Their gardens grew delicious vegetables and the fruit bushes were plentiful with salmonberries, raspberries, blueberries, and many others. It was there among the Tlingit people that Leah had learned about healing herbs and how to treat wounds.

She had also lived in Skagway and Dyea, farther up the inside passage. The pines and spruce were plentiful there and the mountains were impressive. Going north into Canada had been such a great adventure for a little girl. Leah had been a young teenager when she'd experienced the gold fever. Living in Dawson had taught her the dangers of con men and greed, but it had also shown her what wealth could buy.

Leah had experienced much in her life, but this trip had taken the biggest toll. Now all she longed for was the refuge of home and her friends. She missed Ayoona and Oopick and Emma. She wondered how the village children were doing—if they were studying hard and getting excited about Christmas. Emma and Bjorn always made Christmas such a special time.

Leaving her solitude, Leah slowly walked back to the camp. She heard Helaina's voice on the other side of the tent and stopped in her tracks.

"I need to know what you meant when you said you cared about me."

Leah bit her lower lip to keep quiet. She knew Helaina was talking to Jacob. The poor man. How could he have just opened his heart up to tell her that he cared?

"What do you suppose it means, Helaina? I care about you. I've come to care a lot about your well-being, both physically and spiritually. I want to see you happy. I want you to know the peace that comes in trusting God to watch over you and to lead you. I want you to believe in something bigger than yourself, because I know from experience that when the world is crashing down around you, you need something bigger."

"So this is just about preaching to me? You care, but only about my soul?"

Leah wanted to step in and declare that this was indeed the only interest Jacob had, and then steal her brother away before he could open his mouth.

"I care about you, Helaina, but that's all I can do so long as you put this wall between us."

Leah had no desire to listen anymore. She walked away, hoping that Jacob would not hear her footsteps. She pitied her brother for having given his heart to a woman who despised his faith. She pitied Jacob for the pain she knew he would endure when Helaina refused to give up her battle for Chase.

"Oh, God," she prayed softly, "he needs you so much. Please keep him from the misery that will no doubt follow him so long as Helaina's involved."

Jayce had done his best to secure a grave for Chase. The ground was frozen solid, but by using a series of fires to thaw the earth, he'd managed to dig down a short way into the ground. After placing Chase in this shallow grave, Jayce went to work finding rocks to stack on top of the body. He could only hope and pray that the animals wouldn't dig up his brother's remains.

Work seemed the only way to ease his anger. Jayce tried to pray, but while it comforted his heart to a degree, he would inevitably begin to think about the pain Chase had caused, and soon the comfort was lost.

Jayce simply couldn't reconcile the fact that Chase was dead or that he'd raped Leah. It all just seemed impossible to accept. Why had these things happened? What purpose did they serve? It seemed like one of the strange nightmares Jayce had had as a boy. Nightmares where everyone he loved had been lost in house fires or floods. He supposed those things had been borne out of his worst fears, but this was no dream. He couldn't just wake up this time and have it all fade away with the night.

When the grave was finally complete, Jayce packed up his gear and readied the dogs. He had been fortunate in his hunting efforts and would return to Last Chance with two wolf pelts, three fox, and four rabbit furs. The meat had provided well. The dogs seemed particularly fond of the wolf meat. The bear that had killed Chase never materialized again, however, much to Jayce's disappointment.

Moving out, Jayce tried to imagine what he would say to Leah when he saw her again. He wanted no secrets between them and planned to just tell her that he knew the truth. He hoped it would be less painful for her this way. He reasoned that if she didn't have to come to him it would be less humiliating for her. Still, Jayce couldn't help but wonder how they would overcome this obstacle.

How can I help Leah? How can I ever make this right for her? How can she forgive me for not saving her from Chase, when I can't forgive myself?

The questions continued to nag at him all that day. Every time he attempted to clear his mind and refuse to dwell on the matter, something would come along to steal his peace. He knew it was foolish to let his mind wander. The trails were deadly and full of surprises. There were creeks and rivers to cross or follow, as well as obstacles buried under the snow that could wreak havoc with his dogs and sled. Still, it was only by forcing his mind to comply that Jayce managed to even see his surroundings. Leah was all he wanted to see—to think about.

With no little difficulty, Jayce found the native village where they'd left Brownie. He'd gone in the opposite direction twice as he lost his bearings but finally came around right. He was welcomed and cared for, as were the dogs. The people seemed to sense a great sorrow had come upon Jayce. One of the elders asked for his story and Jayce shared his tale with the man. He said nothing about Leah, however, seeing no reason to bring her into the story.

"My brother is dead. A bear attacked him. I buried him the best I could."

The man nodded. "It bad thing. I am pained to hear you speak."

Jayce tried to suppress a yawn. "I thank you for your hospitality—for your kindness."

"You rest here. This good house to sleep in. I know." He smiled and motioned to a woman whom Jayce knew to be his wife. "We let you sleep now." The man pointed to where his wife had created a pallet of blankets and furs.

"Thank you. I will rest very well." Jayce gave them a slight bow and went to the makeshift bed.

Lying there awake well into the night, Jayce knew that he needed a good night's sleep. But he was restless and sleep wouldn't come. He tried to pray, to reason with himself, to force his body to relax—but it was no good. He felt like the biblical Jacob, having wrestled all night with something not of this world. He finally fell asleep just as the man and woman began to stir. His last conscious thought was of Leah. How he longed to hold her—to reassure her that his love for her hadn't changed. He could only pray her love for him had stayed the same, because if she didn't love him anymore—if Chase had driven that from her heart—Jayce didn't think he could bear it.

———————

Leah had never been so happy to see a place in all her life. In the distance, light shone in the windows of a dozen or more houses. Home. Last Chance Creek had never looked more wonderful.

"It's past suppertime," Jacob said as he pulled the sled to a stop. John pulled his sled up alongside, while the other men were already dispersing for their homes.

"My wife will cook for us," John said. "I'll take the dogs. You can take the women."

Jacob laughed. "I think the dogs might be easier to care for."

"We can hear you perfectly well," Leah said, getting out of John's sled basket. Dogs around the village began to bark and yip. "Well, now everyone will know we're here."

It wasn't long before Ayoona came from her inne. "Lay-Ya! You are here."

Leah went to embrace the old woman. "Yes, I am. I am home."

"You come in, and I feed you. We have walrus stew. You like it plenty."

"I do," Leah admitted. "It sounds wonderful, but I'm so tired, I don't know that I can even crawl down your tunnel."

"Leah! Jacob! You're home!" Emma Kjellmann came running

across to greet them. She waved her lantern back and forth. "I've never been so happy to see anyone in my life. Where's Jayce?"

Leah squared her shoulders. "He's gone to find his brother."

"Oh, when we heard it was Chase and not Jayce who'd taken you, we were sick. Bjorn called a prayer meeting and we prayed well into the night for your safety. And here you are, safe and sound. Oh, I'm so blessed. God is so faithful to answer our prayers." She hugged Leah tightly while Leah exchanged a glance with her brother.

"Ayoona was just offering to feed us walrus stew," Leah said, pulling back more quickly than Emma was prepared for.

"Oh, bring the stew to my house. We have fresh sourdough bread and white-fish soup. Please come, Ayoona."

The old woman grinned. "We come for your bread."

Emma laughed. "Oh, what a grand celebration. We should invite everyone, but they'd never fit in our house."

"Speaking of your house," Jacob said, "we wondered if you might be able to put up a houseguest for a time. Like maybe until spring thaw."

Emma looked from Leah to Jacob. "You, Jacob?"

"No. Helaina Beecham." He pointed to where Helaina was just now getting out of the sled. "She's been sick with pneumonia and needs time to mend."

"I'll be fine," Helaina protested. "Stop fussing over me."

"Of course she can stay with us. We have all that extra space, and Sigrid won't come until next June. Of course, Helaina can stay on if she needs because Bjorn and I will take the children south to see their grandparents. Sigrid will have the big house to herself, so Helaina is more than welcome to stay."

"I won't be here that long," Helaina told her. "In fact, if I have my way, I won't be here long at all. I need to get back to the States."

Emma laughed. "Well, unless you have one of those aeroplanes to take you out of here, you'll be hard-pressed to find another way."

"Well, I understand there are men who for hire will take me by dogsled. I intend to find one of them since no one here seems to care enough."

Leah frowned. "It's a matter of feeling the risk to life isn't worth the price," she interjected. "Sometimes the price required is too high."

"Look, it's cold and we're hungry," Jacob said. "Let's discuss this over food."

"Ja. Where are my manners? I'll send Bjorn to help with the dogs."

"No need. I'll have Kimik and Seal-Eye Sam. They help." John moved to take the lines for both teams. "Jacob, pull the hooks."

Jacob quickly released the sleds, and John led the dogs away. They were feisty, but John was quite capable of keeping them in line.

"I get Oopick and we come," Ayoona told Emma.

"Good. Come along, you three. You can wash up before you eat. I have warm water."

They followed Emma to the house, and Leah couldn't help but laugh at the reception they got as they entered the mission home. Bryce and Nolan rushed her and hugged her so tightly that Leah thought for sure they would break her in half. Even Rachel came dashing across the floor to see what was happening. Leah knelt down, but the little girl shyly took hold of her mother's dress.

"She doesn't remember me."

"Of course she does, Leah. She's just going through a stage. She does this with everyone. Even Ayoona." Emma scooped up her daughter and grinned. "She'll be playing with you soon enough. She has to have everyone's attention eventually."

"I'll be right back. I just want to make sure John has enough help," Jacob said, taking off before the women could answer him.

Emma bounced Rachel on her hip. "Helaina, why don't you come with me? I have some clothes that I think will fit you. You can wash up and change from those things and we'll get you tucked into bed. Then I'll bring you some soup and bread. Leah, I have plenty of herbs if you want to mix up something for Helaina's sickness."

"You don't need to fuss over me," Helaina declared as Emma led the way to the back side of the house.

Leah nudged Helaina along. "We just want to get you back on your feet so that you can be on your way. That's what you wanted as well—to get back to the States. Now don't argue with the pastor's wife."

The room they'd added was no bigger than eight foot by six, but it seemed wonderfully large to Leah. A small rope bed stood in one corner. It had been constructed from driftwood and looked quite sturdy.

"It has a feather mattress," Emma said proudly. Rachel fought to get down, and Emma conceded and put her on the floor. In a flash the toddler was off and running. "I plucked enough ptarmigan and duck feathers to make a pillow as well."

"Oh, it sounds divine," Helaina said, rubbing her stomach. "I wonder if you might help me with something else."

Leah and Emma looked at the woman and nodded. Leah felt apprehensive of what Helaina might request, but at this point it would be good just to have the woman settled and out of her hair.

Helaina looked beyond the two women and took a step closer. "I think my monthly time is due. I have terrible cramps."

"Oh, not to worry," Emma said with great assurance. "I have everything you need. I'll bring you tea with the soup. Now you just get out of those things. I'll bring you hot water and something to sleep in. Leah, you come with me to my room. I'll bring water for you too."

Leah hardly heard Emma's words. She followed her slowly, trying desperately to calculate the last time she'd had her own monthly time. A sickening feeling washed over her. It had been just before her marriage to Jayce. She'd not had her woman's time since then.

Feeling weak in the knees, Leah sank onto the nearest chair. She could hardly bear the thought of what it all meant. She might very well be pregnant.

"Are you all right?" Emma asked, her voice heavy with concern.

"I'm fine . . . just tired. The trip was exhausting."

"Well, you were gone for so long."

Just then Ayoona and Oopick arrived, their arms full of goodies. "We are here, Lay-Ya."

Leah looked up and forced a smile, while Emma rushed to help the women. The reality of the moment was almost more than she could bear.

I might be with child. The thought was startling. Worse still was the question that followed.

I might be with child, but who is the father?

Chapter Twenty-one

Leah and Jacob settled into their house and a sort of familiar routine emerged. Jacob rose daily to care for the dogs and later went to hunt or help in the village, while Leah cooked and preserved, tended the store, and worked with hides and sewing. The store took less and less time as the supplies gave out. Most winters Jacob would have already made a trip to Nome, but given the events of the last few months, their regular schedules were completely altered.

"Most of the folks have traded clothing items and furs for the store's food and tools," Jacob said as they finished a breakfast of caribou sausage and oatmeal. "I need to get into Nome and exchange them for goods. We brought some cloth up with us on the *Homestead*. I put it in storage so that we'd have it later. Would you like me to bring some back? I think it might be useful in making shirts and *kuspuks*."

"That would be very useful. Will you leave right away?" Leah saw it as a good way to get Jacob away from Helaina and her constant nagging to help get her to the States.

"Not for Nome," Jacob replied. "I need more furs. One of my suppliers in Nome is big on furs. He has some group in New York that pays him top dollar—especially for beaver, wolf, fox, and such. Oh, and I should lay in a good supply of meat for you before I leave. There's no telling how long it will be before Jayce returns. No sense making John hunt for you as well as his own family."

"No, he's already done so much for me. I still haven't found a proper way to thank him for helping you come after us."

"I'm sure he'd love some of your baked goods," Jacob said, smiling. "I know I would."

"Well, when you bring back supplies, make sure there's plenty of sugar and lard. Nothing ever tastes right when I use seal or whale fat."

Jacob nodded and grew quite serious. "I want you to know that I won't leave if you don't want me to. If you want me to wait for Jayce to return, I will."

"No, there's a greater need for you to be gathering supplies. I'd rather you go. I know it could be some time before Jayce returns, but then again, maybe he'll come back tomorrow. We can't be certain." Leah wanted to keep Jacob focused on his trip. She hoped his interest in Helaina would wane if the two were separated for a time. "Will you go with someone?"

Jacob drank the last of his coffee and got to his feet. "Nutchuk wants to go hunting with me, and I think it will serve him well. His grandfather is constantly giving him trouble over becoming a Christian."

"Well, since his grandfather is a shaman, it isn't surprising.

I'm sure our ways seem just as strange to him as his ways are to us."

"I wish their superstitions wouldn't bind them so strongly. It's hard for Nutchuk to be in that family with his new faith. I know God will give him the strength he needs, but I think getting away on a trapping trip will give Nutchuk a much needed rest from the rhetoric. We can spend time reading the Bible every day, and hopefully his faith can grow."

"I'm sure you're right. I'll put some things together for you."

Jacob nodded and pulled on his parka. "I need to finish up with the dogs. Oh, and we have a new batch of puppies. Angel gave birth last night."

"How many?" Leah asked as she moved to gather the breakfast dishes.

"Six. They all look good and healthy. Not a real runt in the bunch."

"I'm glad to hear it. I hate it when we have to put them down. Seems so cruel, yet I know fighting for an existence out here is also cruel when you're smaller than the rest."

"I don't want you having to be responsible for the dogs while I'm gone, so I'm gonna pay John to help with them. Of course, he won't want to take money, but I figured I'd promise him a couple of Angel's pups for all he's done."

"I think that's a good idea. The dogs will give him better service than my baked goods," she said, smiling. "But I'll get some of those prepared as well."

"Oh, I nearly forgot," Jacob said, turning at the door, "I'm gonna need some new mukluks. These are nearly worn through."

"It's no wonder with you traipsing all over the territory. I'll check around the store and see what we have, and if nothing's large enough, I'll go talk with the women in the village. Ayoona may have even made some for you. You know how she likes to give you something special at Christmas."

"Well, I'd hate to ruin her surprise."

"But you can't go out there on a long hunt without good boots. Let me see what I can find. I think the trip will do you good, and no doubt the furs and meat will keep us well through the winter. I hope you find some caribou. I've really wanted some caribou steak."

He smiled. "That does sound good. I'll see what I can do."

"I know you—you'll probably bring home a whole herd." She wanted to sound as positive as possible about his trip. Leah didn't want Jacob to worry about her or do anything that might delay his leaving. The sooner he left, the sooner he would be away from Helaina, and Leah felt that was the most important thing of all.

———

Jacob had actually been surprised to find Leah so receptive to his leaving again. He feared she'd be uncomfortable staying alone, and maybe worried, too, since Jayce hadn't returned. Instead she was practically pushing him out the door.

He checked on Angel in the partially open birthing shed he'd made for such occasions and found her happily nursing her pups. "Just look at you, little mama," he said, bringing her fresh water and food.

Angel was hungry and quickly shook off her babies to come to where Jacob poured her a bowl of food. It was a strange concoction of mixed meats and commercial dried dog food, something Jacob didn't use often. "Here you go."

The dog, a large powerful animal who held a wheel position

on the sled line, devoured her food quickly, then looked to Jacob as if to question if there'd be more. Jacob gave her a rigorous petting. "You're a good dog, Angel. But now you need to go back and tend to your babies."

She yipped at him as he started to go. Jacob felt sorry for her. She needed more approval and attention than he could offer her right now. He checked the gate of the shed. It was designed to deter intruding wildlife but wasn't all that sturdy. Of course if anything did approach, the dogs would raise a ruckus and someone could deal with it before anything managed to get to the animals.

He thought about how he still needed to talk to John about the dogs' care and make sure he was willing to take on the responsibility with Leah. She would be hard-pressed to see to everything, and Jacob didn't wish to leave her overburdened. Perhaps Helaina could also come over and help. After all, she'd spent the previous summer learning how to care for the animals. But then he remembered she was still recovering from pneumonia.

The thought of Helaina made Jacob momentarily uncomfortable. She didn't yet know that he planned to leave the village. That would be a difficult thing for her to accept. He pondered how he might break the news as he finished with the dogs.

"She won't be happy," he muttered to Marty. The dog cocked his head and gave a little whine as if to agree.

That afternoon Jacob finally made his way over to the Kjellmann house. He brought with him a six-month-old sled dog pup that he'd promised to give to Nolan and Bryce. The pup had broken a leg in a fight with an older dog. The leg had not set right and so he walked with a limp. The boys, however, didn't care. They wanted a pet and Limpy, as they called the pup, seemed the perfect solution. Jayce had promised that as soon as the dog healed completely, he would bring him to live at the mission house.

"Jacob!" Bryce declared at the door. "You brought my dog."

"Doggie!" Nolan called and came running. "Mama, come see!"

Limpy squirmed and yipped as the boys flooded him with attention. Emma soon arrived and laughed at the antics of the boys and dog.

"I hope this isn't a bad time to bring him. I'm going to be leaving for several weeks and wanted to make sure the boys got their dog first."

"Of course it's not a bad time," Emma said. "Come in. Would you like some coffee? I have some good Swedish coffee—strong and black."

Jacob nodded. "Sounds good." He glanced toward the back of the house. "Is Helaina awake?"

"Ja. She'll join us pretty soon," Emma replied. Her Swedish cadence seemed particularly noticeable this morning. "So, you are going away?"

"Yes, I'm heading out to hunt and trap. We need to lay in some of our own supplies for winter, although Ayoona and her family have taken great pains to see us provided for."

"They are good people, as are most in this village," Emma said, bringing Jayce a cup of coffee. "Have a seat. I'm sure Helaina will join us."

Jacob did as she suggested and laughed as the boys rolled about the floor with the dog. "I'm glad you wanted a pet. I worried about whether I'd have to put Limpy down. Up here everything has to be useful."

"He'll be a good watchdog for the boys, I think." Emma looked to where her sons played. "I worry about bears and such when they go out to play. A dog will help guard them."

"I think that's true. These dogs are good about bonding with their owners. He should make a useful pet."

Helaina chose that moment to make an appearance. "I thought I heard voices." She had carefully pinned her blond hair into place and looked quite sophisticated, despite her native clothes.

"I just stopped by to bring the boys their dog before I go." He saw her frown and waited for her comment.

"Are you going somewhere?" She joined them at the table. A smile suddenly lit her face. "Are you going to take me to Seward?"

He focused on the coffee and took a long drink before answering her. "No. I'm going on a hunting and trapping trip. I'll be gone for a while. At first I'll probably just try to get a couple of caribou, and if I do, I'll be back in a couple of days—maybe a week. Then I plan to go out and trap with Nutchuk. We'll probably be gone several weeks."

"But why?" Helaina sounded a little panicked. "I wish you wouldn't go."

Rachel began to fuss and cry from the other room. Emma got up. "Sounds like she's up from her nap. She woke up at four-thirty this morning and wanted to play. Then, when it was a decent hour to wake up, she was ready to sleep again. If you'll excuse me."

"Of course," Jacob said, getting to his feet. "I should probably go."

"No. No. Sit and drink your coffee. There's plenty more."

She left them, pausing only long enough to help the boys with their coats as they headed outside with Limpy. "You stay close to the house," she commanded.

Jacob shook his head. "They'll soon be venturing out everywhere. I can't believe how those boys have grown."

"Jacob, you can't go," Helaina said, not in the least bit interested in the boys.

"I beg your pardon?" He looked at her oddly. "I can go and I will."

"I thought you cared about me. Were those just idle words?"

"This has nothing to do with my caring for you."

"Of course it does. You're deserting me when I need you most."

"I'm providing for my family—for you as well. Emma and Bjorn can't be expected to feed you and keep you without some kind of compensation."

"I'll pay them," she said in a flippant manner.

"Helaina, have you not yet learned that your money can't buy everything or everyone? Up here money is useful, but only when there are products and goods to be had. We are self-supportive people in this territory. We hunt, gather, or make most everything we need. If we don't, we do without in many cases."

"You can't really care about me and just walk away like this."

"I don't recall our marriage," he said sarcastically. "You don't own me, Helaina."

"I didn't suggest we were married, but you said you cared."

"And I do. But that concern is rooted in your spirit right now." He paused. "Well, at least most of my concern is there."

"So this is just about getting me right with God, is that it? You only care so far as helping me to see the error of my ways. You're worse than a preacher."

"Why do you say that?"

"At least preachers are open about the numbers they seek to gather for their cause. You are deceptive with your plan."

"I don't need to listen to this." He got up and headed for the door. "Tell Emma thanks for the coffee."

Helaina followed after him. "Fine. Be like that. At least it tells me what I need to know."

Jacob turned and found her only inches away. "Which is what?"

"That you only care about yourself. That I don't matter to you."

Jacob had had all he could take. Without thinking, he grabbed Helaina in his arms and pulled her hard against him. Then he lowered his mouth to hers and kissed her long and passionately, just as he'd wanted to do for some time. Then just as quickly as he'd begun, he pushed her away. "There," he said. "Think about that while I'm gone and tell yourself that it's just your soul that matters to me."

The house seemed quite empty with Jacob gone and Jayce not yet returned. Leah fell into a routine of work that included finishing off many sewing projects she'd started the summer before. It was hard to believe she'd been gone from home for nearly half a year.

There were plans in the village for a big celebration in honor of Christmas. In years gone by these were always festive occasions where the village would gather at the big community house. Here they would share copious amounts of food and stories, as well as enjoy traditional singing and dancing. The children would show off some of their school papers and put on skits related to Christmas. It was a wonderful time of sharing and fellowship. Even the non-Christians would join in to celebrate the birth of the White Jesus, as they sometimes called Him.

There would also be an exchange of gifts. Usually these were very little items—trinkets, really—that would show respect and consideration for those in the village. Leah always tried to have a little something for everyone, but it would be very difficult this year. Having been gone so long, she would be limited on what she could make or provide. She had planned to bring back jelly and preserves from Karen, but those were all lost when the ship had gone down on Leah's return trip.

But always, even in the midst of planning for the festival, Leah couldn't help but worry about Jayce and wonder about her own physical condition. There was still no sign of her monthly cycle, and Leah was growing more certain that pregnancy was a very real possibility. There had even been moments of nausea.

Against her beliefs, Leah contemplated the herbs that she knew would induce a miscarriage. If she were pregnant, there was no way to be certain of whose child she carried. She couldn't bear the thought of not knowing, but neither could she reconcile the idea of killing her own baby.

"But I don't know for sure that I'm carrying a child," she reasoned. "If I take the herbs to bring on my monthly time, it wouldn't be wrong." But even as she spoke the words, Leah knew it was no excuse. She couldn't pretend that she wasn't pregnant, because the odds were too great that she was.

"Why is this happening, Lord?" she prayed as she worked on a shirt for Jayce. "I'm trying so hard to put what happened behind me—to find a way to not let it come between Jayce and me . . . and now this. How can I bear this blow?"

She had always figured that when she married and became pregnant, it would be the most joyous moment of her life. While cuddling the village infants, Leah had often imagined what it would be like to hold her own baby. With every baby she'd helped deliver, Leah had paid close attention to the things that worked best for mother and child. She wanted to learn so she'd be prepared when her time came.

Just that spring, with the arrival of her thirtieth birthday, Leah had wondered if she would ever know the joy of motherhood. But it wasn't a joy to her now. The very thought sickened her with despair.

"It isn't fair." She looked to the ceiling. "God, this just isn't fair."

Though a visitor was the last thing Leah wanted, when a knock sounded, she opened the door to find Helaina Beecham.

"What do you want?" Leah asked without any real interest.

"I need to talk to someone . . . to you."

Leah shook her head. "I really have no time. I'm quite busy."

"Please, Leah."

Her tone sounded different—almost desperate. Leah knew she'd probably regret her decision, but she opened the door fully and stepped back. "All right, come in."

She directed Helaina to the kitchen and closed the door. Leaning against it momentarily, Leah couldn't help but wonder what Helaina was up to. "Do you want some tea?" she offered.

"No. Please just come and talk with me. I feel so confused."

Leah raised a brow. "You? The epitome of confidence?"

"Don't mock me. It was hard for me to come here."

Something in Leah's spirit softened. "All right. Tell me what's wrong."

Helaina looked distraught. "I can't stop thinking about things Jacob has said to me."

Leah cringed inwardly. If Helaina wanted to talk about her

brother's attraction to her, Leah wanted no part of it. "I don't think I should be the one you talk to. Why don't you wait for Jacob to come back?"

"Because I need answers now."

"But how would I have any of those answers?"

Helaina folded her hands and pressed them to her lap. "Because you are a women who believes in God."

Leah frowned. "What does that have to do with anything?"

"I have questions about God. I never used to care about such things, but ever since I met your brother, he has challenged me with such things. You have as well. I suppose I've simply had too much time to contemplate it all, and now I find myself confused."

Leah felt a sense of frustrated anger. Why should God bring Helaina here? She was living in the missionaries' house after all; why not ask Emma?

"Why do you come to me?" Leah looked at Helaina and saw desperation in the woman's face.

"Because I trust you. You've been through a great deal—mostly because I've caused it, I realize—but your faith has never wavered and you seem to completely understand what God is doing."

Leah laughed out loud at this. "Oh, Helaina, if you only knew. I've been sitting here for days trying to understand why God has allowed certain things to happen to me. Believe me, I'm not the best one to talk to about this."

"But you seem so strong. Even after Chase forced you to join our trip north. You were always talking to him about God's love and His desire for Chase to be forgiven his sins."

"Not that it ever made a difference." Leah contemplated how much to share with Helaina. The woman was still so focused on going after Chase that Leah wondered if it would make a difference. "Let's sit down." She went to the table and motioned Helaina to a chair.

Sitting, Helaina considered Leah's words. "Well, Chase seemed to respect you at least. I think he knew your faith in God made you different."

"Chase respected no one." Leah took a seat and tried to sort through her emotions. She wanted to tell Helaina the truth and hoped that in sharing she would abandon her pursuit of Chase—especially if it involved Jacob. There seemed no easy way to share what had happened, however.

"Helaina," she began, "you were too sick to know what was happening, but one night when he was particularly angry, Chase . . ." She paused and drew a deep breath. "He raped me."

Helaina covered her mouth as a small gasp escaped. Leah decided to press on. "Worse still, I may be pregnant, and I don't know if the baby belongs to Jayce or to his brother."

Leah couldn't comprehend why she was sharing this news with Helaina, but the words just kept pouring out. "Do you understand now why I had to get away from him? I couldn't bear the sight of him. I feared what I might do to him. I couldn't understand why God would allow such a thing to happen to me when I was trying so hard to live a good life for Him. I still don't understand, but . . ." She fell silent and tried to collect her thoughts.

"Leah, I didn't know. I didn't know. I'm so sorry." Helaina had tears in her eyes. "You've often said that I was selfish and thought only of my needs, and you're right. I can't bear it. I never even considered the possibility. I suppose because Chase didn't seem like a threat to me in that way, I assumed he'd be no threat to you."

Leah shook her head. She hadn't expected Helaina to respond with such compassion. What was happening to change Helaina's heart? Leah decided to continue. "I haven't told anyone but Jacob about the rape. I didn't mention the idea of being pregnant to Jacob, because until you spoke of your monthly time when we first arrived at Emma's, I hadn't even thought about it. I tell you this not because I have some great confidence in our relationship, but rather because I am desperate for you to stop your pursuit of Chase Kincaid. Especially if you plan to involve my brother. Don't you see? Now that Jacob knows what Chase did to me . . . well, if he agrees to help you track and capture Chase, he will be guided by his anger and need for revenge. I can't let that happen."

Helaina leaned back in her chair. She appeared to be deep in thought. Leah could only hope—pray—that her words were finally helping the younger woman to understand.

"What will you do?" Helaina finally asked. "How will you trust God, when all of this has happened? See, these are the things I cannot understand. I've heard lofty sermons given by pious men all of my life. I saw no need for such things in my life. Now, in the midst of all you've endured, I need to understand how believing in God works. Tell me in a concise and logical manner."

"I don't know if I can explain it in a logical manner, Helaina. I'm not sure God works in what mortals consider logical ways. All I can tell you is what I know. When I was a little girl, the Bible was respected as God's Word. The people around me believed that God was their final authority. My mother helped me to see, as a child, that trusting God is a matter of faith. My faith is rather damaged right now, but I'm doing my best to let God help me nurse it back to health. I remind myself that oftentimes things happen that we cannot understand. For example, why would God allow so much of the world to be involved with war right now? Why did the *Titanic* sink and take so many lives? Why must children get sick and die? I don't have answers. All I have is my belief that God is good and just—that He will honor His promises."

"But that's exactly what I'm talking about. How do you do that? How can you believe in a God that allows such horrible things? How can I turn to God when He allowed my mother and father and husband to be killed?"

Leah's heart softened toward the woman. They weren't so very different after all. Although they'd been raised in very different worlds, peace of mind and spirit were still dependent upon letting go of all that seemed secure and putting one's faith in God.

"I suppose as far as logic and reasoning go, I would have to ask: What are your other choices? What are the alternatives to trusting God? You could put your faith in money or possessions, but those things aren't any more eternal than human life. We can put our trust in other people, but they, too, will fail us. And when they fail us we're left empty—wounded."

"Jacob said long ago that only God could fill that emptiness," Helaina said, growing thoughtful. "I never believed him, but the last few days I've had a great deal of time to think. Emma won't let me do anything but rest, and I find I'm not very good at sitting idle." She smiled. "I think it has mostly to do with the fact that I don't like myself very much, and when I'm alone and quiet, I only have myself for company."

Leah couldn't help but smile to see Helaina bare her soul and seek help as she reached out to God.

"I want the kind of faith you have, Leah. I want to know how to have the kind of trust in God that you have. The kind of trust that can love Him and believe in Him even after being mistreated as you've been by Chase. I want to know how you go on believing, even when you might be carrying the child of your rapist."

Chapter Twenty-two

Leah looked at Helaina. "The Bible says that God sent His Son Jesus for all—that none should perish. Jesus died on the cross to be a supreme sacrifice for the sins of men—to give us a means of returning to the Father. When we admit our sins and ask God to forgive them, He does. He sees us not in our sinful nature, but through the blood of Jesus and gives us ever-lasting life."

"And then we'll be perfect?"

Leah shook her head. "I wish I could say that were true. I was just asking God to forgive me for the way I've felt toward you."

"Me? Why me?"

Leah got up and stood behind her chair. Gripping the back, she tried to measure her words carefully. "Helaina, my life seemed fairly well ordered until you entered it. It seemed you put a completely new set of complications to our existence in Last Chance, and frankly, I resented the intrusion. But I really resent and worry about the way you use my brother to try and get what you want."

"I have been wrong about that," Helaina admitted. "It's just that ... well ... I'm so confused. I've always been, as you said earlier, confident and capable. All of a sudden I feel that I'm no good for any purpose. I hate the thought of people being disappointed in me."

"I can understand. I just fear that Jacob will get hurt in all of this. But we can discuss that another time. I don't want to deny you your desire to come to peace in the Lord. I can tell you that my belief in who God is and what He's already done for me is all that has gotten me through these bad times. I've been very angry, however, with everyone—God included—for the things that happened. It's hard not to blame someone for what happened, when I feel so clearly that I did nothing wrong. I see no other choice I could have made ... but then I remember I could have exposed Chase from the beginning. I could have said something to the people here, but I feared for their lives."

"So you sacrificed your own life because of your love for them. I think that's admirable."

Leah looked at the wall past Helaina. "Sometimes there are no clear answers. What happened with Chase is done. I can only pray now that Jayce is not hurt or killed as he pursues his brother."

"And I'm definitely to blame for that," Helaina admitted. "I'm sorry, Leah. I'm starting to see all of this with new eyes. Like I said, your brother has given me much to think about."

Leah extended her hand. "Helaina, forgive me. I've wronged you by holding bad thoughts against you."

Helaina took hold of Leah's hand and gave it a squeeze. "I've always known about justice—about seeing the law observed—but now I need mercy. I do forgive you, Leah, and I hope you will forgive me in turn."

Leah smiled. "I do. And now all you need to do is ask the same of God."

———————

Jayce wearily drove the sled the remaining few miles to Last Chance. He felt an overwhelming sensation of guilt upon first viewing Leah's house. How would he face her? What would he say? He wanted to make up for the evil Chase had done but knew there was no way. He couldn't take away what had happened, and he couldn't erase her memory.

"Jayce!" Jacob saw him first and came running. He looked at the nearly empty sled basket. "No luck finding your brother, eh?"

"I found him. He's dead."

Jacob's face contorted. "Did you have to ..." The words trailed off.

"No. A bear attacked him. Might have been Leah's wounded bear. It cut him up pretty bad. When I found him he was half frozen and nearly dead."

"Were you able to talk?"

"A little." Jayce drew a heavy breath and closed his eyes. "Enough."

Jacob put his hand to Jayce's shoulder. "I'm sorry."

"Where's Leah?"

Jacob shook his head. "I don't know. I just got back myself. I'm only here for a short time, then I'm heading out again. I need to get back to camp before I lose all the light. I'm just here to bring in a caribou kill."

Jayce looked to the house again. "I guess I'll start there."

"You go ahead. I'll take your dogs. John's back there helping unload the caribou. We'll get the dogs fed and put away."

"Thanks. That would be great."

"I'll be over directly with some fresh meat. You might let Leah know. Oh, and if she's not home, she might be visiting Ayoona or Emma."

He nodded. "I'll check it out."

Jayce stomped the snow from his boots as he made his way down the stairs to the door. He prayed silently for guidance, then went inside. He heard voices in the kitchen and pulled back the heavy fur. "Leah?"

He saw her startled look. She seemed immediately fearful, then calmed. "Jayce?"

He gave her a slight smile. "It's me." He raised the errant hair that fell across his left brow. "See, no scar."

She appeared to relax. "I'm so glad you're home." She moved to him as if she knew it was expected.

He held out his hands. "Don't come too close. I smell pretty bad."

She smiled. "This time of year most everything does."

"So what about your brother? Where's Chase?" Helaina asked, getting to her feet. "Did you find him? Is he here?"

Jayce looked at the woman who had caused him so many problems. "He's dead."

"Dead?" the women questioned in unison.

Jayce looked first to Leah and repeated. "He's dead. I buried him myself."

"But how? Did you kill him?" Helaina questioned.

Jayce turned back to her. "No. He was attacked by a bear."

"A bear," Leah murmured. "Probably the one I wounded." She

went to the chair and sat down rather hard. "It's all my fault. I should never have left him without a gun."

"That's not true," Jayce said, coming to the table. He halted, remembering that he didn't want to frighten her. "If he'd had a gun, he would have come after you."

Helaina came to his side. "Tell me everything. I want to know the details. I'll need to let Stanley know in Washington."

"There isn't that much to tell, Mrs. Beecham. I found him on the trail; he was nearly dead already. He'd bled a great deal. I managed to set up a tent and unthaw him a bit, but the wounds were too serious. As he warmed up, the bleeding started in earnest. He regained consciousness for a time, then died."

"What was the date?"

"What's today's date?"

"December tenth," she said matter-of-factly.

"Then I suppose the best I can figure is ... the twenty-fifth of November."

"I'm so sorry, Jayce." Leah stared at the table wide-eyed. "It's my fault he's dead."

"No, it's not, Leah. You can't go blaming yourself over this."

"But if I'd tied him up and taken him with us, he'd be safe. If I'd just done what Helaina wanted me to do in the first place—he wouldn't be dead." She buried her face in her hands.

Jayce put his hand on her shoulder. He hoped she wouldn't jump or refuse his touch. "Leah, you did the right thing. Chase was too strong and too cunning. If you'd have taken him with you, he would have found a way to escape your hold, and then he probably would have killed you both."

"I just wanted to get away—needed to get away."

"And you were right to do so."

"Yes, you were," Helaina offered.

Leah looked up and met her eyes. "What?"

"You heard me. It was the right thing to leave him behind. I know I've said otherwise before now, but I feel differently. In thinking about the situation and what Chase was capable of, I think you had to do exactly as you did."

Helaina looked to Jayce. "Thank you for letting me know what happened. I'll go write it up for my brother. Leah, thank you for praying with me. I know it will make things better."

"But not perfect," Leah said softly.

Helaina smiled. "No, not perfect."

Once Helaina was gone, Jayce knelt beside Leah's chair. He hoped his position would make her feel less threatened. "You should know your brother is back for a short time. He's had a successful caribou hunt but plans to head out before nightfall."

Leah looked at him intently. "Thank you for letting me know. It will be good to have fresh meat."

"I thought so too." He gave her a hint of smile.

"Jayce," she said seriously, "I'm sorry for what you had to go through."

"I'm sorry for what *you* had to go through. My struggles don't compare to yours."

She looked at him oddly, then shook her head. "You know . . . don't you?"

"Yes." His voice was barely audible. He felt his words stick in his throat. What should he say? How could he tell her that it didn't matter to him—that Chase couldn't hurt her anymore?

Leah looked at her hands as she twisted them together. "I've worried about how to tell you, and you already know."

"Chase told me."

Her head snapped around. "He told you?"

He heard the disbelief in her voice. "Yes. He was dying. I was talking about God, encouraging him to ask forgiveness. Chase asked me if I could forgive him, and I told him that while difficult, I wanted to try. He challenged that I wouldn't want to try once I knew the truth."

"Then what happened?" Leah asked, her eyes wide.

"He told me he had forced himself on you." Tears welled in Jayce's eyes. "I'm so sorry, Leah. I'm sorry for the pain he caused you—for the torment. I don't know how to say the things I want to say, but please know it doesn't change my heart for you. I'm so afraid that it will change your love for me."

She held his gaze, confusion racing in her expression. "I felt ruined, but God has tried to tell me I'm not ruined."

"You aren't ruined. You are my wife and I love you. Nothing will change that."

Leah shook her head. "There's something that might."

"No. There's nothing. I will always love you. We will forget about Chase and build a new life together. We are just getting started. We can go anywhere and do anything you like. We can live wherever you want to live and—"

"I'm pregnant."

He looked at her in stunned wonder. "A baby? Leah, that's wonderful." He could see she was frowning. "Isn't it?"

"Jayce . . . I . . ." She swallowed hard and he could see this was taking all of her strength. "I don't know who the father is."

And then the realization of what she was saying dawned on him. "You don't know . . . because of Chase?"

She nodded, her gaze never leaving his face. "I have no way of knowing."

"Leah? Jayce?" It was Jacob.

"In the kitchen," Leah called.

"Does he know?" Jayce asked, quickly getting to his feet.

"Not everything—not about the baby," she managed before Jacob entered the room with a chunk of caribou meat.

"I've brought you your steaks, Leah. You'll just have to cut them up yourself."

Leah got up from the table and went to get a baking sheet. "Here, let's set it on the table." She put the pan down first and Jacob put the meat atop it.

"I'm not staying long. I plan to eat and get back to camp."

"Will you eat with us?" Leah asked. "I can get some of this meat frying up in just minutes." She went to the stove and added driftwood.

"That was my plan, unless Jayce minds. I know you two probably have a lot to talk about."

"Stay," Jayce said. "I wouldn't want you out there begging a meal." He smiled and added, "I need to clean up."

"I'll get you some hot water. You can go to the main room. No one will bother you there," Leah said as she took a bowl down from the cabinet. She dipped out hot water from the reservoir until it filled the bowl. "There's some soap in the chest by our bed."

"Our bed?" Jayce asked.

"Kimik made us a bed while we were gone," she replied. She'd turned away so Jayce couldn't see by her expression what she thought of this arrangement. "It's a good bed—very comfortable. I think you'll like it."

Jayce looked to Jacob and nodded. "I'm sure I will."

———

The dinner table was quiet as they sat down to have their lunch. The caribou steaks were thick and juicy, the canned peas Leah served with them seemed the perfect balance, and the sourdough bread tasted better than anything Jayce had had in a long time.

He couldn't help but watch Leah from time to time. She was more beautiful than he'd even remembered. But even with this, in his mind he kept hearing Leah tell him that she was pregnant. That she didn't know who the father was.

The baby could belong to Chase. The baby might be a result of that unholy, evil union forced upon his wife. How could he love and regard the child as his own in such a case?

On the other hand, the baby could be his.

"I have no way of knowing," Leah had told him, the resignation heavy in her voice.

No way of knowing. How could there be no way of knowing? Surely there was enough time between Jayce's last night with his wife and Chase's rape. Surely these things could be calculated and figured. He looked across the table to where Leah sat eating in silence.

I cannot voice my fears about this, he thought. *She is already tortured enough. If I say anything it will only add to her misery—her burden. But, God, how can I bear this?*

"Will you be back in time for the Christmas festival?" Leah asked her brother.

"I doubt it. Nutchuk has plans for us to get into the mountains. He's heard there's good trapping to be had there. I'm guessing we'll be back in January. And I'll leave for Nome soon after checking in here."

"That's good. Supplies are low. There's plenty to eat, but

things like molasses and sugar are completely gone. Oh, and canned milk too."

"Make me a list. I'll get whatever I can. Nome should be in pretty good shape given the load we brought in on the *Homestead*. Plus, we still have the things we put in storage."

"I'll ask around and see if there are any other items people need," Leah replied before turning her attention back to the steak.

Jayce admired her calm. He wanted so much to comfort her—to hold her. He wondered if she'd ever let him hold her again. It pained him to think she might reject his physical touch.

They finished dinner in relative silence. Jacob got up and threw Leah a smile. "Good grub, sis. I'll be thinking of this nice warm meal for a long time. Jayce, I'll see you in a month or so." He pulled on his parka. "Oopick says we're in for a bad winter. Be sure and tell her I said thanks again for the mukluks." He glanced to his feet. "They're sure warm."

"We'll remember you in our prayers." Leah's voice seemed hollow and sad.

"And I'll remember you." Jacob answered Leah, but he looked at Jayce and gave him a slight nod. "God will get us through. We have to have faith."

Jayce nodded. *Faith is all I have.*

Chapter Twenty-three

The Christmas festival held great revelry for the community. The children were delighted to be part of the blanket-toss games and footraces, while the young hunters were honored for their first catches. Mothers and grandmothers had carefully preserved whatever animal their young had managed to track down and now presented it to the gathering as confirmation of the new hunter's ability.

Leah found herself enjoying the native dancing. She watched as the men and women moved in rhythm to the beating of the skin drums. Everyone seemed to enjoy the stories told in the dances, even though they were usually the same stories told year after year. The older folks seemed to be particularly delighted by the abundance of food. Everyone would bring bite-sized portions in huge bowls, and servers would offer them throughout the evening. It was a great time of fun for all ages.

Perhaps the crowning joy of the entire evening was when Bjorn shared the Christmas story with his congregation and with the other villagers who chose not to attend his little church. Afterward gifts were handed out and shared throughout the community. The wealthier would bring in more substantial presents, sometimes offering large pieces of fur or clothing, while the poorer gave only the most meager offerings. It didn't matter, however. No one belittled the poor. In this community they looked out for each other and took care to provide for those who could not provide for themselves. It was the way things were done from generation to generation. Leah loved that about the Inupiat people. They were good to each other. The elderly were cherished and revered, unlike in many white communities. Leah had heard horrible stories from Karen and her relatives in the States.

Days after the celebration, Leah went to see Emma and got the sad news that she'd miscarried. The news took Leah by surprise.

"I'm afraid I'm not good company," Emma said, her eyes still wet with tears. "I was so looking forward to another baby."

Leah had still not told her about her own pregnancy, but realized it was not yet the proper timing for such an announcement. "I'm so sorry, Emma. I wish I could do something to help."

"There's nothing to be done. I told Bjorn last night, and he was ever so reassuring. He said before I knew it, I would be carrying another baby and that we shouldn't mourn too greatly. I know he means well, but I will miss my little baby."

Leah thought of how she'd almost prayed to miscarry. A miscarriage would seem like a gift from the Lord, given her circumstances. If God took her child, then Leah wouldn't have to feel guilty for her thoughts or her negative heart.

"So you seem very well," Emma said, drying her eyes. "I heard about Jayce's brother dying. It's a tragic end, but God's ways are often more than we can understand."

Leah could only nod. She didn't feel that she could yet explain things to her old friend.

"Did he have a family? A wife—children?"

Leah felt the words stick in her throat. Did Chase have children? That was what she needed to know. "No," she finally said. "There was no one like that. He has another brother and a sister too. I'm told they live back east. Jayce tells me the family has never been close."

"Pity. But on the other hand, it's probably best Chase didn't leave a family of his own behind." Emma picked up some crocheting and began to work.

"No doubt," Leah replied softly. Anxious to change the subject, Leah asked about Emma's planned summer trip. "Will you still go to Minnesota to visit your families next summer?"

"Oh, ja. I'm looking forward to it. I can hardly believe how the children have grown. I'm looking forward to showing them off and shopping for them. The mission board has promised us an extra stipend for supplies." Her spirits seemed to lift. "We've taken turns talking about what we'd like to buy. There's always so much to consider."

Leah nodded. "I can only imagine. I was so overcome when we were in Seattle. I guess I'd really forgotten what it was like to be in the city. The choices were more than I could even imagine. There are so many manufactured goods to be had."

"Ja, my sister Sigrid writes to tell me of new inventions and improvements on things already in existence. She's always good to tell me of such things. She's not good to tell of the war or of other things, however."

"Do you think she'll like it here?" Leah questioned. "It will definitely be different from a city like Minneapolis."

"I've told her as much. I've written long letters to explain how her days will be spent up here, just to be sure she still wants to come."

"And does she?"

"Ja. She's certain the wild open spaces will agree with her. She wants to learn to hunt and fish Alaskan style. She loves to do both in Minnesota. She's quite an earthy girl. I suppose her real passion is teaching. She loves to teach school, which is not something Bjorn and I enjoy as much."

"She sounds like a very resourceful woman," Leah admitted. "I will do my best to help her feel welcome. We'll have to have a party for her when she arrives and introduce her to everyone."

"I think that would be great fun," Emma said, glancing up from her work. "I know you two will get along well. I have even wondered if she would be a good match for Jacob, but I think I told you that. Could be they might find a fit in each other."

"I'm certain I would prefer that to the current possibilities."

"Helaina Beecham?"

Leah nodded. "I don't think she really cares for him, but Jacob has lost his heart to her. I'm sure that now this situation with Chase is settled, she'll be bound for the States as soon as possible. She misses her cities and life of ease."

"She does seem to be a good woman, however. She is trying hard to learn what she can."

"I know that's good, but I don't see her being willing to give up everything to live here in Alaska. It just doesn't seem to be her way." She stood up. "I should get back home. I'm working to make some undershirts for Jayce and Jacob."

"Leah, don't worry overmuch about your brother and Helaina. Helaina has been a good help to us. She has the children off on a Saturday adventure. They love her very much. Who would have thought it?" Emma said, shaking her head. "I am glad she's at peace with God." She gave a little laugh and added, "Well there's some peace, and some frustration. She asks poor Bjorn questions day and night."

"She asks me a fair share, as well, and believe me, I'm trying not to worry." Leah hugged Emma. "Come and visit me when you can."

"And you come back when you can stay longer," Emma declared.

Leah nodded. "I promise, I will."

———

Jayce worked to make lashings out of caribou sinew. He braided the pieces together and felt satisfied at their strength. He was making a new *umiak* for summer trips on the water and the lashings would have to be strong to hold the sealskin to the wooden frame.

As he worked, his mind kept returning to the same subject: his marriage to Leah and the baby that she now carried. Jayce found himself burdened with the idea of fatherhood. Would he make a good father? Could he be a loving parent to a child that might not even be his own? He tried to shake off such thoughts, tried to reason that even if the baby were Chase's it would look no different. Jayce and Chase were identical in appearance, and therefore the child could have features that would be the same no matter the father.

Jayce sighed and put his work aside. He didn't want it to matter. He wanted to be the bigger man—the hero of the story. He wanted Leah to feel comfortable and loved. He wanted them to put questions about the baby's parentage behind them. But he couldn't help himself. He dwelled on the issue constantly, and Jayce knew it would only be a matter of time before he said something.

"God, what do I do?" He left his work and decided a short walk would be in order. He took up his Bible and rifle. In case anyone asked, he would just tell them he was out to scout something fresh for supper. Then if the moment presented itself, he'd be ready.

He walked away from the village, heading south along the shoreline. His mukluks crunched against the crusted snow. A storm had come in only days earlier, pushing the salt water over the ice just beyond the shores. This, in turn, pushed the ice toward the beach, forcing it up, breaking it and piling it in what Jayce knew to be pressure ridges. These could be quite dangerous and most people avoided them.

Farther out on the ice he saw several men working with seal nets. They would dig holes in the ice and string nets from one hole to the other underwater, all in hopes of catching fresh meat. Jayce had only learned how this was done a few weeks back. It sometimes proved very fruitful, and other times it was days and days before anything could be caught.

Moving farther away from the village, Jayce's thoughts returned to Leah and the baby. They hadn't talked about the child since she'd told him she was pregnant. It seemed to be an unspoken agreement between them, but Jayce knew it couldn't continue. Soon Leah would begin to show, and everyone would know about the situation. If she and Jayce were not able to deal with this in a joyful manner, there would be further explanations due. Explanations that would no doubt leave Leah feeling ashamed.

Jayce found a spot to sit and placed his rifle across his knees. Reaching inside his parka, he pulled out his Bible and opened it. He went to Matthew, remembering that Bjorn had read from here when telling of the Christmas story. There were verses here that Jayce felt drawn to—Scriptures that told of Joseph dealing with Mary's news that she would bear a child. A child that did not belong to Joseph.

Then Joseph her husband, being a just man, and not willing to make her a public example, was minded to put her away privily. But while he thought on these things, behold, the angel of the Lord appeared unto him in a dream, saying, Joseph, thou son of David, fear not to take unto thee Mary thy wife: for that which is conceived in her is of the Holy Ghost. And she shall bring forth a son, and thou shalt call his name Jesus: for he shall save his people from their sins.

The words comforted Jayce as he read and reread them. Joseph had trusted the Lord and had taken Mary to be his wife. He had raised Jesus as his own child—loving Him and teaching Him, despite the fact that he knew without doubt that this baby was not his own flesh and blood.

Jayce, on the other hand, might well be the father of Leah's baby. He knew this and knew that he had to make a decision here and now that, no matter what, this child was his. This would be his son or daughter and nothing would ever change that.

Looking again at the verses, Jayce felt renewed. *And she shall bring forth a son, and thou shalt call his name Jesus: for he shall save his people from their sins.* Jesus had saved them from their sins. They had asked for His forgiveness and sought His eternal redemption. Neither Jayce nor Leah had done any wrong in the conception of this baby. Furthermore, the child had done nothing wrong. Jayce could not punish an innocent life for the crimes of someone else.

He smiled as a peace settled over him. "Thank you, God. Thank you for showing me the truth." It might not be an easy situation, and there would no doubt be questions to deal with from time to time, but the important thing was to heal and grow in their love as a family.

With renewed vigor, Jayce raced for home. He needed to see Leah—to tell her of what he'd read and reassure her that they would have a wonderful life together, and that their child would be a blessing.

"Leah!" he called as he rushed into the house. "Leah!"

"What is it?" she asked as she came from behind the kitchen fur. "What's wrong?" Her face was ashen.

"Nothing is wrong," he said, pulling her close. He'd momentarily forgotten to be more gentle, but he couldn't help it. "I have something good to tell you."

She smiled. "I'm all for good news."

"Come, sit with me." He led her into the main room of the house. The small table and chairs there would make a good place to talk. When they were both seated, he began.

"I know we've avoided talking about the baby." He saw her eyes widen just a bit as she nodded. "But I need to talk about the baby now. I need for you to understand something."

"All right."

He smiled, hoping that she would be put at ease. "Remember when Bjorn taught about the birth of Jesus?" She nodded and he continued. "He talked about Mary learning that she would bear a son, and of Joseph learning that Mary was with child. Joseph knew the baby wasn't his, yet God sent an angel to encourage Joseph. He told Joseph that it would be all right—that Jesus was God's Son and He would take away the sins of the world."

"I remember that." She seemed to consider his words.

"I was humbled by the fact that Joseph, even though he knew he wasn't the father of Jesus, became the earthly father and raised Jesus as his own son." He reached out and took hold of Leah's hands. "We might not know for certain whether this child was conceived during our time together or not, but there is a good chance that he was."

"So now it's a boy?" she asked, a hint of a smile on her lips.

"Boy or girl, it doesn't matter. This baby is mine."

She cocked her head to the side and raised a brow. "Just like that?"

"Just like that," he said firmly. "I am the father. I will always be the father. The past doesn't matter. We were innocent of any wrongdoing, but even more so, this child is innocent."

Tears formed in Leah's eyes. "I . . . I . . ."

He shook his head and put a finger to her lips. "The past is gone. We are free from its grip. Chase is dead, and he cannot hurt us anymore. We are starting a new life—a new adventure as parents to a wonderful child who will give us great joy. Jesus came to save His people from their sins, and I believe this baby will come to save us from our sorrows and regrets."

Leah took hold of Jayce's hand and placed it against her cheek. "I want that very much. I want to be happy about this baby. Emma just told me that she miscarried her child. She was so devastated, and I felt so guilty hoping God might do that for me as well.

Please forgive me for thinking in such an unloving manner."

He got up from the table and pulled her into his arms. "Leah, I forgive you. Please forgive me for having any doubts about this child. Everything will be all right—you'll see. We'll tell everyone in the village that we're going to have a child, and we'll celebrate."

She nodded and lifted her face to his. Jayce saw the invitation in her eyes. It would be the first time they had kissed since returning to Last Chance. Slowly, so as to let her change her mind if needed, Jayce lowered his mouth to hers. The kiss was tender, lingering, and filled with the love he held for her.

———

Jacob and Nutchuk returned after the start of the new year. They brought a plentiful harvest of skins, as well as fresh caribou meat from a kill made just the day before. The village celebrated and immediate preparations were made for Jacob to make a trip to Nome.

Jacob had done a lot of thinking while away from the village. He'd spent much time reading his Bible and praying for guidance, and now he felt he knew what needed to be done. He approached the Kjellmann house with determined steps. He needed to talk to Helaina.

"Why, Jacob, I thought you'd still be sleeping after our festivities last night. Such a happy time. We were so excited to learn about Leah having a baby," Emma said as she greeted him. "You will be an uncle, ja?"

"Yes, indeed. It's a happy time."

She nodded. "So what brings you here?"

"I need to speak with Helaina. Is she in?"

"Ja. She's putting Rachel down for a nap. Come in. Can you stay to drink some coffee?"

"Well ... maybe just a bit. I need to talk privately with Helaina."

"Ja, I understand. I was just heading over to help Bjorn with school. Helaina is watching Rachel, and the boys are playing down the way at Seal-Eye Sam's. He's teaching them to catch seals." She grinned. "Bryce was certain he would bring one home tonight."

Jacob laughed. "Never underestimate a boy's spirit and drive."

"I won't. It wouldn't surprise me to find a seal on my doorstep when I get back."

"Jacob!" Helaina nearly gasped his name as she came from the back room. "I didn't know you were here."

"I came to speak with you—if you have a moment."

She nodded. "Would you like coffee?"

"You sound like Emma now. That Swedish hospitality has worn off on you, eh?"

"She'll make a good housewife," Emma declared and moved to the door, where her parka hung. "I'll be back after school, ja?"

"That's fine. I'll feed the boys lunch when they come home."

Emma nodded and pulled on her coat. "I'm thinking Sam will feed them. He's probably feeding them all day long. They will be too fat to fit through the door if Sam and his wife have anything to say about it." The trio laughed and Emma quickly departed.

Jacob watched Helaina as she moved comfortably around the kitchen. She seemed somehow changed. Softened. He sensed a newfound peace in her. "I wanted to talk to you. I didn't see you last night at the celebration."

"I stayed here and kept Rachel for Emma." She brought the coffee to the table. "Be careful—it's hot."

Jacob warmed his hands for a moment on the mug. "Well, I'm sure you've heard that I plan to head out for Nome. I'll probably leave tomorrow at the latest. We're out of so many supplies, and while there is still plenty for everyone to eat, it would be nice to have some of the things that spoil us."

Helaina nodded. "I agree. Sometimes I miss fresh fruit more than I can say."

"Well, that's why I'm here. I think you should come with me to Nome. You can get word to your brother, hopefully, and make plans for the spring. Nome will have more to offer you, and while you'll have to pay for room and board, you won't have to worry about feeling too isolated or lonely."

She frowned. "I wasn't feeling isolated or lonely."

Jacob looked down and suddenly felt very confused. He wanted to tell her that she had to go—had to get away from him so that he wouldn't lose his heart any more than he already had. But at the same time he wanted to declare his love for her and plead with her to stay.

"But," she continued, "if you feel that this is what I should do, then I'll go."

Jacob looked up. He started to tell her that he didn't feel that way at all, but something held him silent.

"I suppose I can be ready tomorrow. I don't have that much that belongs to me. In fact, most of my things are still in Nome. At least I hope that the hotel had the decency to hold on to them for me."

Jacob didn't know what to say. He was surprised by her cooperation. There was definitely something different about Helaina Beecham. "I'll be ready to leave by six. It'll still be dark, but I know the trails well."

"All right." She turned away from him rather abruptly and busied herself with something on the kitchen counter. "I'll be ready."

Jacob finished his coffee and got up. "I'll go now."

He walked back to Jayce and Leah's, all the while wondering if he'd made a mistake. With Chase dead, there was no reason for Helaina to remain in Alaska—no reason for her to be in Last Chance. No reason at all.

Chapter Twenty-four

Helaina thought she could be strong and cooperate with Jacob's decision to take her to Nome, but with each mile they passed, she was less certain it was going to work. She'd completely surprised herself by falling in love with Jacob Barringer. What she thought at first was just infatuation with the tawny brown-haired man had turned into something different.

As they traveled she thought of her late husband, Robert, and how he had been her heart and soul. Robert had made her feel protected and loved. She had been a delicate possession in his care. Jacob, on the other hand, expected her to have skill and endurance. While he offered her protection, he also expected her to be independently capable of fending for herself. She liked that. While she'd never thought it possible to fall in love again, that was exactly what had happened.

To her surprise the sled slowed and Jacob leaned down.

"There's a storm moving in. See the heavy clouds to the west and south?"

She looked and nodded. The dark clouds and the sea had closed on the horizon and the wind had picked up, dropping the temperature. She recognized the signs. "What do you want to do?"

"We'll need to make camp for the night—or as long as the storm lasts. I've seen them last for days up here," he announced. "I'll look for a good spot and we'll stop."

In another mile he made good on his word as he brought the sled to a halt. "This will give us as much cover as we can hope for."

Helaina glanced around at the barren landscape. There wasn't much in the way of protection. "I'll help you set up the tent," she offered.

"That would be good. We'll get it done much quicker, and then I can see to the dogs. I think we'll have an hour or so before things get really bad. I'll start a fire first and see about getting some snow melted and some food thawing. It'll be much faster than just relying on the oil stove."

Jacob was quite proficient in his tasks. At times Helaina could almost swear there were two of him. "I'll need you to gather more driftwood once we have the tent up," he told her. Helaina nodded her agreement, all the while checking the skies to see how close the storm might be.

They worked well together. Jacob showed her how to scrape snow from the camp to make a little indention for their dwelling. He talked of using the snow for insulation. "I've been out before with John and we cut ice houses. He's very good at it, and I can hold my own, but it isn't easy. It's not fast either. They are, however, surprisingly warm."

"I was amazed to hear that so many people lived in tents during the gold rush in this area. You said you were a part of the Yukon gold rush. Did you live in a tent?"

"We did," Jacob said. "The tents were pretty large, and we had bigger stoves than the little ones we use here. There were times when we lived with a lot of people in one tent. Other times there weren't but a few. People lived in those tents even when it was forty below."

"I can't even imagine. Everything up here seems so extreme—so unusual."

"It's definitely a life of sacrifice. But I wouldn't be anywhere else. I love Alaska."

She said nothing, not sure that she could respond without giving away her feelings.

"You've probably noted that most of our tents have floors," Jacob said as he fought the frozen ground to secure the stakes. "That's Leah's doing. She felt more secure and definitely warmer. She bought duck canvas and put it together herself."

"I do prefer it," Helaina admitted. "I feel less exposed. It was ingenious. Leah really ought to patent the idea and sell it to Sears, Roebuck and Company."

Jacob laughed. "I'll tell her she can be a tentmaker like Paul."

"Paul who?"

Jacob looked up. "He's in the Bible. He wrote much of the New Testament."

"Oh, the man who was called Saul. The one who persecuted the Christians?"

Jacob nodded. "I'm impressed. You've been reading."

"I've been asking a lot of questions too." She worked to get the tent poles positioned. "Did your sister tell you that I made my peace with God?"

Jacob seemed surprised. "No. No, she didn't. I suppose I really didn't give her a lot of time to tell me anything. I heard about the baby, though. That's very exciting for her. Exciting, too, that you would give your heart to Jesus. What changed your mind?"

"You did. You and Leah both. I was amazed at how you handled difficulties and trials. You always seemed to have such peace. It was quite maddening, actually." She grinned and got to her feet.

"Come on, let's get this thing up so that we can unload the sled. We can talk about this all night if need be." Jacob manhandled the tent into shape and soon had it erected. "There. That ought to hold us."

Helaina gathered driftwood while Jacob saw to the dogs. They were quite efficient, she thought. *We would make a good team—a good husband and wife.* She looked up suddenly at the thought—almost fearful that Jacob would have heard her.

"I've got to stop thinking that way," she murmured to herself. Refocusing on her task, Helaina felt her hands trembling. She tried to pretend it was simply the cold, but her fingers were plenty warm inside her sealskin mittens. She looked to where Jacob finished watering the dogs. The wind was starting to blow harder and it made her steps more uncertain. Jacob didn't seem in the least bit bothered by the weather. He took it all in stride, as though it were nothing more troubling than an ocean breeze.

I've never planned to remarry. I've never wanted to risk loving someone again. This is a dangerous land. It would be easy to lose him up here—see him killed by a bear. Just like Chase. But it had been simple enough for thugs to kill her parents and Robert in an affluent New York neighborhood. Perhaps life was fraught with dangers no matter where you were, and a person just had to endure.

"That's enough wood," he called above the wind. "Go ahead and get in the tent. Get the oil stove lit. That will help to warm up the place."

Helaina slipped inside the tent. It wasn't much more than seven by seven and smelled of old seal oil. She thought of the close quarters and wondered how she would ever rest comfortably knowing that Jacob was just a few feet away. When they'd planned this trip he had figured to sleep in the sled, but with a storm approaching, she wondered if he would spend the night with her in the tent. He would at least take refuge here for a time, and that would put them in very close proximity to each other.

By the time Jacob joined her she had the stove going and the chill off the air. It was still cold, but not so much that she couldn't discard her mittens.

"Feels a lot better in here. Oh, it's starting to snow. I think we've had more snow this winter than most." To her surprise he pulled off his parka and set it aside.

"Won't you get cold? I mean colder?" she asked, motioning to his coat.

"Momentarily, but if I keep it on I'll start to sweat, and that could be deadly. It's important to layer yourself properly up here and pace your work so that you don't sweat. Otherwise you risk freezing even if you're amply dressed. It's a mistake a lot of people make up here."

"It is a completely different world." She thought about her own parka and finally decided to take it off. "I feel foolish," she said, carefully putting it aside.

He laughed. "You won't. You'll warm up with both of us in

here and the stove going. You'll see."

She rubbed her arms for a moment, more out of nervousness than cold. "Emma and Leah helped me dress, so I suppose I'll be fine."

Jacob nodded and started to put together their supper. "I hope you don't mind more caribou."

"Actually no. I prefer it to the seal and whale meat. I suppose we all have our preferences. I can't imagine what my friends in New York will say when I tell them of the things I've eaten. They might even think such things delicacies, but I doubt I'll ever see *muktuk* on the menu at Delmonico's."

"What's that—a restaurant?"

"Yes. A very popular place at one time. Although that poor establishment is having a fierce time of it. The war has changed everything."

"Truly? Even though we're not at war here in the United States?"

Helaina nodded. "It's more felt on the East Coast, I'm sure. The businesses in New York and Boston that were dealing heavily with imports from the European countries are suffering. It affects our economy even if we aren't involved. Although, sadly, I believe we will be involved before much longer. I'm not sure how we can avoid it."

"I guess the war doesn't seem very real here in Alaska. I read up on it in Seattle, but even there it seemed almost the stuff of fables."

"I assure you it's not. I was in England and France at the outbreak and then later when fighting was well under way. It's a horrible situation—one that will require clear heads to prevail. I don't know if that will include American heads or not, but it seems that we must do something."

Jacob warmed the stew Leah had prepared for them, then took out two tin plates. He'd managed to unthaw some sourdough bread by the fire and placed a big piece on each plate before pouring the thick stew alongside. "This should definitely warm us up."

They ate in relative silence while the wind gathered strength and the storm moved ashore. Helaina worried about their safety and about whether the dogs would be able to endure, but Jacob assured her those animals had survived much worse.

"I remember a time when a blizzard held us captive for two weeks. It was something else. I'd tie a rope onto myself and then to the house, and every day go out like that to feed and water the dogs."

"Why didn't you just bring the dogs inside?"

"There were over sixty of them, for one thing," Jacob mused. "But they would also lose their conditioning if I let them live inside. They were fine outside. They all have little houses, as you know, but usually they just sleep outside. They have thick coats and they sleep with their noses tucked against their bodies and their tails wrapped around them. I'm sure you've seen it. They're a hardy bunch to be sure."

"The people are hardy too," Helaina replied. "They are incredible. I wasn't sure how to take them at first. They seemed very quiet and not at all interested in me."

"You were a snob at first," Jacob countered. "You acted rather poorly toward them." ·

Helaina thought back on it and nodded. "I suppose I did at that. I don't feel that way now."

"God has a way of softening our hearts. You'll find that things are different, and they'll keep changing as you grow closer to the

Lord. That's where I see God making a difference in our everyday life. Having eternal salvation is one thing, but letting God make you a new heart for the day-to-day living is something else."

"It's like seeing life through someone else's eyes," Helaina said. "I don't know how it will be once I'm home again."

Jacob frowned, then looked away quickly. "I'm sorry you'll have to wait so long. It will probably be June before the first ships make it up to Nome."

Helaina regretted even mentioning returning to New York. She wanted to take the words back as soon as they were out of her mouth. "I'm in no hurry" was all she could say.

The hour grew late, and once dinner was concluded and everything cleaned up and put away, Helaina felt rather awkward. "Will you . . . are you . . . staying here tonight?"

Jacob looked at her sheepishly. "I hope you don't mind. I'm a very honorable man, however. I'll sleep in the sled like I promised . . . if that makes you feel better."

"No, it's all right that you're here. I couldn't send you out there. It would be too cruel."

"I've slept in the sled on many occasions," Jacob replied. "In fact, I wouldn't have even brought a tent had it not been for you. It just cuts down on my ability to bring back goods to Last Chance. Of course, I could store the tent in Nome since you won't be coming back with me."

Helaina felt heartsick and turned away. "I'm tired. I suppose I'll try to sleep."

"Probably a good idea. If the weather clears we can get an early start."

She nodded. She started to say something about not wanting him to go back to Last Chance without her, but it seemed completely inappropriate, so she said nothing.

———————

Days later in Nome, Jacob was still thinking about how uncomfortable it had been staying with Helaina alone in the tent. He was awake for a long time that night just listening to her breathing and wondering if there could ever be a future for them. There was so much he didn't know about her world—so many ways he didn't fit in. And she certainly had trouble adapting to his world.

To Jacob's relief he found Nome still had a plentiful supply of goods. He left the furs and gave his list to one of his more trustworthy suppliers, then went in search of the Pinkerton agents they'd left behind. He went to the last place he'd left them and found them both still gainfully employed by the Nome police department.

They were content with their jobs and lives in Nome. Maybe too content. Each man indicated he had no desire to leave for the States.

"This is proving to be a good town for me," Butch Bradford told Jacob. "I got me a wife and little place to live. I plan to stay."

"I'm pretty sure I'm stayin' as well," Sam Wiseford added. "I like the isolation."

"What about Mrs. Beecham?" Jacob questioned. "She'll need an escort to the States come summer. Wouldn't one of you be willing to accompany her?"

"Summer's when they'll need us most. I won't be goin' anywhere," Bradford said. "Sorry." The smaller man nodded in agreement.

Jacob spent the rest of his time in Nome trying to figure out what should be done about it. He didn't feel comfortable leaving Helaina to fend for herself until spring, but he also didn't feel that he could take her back to Last Chance.

He sat at dinner, wondering how in the world he could fit all the pieces together, when Helaina came in to join him. He hadn't been sure she would come, but now that she was here he felt mesmerized by her beauty. She was dressed in her Inupiat clothes, which rather surprised but pleased him.

"I figured you'd be anxious to dress in your old things," he said, getting up to help her be seated.

"It's too cold for that." She took her seat and added, "I'm not the same woman I was last summer."

He nodded. "I know." His voice was barely audible.

"Did you order?"

"I did. They have a nice caribou roast, vegetables, and pie for dessert."

She nodded and motioned to the waitress, who looked old enough to be her grandmother. "I'll have what he's having. As well as some hot coffee. I see you've already had some."

Jacob's cup was already empty. "It's good. Pretty strong, though."

Helaina waited until the old woman walked away before beginning the conversation. "Jacob, I came here to say something, and I hope you'll hear me out."

He leaned back in his chair. She had that look on her face, that same determined look she always got when she was up to something. This time, however, it made him smile. "I guess I don't really have a choice, now do I?"

She shook her head. "No, you don't. If you won't listen to me here, I'll follow you all over Nome until you do."

He laughed. "Then you'd best get to it."

"Well," she began, folding her hands and striking a serious pose, "I want you to take me back to Last Chance when you leave tomorrow."

He met her blue eyes. She held his gaze and continued, though he barely heard her words. "I can't stay here, especially when every place I've checked out is costly and hardly concerned with safety. I would be much better off in Last Chance. If I go back with you, I can help Leah and Emma through the winter and then head home in the spring. I could even accompany the Kjellmanns when they leave and be perfectly safe."

"I hadn't really thought of that," Jacob admitted.

"Emma said I was more than welcome to stay with them through the winter. The children are fond of me, and frankly, I've grown quite fond of them."

Jacob knew that what she said made sense. "Are you sure you wouldn't feel more comfortable here? You would have more access to supplies."

"I would be very lonely. Please, Jacob, don't leave me here."

He dropped his gaze to the table. *How can I take her there and stay too?* He wondered for a moment how he might live in the same village—in the same close company—and not make himself completely miserable or act the fool. He was already in love with her, yet he knew she would never be able to adapt to life in Alaska and forsake all she was accustomed to. And he would never leave Alaska. There was no reason to continue the relationship—it would only cause them more pain in the long run.

"Jacob, I need for you to do this for me."

He looked up. "Why?" Something in her tone told him she

had something completely different on her mind—something she wasn't saying.

Helaina was the one to look away this time. "I ... well ... I know I can stay strong there."

"Strong?"

She nodded but still didn't look at him. "Strong in the Lord. On my own, I'm not sure. I just feel like I need time. Time to better understand and learn. I know I can do that in Last Chance. Spending these last couple of days on my own, I've found myself with questions that have no answers. I look in the Bible, but I don't know how to really understand what I'm reading."

"There are churches here. Pastors can help you to better understand Scripture," he countered.

"I don't know these people. I don't trust them. Please, Jacob."

He knew he was losing this argument rather rapidly. It felt like the time he had slid down the embankment of the creek and broke through the ice. He was not on a firm foundation. "Life isn't easy in Last Chance. You know how it is there."

She looked up again and nodded. "I do, and I don't mind. Please take me home ... with you."

He knew she wasn't asking him this to help with any job or obsession as she had before. At least he couldn't imagine what obsession it might be, if she were actually using him in that manner. He knew he couldn't refuse her.

"All right," he finally said. "I'm not sure it's wise, but I'll take you back to Last Chance."

She smiled and it lit up her whole face. "I promise you won't be sorry."

Jacob sighed. *I already am.* But of course, he couldn't tell her that.

Chapter Twenty-five

Winter passed with Helaina actually enjoying her life at the Kjellmann residence. She enjoyed talking with Emma and Bjorn over supper each night and found they generally had answers for her questions. The idea of trusting God didn't seem nearly as foreign to her now. Emma had been good to point out that learning to believe God to be who He claimed to be would come first through faith, and second by letting God prove himself day to day.

"It's no different than learning to trust the man you will marry. Think back to when you met your husband," Emma had told her.

Helaina had done just that. The memory of that developing relationship helped her to understand that learning to love and trust God was no different. She couldn't love and trust someone she didn't know—so she made it her priority to get to know God as well as she could.

Night after night she spent time studying the Bible. With Jacob gone so much, she really had little else to hold her attention. Bjorn led his family in daily devotions, so Helaina used these to be the basis for her studies. That way it was easy to ask Bjorn questions regarding the matter.

Sunday services were another place Helaina thrived. She learned rather quickly that it wasn't just about coming to a place to hear the Bible preached; there was much more. Why she'd never seen it until now was beyond her, but attending church seemed to be like a special refreshment. Maybe it was just because they were so isolated and there was nothing else to do, but Helaina seriously doubted that was all there was to it.

Week after week, Helaina found herself looking forward to the gathering. She longed to be with the people—to sing hymns and to hear Bjorn teach on the Bible. She would never have thought it possible to enjoy church as much as she did now.

June brought the excitement of spring breakup. The villagers were eager for true Alaskan summer, as they knew it, to begin. Helaina, however, dreaded it. Breakup meant the ships would return and the Kjellmanns would head south to visit their family. Helaina would have no choice but to go with them.

It was hard not to be discouraged by this thought. After all, Helaina had hoped to spend the winter getting to know Jacob better, but he'd seldom been in the village. Leah had said he was busy trapping and working with his dogs, but Helaina began to worry that he was merely avoiding her. But why? He'd said that he cared. Didn't he want to know her better—maybe even consider a future together?

"There's so much to do before we go," Emma said, rushing around the little house while Helaina cleaned up after breakfast.

"I can't believe we'll leave in just a few weeks or that Sigrid will soon be here."

Helaina nodded and dried the last of the dishes. "I can't believe the time has already come. It really didn't seem that winter was all that long."

"This wasn't a bad winter. Even if it started early, it didn't torment us as some have," Emma said.

"I think the church services and parties helped too," Helaina said with a smile. There had been several celebrations throughout the dark, lonely months. Emma had told her that these were purposeful parties meant to keep spirits up and prevent the people from becoming too bored.

"Oh, ja. The gatherings are always good. Otherwise we tend to spend too much time thinking of ourselves. When that happens, things can get dangerous. I remember one time right after we came here there was a murder. A man had slept with another man's wife, and when her husband returned from hunting and learned what had happened, he grabbed up his gear and went hunting after the man who'd defiled his marriage bed."

"But what of the woman?" Leah asked. "Did he also kill her?"

"No, but he might have if he wasn't caught first. He killed the man and then some of the villagers found him. They took him to the legal authorities, and he was eventually executed. Bjorn said that we would work to keep the people busy with other things so that they wouldn't turn to such mischief. But you know, people are people. They will do as they please."

"I think you've done a good job. Especially having monthly parties to celebrate all the birthdays that fall during that time. That has been great fun."

"We do what we can."

She seemed to be searching for something, so Helaina dried her hands and came to help. "Have you lost something?"

Emma held up one of the boys' socks. "The mate for this. I'm afraid Bryce is still very bad about picking up after himself. He tries, but boys are boys. My mother often said of my brothers that they knew the clothes hamper only as an obstacle to leapfrog over."

Helaina laughed and helped in the search. "I can well imagine. My brother, Stanley, was none too neat himself. My mother was particularly grieved by the way he would manage to completely ruin his clothes with his rough games. I was, on the other hand, her china doll. She loved to dress me in frilly clothes and have my hair curled. Which," she added, touching several straight strands, "was no easy feat."

"I'm looking forward to having my mother and sisters fuss over Rachel that way. It will do me little good to buy her all manner of frippery. Can you see her dressed in ruffles to run across the tundra?"

Shaking her head, Helaina felt almost sad. Hadn't this been something she'd thought of in regard to herself? She missed her finery. She missed dressing up for parties and being the belle of the ball.

They soon discovered the missing sock under Bjorn's favorite chair. "Here it is," Helaina said, holding it up. "The sock also has a friend." She pulled out one of Rachel's tiny shoes.

"Oh, but I had given up hope of finding that. I thought I'd lost it somewhere outside." Emma laughed as she took both items. "The lost has been found. Always a good thing to declare in a preacher's home."

Helaina straightened up the living room as Emma bustled in

and out, her arms always filled with a variety of things. "We won't take all that much," she declared at one point, "because we always bring so many things back with us. Still, I must have clothes for the children."

Helaina nodded, her thoughts filled with images of stores and establishments in New York. She tried to think of what it would be like to remain in Alaska and never have easy access to shopping and the latest fashions.

But even as these thoughts crossed her mind, she looked at her own outfit. She wore sealskin pants under one of her old skirts. Her blouse was very worn and could hardly be considered fashionable as it might have been just the year before. But here in Alaska function and practicality always won out over decorative style.

Helaina had to admit there was a part of her that was homesick. She longed to relax in her bedroom suite. The room itself was larger than Emma's house. The fireplace alone would take up the space held by Emma's entire kitchen.

Helaina began to prepare tubs with hot water for the wash, yet her thoughts continued to return to New York. She really did miss it. She longed for a thick beefsteak and fresh vegetables. The thought of wearing silk again nearly drove her mad. There were so many things she desired. But even as she thought of these, Jacob's image filled her thoughts. She desired him, as well, but there seemed to be little hope of resolving that problem.

The more she thought about it, the more Helaina needed an answer. Jacob was due back any time now, but it wouldn't be for long. Leah had mentioned on more than one occasion that her brother had made up his mind to honor his commitment to Captain Latimore. He would head north when the good captain came with his ship. Helaina had contemplated imposing herself on the trip. Perhaps if she reminded Captain Latimore that she was to have been assistant to the map maker, she, too, might gain passage on the *Homestead.*

There simply seemed no easy answers. If she went north with the men, she'd never make it back to New York this year. Despair dogged her every step. There was no way to resolve the matter without the need to forsake something she loved.

Why does this have to be so hard?

Leah moved slowly around the house. Advanced in her pregnancy, Leah felt more confident than ever that the baby must be Jayce's child. Just the fact that she was already showing signs of being ready to give birth made this even more certain. By her best calculations, if she'd gotten pregnant on her wedding night, the baby would be due in late June or early July.

Throughout the winter Leah had worked to ready her life and her home for the arrival of this new life. She and Jayce both agreed the house was not big enough for their family, so plans were in the works to build a new house and leave this one to Jacob.

"I've got the money," Jayce had told her. "We might as well use it for our own comfort." And with that he'd accompanied Jacob to Nome to place an order for supplies.

But Leah wasn't sure that Jayce could be totally happy in Last Chance. There wasn't much in the way that he could do to gainfully employ himself, and while he had money in the bank from his inheritance, they certainly couldn't live off of it the rest of their lives.

It troubled Leah, for she knew in her heart that a man needed to have a job that he could call his own. Thoughts of having to move from Last Chance to live in Nome or one of the larger Alaska settlements like Sitka or Seward tormented Leah. She would miss the people in Last Chance, but worse yet, she would miss Alaska if Jayce decided there was no other answer but to move away.

Another troubling thought was how to help Jacob deal with the loss of Helaina Beecham. He'd been gone a great deal throughout the winter, but as he'd told Leah on his last trip home, now nearly a month past, he always knew Helaina would be waiting here and that comforted his heart. But soon she would go back to New York, and Jacob would have to face the fact that she would never come back.

"He can't live there and she can't live here," Leah said sadly.

Leah had never seen Helaina as an ideal woman to be Jacob's wife anyway. Helaina was so willful and headstrong, although that had been tempered by her spiritual growth. Still, Helaina was used to having things her way and living a life of luxury. She was a wealthy widow with a home in both New York and in Washington, D.C. Neither place could Jacob ever call home.

"It seems we are all in a dilemma regarding our home," she told herself. She glanced around at her meager surroundings and realized that deep in her heart, she did want more. She wanted a regular house and a yard where her children could play and have adventures. Of course, the Alaskan wilderness provided the biggest yard of all, but Leah knew the dangers there. Only last week one of the village children had gone wandering off, not to be seen again. The family was still out searching for the three-year-old, but there wasn't much hope of finding him alive. That sorrowed

Leah deeply, for the family, like all families in Last Chance, was precious to her.

"Leah, are you here?" Helaina called from the outside door.

"I'm in the main room," Leah replied.

Helaina came through the hall and lifted the fur that divided the room from the rest of the house. "Do you have time for a chat?"

Leah nodded. "I was just getting ready to sew more clothes for the baby." She patted her belly. "It won't be long now."

"I know. It's all so very exciting. I'm hoping you'll have the baby before I . . . leave." Helaina frowned and took a seat at the table. "That's what I want to talk to you about."

Leah brought her sewing basket and awkwardly lowered herself to the chair. "About leaving?"

Helaina seemed to consider her words for a moment. To Leah she seemed quite troubled. "Yes. About leaving and about Jacob."

"What about Jacob?"

"Leah, I'm in love with your brother. I know that sounds ridiculous."

"Why? Why should it sound ridiculous for someone to fall in love with Jacob? He's a wonderful man."

"He is," she said, leaning forward. "He's the most amazing man I've ever known. He's smart and trustworthy too. He never fails to amaze me with his knowledge."

Leah smiled. "He is quite incredible. He's taught me a great deal. He tried so hard to be both father and mother to me, but as I told him long ago, I preferred he just be my brother, for that was what I needed from him most."

Leah picked up a small gown and began to work on the hem. "But I'm sure," she added, "that you did not come here to hear stories of brothers and sisters. Why don't you tell me what's on your mind?"

"Well, as you know the breakup has started, and the ships will soon arrive."

"Yes. We can expect the first ones within the next couple of weeks. Everyone always gets so anxious for that first ship," Leah said with a grin. The memories of nearly a dozen years flooded her mind. Even the natives had come to appreciate the appearance of the revenue cutters.

"Well, I'm not anticipating it like I thought I would. Truth be told, I'm quite torn about leaving."

"Because of Jacob?" Leah asked.

Helaina nodded and looked at the table. "I long for my home in New York. I sometimes miss it so much that it's all I can think about. But then I think of Jacob, and I know that leaving him will hurt me . . . maybe more than I can bear." She got up and began to pace. "I never planned to fall in love again. Robert was everything to me. To my way of thinking, he was perfect. But now I believe Jacob is perfect, and strangely enough, the two men are nothing alike."

"Jacob is far from perfect, and it's never good for a woman to consider a man in that light. We are all human, Helaina. We will disappoint each other at some point. If you put my brother on a pedestal, he will fall off of it."

"I know that. I know he's just a man, but he's the man I've grown to love. I know you can't understand my point, but when Robert died, a part of my heart died too. I became guarded and protective of myself. I had so many men come calling—all wanting to be my suitor. Most were more interested in courting my bank-books than me, but all were ever so concerned with my being left a widow." She gave Leah a bittersweet smile. "See, I'd not only inherited Robert's money, but Stanley and I split a huge estate left by my parents."

"I knew you were quite wealthy simply by the way you were able to afford outfitting the *Homestead* last fall before we returned to Nome."

"Money has never been a problem. The problem is my heart. I want to stay with Jacob. I want him to fall as deeply in love with me as I am with him, but I know he loves Alaska."

"And he won't leave," Leah said, knowing her brother's thoughts on the matter. "He might relocate to other parts of the territory, but he won't go back to the States. You might as well know that."

"I do," Helaina replied sadly. "I suppose that's why I'm here."

"I don't understand. Do you want me to convince him to go?" Leah put down her sewing. "Because I won't do that."

"No." Helaina shook her head and retook her seat. "You misunderstand me. I suppose I just need ... well ... I guess I don't know what I need." She sighed.

Leah felt the woman's sorrow. There were no easy answers for her in this matter; Leah had already contemplated the situation many times. "Helaina, at first I really didn't want you having any part of Jacob's life. You were troublesome to me because of your job and your focus on justice at any price. Now, however, you've really changed as you've gotten to know the truth of God's Word. Your heart is completely different."

"But you still don't like the fact that I'm in love with your brother."

"It isn't that," Leah said, meeting Helaina's intense stare. "It's that I know Jacob will never leave Alaska, and you seem just as unwilling to leave New York and your old world behind. Jacob would never fit into that world. You need to know that. He would never be comfortable in the city. He hated Seattle and seldom ventured from the house where we stayed. He hates the noise and the traffic—you surely remember that."

"I do," she said in a barely audible voice.

"He's not going to suddenly change and love it all as you do."

"So what you're saying to me is that I must either give up New York and my life as I knew it, or I must give up Jacob."

Leah nodded. "I see no other alternative."

"But if Jacob loves me . . ." She paused and looked away. "Wouldn't he at least be willing to try?"

"At what price?"

"I don't know. I suppose he would have to come with me to New York and sample the life there."

Leah shook her head and got up. "Helaina, he knows what city life is all about. He hates it there. Would you, loving him as you do, cage him like that? He might be willing to try—he might in fact love you so much that he would leave Alaska. But I think that in time it would kill him, and if not that, it would destroy your love for each other. Could you live with that?"

Helaina's shoulders slumped forward. "No. I couldn't hurt him that way." She looked at Leah with tears in her eyes. "I suppose the right thing to do is just go home without telling him how I feel."

Leah's heart nearly broke for the woman. She was truly in love with Jacob—apparently enough to let him live the life he needed to live. Leah had to admire that. She knew from the past that it wasn't easy to let go of a dream—especially when that demanded you also let go of your heart.

Chapter Twenty-six

J acob returned two days later. Helaina watched him from afar
at first. She busied herself with Emma's children and tried to
pretend that it didn't matter. *Leave him alone,* she warned herself.
Don't give him any reason to think you care as much as you do.

But when Saturday rolled around and the village joined
together to celebrate the spring breakup, Helaina couldn't avoid
his company.

"I haven't seen much of you," Jacob said as he came to stand
beside her. Native dancers were just starting to perform.

"I've been helping Emma with the children and packing. We
leave in a few days, you know."

Jacob frowned. "Yes, I know. I wanted to talk to you about
that. I've been doing a lot of thinking out on the trail. Isolation
gives a man plenty of time to consider what's important."

Helaina felt a band tighten around her chest. The last thing she wanted was for Jacob to declare his undying love or, worse yet, tell her that he'd changed his mind and was mistaken about his feelings.

"Oh, look. There's Leah. I didn't think she'd be able to make it," Helaina said. "Come on, let's go help her."

Jacob opened his mouth to speak, but Helaina didn't wait. She moved through the people seated on the ground and prayed that Leah would keep Jacob from further serious talk.

"Leah, I'm so glad you were able to make it," Helaina said, putting an arm around her. "Where's Jayce?"

"He's coming with the food. Jacob, maybe you could help him?"

Jacob looked to Helaina and then Leah. "Sure." He sounded disappointed, but Helaina said nothing.

After he'd gone, Helaina turned to Leah. "I think I'd better stay with you. It seems Jacob wants to talk seriously."

"I wondered about that. He mentioned giving a lot of thought to his future," Leah said, putting a hand to her back. "I'm so tired. I think it may have been a mistake to come."

"Here. There are a few chairs over here. You should sit." Helaina helped lead Leah to a chair. "Can I get you something to eat or drink?"

"No. I'm fine. I'm just tired. I can't believe how big I am. I feel like I'll explode at this point." Leah pushed back a strand of wavy brown hair. "Ayoona assures me it will soon be over and I will be blessed beyond anything I could imagine."

"She seems to be a wise old woman. I think you can trust her to be right. I still worry that you should have a doctor. I mean, what if something goes wrong?"

"The women of this village have been helping each other give birth for generations. There have only been a handful of stillbirths or babies dying during delivery since I've come here. I doubt that's much different than where doctors are readily accessible."

"Still, it's frightening to think that you won't have someone more knowledgeable."

Leah laughed. "Ayoona has helped to deliver over forty babies. Oopick has helped with at least half of those. I think I'm in good hands."

Helaina knew that it was reasonable to believe this. After all, many of the women in the States delivered their children at home with midwives.

The men returned with several bowls and a tray. Leah turned to Helaina and motioned. "Jayce has a tray I think you will be interested in."

"Oh, and why is that?"

"I actually made some chocolate cake."

"Truly? How did you manage it?" Helaina could almost taste the delicacy. Just last month at the birthday celebration she had mentioned craving chocolate cake.

"I managed to hoard some cocoa, and Oopick brought me eggs from their trip up the beach. I wasn't sure I had the energy for such a thing, but it came out quite well, if I do say so." She grinned. "However, once it's learned what's under that dishcloth, you may not have a chance of getting a piece. I think you should go right now, if you want some, and grab a piece before they start to distribute it."

Helaina nodded. "I think I'll do just that. I'll bring you one too."

"Oh, don't. I've sampled enough while making it. I'll yield my piece to someone else."

Jayce and Jacob were heading their way, so Helaina took the opportunity to make her way to the table via a different path. She knew Jacob was watching her, but she tried to ignore him. Instead, she went to the cake and took a piece. Leah had cut the dessert into very small pieces so that more people could have a taste. Helaina popped the morsel into her mouth and smiled. It was like a little piece of heaven. Oh, how she missed succulent meals and fancy desserts. She would make it a priority once she was back in New York to go to all the best restaurants.

Helaina tried hard to encourage herself in this manner. Whenever she was sad or worried about leaving, she reminded herself of something wonderful that she missed. Something that she could have in New York but not in Alaska.

Jacob tried two more times to talk to her privately as the celebration wore on, but Helaina managed the situation with great finesse. She knew it would only hurt them both if Jacob revealed his heart. As the party came to a close, Helaina volunteered to get the Kjellmann children home to bed—something Emma quickly took her up on.

"You're so good to me," Emma told her. "I'm glad you'll be traveling with us. I'm certain to need the help."

"They're dear children," Helaina said, taking a sleeping Rachel from her mother's arms. With Bryce and Nolan in tow, she hurried for the Kjellmann house and the refuge she would find there.

"Please don't follow me, Jacob."

"What did you say?" Bryce asked with a yawn.

Helaina shook her head. "Never you mind. It's not important."

"I think Helaina's avoiding me," Jacob told his sister. Leah turned from the stove, where she worked on making breakfast for Jayce and Jacob.

"She's pretty busy right now. She leaves tomorrow."

"Yes, I know. That's why I'd hoped we might have time to talk."

"Talk about what?"

Jacob drew a deep breath and shook his head. "Apparently nothing."

Leah shrugged. "Well, this caribou sausage is just about done, and the biscuits are ready. Why don't you call Jayce? He's out back sharpening his axe."

Jacob did as she asked, but all the while his mind wandered. Apparently Helaina had no interest in talking to him about their situation. The only explanation for that was that she had considered his words and kiss, and she just didn't feel the same way. After all, she was returning to New York. If she cared, she'd be making plans to stay.

"Jacob!" Emma called from across the way. "The ship has come with my sister. Tell Leah!"

Jacob looked past Emma to the harbor. Out in the water was a three-masted vessel that had also been fitted for steam. "I'll let her know."

"Come for supper. We'll be making merry. It'll be the last time we'll all be together for a while."

Jacob thought of Helaina and knew it would be the last time he'd see her. "We'll be there," he said without enthusiasm.

———

Sigrid Johnsson blew in like a late season blizzard. Her spirit of excitement was nearly contagious as Helaina watched her flit from one room to another.

"It's a perfect house. I love what you've done with the rooms," she declared to her sister.

Emma beamed. "Helaina has been good to help me make new curtains and rugs. I'm glad you like them."

Sigrid looked to Helaina and laughed. "Well, someone that pretty is bound to have marvelous taste."

Helaina didn't know what to think of such praise. She smiled but couldn't figure out what to say. Sigrid didn't seem to mind, however. She continued talking at such a maddening pace that no one had a chance to interject a word.

"Life in Minneapolis has grown so predictable and dull. It's terrible when you come to hope for a summer cyclone just to have a little excitement. Oh, I hope you enjoy your stay there, but I'll bet you'll be ready to return home within two weeks. Last Chance seems like a marvelous place. I'm so excited about the children. How many are there? What are their ages?"

She turned to inspect the kitchen, but even as Emma opened her mouth to explain, Sigrid went on. "Oh, you know Mama. She has sent me with plenty of supplies. Lots of preserves and lutefisk. I don't know how many times I have to tell her I despise the latter." She made a face, sticking out her tongue like a wayward child. "Then I got to thinking that the natives here eat far worse things than lutefisk. I'm sure they'll enjoy it. Anyway, I'm glad Bjorn is arranging for all the crates and baggage. I know I should never have been able to bring it all up."

Helaina felt exhausted by the time Sigrid paused to draw breath and Emma managed to speak. "We're having a special supper tonight. You'll get to meet my dear friend Leah. She's expecting a baby soon and she's promised to help you in any way she can. Her brother, Jacob, will be here too. He's the one I wrote to you about. I think you two will enjoy each other's company."

Helaina looked at Emma as though she'd lost her mind. Realizing how she was responding she hurried to cover her mistake. "I just remembered that I promised to help Ayoona." It was true enough. She'd promised to help the old woman look for early berries.

"Oh, I wish you didn't have to go," Sigrid said. "I'd like to have more time with you both."

Helaina nodded. "I wouldn't mind sticking around myself, but . . . well . . . duty calls." She wasn't sure what kind of explanation she'd offer if Sigrid asked what duty she was speaking of. But Sigrid quickly moved on with the conversation.

"I would very much like to go on some of the hunts. Will the men allow me to come? I think it would be marvelous to go whaling. Do you suppose they would take me with them?"

Helaina quickly slipped out of the house and made her way toward Ayoona's. The thought of Jacob spending time with the vivacious and beautiful Sigrid was almost more than she could stomach. The girl was positively a chatterbox. Jacob would never fall for someone like that. Would he? She stopped midstep and stared at the Barringer-Kincaid house. Maybe she should allow Jacob to speak to her. Better yet, maybe she should just explain the situation. It was hardly fair to go off without a word. How honest would that be?

She thought about how hard it had been to come to the conclusion that she should leave—leave without sharing her heart. *How can I tell him how I feel and still be able to go? How can I hear him speak of love or worse . . . ask me to stay?*

She twisted her hands. *It just isn't fair. Why should life be so difficult? Why can't Alaska and New York be close together? Why couldn't we just live in both places?*

But Leah's words came back to reaffirm Helaina's choices. Jacob was miserable in the city. He hated the noise and the traffic. Helaina knew this firsthand. She had often seen him in Seattle in the gardens at the back of the house, trying to seek quiet and solace.

"Are you all right?"

She looked up to find Jacob watching her. He was leading two young dogs on leashes. "I'm fine. I . . . well . . . I was coming to see you."

"Me? Why me?"

"I . . . uh . . . I know I haven't been very good company. I know you've wanted to talk to me, but I've been so busy thinking about my trip home. I'm sorry if I've hurt you or caused you grief."

Jacob opened his mouth to speak, then seemed to reconsider. For a moment he just looked at her. "I'm fine. You didn't hurt me. I just didn't understand why you didn't want to talk to me. I think I do now."

"Truly?" She wondered what he meant.

"Well, I know your mind is occupied with thoughts of this trip and no doubt seeing your brother again. I know you've wanted to explain everything to him. I'm sure you're homesick, and you desire to be back where you belong."

Where I belong? I don't know where I belong—except with you. She pushed the thought aside. She wanted so much to tell him the truth. "Jacob . . . I . . . well, you should know—"

"I think I know what I need to," he interrupted. His voice

sounded gruff. "Look, I have a lot of work to do before supper tonight. Maybe we can talk more then."

Helaina nodded and Jacob took the dogs and left. She didn't realize how she'd balled her fists in frustration until after he'd gone. *Why can't I just tell him how I feel and be done with it? Why can't I let him know that I love him, but that I love him enough to leave him in Alaska?*

———

Supper that night was misery for Helaina. She watched Sigrid captivate and amuse Jacob with her stories and suggestions for her summer activities. He seemed to think the woman quite amazing as she told tales of rescuing one of her students from a well and saving her young nephews from burning in a fire they accidentally set in the barn.

"Children are amazing wonders," Sigrid announced, "but they are dangerous and destructive too. Especially to themselves. They need a firm hand of guidance and an education as early as possible. And I'm not just talking books. Children need to know their place and to grow in that place. I'm always troubled by the people who hide their children away for nannies and governesses to raise."

Helaina knew many of those people. She had good friends who had children cared for by nurses. "I suppose," she offered, "that their way of life dictates that they provide for their children and enjoy them whenever they can."

"Hogwash," Sigrid proclaimed, renouncing the idea. "It's self-ishness, pure and simple. If you're too busy to be a mother or father to a child—then don't have them."

That caught everyone's attention, but Sigrid didn't seem to mind. "I'm quite serious. You all look at me as though I've suggested we burn down the capitol building, but I assure you, I know what I'm talking about. I worked at a very prestigious school for girls just before coming here. Those young ladies were miserable. They'd spent an entire lifetime barely knowing who their parents were. They had a stronger bond to their nannies."

"That doesn't mean their parents don't love them," Helaina protested.

"Perhaps not, but why then do their parents have no time for them? You see, I believe time spent together equals love. If you love someone, you want to be with them." She smiled at Jacob, who surprisingly enough nodded in agreement. Helaina wanted to throw something.

"It's very easy," Sigrid continued, "to say you love someone, then go about your merry way. Love requires a commitment. It requires sacrifice and sometimes a little bit of disorder in one's life. If you cannot give it, you needn't expect it in return."

Helaina felt as though the wind had been knocked from her. Sigrid seemed to be speaking right to her. It was as if she knew Helaina's situation completely.

"Well, I've always been glad for the time I spend with my children," Emma threw in. "I know Leah will enjoy her time as well. After all, you've had to wait all these years to become a mother."

Leah nodded. "I can't imagine waiting so long and then giving my child over to someone else to raise. After all, what could be more important than being there to love and nurture my own baby?"

"Exactly!" Sigrid declared enthusiastically. "Nothing is more important than future generations."

"Speaking of future generations," Jayce began, "what of the

war in Europe? Have you read much on it—will America go to war?"

Sigrid frowned. "I've avoided immersing myself in that sorry affair. There is much to concern ourselves with regarding the war. I feel that one way or another we will find our men dragged into this fight, but I certainly cannot approve it. It's a waste of human lives."

"Do you have specific news?"

Sigrid shook her head. "None that I care to discuss at a joyous occasion such as this." She smiled graciously. "I would much rather stay on positive topics."

Like nannies raising children? Helaina wondered. She toyed with her food and suddenly felt very frustrated. She used to be just like Sigrid. She thought nothing of stating her opinion and laying out her values for all to see and evaluate. Perhaps that was what irritated her most about Sigrid. It was the reminder of who Helaina had once been.

She glanced again at Jacob, who seemed to be captivated by Emma's sister. And why not? The petite young woman was charming and beautiful. She was also well educated and loved to talk about the things she enjoyed. The conversation had now turned to a trip Sigrid had made to Sweden. She was telling of their relatives and the life they lived in various cities and towns.

"Of course, our family is very close," she said, looking to Emma, who nodded. "We have always been that way and always will be. Nothing will break our ties. We cherish family too much. That's why I shall miss you all so much when you've gone away. I've hardly had time to get to know the children and you will leave tomorrow."

Emma dabbed at tears. "But we shall be back in late August.

We cannot leave for too long, after all. The people here need us."

"Yes, we do," Leah agreed. "I'm so sorry, Emma, but you will have to excuse me. I'm afraid I'm completely worn out." She turned to Jayce. "Would you mind if I went home?"

"If you plan to go alone, then I mind very much." He got to his feet and helped Leah from the table. "Emma, Helaina, the food was wonderful. Thank you for inviting us to share in this."

"Yes, it was a great time," Leah agreed. "I was very fond of the strawberry preserves. I haven't had any in some time."

"I shall bring you an entire jar as a gift for the baby," Sigrid said, smiling. "And since babies cannot eat jam, you will have to take care of it for him . . . or her."

"Thank you, Sigrid. You are very kind. I know we shall be good friends," Leah replied.

Helaina had taken as much as she could stand. In her mind she pictured this wonderful little group—so close and congenial—while she stood on the outside. She was a stranger here, even though she'd spent an entire winter with these people . . . even though they'd gone through hideous life and death experiences together.

A lump formed in her throat, and Helaina knew tears would soon follow if she didn't busy herself with something else. "I'll clean up," she said, reaching out to gather several dirty dishes.

"No," Sigrid said, putting her hand atop Helaina's. "That is my job now. It will be my home, and I will care for it. You must have a wonderful time on your last evening here. Take a walk. Go say good-bye to old friends."

"I'll help Sigrid," Jacob said as he gathered his own things together.

Helaina swallowed hard. All she could do was nod. She wasn't needed here. She'd been replaced.

Chapter Twenty-seven

J ayce looked at the missive in his hand, then raised his gaze to meet Leah's face. "Well?" she asked.

Jayce turned to Jacob and shook his head. "The letter says that Captain Latimore intends to be here next week. The letter was mailed in early May. He's expecting Jacob and me to join him for his northerly adventures. His plans, it seems, have changed again. Now he has someone funding a trip to the Queen Elizabeth Islands. Apparently these are Canadian islands some distance north and east of the Yukon Territory."

"That's a long distance away," Jacob said. "How does he plan to go exploring and get back before he gets frozen in?"

"Well, according to the letter he is merely escorting this team of archeologists, botanists, and geologists to the islands, where they plan to work for the next four years. He has been commissioned to bring them supplies over that time period. He'd like to include us in the project because we speak some of the native languages, you know dogs, and I'm a geologist."

"Will his wife accompany him again?" Leah asked.

Jayce shook his head. "No. Sadly enough she has passed away."

"What? But how?"

Jayce hesitated to say. He took a deep breath. "It seems she died in childbirth."

Leah's hand went to her overextended stomach. "No. How awful. You certainly would not expect such things to happen in big cities where doctors and hospitals are available."

"Nor do I expect them to happen here," Jayce reassured. "Don't let this make you overly sad or worried. It wouldn't be good for you or the baby."

"I feel so awful for Captain Latimore. He's a good man and seemed to love his family very much," Leah said. "And his poor little son is now without a mother."

"It is indeed sad." He paused and looked at the letter again. "It also says that the *Homestead* caught fire and completely burned last winter. He has replaced that ship with a new one and has called it the *Regina,* after his wife."

"I suppose what remains to be discussed," Leah said, looking to her husband, "is will you go?"

Jayce desired to head north and continue the adventure he'd tried to begin last year. But looking at his pregnant wife, he didn't see how that was any longer possible. He was a married man with a child on the way. Those kinds of obligations changed a man's choices.

"I can't leave you like this. The baby won't be born for another few weeks by your own calculations. How could I go without knowing if I have a son or a daughter?"

Leah frowned. "But I know what this means to you. I also know there is very little for you to do here this summer and certainly no employment short of ensuring our own survival. I've already been praying about it, lest I fret over such matters."

"My employment is not your concern, my dear. That is solely my responsibility. I wouldn't have you worrying over it."

"But you do desire to go, don't you?" Her words were quite matter-of-fact.

Jayce wouldn't lie to her. "I would like it very much."

"Then I want you to go. Whether the baby has come or not, you need to do this. Besides, it's just for a few months. The summer will be so busy for me, I'll probably not even notice that you're gone," she said with a smile.

Jayce knew better. "You're a poor liar, Mrs. Kincaid."

Leah laughed. "I'm not lying. Not really. I know that with the baby, I'll be quite busy. Not only that, but I'll help with the fishing and smoking of salmon and seal. I'll help pick berries and greens and look for medicinal herbs and roots. You haven't been here for my summer routine. There is much to do."

"But we were to build a new house this summer. The supplies are to be shipped here by July."

"So I will hire help to see it built," Leah replied. "We have good men here in the village, or I can bring in others from Nome. I'll see it done, or if you prefer, it can wait. The baby won't be so big by next summer that a larger house can't be postponed until then."

Jayce folded the letter and put it in his pocket. "I'll pray about it."

Leah smiled and turned to Jacob. "You must convince him. He needs this adventure—I'm sure of that."

"It would be easier if the baby were already here," Jayce said. "Then I'd know that you were safely delivered and doing well."

Leah laughed and struggled to her feet. "Then I shall pray for God to begin my labor."

Jayce chuckled and jumped up to help his wife. "You go rest and pray then, my love. I want you doing little else."

"I'm much stronger than you give me credit for," Leah declared. "I wouldn't want to drive a dog team, but I can clean up my house."

"Jacob and I will see to everything. And if that isn't good enough, we'll hire one of the girls to come and help you." He accompanied Leah to a bed couch that had been recently delivered from Seattle, a wedding present from Karen's relatives.

Leah stretched out. "Well, maybe I'll rest for a little while. My feet have been swelling miserably of late, and this might do them some good."

———

Emma and Bjorn's trip was delayed by several days when the ship developed some kind of problem with its steering. Helaina was grateful for the chance to spend more time in the small community. She thought perhaps the ship's problems were divine providence—God himself intervening to give her time to change her mind.

Watching the village come to life under nearly continuous sun, Helaina remembered her time the previous summer. Jacob had been a hard taskmaster then, but he'd driven her only so that she might survive. He'd taught her much about the dogs and helped her adjust to life in such an isolated environment. She'd begun to learn the native language, although the natives wanted little to do with her, and she'd learned their culture. Jacob had reminded her over and over again that if she were to live in the village, it would serve her well to learn the ways of its people. Jacob had been right.

Now, however, he seemed just as focused on teaching Sigrid Johnsson. Helaina tried not to be jealous as she watched the couple. Jacob was showing Sigrid one of the dogs, and she was happily petting the animal as though it were her long lost friend.

Helaina couldn't help but remember that she had been quite afraid of the beasts. They were so wild looking—especially the huskies with their intense dark-rimmed eyes. Helaina always felt she was being watched by those eyes. After a time she had come to enjoy the dogs. She loved the puppies, and once she lost her fear of the older dogs, they had come to trust her and love her as well.

Sigrid laughed and straightened. Helaina saw that Jacob seemed amused by the girl's antics. Helaina envied Sigrid's ability to balance her whimsical nature with her more academic and serious side. There was nothing playful in Helaina's nature whatsoever.

With a sigh, she walked away from the scene and berated her heart for its inability to be less attached to things from her past.

"It will be all right," she told herself. "Once I'm in New York, I won't even think of this place. Jacob will be nothing more than a memory." But she knew that was a lie, even as she spoke it. Glancing overhead to the icy blue skies, she sighed. "Lord, I don't know how to get through this. I know Emma says you can see us through all adversity, but I'm more troubled by this than I even know how to pray about."

"Helaina!" Emma called as she came hurrying up the path from the shore. "We leave with the tide. Bjorn was just given the word. We need to get our things together so the men can load our bags on the ship."

So this is my answer, Helaina thought. She nodded and followed Emma home, but her heart was so heavy that it made each step more difficult than the previous one. *I'm leaving. I'm leaving Last Chance and Jacob forever.*

Throughout the day, Helaina helped Emma make sure that they had everything they would need. Sigrid came home shortly after the news had been delivered about the departure. Helaina found she could hardly bear the woman's company.

"I am so looking forward to all the different foods," Emma confessed. "I long for fried chicken, pork roast, and thick gravy."

Sigrid laughed. "You'll be as round as a barrel when you return."

"Yes, but because I won't have a chance to go home again for some time, I'll surely work it right back off."

Helaina helped to get Rachel's little button-top boots secured, then smiled as the child attempted to dance around in them as she had her furry mukluks. She fell down several times as she tried to adapt to her aunt's gift.

"I don't think she knows what to make of such shoes," Emma said, laughing. "You were good to bring them to her, Sigrid. And the dress too. Now she won't go to our parents looking like such a savage."

"Mama wouldn't care if she came naked as the day she was born," Sigrid replied. "You know that very well. Besides, she has been sewing up a storm for the children and will have many outfits ready by the time you arrive. Never fear."

"Oh, it will be so good to see family again."

Helaina felt a twinge of envy at the comment. She would see

Stanley in Washington, D.C., but once she went home to New York, there was no one save her household staff. No one would be there to care whether she might come or go. No one would chide her for staying out unreasonably late. Mrs. Hayworth, the house-keeper, would be happy to hear of Helaina's new faith in God, but it wasn't the same as having family waiting.

I should settle down and create my own family, she thought as she gathered her own two bags. They'd already sent the Kjellmanns' things to the ship, but Helaina had figured to take these herself. They were stuffed full of her native clothes and a few gifts from the villagers who'd finally befriended her. Somehow Helaina couldn't bear to leave them behind.

"Is everyone ready?" Bjorn asked as he came bounding through the door. His sons were on his heels.

"We're going, Mama. The captain is ready for us to board." Bryce's authoritative voice commanded attention.

"Ja, I know," Emma replied. "I am ready for us to board as well."

Helaina stepped from the house, unwilling to put herself through the tearful good-byes that Emma and Sigrid would share. She had hardly taken ten steps, however, when Jacob called her name.

She turned to find him coming toward her. Placing her bags on the ground, Helaina forced a smile. "So you've come to see us off?"

He stopped about three feet from her and said nothing. Helaina thought he looked very much as though he'd like to say something, but he remained silent.

"Is Leah feeling well this morning?" Helaina finally questioned. She couldn't bear the tension between them. She feared if she didn't keep the topic of conversation neutral, she might very well plead with Jacob to join her.

"She's feeling very tired. Jayce has made her stay in bed. She sends her best wishes for a safe trip."

Helaina nodded. "Please thank her for me and give her . . . ah . . . give her my . . . best."

"I will."

The silence fell awkwardly around them. Helaina thought she might just take her bags and go, but something in Jacob's expression looked so forlorn and sad that she couldn't help but whisper, "I will miss this place . . . and the people."

"You know . . . I have wanted to tell you—"

"So you're here," Bjorn said as he came out of the house with Rachel in his arms. "I'm glad to have you see us off."

Helaina could have screamed. She longed to know what Jacob would have said. She picked up one bag and toyed with the latch as she waited, hoping Jacob would renew the conversation once he'd bid the Kjellmanns good-bye.

"We'll miss you," Jacob said, "but I know the trip will do you good. I wish you safe journey."

"Thank you, friend," Bjorn replied. "And you'll look after our Sigrid, won't you?"

Jacob nodded. "We'll make sure she's provided for and doesn't grow too bored."

Helaina felt her heart sink even further. She longed only to be gone—to be done with the good-byes and the heartache. She moved away from the group as Emma came out the door. Didn't they know she cared for Jacob—that her heart was being ripped in two?

You've done a good job of hiding your feelings, she told herself. *No one knows how you feel, save Leah. And she won't say anything. She loves Jacob too much to see him hurt because of me.*

"Helaina!"

It was Jacob again. She froze in place, willing herself not to run. What would he say? If he declared his love for her, she wouldn't know what to do.

"Helaina?"

She finally turned. "Yes, Jacob?"

He met her eyes and for a moment said nothing. She felt her heart begin to race. She longed for another kiss—even if it was to say good-bye.

"You . . . ah . . ." He held up her other bag. "You forgot this."

Disappointment washed over her. Helaina reached out to take hold of her case. "Thank you." Their fingers momentarily touched as Jacob released the handle to her hand. She wanted to say a million things, but the words wouldn't come.

The rest of her traveling companions were walking toward them. Helaina feared that if she didn't leave now, she might not ever go. "Good-bye, Jacob." She hurried away, not even hearing if he replied.

Don't look back, she told herself. *Don't look back.*

Leah could hardly bear the pain of her contractions. "Ayoona, it hurts so much."

"That the way, Lay-Ya. You get great pain, but also great joy. You push now and the baby will come."

Oopick wiped her head with a damp cloth. "It will soon be over."

Leah bore down. She could feel the baby pushing through,

fighting to be born. There was something so wonderful and terrifying at the same moment. What if something happened to the baby? What if he or she wasn't strong enough to withstand the birthing? What if Leah was too weak to live afterward?

Leah screamed as the child was expelled from her body. She fell back against the bed, tears flowing down her cheeks. The sound of the baby's first cry only made her cry harder.

"It's a boy, Lay-Ya. A nice boy. His father be very proud," Ayoona said.

Leah breathed a sigh of relief but almost instantly felt the pains tear at her once again. "What's wrong?" she gasped, grabbing her stomach.

"You have twins, Lay-Ya." Ayoona spoke the fact in such a nonchalant manner that Leah could only stare at her in stunned amazement.

"What?" She cried out against the pain, struggling hard to draw a breath.

Ayoona handed the baby to Oopick. "You gotta push again. You gotta push hard or this baby could die."

"I don't understand." Leah had never once considered herself to be carrying twins. There had been a tremendous amount of activity with her baby, but she had nothing to compare it to and had figured it to be perfectly normal.

The contractions increased in severity, and Leah held her breath and pushed with all her might. Gasping, she drew in another deep breath and pushed through the pain.

"This baby got itself backwards," Ayoona said with a chuckle. "Just like my son John. Comin' to the world the back way."

Leah had helped with breech births before. She knew the dangers—knew that the birthing canal could close in around the baby and strangle it before birth. She found herself praying for God's intervention. She had no idea that she'd carried twins, but now that she knew, she couldn't bear the idea of losing either baby.

The infant came quickly and was smaller than her brother. She had a lusty cry that commanded attention long after her sibling had quieted. Leah stared in wonder as Oopick and Ayoona cleaned her children and dressed them for the first time. Twins. It was almost more than she could comprehend.

An hour after the ordeal, Jayce stood beside his wife and shook his head. "Two babies. I can't believe it. Did you know?"

"I had no idea, though I suppose we should have considered it," Leah said. "After all, you are a twin, and twins tend to run in families."

"They're beautiful, and how congenial that you would give me one of each—a son and a daughter." He grinned at her and gently stroked her face. "Leah, you are the most beautiful woman I've ever known. Thank you for my children."

She tried not to let her fears steal the joy of the moment. They were Jayce's children. As he had told her so many months ago, he would take care of these babies and be their father. They would look like him and her, and they would grow up without questioning their parentage.

"So I suppose the names we picked out for a boy and a girl can both be used," Jayce said, looking at his son. "William Edgar after our fathers. We'll call him Wills."

"And Meredith Patience for our mothers," Leah said, looking at the tiny bundle in her arms. "We can call her Merry."

Jayce nodded. "I like that. Wills and Merry. Perfect additions to our family."

Chapter Twenty-eight

Captain Latimore showed up four days later on the twelfth of June. He was a shadow of his former self, having lost a great deal of weight. It seemed he had aged well beyond his nearly fifty years. Leah felt sorry for the man. His pleasant, almost humorous demeanor was gone, and in its place was a gruff, hard man who didn't care about the pleasantries of life.

"This is an ongoing job for me," he announced to Jacob and Jayce. "The Canadian company that put this plan together intends to see their men living in the Arctic for no fewer than four years. They believe this will garner much knowledge about the north. I will make a yearly run of supplies to them, and given the distance, it will take all summer."

"So the plan this time around is simply to take the party north, help establish their camp, and then leave?" Jayce questioned.

"That and gather a few samples for some of my American scientific friends," Latimore announced. "That's where you come in, Jayce. I will rely upon your geological and botanical knowledge to help retrieve a list of samplings. We will, however, say nothing about it to the others. No sense ruffling feathers since they are paying the bulk of the expenses."

Leah sat in her bed across the room while the men discussed their plans at the small living room table. She wished she might join in but sensed that Latimore wanted nothing to do with her, given the fact that she'd just given birth. He looked at her with an expression of disdain, then nodded and turned away. No doubt she was a sad reminder of his dead wife.

"I have left the Canadian team on the ship. They want to purchase two teams of dogs from you, as well as sleds, harnesses, and any other gear you can spare."

"Well, I have dogs that can be purchased but not many that are trained well enough," Jacob said. "There are quite a few yearlings that show great promise and we might incorporate some of those into a team. We also have eight teams of pups that are being trained to pull, but they'll take time and I'd rather not take any of them. And regarding the gear, I don't have that much that I can afford to spare, but I'll ask around. I know that John had some extra things, and perhaps he could part with one of his sleds for a reasonable price."

"We did purchase one sled and some harnesses and lines in Nome," Latimore told him, "but you know those things are going to wear and it will be necessary to replace them."

"Yes, of course," Jacob replied. "I'll do what I can."

"How big is the team of men you will leave behind?" Jayce

questioned. He offered Latimore coffee, but the captain waved him off.

"There are a total of six. Two are archeologists. They believe there will be signs of some sort of ancient life on the islands. Personally, it sounds like nonsense to me, but they pay well. There is also a botanist, a geologist, a medical doctor, and a meteorologist who is working for the Canadian army, which is surprising given Canada's deep involvement with the war."

"Which brings up another question," Jacob interjected. "What happened to the U.S. Army and their interest in military sites in Alaska?"

"I'm sure the interest remains, but their sight is now fixed on Europe. Things are not looking good. Back in March the Germans torpedoed a French channel ferry called the *Sussex*. That in turn caused an international crisis. Twenty-five of the fifty killed on that ship were Americans."

"How awful," Leah said from her bed. Latimore seemed not to even hear her.

"President Wilson immediately condemned the act and those responsible. He threatened to sever diplomatic relations with Germany. The Germans abandoned their U-boat campaign immediately. They are terrified, in my opinion, that we will come into this war and put an end to their bullying."

"And you believe that to be the case?" Jayce asked.

"I do. That is another reason I've committed my ship to a four-year plan. If there should be a war, and should they need my vessel, they cannot confiscate my ship without compensating me quite well. I would even have the ability to protest any kind of government interference based on the fact that lives would be at stake should I be unable to fulfill my contract."

Leah thought he seemed pleased with himself, and in actuality she couldn't blame him. The idea of sending Americans into a foreign war was outrageous to her. She hadn't understood the Spanish-American War, and she certainly didn't understand this European war.

"There is also the Battle of Verdun. It began last February," Latimore continued. "The fighting goes back and forth between the Germans and French, sometimes with one side winning and then the other. It's a battle for the hearts of the French, as I hear it. Verdun is quite special to them. There appears to be no end in sight, however."

"I am sorry to hear that," Jacob said, shaking his head. "I'm sure many lives will be lost before this war ends. Tragically, I wonder if the people even understand what they are fighting for."

Latimore rubbed his bearded chin. "That remains to be seen. My purpose is to remain in service to myself. We shall leave on the morrow. Can you be ready?"

Jacob and Jayce looked to each other and then nodded. "We'll be ready."

"Wonderful. Now why don't you show me your dogs." It was more a command than a question. Latimore got to his feet and nodded toward Leah. "Mrs. Kincaid, I wish you the best."

Leah thought him without emotion or feeling, and the next morning she had a chance to prove that her summation was correct. She was up from bed finally, tired but needing to show Jayce that she was fully recovered from the birth of their children. She hated knowing that Jayce would leave that day and be away for several months. It was apparent to Leah that he would remain behind should she ask him to do so, but she knew how much he desired to go on this quest. He had talked of nothing else since the sun had returned to last the length of a normal day.

In her heart Leah felt there was little choice. She had to let Jayce go, and she felt almost comforted to know that he and Jacob would look after each other. She would worry less with the two of them together, but in some ways she would also worry more. If anything happened to the ship and crew, she might lose them both.

"Good morning, Mrs. Kincaid," the captain said as he entered the kitchen. "Is your husband here?"

"He will be shortly. He's gone to see someone. Why don't you have a seat and I will fix you breakfast."

"No, thank you. I ate aboard the ship. I have a fine cook there."

She smiled and felt it necessary to speak about her husband's involvement. "I hope that you will make every effort to keep my husband and brother safe. They are all I have now besides the children. Given your loss, I'm sure you can understand. You are all that your son has now."

"My son is no longer my concern. I have given him over to my sister to be raised. I seriously doubt that I will ever see the boy again."

"But how can you say that?" Leah questioned.

"I don't believe I will be long on this earth, ma'am."

The words startled Leah and she found herself gripping the back of the chair as though it were her lifeline. "Why would you believe such a thing? You're not that old, and while you appear thinner than the last time I saw you, you surely are in very good health or you'd not venture north."

"I have no idea of whether my health is good or bad. I simply feel that my days are numbered."

"No doubt you are mourning the loss of your wife. You may feel different in a year or two," Leah offered in a sympathetic tone. "Your sorrow must be great indeed, for I remember the way you spoke of Mrs. Latimore. You held great fondness for her and for your son."

The captain met her gaze and for a moment Leah thought he might contradict her statement. Then his features softened, but only a bit. "I do mourn Regina's passing, but perhaps that is why I have no fear of my life coming to an end. If I am to rejoin her soon, then this interlude will become nothing more than a brief nightmare."

"But if you die, you'll leave your son an orphan. Would it not be better for him to at least have a father than to be without both mother and father?"

One of the twins began to fuss and Latimore took this as his cue to exit. "I will wait for your husband outside. We sail with the tide."

Leah watched the man hurry from the house. He wanted no part of answering her question or of seeing her children.

"Such a sad man," she murmured, making her way to the tiny box bed where her babies slept.

She found Wills awake and quite angry. He was wet and hungry, as usual. Leah changed him, using diapers she'd borrowed from Emma. "There you are, little man. Now come and get your fill while your sister sleeps."

It was there, feeding her son, that Jayce found her. He smiled from the doorway and simply watched her for a moment. "This is the image I will take with me to the north. My daughter sleeping soundly and my wife nourishing our son."

Leah smiled. "I'm certain there will be many such scenes."

He frowned. "And I shall miss them."

"You won't be gone forever. Wills and Merry will still be quite small when you return in September."

He came to sit beside her. "And we might be back as early as the latter weeks of August." Jayce reached out to touch his son's downy hair. "He's so small. It amazes me that we all start out this way." He looked up, their faces only inches apart. "I still battle against myself about going."

"You need to go," Leah countered. "I know that this is important to you, and if you do not go, I fear you will always regret it. And in turn, you may come to resent the children . . . and me."

"Never. You're my life. I cherish you as I do my next breath." He grinned. "I should tell the captain that I need larger quarters and bring all of you with me."

"I doubt Captain Latimore would agree to that. The man is bearing a terrible burden of grief. He has sent his son away to live with his sister and believes his life is not to be long on this earth. That troubles me because I fear he will endanger the lives of his men if he has no concern for his own life."

"Even if that is the case, Jacob and I are strong capable men. If need be we'll reason with the man and help him to see the truth. Pray for us while we're gone, and I'm sure things will work together."

"I haven't stopped praying since you and Jacob decided to go forward with this adventure," she admitted. With Wills satisfied, she placed him in the crib with his sister.

"When the innes begin to flood, you will go to the mission house and stay with Sigrid, won't you?"

She smiled. "I've already promised you that I would. You worry too much."

He laughed. "It's usually me telling you that very thing. Still, I guess I can't help but be worried. You are my responsibility, and now there are three of you. If there are storms or other problems, I won't be here to help."

"Nor will I be there to help you when problems come," Leah said softly. "Oh, Jayce, for years I mourned losing you. I won't mourn your departure this time. Before, there wasn't even the hope that you would return, but now I know without a doubt that you'll come back to me."

He took her in his arms and peered down at her. Leah sometimes still remembered the awful things Chase did to her when looking into his eyes, but the memories were fewer and fewer. Jayce had been a most compassionate, tender husband whose mercies knew no limits. He had never rushed her to intimacy, and in fact had offered her nothing but his undying patience throughout her pregnancy. She couldn't begin to put into words what that meant to her.

"I know you've come to tell me good-bye," she said softly, "but I wish you would not say the words. I'd rather hear that you love me—that you'll be thinking of us."

"Every minute of every day. Probably to distraction."

She laughed. "I don't want that. I wouldn't want you failing to pay attention to some detail and find yourself overboard."

He put his hand to her cheek in a tender fashion. "I promise I will not fall overboard." He kissed her forehead. "I love you so very much. We've been through a great deal, I know. But we've faced it together, and after years of bearing such sorrows on my own, I can honestly say that it is so much easier to walk through life with someone at your side.

"When Chase . . . took you away—when he . . . hurt you—I

feared that I had lost you forever. That I would have to go back to living a lonely existence after finally knowing what was missing in my life. I cannot tell you how I struggled with that. I knew I couldn't impose myself upon you and force you to deal with a constant reminder of the man who had done those awful things, but neither could I lose you."

"You'll never lose me." She put her hand against his. "It hasn't been easy. I won't pretend it has. I know that we agreed you are the father of these children, but it seems that Satan can use this one thing to disrupt me more than anything else. But I am trying, and I'm fighting against such disparaging thoughts."

Jayce leaned down and kissed her nose. "You are a strong and incredible woman, Leah Barringer Kincaid. I will pray that you never stop fighting such lies. I am the father of our children— only me—always me."

He kissed her soundly on the mouth, his arms wrapped around her in a protective embrace. Leah found no fear in his touch and momentarily lost herself in the memory of their first kiss. *There is nothing of Chase in this man*, she reminded herself. *Nothing of the pain and sorrow that I once associated with the name Jayce Kincaid. There is only love.*

"Did you hear me?"

"Hmm?" She opened her eyes and sighed.

He laughed and put her at arm's length. "You weren't even listening to me."

Leah straightened rather indignantly. "I was busy."

"I suppose I'll let it go . . . this time." He walked to where the babies slept and shook his head. "I can't get over having two at once."

"Wait just a minute—what did you say that was so important?" Leah asked.

"Hmm? Oh that." He turned with a nonchalant shrug. "I merely said that I loved you—that I would love you forever."

She frowned. "Oh. That." She couldn't hold the look, however, and began to giggle. "I love you, too, and I shall count the days and hours until you come home to me—to us."

Jayce carried that moment with him as the ship weighed anchor and steamed away from Last Chance. He didn't bother to stand at the rail and wave good-bye. He knew from their agreement that Leah wouldn't be on the shore.

"I'm a fool," he told Jacob as he stretched out on the bed in their cabin. "I shouldn't be leaving them."

Jacob looked at him for a moment, then shook his head. "So why are you going, then?"

Jayce consider the question. "Because your sister is wiser than both of us put together. She knows this trip is important to me. I think it's possible she understands me better than I understand myself. It's at her insistence I go."

"I know how Leah can be," Jacob admitted. "She is wise. Maybe the time apart will do you both good. It will give her extra time for healing. You know what they say about the heart and being absent."

"Indeed." He laced his fingers behind his head. "For my heart is already fonder of her, and we've barely begun our journey."

Jacob threw a pillow at Jayce, hitting him full in the face. "I'm not going to room with some lovesick cow the whole trip. Let me know now if this is how it's to be and I'll go sleep with the dogs."

Jayce laughed and tossed the pillow back to Jacob. "I'm a new father; you must indulge me. I will miss many things in the months to come."

"Yes. Dirty diapers and colicky stomachs," Jacob said, counting them off on his fingers. "Crying in the middle of the night to eat, and crying to be held when they feel neglected. I tell you what: In keeping with your new fatherhood and all the things you will miss, I shall put you in charge of the dogs. They have messes to clean and whine when they need to be fed. It will be just like caring for infants."

"Ha-ha," Jayce said, closing his eyes. "I am so very touched by your compassion. I shall remember it in my letter home to your sister. No doubt it will deepen her regard for you, just as it has mine."

Chapter Twenty-nine

After a brief encounter with a very busy and preoccupied Stanley, Helaina found herself safely ensconced in her New York estate. In this house—mansion, really—Helaina had known many pleasant memories. She tried to find comfort in that as she moved in silence from room to room. For weeks now she'd tried to readjust herself to this once-familiar setting. Everything was just as she'd left it. Having wired ahead to let Mrs. Hayworth know of her return, Helaina found that the furniture had been uncovered, the dust dealt with, and the windows freshly washed. The entire house smelled of oil and polish.

New York society was also as she had left it. They ushered her back with open arms, although there was an underlying attitude that hinted of a mother scolding her wayward child. Helaina found herself making the circuit, explaining her travels much as she might explain her misguided purchase of property in an unfashionable neighborhood.

Some of the men immediately began to fawn over her, telling Helaina what a drudge their life had been without her in the city. Others suggested a desire to come calling, which Helaina quickly declined, much to their disappointment.

There were parties and teas at which she was made the guest of honor and could not refuse to attend. Much of New York had taken their leave to cooler, less hectic climes, but many of the old guard remained and took it as their personal responsibility to see Helaina properly fitted back into society. To Helaina it was all rather mundane and exhausting.

The house, Helaina thought, seemed larger than she'd remembered. Now as she walked its hallowed halls, she felt a sense of sadness wash over her. She was queen over her domain, but it was a very empty domain, and she was a very lonely queen.

She walked into the main receiving parlor. The room was some thirty feet long and twenty feet wide. Fitted with heavy gold damask, the floor-to-ceiling windows allowed a great deal of light to brighten the otherwise dark room. Helaina smiled as she thought of the blinding bright sunlight she'd known in Alaska. It was easy for a person to lose their vision, at least temporarily, from overexposure to sun on snow.

Helaina touched her hand to the ornately carved table. Here, delicate silver frames displayed photographs of her family. She couldn't help but pick up the picture of Robert. The side view of her mustached and serious-faced husband did not do justice to the fun-loving soul she had known.

"So many things have changed," she told him. "You would hardly recognize me."

"Am I interrupting?"

Helaina looked up to find Mrs. Hayworth.

"Cook said you wanted to see me," the housekeeper added.

Helaina smiled. "Yes. We haven't had a chance to sit and talk since I arrived home. I thought if you had a moment . . ."

Mrs. Hayworth smiled. "Of course, deary. You know I always have time for you."

Helaina crossed to one of the brocade sofas. Her plum-colored silk day dress swirled gently at her ankles. It was a marvelous piece, one that made Helaina feel glamorous. "I have missed our talks."

"Truly?" Mrs. Hayworth took a seat on the sofa opposite Helaina's. "It touches me to hear you say that."

"Well, it's true. I know I was unbearable at times, and for that I must apologize. I know that you were only trying to help me in my grief." Mrs. Hayworth nodded, and Helaina continued. "I've had a remarkable year to be sure, but perhaps the most important part is that I have come to understand God's love for me."

"Oh my. It's what I have prayed for." Mrs. Hayworth leaned forward. "Please tell me what happened."

Helaina thought back to the first time she'd met Jacob. "I met a man and his sister." She began her story and tried to cover all of the important details. Mrs. Hayworth was her captive audience, just as Helaina had known she would be.

"I kept hearing some of the same things you had told me, repeated in their conversations. For the longest time, however, I couldn't reconcile it with what I felt was true. I felt the law should be observed at all cost, but Jacob and Leah taught me about mercy. Mercy that extended to me, even though I didn't deserve it. In fact, I'm sorry to say that my actions caused that sweet family much grief."

"But even that can be forgiven," Mrs. Hayworth interjected.

"I'm sure such loving folk would never hold you a grudge."

"No, Jacob and Leah don't hold me a grudge," Helaina said, feeling rather sad. "Leah was somewhat vexed with me for a time, but knowing the truth of all that happened to her, I cannot blame her. Still, I have her forgiveness, and she has mine. Although truly there was nothing I needed to forgive."

She sighed and leaned back, feeling the tight constriction of her stylish new elastic corset. Despite the freedom offered by the rubber webbing, Helaina had not worn such restricting undergarments in Alaska. She found the missing liberty to be quite a loss.

"You seem troubled, if you don't mind my saying so," Mrs. Hayworth offered.

"I suppose I am. I feel ... well ... misplaced. Does that sound odd to you?"

The older woman smiled. "Not at all. Your old life here may seem in conflict with your new life in Christ."

Helaina nodded and leaned forward again. "Yes. Yes, that's exactly the problem. Remember the party I attended the night before last?"

"The one given by the Chesterfields?"

"Yes, that's the one. I remembered them as having the most incredible gatherings. Food and orchestras to rival the best families in New York. I remember the witty dialogue and the pleasure of simply being seen in my elegant clothes and jewelry. But it wasn't the same. It didn't satisfy me at all. Yet, while I was gone, New York and my life here were all I could think on."

"The greener grass," Mrs. Hayworth said with a chuckle. "While you were in one pasture, another seemed better."

"I was certain while in the Alaskan wilderness that nothing could possibly be more to my dislike. There were vast open fields of nothing. No people—no buildings. It was an incredible place. In the village where I lived last summer, I endured the most hideous meals, flooding of the little house where I stayed, and people whom I couldn't understand until I learned their language. I never felt more alone or miserable."

"But to my way of thinking, this was just God's way to get you to a place where He could have your attention. Perhaps here there were just too many distractions."

"I suppose you're right. Just getting into my clothing here takes more time and effort than I ever exerted in Alaska. Although there I was trying to learn how to actually make some of my own things. Goodness, but I wish I'd been more attentive when being taught to sew."

Mrs. Hayworth laughed heartily at this. "I never thought I'd hear you worry about such things. You were far more concerned with the designers who made your gowns or the quality of the crystal on your tables."

"I was nothing more than a snob. God has made that clear to me."

Sobering, Mrs. Hayworth grew thoughtful. "But you miss Alaska, don't you?"

"I do. I find myself thinking of it constantly. And of Jacob. I never thought I would ever fall in love with another man, but I have."

"That's marvelous."

Helaina shook her head. "No. Not really. Jacob could never give up his life there. Alaska is in his blood."

"Sounds to me as if it's in yours as well."

"I think it is, but it would only be worthwhile to me if Jacob were a part of my life there."

The chimes rang from the large ebony grandfather clock. "Goodness me, but it's already five o'clock," Mrs. Hayworth declared. "Aren't you attending the Morgan dinner tonight?"

Helaina sighed. "I completely forgot about it. I'm supposed to be there at seven and I still need to take a bath."

"I'll have one of the girls draw it immediately. I've already seen to your gown. You'll be quite dazzling in that peacock blue creation."

Helaina nodded, but her heart wasn't in it. Mrs. Hayworth surprised her by coming to her side. She gently reached out to touch Helaina's shoulder. "I'm delighted to know you've come to trust the Lord. Lean on Him in this as well. Pray about what you should do. It's very likely that the right thing is to go back."

"But if I do, I would probably have to sell this house and all of my things, because I doubt I would return here. Certainly not to live."

"And what would be so wrong with that?"

"Where would you go?" Helaina reached up to take hold of her housekeeper's hand. "I won't put you on the streets."

"You wouldn't. I've been trying to think of a way to tell you that I'm giving my resignation at the end of the summer. My daughter in Milwaukee wants me to come there and help her with the children. Her husband recently died after a long illness and she needs me."

"I'm so sorry. I didn't know," Helaina said. She got to her feet and faced Mrs. Hayworth. "I will miss you."

"Not as much if you make your way back to Alaska," the older woman said with a wink. "I have a feeling once you are back in the company of your Mr. Barringer, you won't be thinking of this old woman."

Helaina surprised them both by embracing Mrs. Hayworth. "I shall always think fondly of you. You were the first to brave telling me of Jesus. You were the only one who loved me enough to stand up to my nasty disposition and try to explain what was missing in my life. You've been such a dear, dear friend, and I thank you."

Mrs. Hayworth had tears in her eyes as they separated. "You've been a blessing to me as well. Now don't forget what I said. If you are still so very miserable here, perhaps it's because you no longer belong here. God will show you."

That night at the Morgan dinner, Helaina enjoyed the attention of most every single man in the room. She made a striking figure in her gown of blue silk. The high-necked lace inset of her bodice had been trimmed in a braided cord of silver. It seemed a perfect touch with her silver elbow-length gloves.

"Mrs. Beecham, we have positively languished without your company," the gentleman at her right began. "I heard you were traveling extensively. Perhaps you would care to tell us of your travels."

"Mr. Broderick, you are kind to ask," Helaina said, reaching for her water glass. "I did travel extensively as you suggest. In fact, I spent considerable time in the Alaskan Territory."

"Seward's Icebox?" he questioned. The men close by perked up and leaned toward them.

"Tell us about it," the young man across the table insisted. He bent his head to try and peer around a large display of flowers and fruit. "I've heard it's filled with wild animals and nothing but snow."

"It's a very diverse land. I spent time in the far western

sections of the territory, as well as some of the southeast islands. It's amazing that they even exist in the same territory, but you must remember the vast number of miles between locations."

For some time Helaina told of the landscape, people, and the day-to-day existence that she'd known. "I cannot imagine another wholly unspoiled place in all the earth."

"It sounds as though you were smitten with Alaska, Mrs. Beecham. Perhaps you will journey back one day."

Helaina smiled. "I think that is quite possible."

"But what of the food? Surely there was nothing as marvelous as this meal," Mr. Broderick said, lifting a piece of veal to his lips.

"This truly is a delightful meal," Helaina agreed. "I thought often of such meals while suffering through seal meat and oiled greens. Sometimes I thought I would perish of hunger because of the unpleasant things served. However, I grew to actually enjoy the food. Well ... there were things I still did not care for, but many other dishes I came to enjoy. For example, caribou is quite a tasty piece. When the steaks are fried up, as you would a beefsteak, the meat is most enjoyable."

"But what of the luxuries you have here?" the woman sitting opposite Mr. Broderick asked. "Surely you wouldn't forsake such finery. I know you to be a woman of impeccable taste. Your wardrobe is praised in the highest circles and your jewelry rivals that of our best families."

Helaina thought about this for a moment. These were the things she was known for. Praised for her clothing and jewels. Leah, on the other hand, was loved and regarded for her healing touch and giving heart. *I've wasted my life.*

"It has always been a comfort to have every luxury at my fingertips," Helaina began slowly, "but I've come to realize that there is much more to life than those temporary things. I believe God would also have us reach out to those in need and offer ourselves as well as our money. The people in Alaska taught me that. There were so many times when I tried to buy my way out of conflict or trouble, only to realize that money means very little to those people." She couldn't help but remember Jacob's words on such matters.

"I wouldn't want to live where money couldn't buy me what I needed," the woman said with a bit of a laugh.

Helaina made a pretense of eating her dessert. The thick piece of chocolate cake was smothered in a rich raspberry sauce and topped with mounds of fluffy whipped cream. It was delicious, but no more so than the cake Leah had made for the breakup celebration. She pushed the dish back.

"Everything has been wonderful," she announced as the guests began to rise and move into the various rooms for after-dinner drinks and conversation.

The men took their brandy and cigars into Mr. Morgan's study, while the ladies retired to the music room to be entertained by some of the guests. Helaina found herself rapidly growing bored with the gossip that seemed to titillate the other women.

"I'm told that Mr. Hutchinson was seen that very evening with his gardener's daughter," one graying matriarch announced.

"No!" gasped one of the other women. "Did his wife ever find out?"

The matriarch laughed. "It was his wife who told me about it. She spied the entire affair from her bedroom window."

"How scandalous. What did she do?"

The matriarch shook her head and sobered. "Poor dear could

do nothing. It's her husband's money, after all." The women all nodded sympathetically.

Without warning, however, the woman turned to Helaina. "You are blessed not to have to concern yourself with such matters. A woman of means need never be slave to a man's wants and demands."

Helaina shook her head. "Perhaps I am blessed financially, but I cannot say that my money has staved off the loneliness of an empty house. I would very much like to have a husband—a family."

"Why, my dear, you could have your pick of any single man in New York," a rather fragile woman declared.

"And half the married ones too," the matriarch announced. "But, my dear, you mustn't let yourself get taken for your money. You must find a man who is just as rich as you are. You'll never respect him otherwise."

Helaina thought of Jacob and smiled. He owned very little, yet Helaina had never respected anyone more. Pretending to stifle a yawn, Helaina rose. "You must forgive me. I'm still quite exhausted from my travels. The dinner was marvelous," she said, turning to her hostess. "Mrs. Morgan, I thank you for such a delightful evening."

"But we have not yet started the music. Wouldn't you at least stay and play a song or two for us?"

"No, really I must go." Helaina patted the woman's gloved hands.

"I do hope we will soon see you holding one of your famous summer balls," the matriarch declared. "Your parties were always the talk of the town. You can easily dismiss those lonely evenings with a masquerade."

"No doubt. The people in this town truly love to wear their masks." With that Helaina exited the room. She knew the women would gossip horribly about her after her departure. Wasn't that the way she had always known it? And having often been one of the last guests to leave a party, she knew this practice better than most.

Once she was safely in her own house, Helaina reflected on the evening and the comments of her companions. She began to undress and was surprised when Mrs. Hayworth showed up with a cup of hot tea.

"I thought you could use a bit of chamomile to help you sleep."

"You know me very well," Helaina replied, fighting to release the clasp that held her gown closed.

"Here, let me help you. I dare say you were the highlight of the evening, no? The men were probably captivated by your striking figure."

"I suppose so," Helaina said, slipping the gown from her shoulders. "I, on the other hand, have never been so bored in my life." She gave a little laugh. "I felt as though I were playing dress-up in someone else's clothes. I simply didn't belong there, Mrs. Hayworth."

Her housekeeper looked on her with great compassion. "My dear, it really doesn't matter how many places you don't belong. What counts is that you figure out where you do belong."

Helaina let the expensive gown fall to the floor. "You know, you are absolutely right. I think I know exactly where I belong." She drew a deep breath. "We've got our work cut out for us, Mrs. Hayworth. I have an estate to sell, along with a world of goods.

Then there's Stanley. I'll have to deal with him, as well as the townhouse in Washington."

Mrs. Hayworth smiled in such a way that Helaina felt the older woman's approval. She picked up Helaina's dress and walked to the door. "I'll bring your breakfast at seven."

"Better make it six."

Chapter Thirty

Leah enjoyed the warm August day as they gathered berries. With her twins sleeping on a blanket nearby, Leah couldn't help but feel as though she were the happiest woman in the world. It hadn't been easy taking care of her babies without Jayce—the twins demanded much of her time and still weren't sleeping through the night—but with the help of Mary, Seal-Eye Sam's youngest daughter, Leah managed to get enough rest. The fifteen-year-old was a great help to Leah, but so, too, was Sigrid. Sigrid seemed to dote on the infants as if they were her own.

Sigrid had adapted well to the long hours of sun and the lack of amenities. She often talked of her family and friends in Minnesota, but not in a way that suggested she was homesick. Rather she seemed to use the tales in a sort of honoring remembrance that always tied into something she was experiencing in Alaska.

Leah had asked her at one point if she thought Alaska could

ever be her home, and Sigrid had given her a blank stare and responded, "It already is my home."

So with both Sigrid and Mary being quite devoted to the babies, Leah felt herself blessed. Of course there were times when Leah enjoyed time alone with her children. It fascinated her to watch them develop; already they had grown physically and were developing personalities. Wills was very demanding, whereas Merry seemed content to wait her turn. Wills seemed to grow bored with everyone, but Merry appeared happy to watch and listen for long periods of time.

Today was their first outing out-of-doors. Leah had decided it might do all three of them good to enjoy the warm summer day. This also fit well for Mary, who was busy washing clothes back at the mission house and Sigrid, who had decided to can some of the early berries they'd already collected. Ayoona and Oopick, along with several other women, had come with Leah. The day promised to be very productive.

It was nearly time to stop for lunch when the twins began to fuss. They were both ready for their lunch and that suited Leah well enough. She'd actually gotten the trick of feeding both babies at the same time. Sitting cross-legged on the ground, Leah smiled at her children.

"So you decided to wake up," she said, drawing Merry to her breast. Merry's dark blue eyes seemed to watch Leah's face in wonder. Wills would have no part of this. He cried with such intensity that there were actually tears around his eyes.

"Poor boy," Leah said, securing him to feed. "Did you think you'd been forgotten?"

A little ways down the hillside, Ayoona and Oopick were fixing lunch for everyone. Ayoona, though elderly, was quite fit, and Leah was constantly amazed at her stamina. It seemed the old woman could often work long hours after others had worn themselves out completely.

"I bring you food, Lay-Ya," she called, giving a little wave.

"That sounds wonderful."

Leah looked down at her babies. They nursed eagerly, seeming otherwise oblivious to Leah. Even Merry had closed her eyes as if relishing the moment.

If Jayce were here, it would be perfect, Leah thought. She missed her husband more than she could say. She'd heard nothing since early July, when he'd managed to send a missive out from the Point Barrow area. At that time things were going well, but Latimore, it seemed, kept more and more to himself. Jacob had found himself responsible for encouraging the men and keeping morale high.

Jayce, on the other hand, had taken over meal preparations when the cook had fallen ill and had taken to his bed with a fever. As of the time Jayce sent the letter, the man had not yet recovered. Jayce encouraged Leah to pray for them, as the seas were rough and the farther north they went the more ice they would encounter.

Leah tried not to think of the *Karluk* and other vessels that had been trapped in the ice only a few years earlier. Most of the crews had been lost to the elements and starvation. She couldn't bring herself to even consider that the same thing could happen to her husband and brother.

A sound behind Leah caused her to stiffen. There was a rustling in the grass that wasn't being made by the women she'd come with. With her children at her breast, Leah found it difficult to turn but strained to see what might be coming behind her.

Uff.

The grunt sounded not but about ten feet from Leah. She froze. It was a mother bear with a cub that seemed intent on wandering ever so close to Leah and the twins. Uncertain how best to protect herself, Leah started to get up, then decided against it. She had both babies in her arms, and no doubt if she made a sudden move the mother bear would take this as a threat to her cub.

Dear God, help us. I don't know what to do. She didn't even feel that she could call out to the women below for fear of further agitating the bear. The cub gave a whiny grunt and walked within two feet of Leah as he made a beeline for his mother.

Uff.

A low growl followed, and Leah could see that the mother bear had flattened her ears. A sure sign she meant business. She watched Leah with determined intensity.

Leah closed her eyes. She had left her rifle with her other things near the place where Ayoona prepared lunch. It was foolish, she now realized, but she'd felt safe.

Father, you closed the mouths of the lions that threatened Daniel. Please close the mouth of this bear.

Wills, sensing Leah's tension, stopped feeding and began to fuss. Leah felt frustrated, not knowing how best to help her son. If she moved, it might be seen as an aggressive act. Just then a loud boom resounded in the otherwise silent morning. Leah's head shot up as she twisted around to see Ayoona, still shouldering the Winchester 45-90 that Leah had brought along for protection.

Behind her a dull thud sounded as the beast hit the ground. The cub went to his dead mother, while Leah moved quickly to get off the blanket with her babies.

Ayoona walked over to meet them. "Lay-Ya, you finish her. I take babies."

The old woman placed the rifle on the ground and reached out for the children. Oopick was immediately at her side to help.

"Ayoona, you saved our lives." Leah gasped the words, feeling herself near to tears. "I didn't even know you could shoot."

The old woman shrugged. "John teach me. He say it might be useful." Her old weathered face broke into a grin. "Guess he smarter than I figured."

Leah drew a ragged breath and picked up the gun. She looked up the hill, where the cub pawed at his dead mother and was beginning to raise a fuss. "I'll have to kill him too," she said, feeling overwhelmed by the entire matter. "He'll die out here anyway if I don't. I wish Jayce were here."

"We have good meat," Ayoona stated matter-of-factly. "And we get good hide. God has provided."

"The skins will be yours—your reward." She knew the old woman would cherish the grizzly hide.

With new resolve, Leah worked the lever of the rifle to eject the spent shell and went back to where the sow lay. Without giving it another thought, she fired another bullet into the head of the bear, then worked the lever again. She looked at the cub and felt immediate regret. Although this baby would grow up to be just as threatening as its mother, he was just a new addition to the world and quite precious.

Leah took hold of the lever and gave it no further consideration. By the time she'd finished killing the cub, all of the women had gathered not far behind.

"Now we work," Ayoona said, as though the day had suddenly turned perfect. "Leah, you rest. You do enough. Take care of your babies and shoot more bear if they come." She handed the infant in her arms to Oopick and went for her knife.

Leah tried to relax as the women began to skin the bears. She'd nearly been killed—her babies too. *This country holds no mercy for anyone—especially the young,* she thought as she watched the women butcher the cub. *It is a cruel and hard land. How can I raise my babies here?* She shuddered and went quickly to her children. When Emma came back from the States, Leah would have to get her advice on raising infants in the Alaskan wilds. For now, she had already decided this would be the last time she brought the children with her on food-gathering excursions.

"You're to be married?" Helaina asked in surprise. A giddy Stanley—quite a departure from his usually serious demeanor—had arrived to pick her up at the train station that warm August day. When she questioned him, he'd explained his matrimonial plans.

"I know it's rather sudden. Perhaps even more so given that we plan to wed in just a few days."

"Is there a problem . . . a reason that you must rush into marriage?"

He took hold of her arm. "Just that we're in love. She's a marvelous woman. A widow with a young daughter. I shall have an instant family instead of just a wife. She's very smart—you'll like that about her. And she's very beautiful."

They walked to where Stanley's car awaited them. "Do you like it?"

Helaina eyed the contraption. Already the noise of such things was annoying to her. "When did you learn how to drive?"

"Oh, earlier in the year. I just bought it last week, but I'm already proficient."

They were soon wending their way through the busy traffic of downtown. Dodging pedestrians seemed to be one of the bigger challenges. People seemed absolutely oblivious at times to the monstrosities that shared their streets. Helaina was still uncertain as to the value of such a machine. "I think I prefer a dogsled," she said honestly. "In fact, I know I prefer less noise."

"This is the way of the future, my dear sister. You used to see the necessity of such things. I remember your being quite enthused about a more rapid means of transportation. Then there was your argument about how automobiles wouldn't leave behind droppings or kick at passing strangers."

"I suppose I remember saying those things, but Alaska has changed me." She looked at him and figured now would be as good a time as any to mention her plans. However, Stanley was not inclined to let go of his own interests.

"I hope you don't mind, but I thought we'd have lunch with Annabelle." He grinned. "Don't you just love that name?"

"You sound like a lovesick ninny to be sure," Helaina laughed. "But I completely understand and would love to have dinner with your intended."

"I'm glad you agree. We're to meet at her father's house in Georgetown. It's not far from your townhouse. Annabelle moved there after her husband died. She was expecting little Edith when her husband caught the measles and passed on."

"So how old is your Annabelle?"

"Twenty-two. Edith is now two years old and quite the handful. She adores me, though." Stanley fairly glowed with pride.

"I'm sure you'll make a wonderful father." Helaina could see how much her statement pleased him by the way his grin seemed to broaden and his eyes sparkled in delight. "They must both be very special. Where did you meet?"

"We met through her father, Erwin Taylor," Stanley said, maneuvering the automobile through a particularly narrow side street. "He's one of several aides to President Wilson. He made a good fortune for himself in land prospecting. He's just gone abroad on government business, and it worries Annabelle sick, what with the war. He's given us his blessing, however."

"So when are you to marry?"

"On the tenth. I do hope you'll be in town that long."

Helaina considered the timing. "Well, that's just three days from now. I don't see why it won't work out. I should be on my way shortly after that, however."

"Where are you bound this time? With a war in Europe I'm certain you aren't heading there."

"Actually, no. This may come as some surprise to you, but I've fallen in love as well." Stanley turned in dumfounded silence. Helaina pointed to the road. "Stanley, you should watch where you're going!"

He looked back to the road but shook his head. "Who have you fallen in love with?"

"Jacob Barringer."

"The Alaskan? Is that what this sudden sale of your New York estate is all about? Are you planning to move north?"

She drew a deep breath and lifted her chin. "Yes, I am. I wanted to come here and say good-bye, but I also wanted to see if you would handle the sale of my townhouse. I can't afford to wait around. The last ships to Nome will sail late this month, and I must be on one if I'm to get there before the ice makes it impossible."

"But this is all so fast."

"No more sudden than your engagement," she countered.

They passed through impressive gates and up a well-manicured drive that spoke of wealth and sophisticated taste. Helaina was impressed but forced her attention back to the conversation.

"I love him, Stanley. I know it sounds crazy. I never thought of myself as a person who could live in the Alaskan wilderness, but I miss it almost as much as I miss Jacob."

"But it's so isolated," Stanley said, bringing the car to a stop. "I nearly died worrying over you last winter. How will it be when I can only hear from you once or twice a year?"

"Now who's not looking to the future? They are building a railroad to cross a good portion of the state from south to north. There is talk of air travel, and as that industry takes off, who knows what it will afford us? And with so many people moving to settle that territory, the government will continue to speed up the mail. You needn't fear, Stanley. I'm sure we'll be in touch."

"But I . . . well . . . I thought you would be close at hand. I wanted you to be a part of our life here in Washington."

"I'm not saying that I'll never come back to visit. Goodness, I'm a wealthy woman—or did you forget?" She gave him a smile and reached out to pat his arm with her gloved hand. "Stanley, I need to go to him. He plans to return at the end of the month— September at the latest. I need to be there—to see if we have a future. If he doesn't feel the same way, then I'll be back. Probably to move in with you and your young bride."

He laughed and got out of the car. "Then perhaps I won't sell the townhouse right away."

"I think Latimore is wrong," Jayce told Jacob as they settled into their cabin after supper. "He's been frivolous with the supplies, and since the ice has slowed us considerably, I think we should talk to him about conservation."

Jacob had already been gravely concerned about the trip. They'd been able to deliver the Canadians, but the trip had taken much longer than Latimore had considered. They were now heading back to Nome, but it was late in the season and Jacob believed they were in serious danger.

"Perhaps if we remind him of the *Karluk*," Jayce added.

Jacob thought of that poor ship and the disaster that had ensued when they found themselves trapped in the ice some three years earlier. Many men had lived to tell about that adventure, but others had died. The last thing they needed was a repeat of such a tragedy.

"I'm not sure reminders of anything would help. Latimore is, as Leah pointed out, a broken and defeated man. He has little will to live. I thought in all seriousness that this trip would give him a new direction—a desire to break the bonds of his grief. But if anything, I think it's only worsened. I think he's completely unconcerned with our situation."

"The ice is thickening near the shores. Daily we're moving farther from land, and you know that isn't wise."

Jacob stretched out on his small bunk. "He thinks to follow the open lanes of water—believing that this will be our easiest passage home. He tells me the ship has a thick bow and will easily break the thinner ice, but I'm not sure how much the *Regina* can endure. She wasn't created for this purpose."

Jayce sat on the edge of his bed and shook his head. "Jacob, I think we're in serious trouble here. We have a dwindling amount of supplies; no dogs, should they be needed for land travel; and a crew that knows little of survival in the north."

"Add to that a captain who would just as soon die as live," Jacob threw in, "and it spells disaster for sure. I've been praying about it and have even tried to counsel Latimore. However, I'm inexperienced in such matters, according to our captain. He points out that he has successfully navigated the Arctic and dismisses me as if I were a whining boy."

The ship rammed hard, nearly knocking the men from their beds. Jacob shook his head. "We've hit ice again."

Jayce steadied himself. "I've got a bad feeling about this. I think I should have stayed home where I belonged."

Jacob laughed, but there was no joy in it. "Little late for that now." He thought of his sister and the babies, but mostly he thought of Helaina Beecham. He wondered if he'd ever see her again. *I'm a fool,* he thought. *A fool for ever coming on this expedition and a fool for letting her go. When we get back—if we get back—I'm going to find her. She has to know how I feel.*

Chapter Thirty-one

Helaina sat rather uncomfortably as her brother and new wife exchanged their vows. No expense had been spared for the small but elegant wedding. Hundreds of lilies and white roses had been used to decorate the formal parlor of the Erwin Taylor mansion. The bride, dressed in pale pink silk, looked at Stanley as though he were her knight in shining armor. There was no doubt to Helaina that this was a love match. She found herself envious, wishing it might be her wedding instead.

What if I go to Jacob and find that Sigrid has already won his heart? What if I arrive and find that in my absence, Jacob has come to realize he doesn't care for me at all?

The day had turned out quite warm, and Helaina longed for the cooler temperatures of Alaska. She began to think back to the winter and realized she had not even minded the extreme cold as much as she hated this stifling heat. Of course, the fashionable green creation Helaina had chosen for the occasion didn't help. The long, fitted sleeves and high neckline seemed to hold the warmth of the day to her body. She waved her ostrich feather fan, but it did little but move the damp, warm air around her.

When the ceremony finally concluded, the entire group was ushered into the main dining room for a wedding luncheon. Helaina found herself swarmed with friends of the happy couple as she made her way through the house. She tried to offer reasonable small talk, but her mind was ever on the train she would board that evening.

"Your brother mentioned at supper last night that you intend to leave us," a young man in a navy blue suit declared. His accent bore a distinct southern flavor.

"I'm afraid so," Helaina replied with a smile. "I will take a train bound to San Francisco tonight."

"I hate train travel," said the maid of honor, Amorica Smythe. She seemed bored with the entire matter. The spoiled young woman was the exact opposite of Annabelle, whom Helaina had found to be simple and unpretentious.

"Well, my dear Amorica, you'd hate wagon travel worse," the young man replied. He looked to Helaina and smiled. "My manners are atrocious. I'm David Riley."

"Very nice to meet you. I'm Helaina Beecham."

"Yes, we all know. Your brother has told us much about you, including the fact that you've worked in the past for the Pinkertons. That must have been most sensational."

Helaina could see that several other gentlemen had joined her circle. They all seemed very much interested in knowing about her adventures. "I wasn't a true agent. I merely helped Stanley with some select cases. My finest adventure was in Alaska. And I found that I enjoyed that dear territory so much that I'm heading back tonight."

"To Alaska?" Amorica asked in surprise. "I've heard there's absolutely nothing there. Is that true? Where will you live? How will you manage?"

Helaina shook her head. "The territory is vastly unspoiled by man. There is great beauty and riches beyond compare."

"Yes, they still have great veins of gold, I'm told." David seemed quite excited. "Perhaps I will come and visit you there."

"Your mother would never let you leave the area," one of the other men teased. "You know how she dotes on you."

"She'll have to part with him if we go to war," another said.

"Hardly that," Amorica countered. "She'll merely buy his way out of that responsibility like she does all others."

David seemed rather hurt by this. "She needs me—I'm all she has."

The others laughed as though in on some big joke.

Helaina saw that Stanley was by himself and excused herself. "I must apologize for ending our conversation, but I need to speak privately with my brother."

They were noticeably disappointed but nodded their consent. Helaina was never so glad to be away from a group in all her life. They seemed so much younger, although she doubted David was more than a year or two her junior.

"You look handsome," she told Stanley, standing on tiptoe to offer him a kiss on the cheek.

"Thank you. I'm so hot, I thought I might well give up the ghost during the ceremony. Maybe it will rain and cool things down," Stanley said, pulling at his collar.

"Perhaps. It would be nice for you." She noted the clock. "I'm going to have to be on my way. Would your driver take me to my townhouse and then to the station?"

"I've already arranged it," Stanley said, sounding sad. "I do wish you would stay. At least for the luncheon."

"I can't. I'll be late for my train."

"But I worry about you. I don't want to see you get hurt."

"I know, little brother." She smiled. "But I have to follow my heart, just as you did. I pray you'll both be very happy."

"I hope Jacob is worthy of your sacrifice," Stanley said, shaking his head.

Helaina laughed. "I suppose because I love him so much, it doesn't feel like a sacrifice at all. The sacrifice would be in staying here."

"Well, if you are sure of this." He frowned but leaned down to kiss her cheek. "I give you my blessing."

"Thank you. And put your mind at ease. I've never been more sure of anything in my life."

Chapter Thirty-two

September arrived without any word of the *Regina*. Night after night Leah waited and prayed, always hoping that the dawn would reveal the return of her husband and brother. The nightmares made her wait more difficult. She often dreamed of bear attacks—huge white polar bears that would come out of nowhere to devour Jacob and Jayce. Other times she saw them drowning in icy waters—their ship crushed to kindling in the background. Her worst fears were confirmed when a whaler bound for Dutch Harbor made a stop in the Last Chance harbor.

Leah had heard of the ship's arrival and left the babies with Mary and Sigrid to make her way to the shore. She hoped the ship's captain might have seen or heard of the *Regina* and have some news to share. What he had to tell her, however, was not what she wanted to hear.

"We heard tell the *Regina* ran into trouble west of Point

Barrow. She's stuck there in the ice, out to sea. She's moving with the floe but has no chance of breaking free."

"Is something being done?" Leah asked. "Has the government been notified to send help?"

"There's no help to be sent now. No one's going to risk their vessel to save a few foolhardy explorers. They should have known better."

He had little else to offer, and Leah walked back to the mission house feeling a great sense of dread. Stories of the various ships stranded in the Arctic came back to haunt her.

"Well, did you get word?" Sigrid asked. She sat on the floor, playing with Wills, while Merry slept peacefully nearby.

"The captain said he'd heard that the *Regina* is stuck in the ice."

"Well, that would explain her delay," Sigrid said, smiling. "Surely it won't be long before they manage to break free of that."

Leah shook her head. "No, this is most serious. It won't be possible for them to get away from the ice—not now. The season is too far gone. The temperatures have dropped drastically up there, and ships won't be able to maneuver." She sat down and tried to figure out what might be done.

"Do we know for sure that they're stuck? You said the captain only heard this. Maybe it's just a rumor."

"I suppose that could be true, but there's been no other word from them. I would have expected them to return by now. The open water lanes won't be available much longer. If they are free to maneuver, they would be headed to warmer ports by now."

"I suppose you're right. What then can be done? How would you go about finding out for certain that the rumors are true?"

Leah shook her head. "I suppose I shall have to go to Nome.

That will be the closest place where I can get reliable information. They may have heard more official reports. If the government ships have seen the *Regina* or taken reliable accounts of her fate, they would report it to the officials in Nome." She looked to her children and knew she couldn't risk taking them with her. Oopick and Ayoona would no doubt be willing to care for them. Mary, of course, could also offer a hand.

"I need to speak with John. He'll be able to help me. We can make a supply trip and bring back goods." Leah got to her feet. "I'll be back in a few minutes. Will you stay with the children?"

"Of course."

Leah hurried to find John. She was breathless when she reached him where he sat working on building a sled. "John, we have a problem," she panted.

He looked up, his round brown face appearing serious. "What's wrong?"

"I was just talking with some men from a southbound whaler. They said rumor has it that Jayce and Jacob's ship is stuck in ice. He didn't know anything for certain, and I must have news. I'd like to make a trip into Nome. I know there isn't enough snow to take the dogs, although I would expect it soon enough. Still, I need to get there. Do you suppose we could go by umiak and bring back supplies as well?"

"Sure. We can get there pretty fast that way. It won't freeze over too bad if we go quick."

"I can be ready within the hour. Will that suit you? Can you arrange for the dogs?"

"Sure. I'll get Kimik to take care of them."

She nodded. "I'll speak with Oopick and your mother. I'll have to leave the babies." Even the thought of being separated from her twins left Leah questioning the sanity of this trip. "I'll meet you on the beach."

Leah hurried to attend to every matter. She spoke at length with Oopick and Ayoona, who assured her that they would care for her children.

"You no worry, Lay-Ya. We keep them safe and feed them plenty. They can chew muktuk soon."

Leah smiled. "I'm sure Wills would love that. Sometimes I worry that he's not getting enough to eat. I've been supplementing their nursing with bottles of canned milk for weeks now, but they always seem hungry." She sighed. "I shall miss them so much, but I have to know what's happened to Jayce and Jacob. I see no other way."

Leah wrestled with her decision from the time she left Last Chance until she stepped foot in Nome. This was the first time she'd been separated from her babies for any length of time and it felt completely wrong.

Seeking out information, Leah made her way from the harbor to the telegraph office and then to the military officials.

"We have no official word, ma'am."

The officer was sympathetic but completely useless, as far as Leah was concerned. "I need to get information about the *Regina*," she reiterated. "If the reports are true and she's stranded in ice, those men will need a rescue."

"I can understand your concern, ma'am, but if they are moving with the ice, we have no way of knowing their exact location. Furthermore, the dangers are too great to risk a rescue. The situation would probably just leave two ships stranded."

Leah clenched her fists. "But my husband and brother are on that ship."

"Yes, ma'am. You told me that."

Leah finally gave up and went back to find John. "Nobody knows anything officially," she told her friend. "Everyone has heard the same rumors and believes them to be true, but they cannot act upon them. It's too risky."

John's expression never changed. "Alaska too risky, but I don't see them leaving."

Leah smiled, despite her worry. John always had a way of easing the burden. "I suppose I'll check into the hotel. It's kind of late to head back. I'll be ready bright and early. We'll tackle the goods together."

Walking with less enthusiasm than she'd known earlier, Leah made her way to the hotel where she and Jacob had stayed the year before. The place hadn't changed. There was still a musty odor of cigars and unwashed bodies.

"I need a room," she told the man behind the counter.

"Just you?"

"Yes. And just for tonight."

"Sign the register."

Leah turned the book to sign her name. She saw only two names listed on the page above hers. One belonged to a man, and the other was Helaina Beecham. She thought for a moment she was imagining the words. Leaning down, Leah looked again.

"Helaina Beecham." She looked to the man. "Is she still here?"

"Sure. She's in room 211. You want a room next to hers?"

Leah nodded. "I'd like that very much." Hope surged anew. Helaina had money and contacts. If she was back in Alaska, it could only mean that she'd come here to be with Jacob.

Only Jacob isn't here.

Leah knew once Helaina realized the situation, however, she would take charge and figure out what needed to be done. Leah might know the wilderness and be able to treat a case of pneumonia, but Helaina would know how to cut through the bureaucratic nonsense of government and get some answers.

Racing up the stairs, Leah didn't even bother to stop at her own room. With her pack sack in hand, she went straight to room 211 and knocked.

"Who is it?" Helaina called from behind the closed door.

Leah could have cried for joy. "Helaina, it's me. Leah!"

"Leah?" Helaina immediately opened the door. The women embraced. "I can't believe you're here," Helaina declared. "I have been trying to secure some type of transportation to Last Chance. This is answered prayer. What brings you here?"

"We have a problem—a very serious one," Leah said. "May I come in?"

"Of course." Helaina stepped back and opened the door wider.

Leah smiled to find the woman dressed in native fashion. "Where are all your pretty city clothes?"

"Back in the pretty city," Helaina said with a laugh. "I have a great deal to tell you. Is Jacob here too?"

Leah frowned and shook her head. "That's what we need to talk about."

Helaina closed the door and leaned against it. "What's wrong? Where is Jacob?"

Leah put down her pack. "You know that Jayce and Jacob went north with Captain Latimore."

"I knew that was the plan."

Leah heard the questioning in Helaina's voice. "They've never come home, Helaina. The ship is missing somewhere in the north."

Helaina moved her bags from the only chair in the room. "Sit down and tell me everything." She placed herself on the edge of the bed.

"I'm afraid what I know isn't much. No one seems to have any real knowledge. I've talked to all the officials in the area, and while they've heard rumors that the *Regina* is trapped in ice moving with the floe, they have no other proof or information about her location."

"When was she last heard from?"

Leah shook her head. "No one can tell me. It's almost as if the ship doesn't exist."

"I'm used to dealing with that kind of thing," Helaina said with a wave of her hand. "We won't let that slow us down. First things first." She pressed one index finger down on the other. "We will talk again to the officials. Sometimes you don't get the right answers because you don't ask the right questions. I know it may sound strange, but sometimes details are easily forgotten. There might be some information to be had that we just haven't learned about."

"I knew when I saw your name in the hotel registry that you would know what to do," Leah said, tears forming. "I can't manage this on my own. I have to get home to the children."

"Children?"

Leah nodded and forced a smile. "I had twins right after you left. A boy and a girl."

"Oh my. That must have been quite the adventure."

"It was. They are such dear babies, and I'm anxious to return to them." She shook her head. "What are we going to do, Helaina?

Winter is no time to get things accomplished up here, and the snows and storms will soon be upon us. Communication will be difficult at best."

"I didn't sell everything I owned to move here only to see my dreams crumble. I've come too far to lose Jacob now," Helaina replied. She met Leah's gaze. "I won't give up. I'll wire Stanley and use whatever resources are available to us. I don't care if we have to go to President Wilson himself."

"You know the president?"

"Not exactly, but Stanley just married a woman whose father is an aide to the president. I'm not afraid to use family ties to get help in this situation. Those men can't manage a winter out there alone—without supplies."

Leah considered the stories she'd heard. "It has been done before. That's the only thing that gives me hope. They can hunt on the ice and Jacob knows plenty about that. Jayce even knows something of it. They are both very knowledgeable about surviving the harsh temperatures and storms that accompany life in the Arctic. I have great faith in their ability."

"I have faith in their ability too," Helaina agreed, "but I also know it doesn't hurt to work on things at this end. I can't sit idly by and do nothing."

"But what if that's all we have until spring?" Leah asked seriously. She'd already given this plenty of thought and knew the odds of any kind of winter rescue would be difficult, if not impossible.

"I don't know, Leah. I suppose we'll deal with that when we know there is nothing else to be done. Either way, I have plenty of time and money to put into bringing our men back safely. If we have to purchase our own ship and outfit it for the Arctic, then that's what we shall do."

Leah couldn't help but smile. "And you can be the captain and I'll be first mate."

"Whatever it takes," Helaina replied with a grin. "For as long as it takes."

———————

"There must be something we can do," Jacob said as Captain Latimore sat reviewing his log.

"I know of nothing. This is the end for us. I've read too many other accounts of ships crushed in the ice. We can't hope the *Regina* can last long."

"Then we should make ready to abandon ship when the time comes," Jacob countered. "We should start setting out supplies on the ice. We can even pitch our tents there." The ship moaned as an awful cracking sound echoed in the cabin. "See what I mean? One of these times the ice will break through. You can't just sit here and do nothing."

"I am the captain. A good captain stays with the ship until the bitter end," Latimore said.

"Well, I'm not the captain. With your permission, and even without it, I intend to see our evacuation begun." Jacob got to his feet and looked at the poor man. "I'm sorry it's come to this."

Jayce waited for Jacob outside the door. "Well?"

"He's given up. He no longer cares. I told him it was time to off-load as many supplies as we are able to handle. I suggested we pitch tents and get away from the ship in case she caves in and sinks. He's oblivious to it all. Says he's the captain and he'll go down with the ship."

Jayce shook his head. "The crew has gathered to eat. Shall we go and speak with them?"

"It's mutiny."

Jayce met Jacob's eyes. "I don't think we have any other choice."

Chapter Thirty-three

As the end of October approached, Leah waited anxiously in Last Chance for John to return with Helaina. In Nome the women had agreed that it was best for Leah to return home to her babies while Helaina waited for any information Stanley might be able to garner for her. John returned to Nome around the twentieth of October to bring Helaina back to Last Chance. Hopefully she would have some idea of how they could best help the men of the *Regina*.

It was already dark when Leah heard a commotion in the village, signaling Helaina and John's return. She had kept food warm on the stove every night for the last few evenings, thinking they would be back any day. Tonight's meal would be pleasing to Helaina. Leah had fixed canned roast beef with potatoes and gravy. It was a far cry from the usual Inupiat fare.

Checking quickly on the children, Leah made sure they were

asleep before heading outside. Helaina met her at the door, her bags in hand. Leah reached out and took the larger one.

"Come in. I have supper for you."

"It turned kind of cold this evening," Helaina said, a bit of shiver to her voice. "Otherwise we had a good time of it. We're delayed because I was waiting for information from the coast guard; they seemed to be the ones who would have the most official word."

"Come into the kitchen and tell me everything."

Helaina pulled her parka off once inside the house. Her long blond hair fell from its once carefully arranged bun. She began pulling the rest of the pins and put them on the table while Leah went to get her food.

"I hope you like this. It's roast beef—not seal or walrus."

"Sounds divine. I had John bring back more food supplies. I just can't help but think it's better to have too much than not enough."

Leah put the plate on the table and Helaina gasped. "Those aren't potatoes with gravy—are they?"

"Yes. I figured you should have something special. I've had some ready every night for the last three nights. When you failed to show up, I simply ate them myself." Leah brought Helaina a hot, wet towel. "Here, I thought you might like this to wash up with."

Helaina sighed. "This feels wonderful." She began to wipe her hands and face. "Do you want the good news or the bad news first?"

Leah felt her heart skip a beat. "There's bad news?" She drew a deep breath and steadied herself. "I'd rather have it first."

Helaina put the towel aside and sat down at the table. Leah

joined her. She could see that Helaina was quite tired, but there would be time for sleep later. Right now, Leah needed to know everything.

"There is still very little information and nothing can be done until warmer weather. That's the worst of it. Not knowing and not being able to do anything.

"I've had communication with everyone possible, and no one can say for certain that they know anything more than we do. The coast guard, which now runs the revenue cutter service, does have an official report of the *Regina* being stuck in ice and moving westerly with the current. The confirmed word states that they were last seen on August fifteenth."

"That's over two months ago," Leah said, shaking her head. "A lot could have happened between then and now."

"Exactly. Especially since they were still moving with the ice."

Helaina began to eat the roast, a smile touching her lips. "This is wonderful. I was already tired of dried salmon. I don't know how I'll ever adapt to the food here, but I will."

"So what's the good news?" Leah braved the question.

Helaina sipped her coffee before answering. "The good news is that we have everyone from the president in Washington, D.C., to the governor of the Alaskan Territory involved. Stanley is leaving no stone unturned. He's even managed to reach some of the men from the *Karluk*. He's hoping with the help of that ship's log, as well as that of another ship that was stranded just last year, they might put together a chart of currents and events that took place and help establish where the *Regina* might have drifted."

"But we can't help them at all until spring? That's a long time." Leah knew that the Arctic would be ruthless and that the lives of the men were in grave danger.

Helaina stopped eating. "I know. I've wrestled with this myself. It's so hard to imagine that nothing can be done, but as everyone, even my brother, pointed out—where would we start? Even if you managed to put together a team of natives and dogs with plenty of supplies, where would we even begin to search?"

Leah slumped back against her chair. "I know. That's already gone through my mind—because believe me, I did have all kinds of plans in the works."

"They could be clear over on the Siberian coast by now."

"I just don't understand why this happened," Leah said, shaking her head. "I keep trying to reason it out, but it makes no sense."

"Well, the word I was given was that the temperature dropped sooner than expected. Everyone figured to have at least until September before things turned truly bad, but the ice came early and cold weather set in so as to drive everyone south. Even the revenue cutters and whalers returned well ahead of schedule. You probably saw that for yourself. Apparently Latimore didn't realize how dangerous the situation had become."

"Or he didn't care," Leah replied. "I know he was grieving his wife's passing. He should never have led this expedition."

"No, that's for certain."

Helaina continued to eat while Leah thought on the problem at hand. "I know Jacob and Jayce will be able to take care of themselves and anyone else. But even that will depend on supplies. I don't know how well situated they were for Arctic survival. Latimore probably gave it no real consideration."

"But Jacob would have," Helaina said. Her voice revealed that she had no doubt of this fact. "Jacob wouldn't go off without making sure that they had adequate supplies and gear."

Leah nodded. "That's true. And Jayce would have insisted on no less. Between the two of them, Latimore would have had to listen. At least we know they have that much."

———

"What do you mean we don't have any ammunition for the 30-30?" Jacob asked. He'd had the men taking a meticulous inventory of what goods were still available on the ship.

"All I can find is just under a thousand rounds for the shotgun," a young man they called Bristol announced. "I know the captain has a revolver, but I couldn't say what kind of extra rounds he keeps."

"There's got to be ammunition for the 30-30. We'll never be able to take down large animals with the shotgun." Jacob looked at the list of equipment and inventory that they should have had. "Do you suppose the Canadian team took more ammo than belonged to them?"

Jayce shrugged. "It's always possible, but I say we keep looking. It's easy to miss something on a ship this size. It could have been stashed somewhere just to get it out of the way."

"We need to find it, then. If things get bad and we have to abandon ship, we'll need those rounds."

Jayce nodded. "I'll make it my job to find them."

Jacob looked to Elmer Warrick, the first officer. The tall, skinny twenty-four-year-old had also served with Latimore on the *Homestead*. "What can you tell me about the food supplies?"

"It's a little more encouraging," Warrick reported. "We have ten cases of smoked or dried salmon, five cases of tomcod, and one hundred fifty cases of sea biscuits." He looked up and grinned. "Hardtack, as you landlubbers call 'em."

Jacob smiled. "Go on."

Warrick nodded. "There's nearly a dozen cases of canned peaches, thanks to the captain's love of 'em. There's ten casks of beef, six cases of dried eggs, twelve barrels of molasses, enough coffee and tea to float us home, and an odd assortment of canned goods, flour, pemmican, and seal oil. I can get you exact counts on those things later."

"All right. Be sure that you do." He turned to Jayce. "What did you find regarding some of the other equipment?"

"Well, we have the obvious bedding supplies we've each been using. There are also another two dozen blankets in storage, along with two wood stoves, two coal stoves, two sleds for which we have no dogs, thirty cases of gasoline, a case of matches, and three hundred sacks of coal." Jayce looked down to the list he'd made. "We have a good collection of tools—axes, hammers, shovels, a couple of saws—all of which I figure could serve us well in ice fishing and even making ice houses."

"If we can find some solid land instead of ice floes," Bristol interjected.

"All of this gear will help us in some manner to stay alive," Jacob said. "We have to remember that nothing goes to waste. When the time comes that the ship is destroyed, we will need every bit of it. Even wood from the ship itself."

"What about water?" one of the other crewmen asked. "We can't live without water."

"Very true," Jacob said. "The natives taught me a most valuable lesson. The old ice floes can be used for drinking water. Something happens from their long exposure to the sun—somehow the salt is drawn from it. We will melt ice from the older floes and keep our water source until we manage to find land."

"But how will we survive, Jacob?" Bristol asked. "The captain's gone mad and we can't even find half the supplies we should have. We have no dogs to take us by sled, and the lifeboats are useless to us without open water, which we probably aren't going to see again until June."

"We will survive by trusting first in the Lord and then in the wisdom we each have. All of us know things that can help in our survival. I've lived in the frozen north since my teen years. I'm not about to let this stop me. I hope you won't let it stop you either." The men around him nodded. "We will have to work together— to trust each other and to be trustworthy. There can be no thievery. No hoarding. We must share and share alike. Do I have your word on this?"

The men nodded again, and Jacob could see that they were desperate to have hope. He smiled. "Physically, we are good, strong, healthy men, but I've seen such men defeated because their spirits were not also strong." Jacob dropped to his knees. "I, for one, will not be weak spiritually."

The crew joined him on their knees. Not a single man protested as Jacob began to pray. "Father, we seek your guidance and wisdom. We ask for direction and knowledge as we deal with the days to come. Watch over us. Keep us in your care. Let our minds be clear and our bodies strong. Renew our spirits and our hearts, that we might be generous with each other, practicing kindness and mercy. Lord, the way looks so very difficult, but we know that you are a God of infinite power. We trust you now for all that we need. In Jesus' name, amen."

Jacob heard the men murmur in agreement. Opening his eyes, he looked overhead and saw the aurora dancing in a brilliant display of color. Some might consider it a bad omen, but Jacob felt as if God were answering him, reassuring him that all was not lost.

"Leah's out there . . . somewhere under the northern lights," Jayce said as he and Jacob walked to the ship's rail. "She's worried about us and probably mounting up an army to come find us."

"If I know my sister, she'll be trying to lead the whole bunch."

Jayce sighed. "If I know my wife, she'll not rest until we're both back safe and sound."

Leah stood under the northern lights, watching the show as if it were the finest entertainment in the world. Helaina soon joined her, awestruck by the display.

"They're truly beautiful," she told Leah. "I've never seen anything like it."

Leah thought of all the times she'd seen the aurora before. She never tired of it, but tonight they left her feeling rather sad. "The natives have a legend about the lights. They say they are caused from the torches of spirits who are looking for the souls of the dead. The people believe there is a narrow path to follow over to a land of plenty. It's their heaven—where there is no sickness or hunger. They believe the noise made by the aurora is because the spirits are whistling to them. Some of the people believe they can send messages to the dead through these spirits." She sighed and wrapped her arms to her body. "But always they think of those who've just died. This is their light home."

Helaina put her arm around Leah. "But it isn't Jacob's light home, nor Jayce's. They aren't dead—I know they aren't."

Leah looked to Helaina and nodded. "I know it, too, but I don't know anything else. I don't know if they can hang on—or if they have the things they need to live. I don't know if they are sick or if . . ." She let the words fade away.

"You taught me, Leah, that faith is believing even when it's hard to see anything to believe in. We both know that God is with us—just as He's with Jayce and Jacob. God must have a purpose, even in this."

"You sound so wise," Leah said with a smile. "Almost as if you'd spent a lifetime believing in God."

"I have. For I didn't really live until I found Him."

Leah embraced her friend. "Thank you for coming. I think I might lose my mind if not for you."

"We will keep each other strong," Helaina said. "We look to the only light that matters—the true light."

Leah looked back to the skies. "They're out there . . . somewhere . . . under the northern lights. And they're thinking of us—hoping to see us again, just as we hope for them to come home."

"And we won't give up hope," Helaina whispered. "Because they won't give up."

Leah thought of her babies and of the comfort they had already offered her. God had a way of loving His children through other people. He had sent her Helaina, a woman Leah had once considered her enemy. A woman she now called friend.

"Nothing happens by chance," she murmured. "Not even this."

"Especially not this," Helaina replied, looking to the brilliant display of lights. "I think the aurora is God's way of reminding us that He's still in control—that we aren't forgotten. That they . . . aren't forgotten."

Leah felt strength anew. "I think you're right." She smiled and warmth spread throughout her body. "No . . . I know you're right."

CROSSINGS®
THE BOOK CLUB FOR TODAY'S CHRISTIAN FAMILY

A Letter to Our Readers

Dear Reader:

In order that we might better contribute to your reading enjoyment, we would appreciate your taking a few minutes to respond to the following questions. When completed, please return to the following:

Andrea Doering, Editor-in-Chief
Crossings Book Club
401 Franklin Avenue, Garden City, NY 11530

You can post your review online! Go to www.crossings.com and rate this book.

Title _____ Author _____

1 Did you enjoy reading this book?

❑ Very much. I would like to see more books by this author!

❑ I really liked_____

❑ Moderately. I would have enjoyed it more if_____

2 What influenced your decision to purchase this book? Check all that apply.

    ❑ Cover
    ❑ Title
    ❑ Publicity
    ❑ Catalog description
    ❑ Friends
    ❑ Enjoyed other books by this author
    ❑ Other _____

3 Please check your age range:

    ❑ Under 18   ❑ 18-24
    ❑ 25-34   ❑ 35-45
    ❑ 46-55   ❑ Over 55

4 How many hours per week do you read? _____

5 How would you rate this book, on a scale from 1 (poor) to 5 (superior)?
_____

Name_____

Occupation_____

Address_____

City_____ State_____ Zip_____